PRAISE FOR *KEEPER OF THE KEYS*

"The book is a welcome breath of fresh air.... A well-paced, smartly written thriller with an ambiguous protagonist and a genuinely mysterious mystery to be solved." —*Booklist*

"Breathtaking. The action is nonstop.... The mysteries blend together seamlessly.... It was definitely worth it for O'Shaughnessy to step out of her comfortable series world for this book." —*Romantic Times*

"An entertaining change of pace from the authors' popular Nina Reilly mystery series."
—*Monterey County Herald*

"There are some slick twists, and the ending is quite a surprise." —*BookPage*

PRAISE FOR PERRI O'SHAUGHNESSY'S NINA REILLY SERIES

"Will keep you turning pages into the night."
—*USA Today*

"A real puzzler, with twists diabolical enough to take to court." —*New York Times Book Review*

"Stylish and elegant...compelling."
—*Cleveland Plain Dealer*

"An ambitious, sprawling novel with a switcheroo ending." —*Boston Sunday Globe*

PERRI O'SHAUGHNESSY

KEEPER OF
THE KEYS

A DELL BOOK

KEEPER OF THE KEYS
A Dell Book

PUBLISHING HISTORY
Delacorte Press hardcover edition published November 2006
Dell mass market edition / September 2007

Published by Bantam Dell
A Division of Random House, Inc.
New York, New York

This is a work of fiction. Names, characters, places, and incidents either
are the product of the author's imagination or are used fictitiously.
Any resemblance to actual persons, living or dead, events,
or locales is entirely coincidental.

Library of Congress Catalog Card Number: 2006048481

Dell is a registered trademark of Random House, Inc., and the
colophon is a trademark of Random House, Inc.

ISBN 978-0-440-24183-6

Printed in the United States of America
Published simultaneously in Canada

www.bantamdell.com

OPM   10   9   8   7   6   5   4   3   2   1

For Brad Snedecor,
generous soul and benevolent spirit,
who has done so much for our family

KEEPER
OF THE KEYS

S he felt sick all the time now, and it was guilt making her feel that way. The guilt had spread like malignant cells throughout her body. Now it squeezed her neck until she choked, and couldn't breathe, and couldn't speak truthfully. She didn't want to live like this, and she couldn't anymore. She would rather die. She felt she was dying anyway.

In the shower, a glassed-in space with a glass tile floor that hovered gorgeous as a transparent butterfly over dark Topanga Canyon, Leigh Jackson scrubbed away the sweat of her day's labor. Brushing a stiff loofah over her arms, she realized the pointlessness of worrying about what came next. She had to confess, outcomes be damned.

Although tonight could ruin her life, and his.

Correction: it could ruin her life more than it was already ruined.

She heard him sawing downstairs. Her husband, Ray, had followed his latest routine tonight, the routine that made her crazy, made her act out, forced her to—

No. Unfair to blame him.

By the time she had come home, he had already eaten

and disappeared into his dungeon workshop downstairs. He loved it; she hated the space, finding it as claustrophobic and as hard as an animal's cave. She had never told Ray that, although he must know. He used to know her so well. He used to study her smile and the slight wrinkles around her eyes that had suddenly appeared when she reached thirty a few years before. He used to touch them almost—reverently.

Well, that had stopped.

Culpability. Not all hers. Not entirely unfair to allow that he played a role in her unforgivable behavior. Once locked together as tightly as barnacles on a rock, they had pulled apart. The parting cracked things: shells, muscle, tissue, heart.

Wounded when he didn't touch her anymore, unable to pierce the dark hood over eyes that had once looked at her so openly, for some time now she had pondered what had triggered his withdrawal. To her surprise, she traced the changes to when his architectural firm began to get truly successful. Newspapers covered their projects. The latest article featured her handsome husband, looking somewhat bewildered at the attention, with a foot up on a concrete pediment in front of a gigantic new structure.

He had become the public's toast, any crazy design idea accepted, no, even celebrated by the press. Jobs poured in.

"We've got a cushion now. I could take some time off, have a baby," she had said happily a few weeks before, reading the story with the color photo in the morning paper.

He hadn't said anything, but it was right after that he started in on the infernal model-building.

She plucked a towel off the brushed-nickel rack and started on her hair. Ray had designed this house, right down to the metal plate behind the toilet paper roll that you could tilt out to hide things behind. How they had laughed about that, holding hands and poring over the plans. "My mother always had hiding places in the houses we lived in, so I guess I always expected every house to have one. I'll buy you diamonds to hide in there," he had said, taking her callused hands in his. "You'd like a big fat diamond, wouldn't you?" He twirled her hair between his fingers as they kissed.

She told him, Make it a diamond-headed saw. That, she could use. Still madly in love, she let him have his way with her anytime he wanted, along with letting him have his way with the design of the house he called their dream.

Only later did she realize what that cost her. She felt uncomfortable, out of place in her own home, preferring curvy organic forms like the furniture she designed and built in her business.

So she didn't care about diamonds, but she always thought they would have a child, half of each of them. She didn't understand people not having kids. In her view, if a plan existed for human beings, it was to reproduce and raise a flock of terrific new human beings. She didn't intend to drop the subject.

The next time she broached the topic of getting pregnant, she picked a moment she thought propitious, her on top, him enjoying her body the way he always did. They had eaten a lovely meal, cooked by her. She had changed from her usual working togs after work to look pretty for him, and she could see by the appreciation in his eyes, he liked the silvery sandals and short black dress, and had, even more, enjoyed removing them.

They lay together in candlelight and she, warmed by the moment and the caresses she could still feel on her naked skin, said, "I love you. Now, let's do it again. Make me pregnant, Ray."

He pushed her off and pulled on his jeans. "It's not a good time for me."

But time was starting to work against her. A thirty-five-year-old woman had to consider such things. She tried to raise the issue several more times, but each time agitated him more until finally he refused to discuss it.

In her contemporary-as-hell bathroom, sticking dangling purple earrings into the holes in her ears, Leigh allowed herself a few moments to mourn. She might never have a child after all, not with Ray anyway, and this thought reminded her of other people she had lost through death or distance.

Tom and his sister, Kat Tinsley.

Brushing a little powder over her shiny nose, she wished she hadn't run from Kat, who had been her closest friend once. They hadn't seen each other in years. Every time she went to Tom's grave, she expected to run into her. In the six years since he died, she never had.

Ray used to like the smell of gardenias, like the ones she had carried in her wedding bouquet, so she pulled out some cologne he had given her in more sensitive times and squirted herself liberally. Who knew whether she might gain a subtle, unconscious advantage? As she selected a cool cotton blouse and knotted it above her navel because she still could get away with that, just barely, because her work was often physical and kept her in good shape, she could not stop a fleeting memory of his arms around her, how good they used to feel, how safe.

She didn't feel safe anymore. Ray, her Ray, had gone away, to be replaced by a man she didn't know and could no longer predict, subject to fits of temperament, fits of temper, in fact. When she arrived late to a restaurant date the previous week, he had already gone home. He bolted the front door from the inside. He made her wait outside the exact amount of time she had been late, as he explained later, as if somehow that made his reaction entirely sane.

She yanked on her favorite purple T-shirt and fresh shorts, gave her hair a shake, and walked barefoot into the stainless-steel kitchen, punching at cabinets that had no handles because they might ruin the "line." Frustrated even more than usual, she finally opened the wine cooler with a good hard kick. She pulled out a bottle of something red, uncorked it, and poured two glasses, setting them on the table in front of the couch, then called to him, "I'm coming down. You need anything from up here?"

"No."

She felt afraid but would tell him, whatever it cost her tonight. Whatever their problems, he deserved an honest wife. How could they ever love each other again without that much?

She used to love sneaking up behind him, enveloping

him in her arms, feeling how his heart and breathing steadied as he relaxed against her body. Now, she didn't dare surprise him because, well, who knew? Considering that strange tantrum last week, he might even strike out at her.

Clutching the railing, she prepared herself. Rip everything apart. Only then could they mend.

Ray watched his wife's muscular, long legs slipping down the stairs to his studio, telling himself, don't say anything. Don't let her get to you.

But it wasn't easy. The epic nature of his feelings frightened him, like his first sight of Godzilla had when he was a child. Big, mean, and evil. That described him lately, and he didn't like that about himself, but didn't know how to change it, either.

At nine o'clock on a summer night, the dark already frank outside, Ray's bright white basement workshop remained timeless and chilly. Although tonight, caught up in a bigger emotion, he felt immune to its pleasures, usually he liked it that way, bland. He concentrated best in a non-distracting environment. Leaning forward in his Herman Miller chair, he pasted a small stick of plywood meant for model airplanes onto the model house he was building out of balsa and Styrofoam, remembering the way the garage on Bright Street had always listed slightly to the side.

"Hi." Leigh lingered at the bottom of the stairs. Specs dangled around her neck and long, light hair drifted down over her shoulders. Silky nylon shorts cut into her pale skin. She chewed her lip.

"Hi." Give her that much. Reveal nothing because he dreaded another confrontation with her. They got nowhere, except farther down the downward spiral. He had an awful feeling they were close to saying something irrevocable, and it scared him so much he felt afraid to talk at all.

Looking down at his architectural model, she walked over to the table. She placed a hand on his shoulder. Her touch felt forced. His heart beat harder.

"Which one is that?"

"From when I was ten. There were three that year."

She tilted her head. "The foundation seems to be slanting."

"Just like the real thing." Six other models sat lined up on the shelf above the massive wooden table. He continued to work, lining up a few dozen tiny shakes for the garage roof. He squirted some glue onto one, then tried to place it, but his hand fumbled, and the shake went on crooked. He took a deep breath, then adjusted it.

He wanted her to go away right now, give him an opportunity to cool down and put his vile feelings where they belonged, somewhere besides in this room with them. "Is it still hot outside?"

"Down to ninety-two," she said. "I turned the a/c down a little."

"Good."

Leigh sat down on the leather daybed, a fair copy of a van der Rohe original.

She was not going away.

Ray finished pasting a few more shakes. Leigh watched, although she appeared preoccupied. "You missed dinner." He tried for a normal tone. He did not want her to have the slightest clue about how very, very upset he had been about the images that arose in his mind during her absence. See, this was the thing about relationships. His mother had warned him that the heart was the nastiest place in the body, not the genitals. She had encouraged him to have loads of girlfriends but to keep his heart private, but then Leigh had come along and plucked it right out of him as easily as if she were picking a wildflower along a road.

How could she?

"I thought you said you would cook tonight," he went on. How surprising, to continue operating as if they had something to salvage.

Did they? The thought confused him, and for a moment, he stopped working and tried to think.

She looked startled. "I did? Oh. I guess I did. Sorry. I forgot. I really am sorry, Ray, but I had something else to do, and so I just—" She tried to squeeze his arm, but he moved away. Instead, she picked up a piece of balsa he had formed into an intricate porch trim, then put it down when she saw the look he was giving her. "I stopped by the drugstore to get a few things."

"That took, generously, one hour," Ray said. He tinkered with a small step leading up to a porch. He couldn't seem to get the porch right. Memory failed him sometimes. How many people could remember such detail, going back twenty-five years or more? He did pretty well, considering how the mind worked, how emotions colored and distorted memory.

He tried again, but couldn't get the stair to sit right. He had trimmed it too tight. He pushed through it with his thumb, breaking the lightweight wood in half. "What else did you do?"

A wrinkle between her brows registered something in his voice. "Errands," she said. She eyed the now ruined porch step.

"Must have been a lot of them. Errands."

"I drove around, okay? I wasn't ready to come home."

"It's the anniversary of Tom Tinsley's death, isn't it? You went to the cemetery. You always do, Leigh. I've known it since we got married."

She didn't answer.

"Brought him flowers. Had a chat with a dead man. I never could understand that routine. See, it seems to me you should celebrate someone's life, not their day of death."

"It wasn't a celebration, Ray."

"No. I guess not. But I get tired of eating alone, Leigh, and it seems I eat alone an awful damn lot these days."

"Look, I didn't come down here to fight with you, okay? I poured us some wine. Why don't you put this stuff away for now. Let's talk, okay?"

The glue flowed, balsa wood meticulously slid into place. He had it exactly right this time, and stepped back to admire its perfection. "Maybe later." He suppressed the urge he felt to start in on her, but that didn't stop the heat rising inside him or the emotions preparing to launch like fireballs. He studied the architectural model of the house, the tiny floor plan fully visible as though a hurricane had blown the roof off. He admired its neatness, although possibly the front window should be larger?

"Damn it!" She slapped at his hand, knocking a small piece of wood out of it. "What is wrong with you? What is all this crap? Your own sick celebration? I mean, you lived in a bunch of houses when you were a kid. Millions of kids do, but they move on, not pissing life away on a screwy hobby, trying to resurrect a screwy past!"

He picked up the piece that had fallen and laid it carefully on his table next to a pile of scraps. "I've explained it to you," he said, with what he thought was amazing restraint. "I developed my love for architecture living in these funny little boxes. It's a hobby, like boat-building or hunting. It makes me feel good."

"You used to say every house you lived in had an aura. I thought about that. I thought, what, was this one warm? Did this one protect him? Did this one scare him? I forgave that thing that took you so far away from me. But you've become obsessed. You're at it all the time. You won't even go to the movies with me anymore." She stopped and he saw the effort she expended calming herself. "Look, Ray. I just can't live so disconnected from you or from how we used to be. We were so close. We told each other everything!"

"Not anymore, we don't."

"I'm trying, okay? I've got things to say. Things I need to tell you."

"Okay." He slammed his fist down on the table, keeping his voice steady but unable to unclench his hands. "You want to talk? We'll talk." Fear came up in her face, and while he hated himself, he also could not stop himself now. She wanted an adult. She had one, had his full fucking attention now.

"Not here. Come upstairs. Please."

"First why don't you tell me about where you go when you don't go to the store or to work or to the cemetery. How about let's start with that?"

A silence as palpable as the haze hanging over the canyon outside sucked the oxygen from the air. Ray let his hand dig down into his pocket.

Her voice sounded small. "I get lonely."

He pulled out a key and threw it on the table. It spun, then landed in front of the miniature garage.

"I was going to tell you, Ray." She wiped tears from her eyes. "Tonight."

"You left it on the TV." The cheesy motel on Pacific Coast Highway still used old-fashioned keys, which had surprised him. He thought metal keys were becoming as obsolete as dial phones.

"But you didn't say anything." She put her face in her hands.

"Neither did you." Pain crept through his heart like a slow-motion bullet.

"I want to explain—"

"You gave yourself away so cheap," Ray said, pacing around the table. "It's totally mechanical to him, attracting other people. He's not even that good-looking; he's just a smooth salesman. We used to laugh about him, Leigh! Remember? Now you— How could you?"

Her hands combed through her long hair. "I don't know."

He put both hands in his pockets. His left hand landed on a coil of copper wire. How quickly he could coil this wire around her neck and end this pain forever.

He pictured the whole thing. He could do this, yes. The love they once had, now compromised; the pain so intense he couldn't think straight; the fear he had of the future; all emotions could be shoved back into memory, safe as an old letter gathering dust in a box.

He reached up and slid his hand behind her neck and pulled her down toward him, the other hand still in his pocket, holding the wire tense. He buried himself in her hair and the scent of her skin. He could. He could kill her. He could easily kill her. Keeping her close as he stood up, he thought about exactly how.

1

A white yacht floated deep in smooth water not a hundred feet away, separated from Kat and Jacki by the sheet of glass that made up the back wall of the restaurant. A man in a white cap moved about on deck. Blinding white boats floated at their moorings a long way out under a hot cloudless sky. Kat took off her cotton blazer and nudged off her dressy shoes under the table. Her sister, Jacki, sat across from her, marine-blue eyes hidden by huge sunglasses, lipsticked, wearing a sleeveless blouse that overhung her eight-months-along middle like a steep-eaved roof. "Have a good morning?" Jacki asked.

"The usual schizoid Sunday in August. I read the paper in my jammies and enjoyed myself until I made the mistake of returning a business phone call and had this knockdown fight with one very angry owner in La Cienega who thought his house should be worth double my appraisal. Sorry I'm late. I couldn't find legal parking so I'll probably get towed."

"The walk nearly killed me." Jacki lived right here in Marina del Rey, only two blocks away in a loft condo with her husband, Raoul, who taught bioethics and biology at

UCLA. Kat couldn't afford this area on one income, so lived several miles south in Hermosa Beach.

"Braggart. I should have had a margarita instead of this latte," Kat said, taking a sip. "Things always go better with tequila."

"You drink too much."

"So do you when you're not pregnant."

"Already the low blows," Jacki said comfortably, offering her a napkin, "and you've only been here"—she consulted her watch—"three minutes."

"You started it."

"So I should get the last word."

Kat nodded. "Always end as you start. I remember that from the one creative writing course I took at Long Beach State."

"I ordered a turkey on rye for you, okay?"

Kat nodded again, taking the napkin and setting it beside her plate. She made a note to herself to stop for a bottle of wine on the way home. Evenings had been much easier to get through lately, what with this new habit of getting slightly shitfaced every night. Yes, later she would undoubtedly violate the Buddha's Fifth Precept against intoxicants once again this evening, because she didn't seem to have any control over anything anymore, but the main thing was to be on the path and do the best you can at any given moment. She was drinking coffee right now and not hurting anything, not engaged in any sexual misconduct, not stealing, not getting whacked on chardonnay, piling up merit to piss away later tonight.

Jacki had just started her maternity leave, and she was

becoming quite irksome now that she didn't have a job on which to expend her prodigious energies. She called Kat a half-dozen times a day.

Leaning back in the blue-trimmed wicker chair, Kat decided she didn't really mind. In fact, she didn't have much of a life outside her work and Jacki these days. Her sister's phone calls gave her a sense of normality. "I love the air here," she said, breathing deeply, as a sea breeze swept across the patio. "I heard it was a hundred and eight in San Bernardino yesterday. Imagine being there next month, in September, when it really gets hot. We're lucky, living on the coast. They say being near large bodies of water makes the air heavier or something and so it's healthier for you."

"Fewer cooties is what I hear."

"Ask Raoul, and be sure to use the word 'cooties.' He knows all that special science stuff." Kat checked out the nearby tables, but they were full of women just like her and Jacki at this time of day. The pasty and pudgy waiter wasn't hot. His dress shirt gaped enough to display part of a blue tattoo she really didn't want to see the rest of. It took the pressure off, not having to be aware of him or to wonder what he thought of her.

"Hey, you know, Kat," Jacki was saying, waving her hand at the cloudless sky and ocean beyond, "if we have no other legacy when we die, at least they can say we got the hell out of Whittier."

"That's such a Whittier thing to say," Kat said.

They laughed. They had grown up in a two-story house with a living/dining combo, three bedrooms, and windows closed off at all times with dark drapes against the hot, dusty outside. The town had become a scapegoat for them. Once there had been orange groves, times their parents nostalgically remembered, before their time, before the World War II vets arrived with their new wives and big families, hungry for safe, cheap housing. The old Quaker town thirty miles inland became just another suburb bursting with tract houses, absorbed into the basin-wide suburb which was L.A.

"If Daddy had only let us fix the place up—get some—"

"A/c," Kat finished. "God, what he inflicted on us, and I don't mean his sense of humor." Kat and Jacki both kept their condos frosty in summer. They would go without food before they would give up air-conditioning.

"Remember? He said it was to save the earth when what he was really doing was saving to buy the girlfriend a Camaro," Jacki said.

"Which she took with her. We never thanked her enough for leaving him."

"You did pretty well. Even Ma got a kick out of those roses you sent her," said Jacki.

But for months after her husband left and again after their brother, Tom, died, their mother had just sat dully on her couch, exuding, in that dim overhot room, the familiar smell of what Kat secretly called Eau de Dumped, the smell of the lonely women of Southern California. No emollients, no deodorant, could disguise that stink of loneliness.

I ought to take a whiff of my own armpits, Kat thought

glumly, and tasted the hot milky drink the waiter had just brought.

In her working life as a realtor, Jacki had always appeared supremely coifed and styled. Today she wore her streaked hair snapped into a clip, the dark roots shiny and clean but untreated. Her skin looked pinker these days, no doubt due to the pregnancy, but the color didn't hide the million freckles she usually erased with foundation. Kat said, "You're starting to look just like Ma when we were little. I expect you to say, any second now, 'Pick your nose again and I'm calling the cops.' "

Jacki swatted at her.

"You said you wanted to talk to me about something?" Kat asked.

But Jacki, relaxed since leaving her job and under the spell of a modified endocrine system heavy on the maternal hormones, appeared in no hurry to discuss whatever was bugging her. "I ordered myself a salad, nothing heavy. I'll graze like the enormous hippo I have become and continue with meal number six of the day when Raoul gets home. You have plans tonight?"

"Not really, no." Unless maybe getting laid by someone Kat had not yet met counted as making plans. His name was Nikola and he had a promising twinkle in his eye, at least in the one-inch shot he had posted on Match.com. They were on for dinner at a bistro in Hermosa.

"What do you do for fun these days?" Jacki asked.

"Work sixteen hours a day, as you well know. I looked at six houses today desperately seeking comps for an old thirties shack on the beach at Zuma that only has one bathroom."

"Some fun," Jacki said. She too had always worked long hours, but somehow had found time to date her husband, cook elegant dinners, host quasi-scintillating friends, see all the latest movies and concerts, and it seemed, organize good weather wherever she went. Now, she would have her baby at age thirty-six, just like she had always planned. "So how much did you decide it was worth?"

"A million three. A teardown."

"Who's listing it?" They talked about their favorite subject, residential real estate, for a few minutes. Kat worked as an appraiser, comparing ineffables. Jacki was a realtor. Real estate cluttered up their genes, and besides, with the market smokin' as it was, they were both making enough money to live and sock away a little, and to hope for The Big Lebowski, the monster hit, to come someday and wipe out all their financial insecurities.

Jacki was definitely working up to something, Kat could tell by the thoughtful way she dropped her ice cube in her coffee and swished it around. Finally she cocked an eyebrow and said far too casually, "What happened to that Internet guy you were dating?"

"That didn't work out."

"Really? You said the sex was so hot and he had the potential to become real someday."

"I never."

"You implied it." Jacki's eyes narrowed. "You don't even remember who I'm talking about, do you? How many men do you see in a given month?"

"Make up your mind, willya? First you insinuate I'm a drudge. Now you're mad that I do just wanna have fun."

"Okay, intervention time."

"Not again."

"Kat, you have to be careful. It's crazy—in these times— for you to be running around like a . . . like a . . ."

"Hooker too stupid to demand her money up front?"

"You prowl mindlessly. It's not going to get you a man who loves you and wants to spend the rest of his life with you. You have to know that." Lunch plates appeared. Jacki hunkered down to her Shrimp Louis, crunching loudly, not like a single woman, but like a complacent one.

"You're just jealous, stuck for life with an accomplished egghead who loves you madly," Kat said.

"Take the advice of your wise older sister, who, yes, figured out what it takes to be happy. And it isn't all Raoul's doing, I'll have you know. A person has to achieve a certain integration of self."

"You know it all, big sister."

"I do know a few things—"

"You're getting smug."

Jacki smacked her hand down on the table, spilling a few shreds of dressing-soaked lettuce. "I'm worried, okay? I can't tell you what's going to make you happy. I know what makes me happy: a solid relationship. I love Raoul. He holds me up. I don't have to spend all my time trying to find renters to lodge in my heart, like you do. You exhaust yourself and you waste your time being unhappy."

"How else am I going to find love? I don't know anybody in my condo development. I quit going to church when I was fourteen; going clubbing alone is dangerous. I don't have friends except you—at least, you were my friend up to five minutes ago. I'm rethinking that now. Everybody meets online these days. It's safer than you might think."

"I figured it out," Jacki said, with the infuriating gaze of an older sister who *had* figured it out. "You don't know what will make you happy, do you?"

"You're about to let me know, though, aren't you?" Kat's turkey sandwich was huge enough to satisfy King Kong, and was accompanied by a vast pile of fries. Kat poured on the ketchup, hungry.

Her sister speared a soggy shrimp, her steady chewing implacable. "Well, do you? Know?"

"Sure."

Jacki put her fork down and folded her arms. "Okay, then. What will make you happy?"

Kat said, "Questions are demands, did you know that? Like e-mails. You have the right not to respond. In fact, I recommend that strategy. You can't imagine how annoyed people get when you don't respond to e-mails; ergo, fewer e-mails, fewer demands on your time. In other words just because you ask doesn't mean I have to tell you."

Jacki smiled evilly. "Meaning you don't know the answer."

"It's insulting, you implying I'm unhappy, you know."

"Tell me you're happy. With a straight face."

"Quit nagging, Jacki."

"Like you said, I'm your only friend. It's what friends do. Plus, hey, I brought you something. Damn, where did

I put that thing? I cut it out for you." She pulled out an enormous wad of cash, receipts, gum wrappers, hard candy, coins, and pens from her tiny Chinese silk purse and sorted through it. "Guess I forgot it," she said, stuffing everything back in somehow. "It was in the *Times* real estate section last week, this article about a mansion being built at Laguna Cliffs. Ultramodern, you know, mucho concrete-o, geometric palm trees, and an infinity pool. Probably list at around four and a half million."

"What about it?"

"It's being designed by her husband. Leigh Hubbel's. Remember, we heard he was an architect? Now I can't remember his name—sort of common like Jones or Johnson. Shoot. His firm is doing really well. They designed the new history museum in Pasadena, the one with the Native American mummy. Did you know the Chumash buried people in urns, all curled up in a sitting position?"

"No stranger than draining their blood and replacing it with fixative, putting makeup on their poor dead faces, stretching them out in a coffin in some fine outfit, then burying them surrounded by concrete."

"Geez," Jacki said, placing a hand on her tummy. "You've given this entirely too much thought. So listen, to return to my actual point, Leigh's husband is described in the news as the next Hockney."

"I doubt that. Hockney's the artist, the swimming pool painter, photo-pastiche master. Could you mean Michael Graves?"

"That's our man. I swear"—Jacki stretched down and

rubbed her foot—"all the blood flow gets hijacked down to here." She tapped her stomach. "I can't think straight anymore."

"Did you ever?"

"But let me tell you, the universe is conspiring and even you should listen when that happens. It must say something in your Buddha studies about how the universe tells you things and you should listen." Jacki, who attended a Quaker church, treated Kat's interest in Buddhism as an aberrant phase.

"I haven't got to that part yet, I guess."

"Anyway, last Friday I went to the cemetery. You know, it's been six years since he died?" She wiped away a sudden tear as easily as someone brushing off a fly.

"Oh, Jacki. Was that such a good idea?"

"It doesn't make me sad. It makes me happy to visit him and the folks. You never go, do you?"

Kat did go at times, although never with her sister. She had marked that awful anniversary in private again this year, at home where she could howl into a pillow observed only by the birds outside her window. Death made her so angry. She would never make her peace with it, never.

"Anyway, I wasn't the only one, turns out."

"What are you talking about?"

"Well, I was gathering up a bunch of chrysanthemums from the back seat, and who should I see in the car window?"

"You saw Leigh."

"Yep." Jacki sat back, smiling as if delivering a wonderful gift. "I got out as quick as I could, but she took off. It takes me a long time to get out of a car these days, you know. Anyway, I thought she looked like hell, haggard, her eyes all swelled up. I know she saw me, but she left anyway. When I got to Tommy's grave, I found the most beautiful bouquet of irises. She must have left them there. He liked them, remember?"

The bouquet of irises in his kitchen had wilted and died by the time Kat and Jacki had gone to clean out his apartment. "Of course."

"You two used to be close. You should call her," Jacki said.

"Oh, you do make it irresistible, reconnecting with a haggard, crying former friend who—Tommy never would have died if—!"

"You're too harsh—"

"She's old business. Not your business, by the way. I haven't seen Leigh since his funeral." However, the image of Leigh standing by Tommy's grave did rise up like a ghost before her, strange, unwelcome and compelling, a blurry image seen through a screen of tears.

"Exactly." Jacki ate her last shrimp. "So I saw her at the cemetery, then I read this article, and I started thinking about the three of you, how golden you were. I was always jealous of how close you and Leigh were, and I don't think I've seen you happy, not really, since Tommy died and you and Leigh quit being friends."

Kat rolled her eyes and motioned to the waiter. "Margarita, no salt," she said. "I get it, Jacki, I'm an anti-social flake. Can we move on?"

"Oh, get over yourself. I'm not going to compliment

you for your terrific professional success, your ability to be independent and strong and fun and"—Jacki reached over and stroked the edge of Kat's blazer—"fashionable and loyal and the best friend I could have on earth. But see how cranky you got just then? You have issues and they'll never go away until you deal with them. What's the harm in giving her a call?"

"I don't want to see her. I hate her." She threw cool margarita down her throat.

Jacki shook her head. "You hate yourself."

"I gotta go." Kat put a lot of cash on the table, because although Jacki and Raoul were okay financially, she knew they worried about the baby coming and how they could survive without Jacki working for a while. She reached down and pulled on the leather stacked-heel shoes. "I gotta rush now, off to the liquor store to stock up for the evening's debauchery. Give the clerk my phone number while I'm at it. Thank goodness wine's so cheap in California. I'm not yet reduced to drinking plonk from someplace in the world where you wouldn't even drink the water." She drank the rest of her drink standing up.

Jacki patted her hand. "You deserve much, much more out of life than a little apartment, a stressful job, and the memory of our brother to keep you company."

Kat jumped up, hugged her sister, and said, "Enough, okay? You give good advice. If I were an integrated person like you, I would do whatever you say. I'd have two-point-six kids, an eight-hour workday, and a kindly rich fella by my side, hanging on tight to make sure I didn't slip on an old banana peel."

Jacki looked her in the eye. "I'm telling you, the stars are aligning. I dreamed about us as kids last night, you and Leigh swinging in the backyard on Franklin Street. You pushed her, and she—oh, she laughed in this itty-bitty-little-girl voice, and then she tickled you until you fell. It's precious, what you had."

2

Esmé Jackson bustled around, wiping down the granite countertops in her kitchen, slipping a serrated knife through tomatoes. Her son, Ray, was due for their usual Sunday meal. She had considered something elaborate for dinner but rejected the idea, settling on strata—baked layers of bread, eggs, cheese, vegetables, cooked sausage, and crumbs. Peasant fare. He liked that sometimes.

Fifty-nine, tall, still strong except for occasional breathing problems, she swung around her generous kitchen feeling lucky, so lucky to have a son like Ray, who loved her, who still came to dinner once a week. He was as dutiful as she had been to her own mother, sometimes at great personal risk. Her mother's old flowered apron, stained with curry from last night's dinner—or was it the night before's—covered her carefully chosen slacks and blouse.

She flipped open the cupboard where she kept baking ingredients. She would make chocolate pie, his favorite, she decided, pulling out a box of graham crackers along with a pudding mix. He had eclectic taste in food, liking boxed macaroni and cheese as well as homemade pasta with a creamy béchamel. He loved pudding pie. Big baby, she thought, smiling to herself, stirring whole milk into the pudding mix in her non-reactive aluminum pot.

Humming a show tune, she turned the fire down to medium, stirring with a wooden spoon so that the pudding would not burn. When she finished, she crushed graham cracker crumbs with butter and sugar into a glass pie plate. She dusted the top with crumbs, too. Make it look fun. Ray needed bucking up. Her job made it hard to do the things she had done for him when he was young—she always tried so hard to make him happy, had devoted her life to it, in fact.

Ray filled a glass of water at the sink, then opened the cupboard door and peered underneath. "I sent Lamont over to fix that leak. He said you sent him away. It's running down the back wall, Mom. Probably down behind the bricks in the basement by now. That's going to be hard to fix."

Esmé bristled. "I don't need your fancy plumber, although of course, I really appreciate how you always want to help me. But as I told you, let me take care of my own home, okay? I'm not entirely useless, you know."

A dozen maintenance problems always hung like spiders behind the newly painted exterior of the fifty-year-old house on Close Street, Whittier. In the past year, Ray had designed a garage to replace the sagging carport. He had built a gazebo in the backyard, had established plants in the front yard, and added shutters to the windows, creating what he jokingly called "curb appeal." The house did look good, better than most old houses. However, the chimney blew smoke. The floors were so uneven you could roll a ball up and down them.

"I could build you something nicer," Ray said, looking around.

"Admit you love this place."

"Kind of. This kitchen. The old range. Even though the outside changes, the inside stays the same."

He always said that. Although he wished she would move on, he took comfort from what didn't change, just like she did: the pink and green bathroom tile, the checked curtains above the kitchen sink, the linoleum on the floor of the den. This was the place where they had stopped moving and Ray had finally made some friends.

For his own home, he had designed a showplace. *Architectural Digest* had featured it last spring. Of course, Ray's house had too few lamps, Esmé thought. The couches weren't comfortable. You couldn't leave a book lying around without the place looking messy. Too big and too clean, it was no wonder Leigh had problems with it.

Ah, but here they could relax. Home.

Leigh never did understand Esmé's house on Close Street. So many times she had harped on replacing the fixtures in the bathroom, installing a new stove, insulating the attic, removing the old asbestos, rebricking the uneven basement walls. Esmé had refused and Ray had backed her. "Leave it true to its time period," he said.

"Why not cherry it up?" Leigh had persisted. "A Nelson sunburst clock. Basket chairs. Let's turn the back patio into a real lanai, with netting and colored-glass balls." This was not long after she and Ray had married, and their hands had always touched as their bodies leaned toward each other.

"No, thanks, Leigh, although you are always so full of helpful suggestions, aren't you?" Esmé had said as kindly as she could considering how upset these suggestions made her. "I come home after a long day of checking out people's groceries and water the sweet peas against the back fence. I run the water in the sink, which fills up a lot quicker than your water in your fancy new house. My toilets don't spare the water, either, and the wall furnace may be rusty, but by God it heats the place in two minutes flat."

"In other words, don't touch," Ray had told Leigh, smiling, looking into her eyes, squeezing her hand.

"What a summer we are having," Esmé said to Ray, as he took his place at the bird's-eye maple dining room table. She thought to herself, he isn't sleeping. He looked scruffy, like he had slept in his clothes. Masking her concern, she went on, "My pink roses are in bloom. Have you ever noticed how much scent affects mood? It sure does mine. Surely there's some research on it. These sweeties smell like . . . the ocean at dusk." She stuck her nose into a cluster she had placed in a handblown vase she had bought at a flea market that harbored an invisible crack on the underside. "They smell like a world striving for perfection. Better than incense. Better than Chanel No. 5. More delicate."

Ray began to eat.

Esmé talked for a while about things that interested her that she thought might interest him, but Ray fiddled with his meal in almost total silence.

"What's the matter? You're hardly eating."

His fork rattled against the table as he set it down. "What kind of a man was he? My father?" He looked so healthy and young, so—unhappy.

She put her fork down, concentrating on her answer. Wasn't it strange that even a grown man like Ray, in his late thirties, married, was still mourning the loss of a father he hadn't seen since he was two years old? "You haven't asked about him in years. What's going on with you, Ray?"

"I've been thinking about my life. I would like the information. You never told me much. All I really know is that he left before I was born and died when I was two. You weren't married long."

She sighed. "Like I've told you before, Henry looked like you, but not so tall or good-looking. His hair was dark like yours. Had a job in a bank."

"Why didn't you keep photographs? Wedding photos, at least?"

"I told you, when he left, I was very upset, Ray. I put them in a box and somewhere along the line the box got left behind."

"And he had no family?"

"An aunt in South Dakota or somewhere. Ray, I have told you all this. He had left home very young to come out to California. He never got along with his parents. I can't remember what the problem was, anymore. He was... hard to get along with."

"Why did you break up? Was it me?"

Esmé sighed. "What do you mean?"

"Was he... afraid. Or maybe he didn't want kids."

"Maybe he was afraid, but he never knew you. It wasn't personal, honey. I'm sorry you grew up without a father, but I've tried to make it up to you." Her breathing wheezed slightly. She got up, opened a sideboard drawer, took out her inhaler, and took in a long breath. She was feeling disturbed by his haranguing, all this ancient history they had been through so many times before. Ray always went back to the past when things went wrong in his life. The medication went into her lungs, relaxing the bronchi, but making her feel a little dizzy.

She said softly, "You know I don't like talking about those years. It was hard, raising you, feeling like I had so much responsibility and no support. I love my life now. I love thinking about what good things might happen today. Like a visit from my son."

"Why did we move so much when I was growing up?"

She shrugged. "We had good reasons. Can we talk about something else?"

"Sometimes we left in the dead of night. Were we evicted?"

"Maybe once or twice. Usually not."

"Until we moved to this house, I never had a friend for more than six months."

"We had each other."

"When you're a kid, however you live is normal. If you have a parent that screams at you, well, that's life. If you're poor, you don't notice. But I look back and I wonder. You had jobs that barely covered the rent. It wasn't like your career forced us to move constantly. Eight schools before high school. That isn't normal."

"Nobody in Southern California has what you would call a normal childhood," Esmé shot back. "It's a place you come to change your life. Everybody came from somewhere else, Mexico, Oklahoma, Texas. Here you get to be who you want, and you've benefited from that, by the way. Thank God for the great public universities. Like the Marines say, suck it in, soldier. Move on. Anyway, we did settle down, staying right here from the time you were twelve."

"You know, I used to play a game with myself. At each new place, be a new guy. Be friendly; stay aloof. Be smart; play possum."

"Well, that sounds like a strategy. You had to fit in somehow." Her patience had about given out. She wondered if Ray, always a little obsessive, was developing a real problem.

"It's bothering me. I think about this house or that one, and try to remember the day we left. Who was I that day? Why did we have to start all over again? You know, I've been building models in the past few months of all the houses we lived in."

Esmé frowned. "Why?"

"Leigh and I . . . had problems."

"I'm sorry to hear that." And deeply surprised, since this was the first time she could recall Ray ever mentioning anything so personal about his marriage.

"Life gets to a certain point—" He stopped. "She wanted—" He stopped again. "I wish I knew some things, that's what I came here to tell you."

"Don't get bogged down in things that happened a million years ago, that's what I want to tell you." She got up from the table to get coffee and cups. "Hey, after supper, I have a treat for you. Remember how you threw some cantaloupe seeds into the gully behind the house one year, and they sprouted and fruited? Well, I did it again. Three baby cantaloupes—"

His hands were fists. They sat on the table as if he were holding forks in them, and he was staring at the old fruit-design wallpaper, his brow lowering. Alarmed, Esmé stopped talking. She could hear the clock in the living room ticking.

"Mom, listen. Leigh's gone."

"Gone?"

His eyes moved to the red vase, then he leaned over, re-organizing flowers, stretching out leaves with his long sensitive fingers. "Didn't you wonder why she didn't come tonight?"

"Well, I thought— What happened, Ray?" She sat down heavily in the kitchen chair.

"Did she say anything to you about us, what was happening with us?"

"Leigh doesn't confide in me. Thinks I'd be too much on your side, maybe."

"We had a fight."

She wiped her wet hands on the dishrag, preparing herself for a sleepless night, hating to see him in such pain.

"A physical fight?"

"An argument. Serious."

"Don't blame yourself. It's not your fault."

"I'm afraid it is my fault. Most of it, anyway."

God, she hated seeing her boy like this. Why did women and men, whom nature presumably meant to put together, clash so violently and do each other so much harm? "When did she leave?"

"Friday night."

"Well—where is she? Is she back here in Whittier with her parents?"

"No."

"Are you going to try to find her?"

"No point in that. It's over."

She put her hand on his arm. Only after he gently wrestled out of her grip did she realize she had squeezed so hard it must have hurt.

Kat's date that night came from Czechoslovakia, or, as he explained it in his e-mails, Slovakia, since Czechoslovakia had disappeared into history. They met at an outdoor café across from the beach in Hermosa. Tired of the brain-numbing hunt for parking, tonight she splurged on a lot, paying six bucks to cover the two hours she thought dinner might take. Gathering up her small bag, hustling down the street on her spike heels, she made it exactly on time, fifteen minutes late.

The prospect had secured a corner table with a glimpse of the sunset over the sea. He faced it; she faced him. She liked how tall he was when he stood to greet her. She even liked the way his eyes scoured her, her spiky red hair, as shiny as expensive products could make it, and her excellent rack neatly packaged in a Calvin Klein bra. She hoped he hadn't padded his online profile as much as she had padded her physical one.

He ordered the cheapest thing on the menu and skipped salad. Nik did not bike. He did not hike. He did not have an interest in exploring small towns for unusual crafts.

What he liked very much was to smoke, apparently. Since he could not smoke in the restaurant, he instead held on tight to his pack of cigarettes, flicked his lighter, complained about American puritan mores, and reminisced longingly about a past in good old Bratislava or some damn city where you could light up anywhere. He made an effort to amuse Kat with his tales of growing up. He had come over as a young boy before the Cold War ended.

She found herself looking at the door, wondering if Leigh might eat at this restaurant, what she looked like these days, examining people coming and going, watching for someone familiar to arrive and plunk down next to them, ready for a showdown. Jacki had really got her going.

When their coffee came, he took her hand in his and gave her a soulful look, saying, "How I loff American girls." Meanwhile, blonde, athletic, blithe, his American girls jogged along the boardwalk in the Hollywood sunset, movie-star skin glowing, minds free of archives, not like Kat here, thick with feeling and in a twist about an old friend. And thirty-five years of age, twice the number of years on some of the females he couldn't keep his eyes off.

However. He seemed interested enough. Except for the lingering tobacco on his clothes, he smelled good. A pushover for a decent aftershave, she had nobody else going and would welcome some peace from the nagging memories. Glad her fingernails had been painted red that very morning, glad her hands still felt soft from all the lotions, Kat rubbed his hand back, thinking, hey, I could settle for a night out of him. He'll hold me, kiss me, touch me. I won't feel lonely. I won't think about Tom or Leigh, or how it all went so wrong.

Excusing herself, she went to the restroom, where two women years younger than her primped, worrying about their wrinkles. Washing her hands with the cheap pink soap, wiping them with the harsh paper, she decided to go for it. If he wanted, he could have her, backwards, forwards, upside down.

She returned to the table, offered to split the bill, stood up, and said, "Well, time to go."

Surprised, he stood, too, then shrugged and blew kisses

on her cheeks, continental-style kisses o' death. "My treat," he said. "Nice meeting you."

As Kat walked out, she saw the reason for his insouciance. Nik had pulled a smooth switcheroo, turning his attention to the tall, slim waitress-until-she-hit-it-big, who had winked at him when they ordered. He held his credit card teasingly out of reach. She leaned over him with a big smile, pretending to grab for it.

Kat left him basking in the glow of the waitress's remarkably white teeth. She wasn't insulted, exactly—dating had become a practical matter. She could cope with the night without him or any man. Fine.

On the way home, she picked up wine, several bottles. She drove by a couple of her favorite places, but mentally perseverating on the conversation with her sister, she went home instead of finding a cool barstool on which to get blitzed.

She had been living at Candor Court in Hermosa Beach for almost eighteen months. She didn't like all the townhouse association rules, especially the no-pet rule and the no-park-on-the-street rule, but her red geraniums on the second-floor balcony, lit by the Chinese lamp she always left on in the living area, made her feel welcome. She petted a few new leaves, said hello, but the geraniums didn't talk back. Fine, fine.

Tossing her keys into the antique plate and her clothes on the floor, she decided not to open up the wine after all, to use this opportunity to work on her spirit. The sun lingered while the moon came up, and the air on the balcony cooled. The year had fallen into its deepest, truest season, ripe summer. Out on the lawns, sprinklers started up, and not a breath of air disturbed the yellow sycamore leaves.

Kat slipped out of her work clothes and into her robe and went into her walk-in closet, closing the door firmly. She had set aside this space with its tiny window to use as a shrine room. A picture of Rinpoche rested against the small brass Buddha, a tea candle in a dish in front. She lit the candle and some incense, sat down, crossed her legs, checked her posture, and began counting her breaths, letting her body calm itself.

She closed her eyes and of course there was Leigh the last time she had seen her, six years before, standing by Tom's grave, hair uncombed, hand over her eyes. So Leigh still returned to his grave to bring him flowers and mourn. Kat felt a wave of sympathy and longing for her old friend. Leigh had known and loved their beloved Tommy, who was now a fading memory for all but his close family. Kat let the emotions rise and noticed them, and now they were supposed to pass away, but they remained and built on themselves. She remembered Tom, too, what he did for her, and what she had not done for him.

All three siblings and Leigh had attended California High School, "Cal High," in Whittier. Jacki loved school, and caused Kat and Tom numerous problems later with her expectant teachers as they followed behind like muddy dogs trampling over her hallowed footsteps.

Kat studied sporadically but did well enough to take a few advanced courses. Tom studied rarely, but excelled at sports and was therefore forgiven many transgressions, and managed to advance year by year in a predictable fashion. Like Kat, he appeared college bound, although if you asked him, he would say he planned to travel the world, goof off, surf, and skateboard through life.

For some unknowable reason, in Kat's junior year, a pack of senior girls decided to hate her. She never knew if it had to do with a brief fling she had with one of the point guards on the boys' basketball team or if she had merely worn the wrong perfume one day. Or said something negative about a certain hairstyle. Or worn a T-shirt in the wrong color. At any rate, some days, when she missed the bus, she had to walk a long, long way home, a couple of miles, much of it up busy Whittier Boulevard. Tom and her best friend, Leigh, stayed late for sports or they would have walked together.

Instead, she bore alone the greasy-faced boys who recognized her and offered her rides she knew better than to accept, and the middle-aged men who stopped, goggling, wanting her in their cars where they would have power and she would have none. God only knew what would happen if she ever accepted a ride from them.

Many of those unhappy days, three girls followed her,

harassing her. Kat thought about telling Jacki, but by then Jacki was in college, not living at home, useless. She told Leigh but Leigh, being Leigh, totally overreacted, insisting she get them expelled, kick their butts, etcetera, absurd suggestions in Kat's opinion. She told Leigh she would, just to shut her up. She considered complaining to her mother, but Ma had problems of her own, an overworked husband and not enough money. And what would her mother do? Call their moms?

Then one day, the girls had come up quite close behind her, so close they didn't need to shout epithets, they could murmur them, intensely more menacing.

"We could cut you right now," one said.

"Walk faster," the last one warned, "or we'll catch you." She ran as fast as she could.

"Why are you running?" Tom said, catching up to her as she ran, sweating, the last steep hill.

"Where'd you come from?"

"Got a reprieve today. Coach got food poisoning."

"Ah." She slowed down.

"It's too hot to run."

"You're so right." She looked behind her, but the girls had disappeared, probably when they saw Tom, the quarter-back, who, over six feet by the time he was fifteen, had the exaggerated musculature of a *Batman* comic character. She breathed deeply, trying to catch her breath. A jacaranda tree bloomed big and purple between the sidewalk and the street. Even in Whittier's yellow air, no doubt stunted by pollution, by dry soil, by neglect, these curbside trees displayed themselves like Vegas showgirls wearing their best feathers.

"So why?"

"No reason."

"Liar. You never run for no reason. You look like shit lately, Kat. Even Ma noticed."

"Thanks. I hate you, too. Did she tell you to talk to me?"

He nodded.

"I've got problems. Three of them. But you can't tell Ma."

"Never."

Confiding in her younger brother for the first time in her life, trusting him for the first time, she told him everything.

The skin on his jaw tightened, and she, horrified, realized she might have unleashed a bad, bad genie. "Promise me you won't hurt them."

"Geez. Okay, but man, I don't like things that force me to think hard."

However, he must have, because, amazingly, after that day the girls avoided her in the hallways. They didn't follow her home. No nasty notes got taped to her locker.

"What did you do?" Kat asked Tom after a few weeks.

"Gave them something else to think about, the friendly attention of a couple of guys on the team who owed me. Make your enemy your friend, right? They won't bother you again."

She had always thought of him as her little buddy.

Right now, he was her hero. "Tommy, thank you. I mean it. If I were God, I'd put you in heaven."

"But that won't help me right this minute. Right this minute, I have this big paper due in American History," he said.

"Done. And don't worry, I'll disguise it by spelling a few things wrong and making egregious grammatical errors." She stayed up all night finishing his essay.

After that, she depended on him for everything, confidences, a shoulder to cry on, a minor revenge to be taken.

He protected her, but she had failed to protect him from falling in love with Leigh.

Kat returned to her breath and was mindful for about one split second, and then she was mourning Tommy again, missing him, slumping, so sad. Then she moved into the next usual phase, hating herself just like Jacki said. It wasn't all Leigh's fault, as she well knew.

She should make peace.

Breathe ten times, in and out, observe the breath coming in cold at the nostrils. Thought coming, thought going, how much longer ...

The little oven timer rang. Phooey.

Later still, not sleeping, she Googled Leigh Hubbel, now Jackson, discovered Leigh made custom furniture—of course!—and then sought out the husband, who had hundreds of mentions. Kat looked at a few, admiring the buildings and his face, which was vaguely Italian, strong-nosed, framed by a lot of dark hair. Then she downloaded a map but did not print out the directions because she liked maps and liked deciding some things for herself. Leigh and her husband lived in Topanga Canyon, in a fine house which sounded not far from what Jacki had described, but she had an office in Venice Beach, near Santa Monica, where Kat's appraisal company had its office.

Kat thought about haircuts, the ones they had gotten when they were fifteen.

Leigh had long blonde hair then, a perfect platinum running like a rushing stream, glistening in sunshine down her back. The two girls had hit a designer haircutter on Greenleaf Boulevard. "I'll give you two dollies a break on the price just for the pleasure of slipping my fingers through your hair," the haircutter had said. Kat thought he was nasty but Leigh thought he was funny, and she liked funny. Maybe reading their minds, he trimmed Leigh's hair respectfully, then crew-cutted Kat's red hair into a short fuzz.

Kat's parents flipped, which Leigh loved. "It's a fundamental requirement for kids our age to make our folks regret giving birth as often as possible." She plucked at Kat's scalp with fire-red fingernails. "When it grows back," Leigh said, patting the fuzz critically, "let's get that jerk to dye it blonde."

"Why would I?" She liked her fiery hair.

"Men like it."

"I ask for a good reason and you lob me crap?"

This was when she still loved Leigh more than anyone else, and long before Tom fell in love with Leigh.

Kat had a home address for Leigh and her husband, and a phone number for Leigh's business. She called Leigh's business number and left a simple message, asking for a call back.

3

Ray left his mother's by eight. The drive from Whittier to Topanga Canyon at that hour on a Sunday night took him an unusually grueling two hours due to a pileup on the 605. He pulled his blue Porsche into the expansive, decoratively paved driveway of his home, pushed the remote to open the garage, drove in, and turned the key to off. He sat in his car.

He should be relieved. Leigh hadn't said anything about anything to his mother. Instead, he felt a familiar—what he was starting to call—craziness. Confusion. His mother fed him, loved him, and never pried into his private life. She also never shared her own. He didn't believe there wasn't something behind all that moving they did, more than just wanting a change of scene or boredom. It didn't make sense. And he didn't believe her when she claimed it did.

At first, a year or so ago when he had started on the models, Leigh had laughed, saying he was saving a pile, doing his own therapy. Then things changed.

He had a strong feeling that his work in the downstairs studio was important, but he didn't know why. He even

believed it could somehow bring him and Leigh closer together, help them resolve the issues driving them apart.

Instead, his models destroyed what they had.

Heaving himself out of the car, he clicked the remote
lock. Outside, he pushed the button to close the garage
door, carefully avoiding the light sensor, stepped onto the
driveway, then stopped to study his house.

The big home and eccentric plantings, bulleted by low-
lighting that had taken him months to design, loomed
over him, imposing, fearsome, if you had imagination.
The house spoke to him, with grass-paper walls, sanded
timbers, the glass lit from behind to act as a divider, all angles, sharpness, stone.

Leigh hated what she called the razorblade feel of the
outside iron fences and the minimalist furniture inside,
saying all these affectations of design made her bones
ache.

She had never felt welcome here. He knew that. The
painstaking hand-finished furniture she made mostly
stayed in her shop and out of his realm, with a few personal exceptions. Walking up to the house, he brushed a
spiderweb from the ornate woodwork flanking the eight-
foot-high front door. Its key, an anachronism that looked
Victorian, rattled on the same ring as his plastic-topped
car key. He had intentionally bought an antique lock, and
then found a locksmith to create the proper key. He had
always loved keys. This one kept the frivolous away. No casual burglar could easily break through this particular co-
nundrum. Hell, if someone did, I'd be the first to applaud
him, Ray thought, pushing open the door.

Inside, he barely glanced through a glass wall that showed sprawling brown-green hills and, in the far distance, the shimmering ocean, spotlighted by a large, low moon. He had the new fancy seamless corner windows, the better to expose the view and create a floating environment. The house, which he privately called "Eyrie," had gotten him his start. Clients came there and were properly inspired and intimidated into paying the high prices his firm charged for its vision. If the place ever sold, over his dead body, he could retire and live a long, comfortable life on the proceeds.

He dumped his keys on the massive slab table in the entryway. Negotiating his way toward the kitchen, he remembered his tight-lipped refusal of every one of Leigh's suggestions. He should have encouraged her. Things could have gone so differently. He had been stingy, secretive, protective, like his mother. Strange, human, autonomic, to reenact in his personal life the same repression that had enraged him since childhood.

The egomaniac poured himself a glass of Obester Sangiovese from the Half Moon Bay tasting room. He tasted it, but might as well have sipped water. The rich depth of this particular vintage was wasted on him in his present mood. Taking his glass along, grabbing a hunk of cheese and a few crackers, he headed toward his workshop.

Stepping carefully down the treacherous staircase that he had designed without railings, that paid no heed to the fact that people got drunk and fell off, including himself one notable night, he entered his lair, a room nearly fifty feet long. He flipped on the overheads, concentrated halogen beams that kept the room warm without overheating.

Right now, he had four models going of the earliest houses he could remember, the ones he had lived in from the time he was four until he turned eight years old. He sipped his drink, then he set his cut-crystal glass down. He ate cheese on a cracker, then picked the glue gun off a shelf at the end of the room. He wanted to tackle the railroad tracks behind the house on Dittmar, in Whittier. The house alone didn't tell the whole story. Precisely, carefully, consulting the blueprints he had obtained a few months before, he laid a long line of hot glue behind the tiny lattice backyard fence. Every morning and many nights the train had roared by, sometimes more than a hundred cargo cars long.

He had counted them endlessly. He should know.

He stroked his chin. The bedroom window was too high for a little boy inside to see anything outside. Adjustments needed to be made to the elevation. The blueprints were wrong; he remembered his bedroom window, the white curtains Esmé put up every time, the old thrift-store bed that made his back hurt.

He ate another cracker and set to work. However, the painful truth was, he couldn't remember the details so well anymore. About midnight, he tried to sleep on the daybed, but couldn't. Halogens burning down on him like pink-tinged eyes, he went to the bookshelf and knelt on the industrial carpet, pulling out a heavy plastic container that contained his deep past, pre-Leigh.

His mother took few photos of him as a child. Each

time they moved, he was allowed exactly two boxes for papers, toys, and books. He found his youthful drawings along with color photos of many faded houses that looked so similar now, so shabby to his educated eye, snapshots of him doing flips in various backyards, his mom hysterical while he nearly cracked his skull open. The tire swing at some house. Where? Maybe on Ceres Street?

No pictures of his father. His mother must have retained feelings for him; she had never gone out with anyone else again. She wasn't bad-looking even now for a woman in her late fifties, but she had that air: I've put that behind me.

He imagined his father with a flat-toothed grin just like his, flanked by sharp canines. Leigh had called him vulpine once. He had been vaguely flattered. Another girl had once told him he looked like a young Jack Nicholson. Unearthing several pictures of himself in his teens, he wondered what he had really been thinking all those years when most of his energy went into fitting in. At Hillview he had been a doper. At Cal High he had made himself into a preppie. When they moved, he would start the new school circumspectly, laying low until he could figure out a harmless persona that would permit a smooth year.

He regretted not knowing his father, if only to see the color of his eyes in memory, and whether the man had a mind for physics or physical labor. He moved on, to his small collection of plastic toys—colorful cars and trains.

Also, he found a list on the endpaper of a book that he read over and over every summer of his life, wishing he could live it, an E. Nesbit story called *The Phoenix and the Carpet.* He didn't know why his mother saved this particular favorite, but he felt grateful. She had read it to him several times. He thought maybe she loved it, too.

Then, jumbled at the bottom of a box, he found the keys.

He picked them up for inspection. Every house they stayed in, whenever they moved, he had kept the key. His mother, who held many day jobs, insisted he have a key to any house they lived in, so he did. She was always careful with keys. The houses were kept locked. Keys were precious. "Protectors," she called them.

His younger self had assembled the collection onto a large silver key ring, which jingled promisingly. Some of the keys still bore traces of labels in Magic Marker or squiggles on masking tape.

He shook the key ring, enjoying its jingle. Then, opening the book to its blank front page, he read the addresses he had painstakingly printed, one after another and another:

Norwalk, Whittier, Downey, Redondo Beach, Yorba Linda, Placentia, Fullerton.

The list went on, scattering his past through all the bleak suburbs of Los Angeles and Orange County. Sometimes they only moved a few miles, from tract to tract. So his mother could keep her job?

Eight schools by the time he started high school, he told himself again.

Why?

As he sat there, his chest filled with a nameless emotion, he heard the doorbell ring upstairs. He checked his watch: one-thirty. From a bin in the closet he grabbed a baseball bat, then jumped up the spiral stairs. He didn't want to answer the door, but if he didn't answer, they might think he wasn't home and decide to break in. Imperiously, the bell rang again.

Without turning on any lights on the main floor, he crept toward the front door. He peered outside, then unlatched the lock.

In burst James Hubbel, Leigh's father. He must have come straight from work, because he wore his dark blue cop uniform and appeared tired. "Put the bat down," Hubbel commanded.

Ray put the bat down. "It's late."

"I see you can't sleep, either," Hubbel said. "You think her mother and I are sleeping? You think that?"

"What's the problem, Jim?"

"Where's my daughter?"

"Not home."

"This is no time to play games, Ray."

"Don't tell me what to do."

"I'm not here because I insist on pancakes instead of eggs for breakfast!" Hubbel yelled. "I'm not here wondering why no grandkids yet!"

Ray was happy he was still dressed. He would hate to be wearing his skivvies, facing this six foot three ex-Marine-turned-policeman with eyebrows as thick as overgrown grass. Leigh loved her father, describing him as a tough guy with a good heart.

Hubbel pushed his way past Ray, more bully than heart at the moment, looking around. The living room, serene, bare, full of textured beiges, remained empty and did not speak. He went to the white granite fireplace, and pulled the LCD screen aside.

"No sign of her in there," Ray said. He knew this was not the right thing to say to Leigh's father, and yet he could not help himself. He felt terribly defensive.

"I'm going upstairs," Hubbel said. He climbed the main stairway, the cantilevered concrete stairs that seemed to float upward, to the second floor. Ray heard him above, opening doors and drawers, slamming them shut. He sat down on the couch and stared dully at the fireplace. The uncurtained windows felt like black holes sucking out his insides. I'm having a breakdown, he thought, but found it hard to care.

Moments later, Hubbel marched down the stairs again, long arms swinging. "This is goddamn dangerous, this stairway. You have a problem with rails?"

"They're ugly."

"Aw, I hate this aesthetics over function crap." He landed in the entryway, and stood close to Ray, who had gotten up and opened the front door.

"You satisfied?" Ray said.

"You kidding? Where is my daughter?"

"She hasn't called you?"

"Not since Friday. Her mother's upset. She was supposed to go shopping with her Saturday. Aren't you listening to your phone messages? You two have a fight?"

The unwelcome memory of Leigh's last night at home assaulted Ray. "An argument, yes. Look, I don't know where she is, okay? She's gone."

"She left? When? Did she take her car?"

Ray answered the questions. Hubbel never let him lower his eyes, look away. Yes, she took the car, took her purse, packed a bag. No, she didn't say where she was— she was very—he thought she'd come back after clearing her head for a while—no calls. No, no calls, no e-mails, no notes.

"Why wouldn't she call us?" Hubbel said, thinking out loud. "She knows—she knows—"

"It's just the weekend. I'm sure we'll hear from her tomorrow. Come on, Jim, she's an adult and it's really late and I have to work in the morning."

"You should have let us know. I've seen some things I can't even talk about in my business, Ray. You hear? I don't let people I love go off the radar for days. I'm going to call some people, some hospitals."

"If you talk to her, tell her—"

"Tell her what?"

"To get in touch."

"I don't like the sound of this. I don't like the lame way you're talking. It's like you've given up on ever seeing her again. She comes back, she calls, you tell her to call her mother." Hubbel stood very close to him at the doorway, his big hard stomach pressed against Ray. "If I find out you harmed a hair on her head—well, I'll kill you."

4

Monday morning before work, Kat listened to two messages from Jacki. Nothing from Leigh yet. Well, it was only eight-thirty. Still, she had always been an early bird.

She punched in some numbers.

"Leigh Jackson Designs," a girlish voice chirped.

"Hello. I'm trying to reach Leigh."

"She's not in yet. Can I leave her a message?"

"Hmm. This is an old friend, Kat Tinsley. She might remember me. I mean, in case she's there and just busy. She might want to talk to me."

"She's not here. What's your number?"

"I need to talk to her right away."

"Are you interested in custom furnishings?"

"No, but I do need to talk to her."

"She'll get back to you when she can."

"When might that be?"

The receptionist sighed. "When she can."

Frustrated, Kat left her number again. With no time to call Jacki, Kat rushed to her office in Santa Monica.

She had a Superior Court appearance, then two houses

to evaluate, one in Topanga, the other in Long Beach. In both cases, a divorce was imminent. Distraught parties awaited her report as to value. She needed to be scrupulously fair or she would be challenged or impeached in court.

As she scurried through the traffic, feeling the heat already working to melt her windshield, she wondered what it would be like to have owned a property in Topanga for many years and to have watched that property's value skyrocket. As a child, she had visited a friend who lived in the canyon, and what she remembered was her friend's mom chasing a rattlesnake up the street with a rake, trying to cut off its head. The family used to drive to a roadside spring and fill their bottles with pure water every Saturday.

How times had changed. The decrepit cottages had morphed into estates. The estates had transmogrified into feudal fiefdoms. Topanga had become très chic, as close as you could get to L.A. without having to play L.A. games. And Leigh's house was a work of art. Leigh's mother had money, Kat recalled. She had grown up in the big house in Whittier across from Kat's little house. It wouldn't seem strange to her.

Tinsley Enterprises in Santa Monica wasn't a long way from Hermosa Beach, it just felt that way because of the daily life-risking commute. Kat pulled into the small parking lot next to the office on Santa Monica Boulevard, pleased to get a spot so easily for a change, picked up her things, and ran up the two flights of stairs to the office, where the receptionist greeted her with a cup of coffee, half milk, just the way she liked it.

Kat and Jacki's dad, Gus Tinsley, had opened this real estate appraisal firm in the seventies and muddled along for decades until he died suddenly, still young, not long after divorcing their mother. Kat had first gotten involved in the business during summers starting in high school, following her dad around and watching, with astonishment, as cheap fixer-uppers ascended into properties worth millions.

She continued to work for his successor, Micky Gowecki, finally passed the test to become an appraiser, and now felt confident in her work. She knew the market, the psychology, and the loopy, blustering desire and greed that drove people to question her judgment, and she was good on the witness stand in disputed cases. Her work had swiftly become almost unassailable, and she was earning a rep for fairness.

She spent the late morning in court wearing her credibility togs: fake diamond studs, fake diamond solitaire at her neck, black silk suit that nipped snugly at the waist, making her look thinner. Up on the chopping block today, a house in La Habra, an utterly basic, roofed dwelling.

People who didn't have much often fought the most brutally to hold on to what they had.

The soon-to-be-ex–husband started off with some dignity. He answered his own attorney's questions calmly. Then his soon-to-be-ex–wife's attorney, a female, picked away at him. The man appeared to be choking, the way he worked the tie at his throat. His face fluctuated between pasty and blotched as the emotions ratcheted up. He had a right to that house! He grew up there! His father built it! He had happy memories galore! This greedy witch would fix it up and flip it, destroying a family legacy!

The ex-wife took the stand. She still lived in the house. He had left her, cheated on her, broken her heart, and she couldn't see why she should have to move. Why should he be rewarded for being such an asshole? He hated the house and complained constantly about it. He'd sell it for a bundle and make a huge profit.

Kat took the stand, trying to remain objective, answering questions about square footage, coverage, comps. This house had lovely landscaping, which added an extra thirty grand to its value.

She explained how she had arrived at her valuation, describing the number of bedrooms, legally only two, not three, since one had no closet, the state of the paint and rugs, poor, the repairs necessary to bring the property up to snuff. She testified that having only one bathroom cut into value, showed pictures of the street that revealed a run-down, undesirable ambiance.

By the time she was done, not a single person in the courtroom liked her.

On the way to the house in Long Beach, she called the Jackson house. When a machine answered, she hung up without leaving a message, a little nervous about her mood and what she might unleash if she let her mouth start up.

What would she blurt? "Hi, Leigh? It's me, Kat. Let's meet up and see a movie and hang out together like we used to do a hundred years ago, when my brother was alive and we were younger and hadn't done reprehensible things."

She called Leigh's business number again. "Sorry to bug you but—I'm Leigh's old friend—"

"Oh, yes, you again," said Leigh's receptionist, suddenly not sounding so certain, suddenly young. "I'm sorry. Leigh hasn't been in."

"Is she sick?"

"I don't know. I haven't spoken with her. In fact, I don't know what to do. I'm stuck here with no boss, you know? It's strange. And the really strange part is—" She stopped.

Maybe she had thought twice about unloading her troubles on a stranger.

"Tell me." Kat used her most authoritative voice.

And the younger woman caved. "She never misses a day, unless she tells me. See, on Friday, she left early for a funeral or something—she was upset and said she wouldn't be back, so she asked me to come in yesterday."

"On a Sunday?"

"We had some work to make up and she said she'd pay me double! She never showed up. Now here it is Monday, and she doesn't come in and I can't reach her. No one answers her mobile phone. This is weird. And I'm due a check today. I need my money for rent. What should I do?" the receptionist asked.

"Have you spoken with her husband?"

"I finally called him at work. He sounded mad and said he didn't know where she was. I don't even know if I should come in tomorrow. I mean, I don't run this place. She's my boss. She's supposed to tell me what to do."

It was strange, Leigh not showing up for work and not calling. "You should continue to come to work until you hear either from Leigh or her husband," Kat advised, again slipping into her older, wiser persona.

"We have clients calling, wanting to know how the work is going. I don't know what to say."

"Tell them it's in progress. There will be a slight, a very slight, delay. And you'll get your check soon; don't worry."

Relieved sigh. "Okay."

"Do you know Leigh's husband?"

"Not really." A pause. "She brags about him sometimes, how successful he is, how smart. But she makes as much as he does. Sometimes more."

"Really?"

"She's not famous like him. She's nobody as far as his world is concerned but she has a fabulous reputation around here. People adore her furniture. That's what this town worships, quality. You wouldn't believe some of her clients. Movie stars, directors, producers—"

"So where is she, I wonder?"

"If you talk to her, tell her Ashley is having a fit. I mean, I hope she's okay, but damn. I can't run this place alone, and I can't work for nothing."

Ray worked at Wilshire Associates, an architectural firm, in an office he kept intentionally low-tech. Other than a laptop and a big flat-screen monitor he attached when needed, he spent most of his time at a large, north-facing drafting table that overlooked the tall shining glass windows with a view of West L.A., drawing freehand with soft, smeary charcoal pencils. The architectural offices, on the fifth floor of a building on the boulevard, featured one whole wall of windows almost two stories high. He and Martin Horner, as partners and senior architects, had the views. Associates and assorted other support rabble skulked on the darker backside of the floor, which, true to the classy image the firm enjoyed cultivating, also had windows, only smaller.

Today he worked at his tilted table on the Antoniou mansion. Deadline for the preliminary drawings was only three days away, on Thursday. Achilles Antoniou, a restaurant owner originally from Athens, thought Ray was designing the Parthenon warmed over for his eight-bedroom spread in Laguna Cliffs, and Ray had started out with enough Doric columns to satisfy him, but this morning he had tossed the preliminary drawings and started over with a stunning modern structure that would give Antoniou the thing he was actually looking for, social cachet. Ray could talk him into the new design, he was sure.

He had never done this before, ignored the client's vague wishes. He had always teased them out and brought them to life before.

Today he felt unable to do that. Everything else in his life had gone to hell. He did not want this project to go the same way. Antoniou would get what he needed, not what he thought he needed. And so would Ray.

People knew better than to interrupt him when he was sketching, and Suzanne fielded his calls, so he spent most of the morning alone. At quarter to one, he put his pencil down. He would grab something from the vending machines, then take off. He checked the hallway. No one. Good.

Too late, he spotted Martin, and Martin spotted him.

"Hang on, Ray. I need to talk to you. I'll just be a minute here."

Ray grunted and sat down in a chair at a messy desk. Meanwhile, Martin, continuing a process that had gone on for quite some time already judging by the client's fatigued look, worked his charm by the overgrown acacia tree in the far corner, where the windows were high and the view awe-inspiring. "We create a vision for you, something supremely yours, something that says, hey, I've made it, and I get to make things look how I think they should look."

The potential client, a director with fashionably thick intellectual glasses and a beard, who was famously rich and image-conscious, nodded.

"You want an indoor-outdoor pool, we provide it. The parties will never end."

The potential client took off his glasses and wiped them with a sparkling clean ironed handkerchief.

That's a no, Ray thought to himself, but not to worry. Martin was on top of it. "Or a Japanese garden with pines imported from Kyoto and nephrite boulders taken from the coastal waters off Big Sur. We can do that, too."

The beard moved as though the guy was preparing to smile. Bingo.

"A teahouse," Martin crooned. "Wabi-sabi walls, golden bamboo. Gravel walks. Ginkgos. Peace. A wonderful torii gate. We can build you that."

"I have always wanted to visit the temples at Kyoto."

"You could look for some very special addition to your garden there. Or look for tea-bowls. I know a dealer in the Ginza who has eighteenth-century bowls from a Zen monastery. I'll call him. You are gonna impress the hell out of your neighbors. Not that you care about that." Martin got a full nod there, wild enthusiasm from this cautious man.

Not a great architect, Martin was a great people-reader. Ray often watched client sessions with reverence. These people danced with Martin, and they danced to Martin's music, however vulgar and jerky.

"Look, I know you've interviewed a few other firms. That's just smart business, and you're a savvy guy; everybody knows that. An investment like this, of course you've got to be careful. But here's what we can give you that they can't."

Ray was dying to hear what that could be.

"A chance to play God."

An eyebrow raised slightly.

"A chance to create your personal universe. You are part of the creation, every step of the way."

The guy totally bought Martin's horseshit. When Ray next passed the desk, Martin was shoveling paperwork toward the client, smooth-talking in between signatures, chuckling like a little kid.

"How come he got born under the brightest lucky star?" Martin said after the new client left.

"You're doing okay, last time I looked."

"Yeah," Martin said. "Thanks for waiting. I hate waiting and I know you do, too."

"No, it's a rare privilege to get a close-up view of a sea lion devouring an otter. Nature at its most bestial." Ray looked at his watch. "I'm in a rush. I have to run."

"What's up?"

"I have an appointment on the museum project in a few minutes." In fact, the appointment wasn't until the next morning, but he didn't want to talk to Martin, didn't want to spend time with him, didn't want to deal with him. At some point, he was going to have to figure out what he did want to do to Martin. "One of the directors asked for another model on grounds that ours is white Styrofoam and looks it. Our competitor spent at least thirty grand on their model and it shows."

Martin shook his head. "I hate losing that competition, but that's more money than we can front on spec. These people have no idea how much time, money, and expertise goes into building a model. Also, they have no imagination."

"Don't worry, we can talk him out of it. Models are a thing of the past." Funny thing to say, Ray thought, interrupting himself momentarily. "Wait until he gets a load of the computer renderings. I'm taking along the Parks project, too, just to shut the director up. Denise says the final presentation's coming along well, although you know Denise. She never panics until the last minute."

Denise Bell, one of the windowless-office denizens, took their models and made them look absolutely real by combining real photos with computer jazz. Then she created presentations that were more like mini-Hollywood films, including music, interviews, narration, and sound effects. Her talent brought them a lot of business.

"We ought to start giving Denise bonuses on the big ones," Ray went on.

"Maybe," Martin said, which was a surprising concession, since he never spent a dime he didn't have to.

"Okay. So I'm out of here."

"This will take just a second."

Conspicuously, Ray checked his watch, then gritted his teeth and sat down in the high-backed plush chair opposite. "Snap. Snap."

"I need to ask you something," Martin said.

Ray tapped his foot.

Martin knocked the end of a drawer twice, then pulled it open. Inside, he had told Ray once, he hid problems and, sometimes, solutions.

He pulled out a bottle of wine.

"Hey, Martin, what the hell. Are you joking? It's the middle of the day! And I told you—"

"I promise this won't slow you down. It keeps me creative," Martin said. "Check this out. It's lunch." He poked his head around a door. "Suzanne's gone. She always locks the outside door." The clock had clicked one, and everyone had rushed right out the door by the time it clicked one oh one. "It's just you and me this fine warm afternoon." He uncorked the wine, pulling two crystal glasses from the drawer.

Ray shook his head. "No thanks. You're an idiot, Martin."

"It's medicinal."

"I don't need medicine to feel creative, pal."

"Well, your loss. Still, I'm surprised."

"Why?"

"Leigh likes it so much." Martin poured his glass full and crossed his leg. "Glug glug," he said, smiling, and let his handsome head with its thick brown hair fall a little back so Ray could see his Adam's apple bobble as he swallowed. It reminded him of Leigh on the night that—

It was then that Ray realized how much he hated Martin. The hate burst into full and complete existence, undeniable, hot. He could feel his face reddening. He couldn't hide it.

So Martin wanted to talk about Leigh, and drinking gave him courage. Okay, Ray thought. He'll get more back than he expects on that subject.

"We're different, Leigh and I," Ray said in a hard voice that Martin should have noted.

"In my opinion—not so much," Martin remarked. "You're yang, aggressive, male, and all that, and she's yang, too. Yang yang. Like clashing bells." He breathed in deeply.

Ray felt the bloom of blood vessels flaring in his face and said nothing.

"Is everything okay between you two?"

"What fucking gall, asking me that."

"Are you two fighting?" Martin asked. "Because you should tell me. We have mutual clients and Leigh doesn't answer her phone at work—the receptionist told me she hasn't come in at all today. In fact, she's worried."

"Poor, neglected Martin," Ray mocked. "Did Leigh miss an important date?"

A pause. Martin poured himself another glass, figuring things out. His hand was shaking. "What?"

"A date."

"What do you mean?"

"You've been sleeping with her. I assume that involves arrangements."

Air blew from between Martin's sensual lips. Had that attracted Leigh, the exaggerated definition of Martin's upper lip? Ray rubbed his own with his fingers.

"Oh, shit, Ray."

"I followed you. The Camelot Motel, Torrance, Pacific Coast Highway. Like a country tune. I watched her going in there, wearing that black lace shirt she wears that makes her breasts look big."

"Hell. Ray, you're hurt, man, but I've never known you to be mean-spirited—"

"I watched you leave the motel first a few hours later. You have a nasty five o'clock shadow at the end of the day," Ray said. "You ought to shave twice like Nixon did."

"You probably want to punch me out. I can't blame you for that." Martin was already moving into his smooth-over mode; he obviously felt he would not get punched out, that Ray was a professional, for God's sake.

Ray continued his own train of thought. "She came out ... disheveled. Her blouse hung low on the left and her jeans, they weren't buttoned all the way up. She was still messing with them. When she came home that night, she said she had worked late and accomplished a lot. I wondered what she thought she was accomplishing at a motel on a noisy highway on Wednesday night with my partner, my former friend. Designing a one-of-a-kind armoire?" He laughed.

"So you caught us."

"Yes."

Martin set his glass on the desk and licked his lower lip back and forth, apparently trying to think about how to approach this catastrophe.

He was so predictable, Ray could have mouthed the words he would say next.

"It's completely over. I swear it. She dumped me. She loves you, Ray."

"Go on," Ray said.

"No need to get worked up about it," Martin said, and to Ray's satisfaction, he began to look apologetic. "We're a good team. Can't let a mere woman get in the way, even one as outstanding as Leigh. Leigh and I—we never had a regular thing. She was a slipup. Very brief." He cocked his head as if waiting for Ray to refute this obvious bull. "I'm sorry. I hope we can get past this."

Ray said nothing.

"Can we?"

"No."

"It will never happen again," Martin said. "Our

relationship—yours and mine—is much more important. I can't believe I put that in jeopardy. I hope you can
rethink this once we've all had a chance to cool down
about it." Then he asked, "But, Ray, where is she? Her receptionist at work is having to close up the office today. Is
she sick? Did she—leave you?"

"Did she want to leave me?"

"I can't speak to that."

Had Leigh maintained some feeble level of discretion
after all? Had she refused to talk about her relationship
with Ray to her lover? Ray hoped so. The woman he
married, the one he thought he knew once, would never
have betrayed him like that. "When did you see her last,
Martin?"

"Wednesday. We went to the movies. She wanted to
end it. Wanted to tell me all about you, how much she
loved you." Gesturing, glass in hand again, he needed to
explain some more. He didn't seem to notice Ray's hands,
fists now, the tension in his body.

This fury—Ray loved this fury. He felt like he was being defrosted by this murderous heat radiating inside
him.

Martin said urgently, "Ray, listen to me. I'd like to be
honorable, insofar as a bastard can be honorable under
these circumstances. It was only a few times. When she felt
neglected. Trivial. No effect on your marriage, you know?"

Ray recalled the moment he knew, not the moment he
confronted her, just the instant he saw what was going on.

Leigh had come home, not too late, around nine, on a night a week or so before their final fight, bedraggled, heading for a shower.

"Come to bed," Ray had said, worried. "Wrap me in your lovely arms."

Her skin under the badly buttoned clothes glowed. Her eyes had a luster.

Ray recalled that look. Postcoital. He knew instantly. He stepped back from her.

She didn't notice. "Okay, sweetie," she said, needing transition time, grabbing a towel from the linen cupboard, running toward the bathroom. "Just let me take off the day's grime."

So, for ever after, he would think of Martin Horner as the day's grime.

"No effect on our marriage, huh?"

For the first time that afternoon, Martin really looked at Ray. "That's the last time we got together. I swear it."

So, they went to the movies together, not just to creepy motels. The idea of them sharing such casual intimacy crushed Ray. "What did Leigh say?"

"About?"

"The future. Ours."

Martin sucked unhappily on his wine. "She doesn't like talking about you, okay? But this one time, she was crying. She broke down, said you'd changed lately. Got cold on her. Scared her sometimes, because you always seem angry lately."

"You fucking asshole. You're a bad friend, an unfaithful husband, an absent father, a lousy architect. I ought to walk out of here and never come back."

"Oh, hey, Ray, no." Martin looked around as if seeking a miraculous solution to his problem. "I screwed up, okay? I'm truly disgusted with myself. I took advantage of her when she was down and I—betrayed a friend. It's unforgivable. Yes! But this is business, Ray! This is not about the sorry state of your marriage. This is important!"

Ray stood up to go. Now truly alarmed, Martin grabbed for his arm. "You're overreacting! We've got legal obligations here, Ray! Clients I sold on you!"

Ray clenched his jaw, took his right fist and hurled it, enjoying the crack it made on contact with Martin's chin, although it hurt his hand more than he could have dreamed. He might have actually broken bones. He stared at his hand, wondering if he had.

Martin staggered back. "You think you're some big creative designer?" he shouted, rubbing his chin, eyes watering. "Let me tell you how it is, Ray. I sell product. You produce it. You're a fucking technician. I've watched you for years stealing left and right from every genius who ever designed a building before. You're a great mimic but that's it. Ten years from now, I guarantee you, nobody's going to be saying breathlessly, 'Oh, there's a Ray Jackson building.' They'll be saying, 'Oh, after Louis Kahn. After I. M. Pei. After Frank Gehry or Michael Graves.' After ever after."

"To hell with you. Die, Martin."

"You're the one who's dead! That's just what she told

me after we made love. Twice! I took her from the rear!"
Martin shouted. Ray walked out into the hallway.

Where big-eyed Suzanne, holding a handful of letters,
gulped. "I stayed in to finish his letters, Ray," she said. "He
told me to show some initiative or start looking for another job."

Martin now stood in the doorway, still breathing hard.
"Leigh told me she was afraid you followed her," he said to
Ray's back as Ray walked toward his office. "I laughed it
off. Called her paranoid."

5

Back in his office, door closed to the world, Ray gathered up the museum plans, breathing hard. Maybe he was having a heart attack, and his hand was puffing up.

His life was falling around him. First Leigh, and now his work, his refuge. Recalling Martin's graphic sexual imagery, Ray shivered, thinking that Leigh was so unhappy she had let Martin—let him—damn Martin! And damn her!

Glad he had lied about having to leave early for a meeting, he tidied his desk quickly, stowing his current projects in one of the enormous flat drawers that held dozens more. Martin's words replayed through his mind. They had gone to the movies like teenagers!

Oh, Martin was good, had slashed at him so accurately with words that were only now starting to bleed inside him. "Mimic" in particular, that hit hard. Ray wasn't thinking so much about himself as an architect when he replayed the word. He thought about himself as a man.

He went to his window, the one he had sacrificed so much for. Every unhappy adult probably started off as an unhappy child. He must have had happy times. Esmé swore he did. What he remembered instead was taking one step forward and getting yanked back two steps, painfully. He would be a different person now, the man who could have held on to his wife if he hadn't been ripped out of the soil over and over when he was young, until he'd lost track of who he was and where he was, rolled himself up like a bad set of blueprints, and stopped growing.

He closed the blinds and flipped off the light, trying to calm himself. Maybe Leigh and his mother had the definitive line on him: he had an unhealthy obsession with the past. Maybe he needed a good shrink to unload on for the next fifty years to work things out, inching toward a wholeness in minuscule increments.

He couldn't wait for that.

Closing the door to his office behind him, he told Suzanne he would not be back. If she wondered why he wouldn't be back, she didn't say, keeping her head down over her desk, avoiding his eyes.

Martin, like any sneaking skunk, had slipped off to some dark place.

Ray was splintering. Nothing held him together anymore.

In the parking lot below the building, he ran his hand along the hood of Martin's Ferrari, admiring the amazing custom paint job, duotone black and blue, so swank the vehicle could be framed and hung on a wall as art. These designers shaped cars like jungle predators, tight-haunched and ready to pounce. Martin kept his baby spotless.

Ray looked around; he was alone for the moment. He

took a key from the immense collection in his pocket, choosing one that was particularly exotic and jagged, and then he ran it hard along the driver's door, feeling a puerile burst of joy at the sight and sound of such destruction. It left an ugly metal scar, deep. Martin, with two children, a house in Brentwood, a beautiful wife, and many affairs under his belt, ought to appreciate the moronic gesture, since Martin frequently behaved moronically.

Ray's own sleek Porsche welcomed him inside, its pleasant cool air blowing around his legs and over his overheated face. He opened the glove compartment; yes, the keys from his childhood were nestled there like old friends. Real friends, sheltering friends. His hand flexed okay, no broken fingers. Martin hadn't even fallen down. The anger that had propelled the blow had been so powerful it was remarkable that the blow hadn't sent Martin sailing through the window.

Ray drove through the dense maze of Los Angeles, along several freeways for forty-five minutes to reach the first address on his list. Ten keys on the ring gave him no indication which key fit what house, but he did have a certainty that each one meant something.

Norwalk, Bombardier Avenue. The name must have derived from World War II, he decided, plodding up the stark, hot sidewalk. Strange thing to name a street. The Santa Ana winds had been blowing for days, and today the wind blasted furiously and randomly, crazy-making, pricking at his skin, insinuating itself, burrowing disturbingly underneath like unclean parasites. He forged on, wiping dirt from his eyes, excited and fearful at the same time.

The block seemed deserted. The residents marched out to their cars at seven-thirty and drove through heavy traffic to office parks, where they would attempt to be productive. Then they drove home through heavy traffic to watch the hypnotic blue-lit object in the living room, where they attempted to forget their efforts of the day. The routine hadn't changed since Ray was a kid. He looked at swing sets in the identical backyards, the scorched plots of grass in front, paint peeling along the gutters, roofs patched, an indescribable decrepitude in a place that must have seemed hopeful fifty years before.

The builders of these subdivisions hadn't thought a half-century into the future. They had thought: how fast can we get these things built? The ranch houses showed their lousy construction ethos. Or maybe Ray just knew more now.

He didn't know the exact number. As with so many houses in L.A. County, the numbers had changed over the decades. He tried to latch onto the right house based upon his memories of the place, but things had altered too much.

At the end of this street was the school he had attended in kindergarten. His mother had told him she always tried to move within walking distance of a school. He recalled his teacher, Mrs. Cangi. The five-year-olds called her Mrs. Candy, and thought themselves hysterical.

He walked on, remembering. He had come home from kindergarten, marched up to the porch, and knocked on the door to his new home. No one answered. His mother, usually reliable, had not opened the door. At first merely frustrated, he had sat down on the steps. Eventually, a neighbor walked by, staring hard at Ray, as if he didn't belong. Several more minutes passed. No one else came by. The grown-ups were all gone. Planes and bugs buzzed in the stifling sky; otherwise, all was still and very hot.

Ray began to experience a hollowness that frightened him, as if the bravado was draining from him. Invisible, he only existed like one of the plants in the yard, waving in the wind, unnoticed. He had no way to get inside, no home to go to, no mother to greet him. She had left him, vanished. Reduced to nothing, a bubbling mass of fear by now, he had pounded on the front door.

He had screamed.

Moments later his mother, hands full of papers, had torn up to the porch and gathered him into her arms.

"Where were you?" he cried.

"Mailing letters."

Was this house, on the right side of the street, with a small porch that didn't look right, the correct place? What about this one?

Finally, he decided he spotted something familiar, that porch. The one he had screamed upon. Yes, here was the place, painted dirty adobe orange now, with yellow trim, closer to the school than he expected. On the right-hand side he could see the bedroom he had slept in as a little boy, its window covered by a flowered curtain.

Recognizing the tiny tract house sent a pang of sorrow through him.

So it was real. He had not seen this place since they left it. The model he had built of this house was all wrong—the model made it look significant, too clean. The ordinariness—how could he capture that?

He took a position across the street to observe.

Nothing happened for some time. Heat waves rose, Hollywood-style mirages above the melting asphalt, unreal, strange. An ice cream truck tinkled in the distance. He remembered the tune. From behind a picket fence two houses down, a dog pricked up its ears, observing him. I don't know what you're up to, the dog's eyes seemed to tell him, but I'll swear you're in the wrong.

At two-fifteen, two children drifted in single file up the road, much as he had done as a child, hot, unhappy, army privates on maneuvers, heavy backpacks already damaging their spines. Marching up to the house, they climbed the steps to the porch, looked around, collected the key from under a pot next to the front door, and entered the dark house.

Nobody home but the children.

Ray rattled the keys in his pocket. Probably one of them still matched that front door lock. In California, in suburbia, almost nobody changed locks when they moved into a new home. Why not? Well, people hated spending money. People never thought about trust, about fear. They loved buying a house. They loved getting the key to this new, at least to them, house.

The suburbs induced a kind of psychotic lethargy. The

blandness, the sameness, made it hard to believe anyone would bother to rob you. In the same way, schools of fish flew around the sharks in their patterns, multitudinous, identical. What were the chances you would get picked for dinner?

These kids, well-trained, had put the key back into its hiding place. Ray watched them place it carefully there.

Hi-ho.

He could take their key, not even bother with his, go inside whenever he wanted. And he did want; he wanted badly to see what he would feel like on the inside. Dead, or alive?

He heard faint crashings and maniacal laughter from the living room. The kids were watching television.

He watched until another dog, this time right next door, came out for a walk, leading its sharp-eyed elderly owner, biting at its chain, not glancing Ray's way. He retreated down the block to his car, which had probably reached a hundred twenty degrees by this point, furnace-level. Using his shirtsleeve to move the steering wheel, Ray turned the car engine on, drove around the block, let the a/c cool the vehicle, and returned to Bombardier Avenue, this time parking several houses beyond his old house.

Good. The big dog and vigilant owner had retreated back inside.

He approached. Although he didn't need the key to this house because he knew where they hid it, he had an urgent desire to try his own old key. Would it fit?

Cartoons blared inside. He twiddled key one in the lock, then key two.

Etcetera.

Nothing moved on the street, no other beings stirred. Only the heat shimmered off the sidewalk and parked cars, and the smelly black tar mending cracks in the street melted.

The fourth key worked. A rush hotter than the weather stopped him. Wet and nervous but under the influence of a compulsion he could not control, he turned the key in the lock and pushed gently on the door.

He recalled that this house had no entryway, no gracious hello. It dumped visitors directly into the living room. He opened the door gently, locating the TV by its sound, aware that the two children inside were vulnerable and might get scared.

"Oh, hi!" he said, as if surprised to see them, exulting in his heart at gaining entrance so easily. The old key had worked!

He had the funniest feeling looking at the kids on the floor. He felt he belonged. So uncomfortable in his own skin lately, he had forgotten how fantastic that felt.

"Hi," the oldest one, a boy maybe eight years old, said. "Who are you?" They were sprawled on the carpet facing away from him, and now they had both twisted around, their faces so similar with their blinking bug eyes that he resisted an impulse to laugh. He stayed at the door, harmless-looking.

His heart pumped out of control. "Where are your folks?" he asked.

"At work," the younger one, a towheaded girl, ventured,

then turned back to the television. On the screen, a pink character rode around in a vehicle that flew.

"I'm sorry," he said. "I must have gotten the time wrong. I thought they would be home by now."

"Nope," said the boy. "Mom works 'til four."

"Nearly two more hours," Ray said. "I'm really early."

"Yeah." The boy studied him, as if realizing he should be asking questions. He apparently couldn't think of what those questions might be. His eyes flicked back toward the TV.

"Hot day," Ray said, noticing the fan going, but no air-conditioning.

"Yeah," the boy said again.

"You know, I used to live in this house."

"You did?" Both children actually cared more about the cartoons. Any interest came out of sheer trained politeness.

"I had the room right off that hall there. On the left."

"My room," the boy said.

"And out back, we had a tetherball pole."

They didn't know what a tetherball pole was.

"There was a patio with a kind of—um—shade thing over it. Lattice."

"Plants grow all over it," the girl volunteered. "What a mess. Leaves all over the place," she said, obviously quoting her harried parents.

"Mind if I look around?"

They didn't. Certainly not properly advised about strangers by their parents, they turned their attention back to their cartoon while Ray wandered freely around the house. He made mental notes for his model—this window he had not remembered, that closet in a corner, not along the side.

Not much had changed, sad though, because what had been shiny and new in his childhood had turned shabby. Out back, the wooden lattice over the concrete patio had missing pieces, although, with a heavy, untrimmed wisteria, it actually appeared almost charming. Someone had tried painting the concrete below, but the paint was faded, chipped.

His bedroom, apricot-colored, no longer blue like he remembered it, now held a bunk bed. Apparently the boy had friends over, and an obsession with moving vehicles. Car stickers crawled randomly up and down the walls.

In the kitchen, blue Formica showed cracks from hot pans that should never have been set down on it. His mother used to shout at him if he came near the counters with something hot. He looked under the sink. She used to hide things there. Once she told him she kept twenty dollars in a can down there in case a crazed drug addict came knocking.

Bleach. Cleanser. Sponges in shreds.

But in the master bedroom, he found something that made this entire mad journey worthwhile. He easily discovered the wife's stash of jewelry fatheadedly hidden at the back of her dresser. She had a few pathetic gold pieces, some mementoes worth nothing—really, if you judged people on such things you had to feel life was sad and paltry. But what caught his eye in that room was the crooked slat in the wide-planked flooring.

He recalled the slat, and his mother pushing on it.

She always had a hiding place. She called them her "safes." Protectors, safes...he supposed it was common for single mothers to think this way.

He punched the unnailed side. The slat flew up.

Below, a dark, cobwebby hidey-hole exposed itself. He reached inside.

Back in the living room, he asked the children if they might want to go out for ice cream.

With pleasure he recognized as socially unacceptable, he pictured in his mind the fear their parents would feel, coming home and finding the children gone.

Sadistic, yes, but also just plain righteous.

He had come home to an empty house. He had known fear.

"No," said the boy regretfully. "We're not allowed to leave the house."

He didn't press and said his good-byes to the children, who appeared relieved to see him go. Did they somehow understand him to be an anomaly, not an acceptable part of a typical afternoon?

They seemed like nice kids, and he would have enjoyed teaching their parents a damn good lesson. Of course, the whole idea was nuts—he would have been caught. What on earth was wrong with him?

Pulling open the front door, since the children remained inert in front of the television, he felt satisfied with his activities of the day. He didn't want undue attention. He pictured the parents coming home, their panic. It would be enough that he had come in, looked around, taken nothing, at least, nothing they knew they had.

"Who should I say came over?" the little boy asked as Ray prepared to leave.

Ray cracked the door open long enough to say "Clint Eastwood."

He did not have a cowboy hat to tip, so he merely nodded and let himself out, fingering the object he had found, which was now safe in his jeans pocket, and locked the door before pulling it shut.

On his way back home, he stopped in downtown Los Angeles, waiting patiently at a hydrant until someone on the street left a spot, then whipping into it, cutting off an Acura and an Infiniti, because unlike them, he didn't give a damn if they scratched his car. What he gave a damn about was getting the goddamned space.

He breathed a few times, locking the doors remotely, ignoring the bitter invective spewing noisily from the Acura, accompanied by a hand pounding on the car door for emphasis. Two doors down, a dusty shop quaintly spawned in the days when even radios had sex appeal held a jumble of cheap electronics.

"Can I help you?" said the clerk in a three-piece suit, as unsuited to his surroundings as an arguing attorney at the beach instead of the bench.

"I need a cassette player."

The clerk chewed his mouth. "Hmm." He gestured for Ray to follow, and Ray did, down past aisles of plastic parts, earphones, wires, gadgets for every conceivable purpose, and some probably inconceivable.

He showed Ray car cassette decks.

"Portable," Ray said.

The clerk's brow furrowed. "Man, why you want one of them old things anyway?"

"You don't have any?"

He put up a hand. "Of course we do. Just not much call for them these days. Wait a sec." He turned his back to Ray and disappeared through a door at the back of the store.

Ray browsed the aisles, finding himself interested in a number of things that might be useful at some point, including miniature lighting fixtures for his models. He piled a few things on the counter. By the time the clerk returned with a very old-fashioned boom box that would run on batteries, he had managed to run up quite a bill.

"You'll need headphones."

"I have some."

Outside the store, the Acura had disappeared. At Ray's old hydrant spot, another car waited to fill another empty parking space, nature abhorring a vacuum. Ray put his purchases into the trunk of his car, slammed it shut, and drove off. The other car, with only inches to spare, slipped in behind him.

Back to Topanga, speeding, braking, tailgating, cursing. It was five in the afternoon and Ray was out of control, weeping and shouting in the car, not knowing what he was even shouting.

A cold shower. Ignore the phone messages and the computer. He pulled on running shoes and went outside and ran through the hilly neighborhood like the wind.

It worked. He came back to himself.

Calm now, walking back up the drive, he thought of the innumerable anonymous tenants who had lived on Bombardier Avenue over the past decades. Someone else must have found the loose board, used the opportunity it presented.

But he had proof they had not. He had seen his mother putting that board into place. He had been watching her. He always watched her with the jealous attention of the only child. That house hadn't been renovated in thirty years. He had established that personally. The board merged with a thousand other rickety things that developed, and never merited special attention.

He went inside, found the museum plans where he had left them by the front door, and pulled a black cassette tape out of his pocket, turning it over and over in his hands, scrutinizing it. No label. Normal bias. Sony. At the bottom he could see where the white part of the slender tape met brown. Someone had rewound the thing, but the tape was loose.

In the kitchen, he located a pencil and wound the tape tight, using exaggerated care.

He kept headphones in the entertainment unit in the great room. Not wanting to be interrupted, he went around the house locking doors and even arming the alarm. He put the headphones on, adjusted them for fit, then plugged them into the cassette player. Static, then:

"*You know why I'm calling,*" what sounded like his mother's voice, reedy, younger, said.

"*Did I scare you?*" said a male voice.

"*Yes! Yes, you scared me. I looked outside—*" She paused, sounding terrified, and said, "*Please don't do this. You're ruining our lives. I'm begging you—*"

"*You can fix this. I'll never call you again. Never follow you. You know what I want.*"

"*Next time I'll call the police!*"

"*Oh, no you won't.*"

Click.

Ray listened all the way to the end of the tape, flipped it, and listened to the other side. Static.

He listened to it again. Then he stopped and started it, writing all the words down.

6

The morning presentation wowed them. After Ray and Denise offered up their goodies and Martin wheeled out the rest of the irresistible feast, the museum people stopped just short of signing the deal on the spot. Ray ignored Martin privately while putting on an attentive face. Afterward, Martin flew through the office making more noise than usual, playing up how normal everything was. The rest of their coworkers cowered and ran away when they saw him coming.

"You have a phone call," Suzanne said to Ray when the meeting finally broke up, "on hold."

Back in his own office, he picked up the phone. "Yes?" He spent most of the next hour coddling Achilles Antoniou, who had a million questions and doubts.

Once he hung up, consumed with the voices he had heard on the tape from the house in Norwalk, while he should have been noting changes that had been suggested during the meeting, he thought about weapons. He sketched the knife his mother kept sharp. He drew a gun going off. Now, this was confidence. This was power. You could destroy somebody like Martin, who was a plague on the world, in an instant.

He drew a noose.

Twenty-eight miles from her office in Santa Monica brought Kat to the house on the eastern edge of Torrance near the 110. She noted the mileage in her book, then stepped out into the blazing afternoon. The moment she closed her car door behind her, her ears reeled from the freeway roar and she imagined filthy, invisible particles rushing on the wind, forcing their way into her lungs.

After taking photographs, she walked around the house for a closer inspection. Mildew on the window ledges. A thirty-year-old-roof that had seen too much sun, too much rain, and no repair, ever. No sprinklers and a scarred, scorched lawn showing recent signs of visiting dogs. A one-car garage that probably started out as a shed, and still looked it. This was a neighborhood in transition, as it had been since the day it was jerry-rigged into existence. Nobody wanted to live here, so close to the freeway. They chose this place because houses here, in the under-a-half-million-dollar range, remained affordable to people who had sold other houses in scarier areas of L.A.

She got out her disto, shot it around the perimeters, and wrote down her measurements in a thick notebook that worked both as a record and as a useful reference.

She made one last stop for the day in Gardena, this time to act as second to her boss on a particularly contentious evaluation. Feeling bedraggled, finding the water in her bottle had reached an unsavory warmth, she drove north on the 405 back to the office, cranking up the a/c.

But the always feeble a/c in her Echo had crapped out. Was the whole system, the whole interlacing network of televisions and freeways and air-conditioning systems going down? Was this the end of the world? The traffic reporter sounded cool enough, maintaining that chipper air of a guy with bad news, but hey, folks, not so bad this time. He told of a four-car accident on the 405 near Rosecrans with minor injuries, "everybody on the shoulder, CHP in attendance," then broke for a cheerful advertising ditty. Jaws clenched, hands glued to the steering wheel, radios spewing poor advice, everyone kept their windows up and their air-conditioning blowing.

The ordinary twelve-mile-an-hour afternoon traffic, worsened by the action just north of her, got hellishly worse because someone as stressed out as she was but less resilient chose that moment to have a heart attack or stroke or something. She breathed in and out and reminded herself about wisdom and compassion, and her own stress eased. Three highway patrol cars in front of her began their halting, swerving dance that was designed to slow traffic even more. They stopped about three hundred feet ahead of her and everyone else on the freeway stopped, too. Minutes later, a helicopter punched through the smog and landed on the road in a whirl of dust.

While she watched for the poor soul to get airlifted, windows open to the smoggy oven, Kat was reminded of the fierce summer days of her childhood in Whittier. The highway patrol cleared them for takeoff at last. Traffic, now permanently logjammed, snailed along. Defiant, she pulled her shirt off. The man on the left of her stared at her expensive push-up bra and gave her a thumbs-up before dropping back in the next lane.

The woman now on her left, driving an AWD Audi two-door, who also perhaps lacked freon or whatever the current additive was, hair neatly secured by a clip, in a blouse so soaked it left nothing to the imagination, was inspired. Catching Kat's eye, the Audi woman pulled her shirt off, revealing a modest gray sports bra. Fuck 'em if they can't accept a hot woman, they tacitly agreed, giving each other respectful nods.

Traffic slogged along. The two misfit women in fact drew very little attention from the people locked inside their atmosphere-controlled, tinted-windowed vehicles.

Why did Kat love Los Angeles? Because the spicy salt waves of the Pacific rolled in over the town, washing away all sin, cleansing and hopeful? Or was it just plain stubbornness? *Miserere,* but I'll take life anyhow, she told herself, and popped Andrea Bocelli into the CD player.

Kat called her home phone for messages. Nothing from Leigh. She called information and had them dial Ray Jackson's house. No answer there, either. Grimly purposeful, she called his office, but was told he was on a conference call and couldn't be disturbed.

Frustrated, Kat decided to drive to Topanga to meet this mystery man Leigh had married, right after she made her last check-in at work.

Did Leigh miss her? Leigh had never made friends easily. Kat remembered opening the front door of the

Franklin Street house one day and finding a sack and a card that said "To my *amiga*." Inside was a tiny framed painting of two little girls, standing at the shoreline, backs to the camera.

Leigh gave presents like that, things she worked on in secret, never on birthdays or at Christmas.

Was there a right moment back then for Kat to change history instead of just letting wrong things happen?

After leaving college, Tom had discovered the lovely work prospects available to a political science major. He worked for a year at a ketchup factory. Coming home for months slathered in the sauce, looking like a murder victim or perpetrator, he finally quit, then operated a forklift at a container company. Evenings and weekends, he dabbled in community theater, using his muscular young maleness to earn him many supporting roles.

As he got better, he got a couple of big parts and found an agent, who, one fine day, finagled him a part in a movie. Kat dragged Leigh along to see him, dressed in a red jacket, hold a door open for Dennis Quaid, speaking an actual line: "Right here, sir!" They giggled and teased him all night about landing a major motion picture and what a fine actor he had become. "*Right* here, sir!" they said, and "Right *here*! Sir!" until all three of them were incoherent with their own idiocy. Leigh thought it was hilarious that he had been bitten by the movie bug.

He got parts in some big plays and some fair write-ups in the *Times* and then one night—

Kat was barely twenty-six and a half, Leigh twenty-six, and Tom twenty-five. He came out of a performance of Tom Stoppard's *Jumpers* at the Ahmanson, grinning, gathering up the bundle of flowers someone handed him. While they waited for him, he cheerfully signed a few autographs, flirting and kind to his fans, and Leigh hung back with a funny look on her face.

"Uh-oh," Kat said, watching her friend.

"Have you ever looked at your brother, really?"

"Not the way you're looking at him."

"He's turned into—"

"I guess I shouldn't be surprised."

"He's beautiful."

So Leigh and Tommy finally got together. They had known each other for so long as kids—Tommy, Kat's silly kid brother—that their relationship blasted off fast. They double-dated with Kat and her then boyfriend, and she spent as much time as always with the two of them. After two months of increasing heat Leigh moved into Tom's bachelor domain on Balboa Island in Newport.

Of course, there was a problem. Leigh's father, James Hubbel, didn't like Tommy. Vain and poor, he called actors in general. Not marriage material, he would advise Leigh in private, away from Tom.

"I do it for fun," Tom said once at a family dinner with the Hubbels, oblivious to Mr. Hubbel at the head of the table, shaking his head with dismay. "What I really want is to go to Fiji or the Marquesas, find some peaceful spot, and set up a farm."

"How practical," Mr. Hubbel said. He was smiling, not in a good way.

Tom said, "No, Jim"—another provocation—"I've looked into this. You pay the government to lease lagoon space, hire a guy who knows how to seed the oysters, and you've got pearls. A whole world market. Or you could grow vanilla beans."

For a long time, Leigh thought Tom said these things to be provocative, and only as time went along did she pick up that, yes, he meant every word.

"What if I don't want to go to live on an island?" Leigh and Tom were swinging on the front porch glider at his apartment house on Balboa. They had just finished eating barbecue, and were preparing themselves for a walk on the beach by drinking beer. Kat sat on the steps painting her toenails.

Tom kissed Leigh, then nuzzled her hair, saying, "That's okay. There's always a plan B."

"What is it?"

"No idea. Whatever you want."

"You don't even have a savings account."

"Money goes and flows too fast these days." He waved toward the glowing sunset. "We're doing all right, aren't we?"

But they weren't. Leigh tired of the parties and Tom's erratic and, to her, aimless existence. Between jobs, between auditions, he played volleyball on the beach or visited with his buddies while she slogged away, installing cabinets on construction jobs, the only steady paycheck.

Leigh confided in Kat, "I can't stand the way he just

hangs around! He offered to get a real job the other day, but I know how that would go. He'd hate me in the end."

"He wouldn't," Kat had replied. "Oh, Leigh, I wish you had never hooked up with him. He's so crazy about you. He'll do anything you want, just so he has you."

"I don't think Tommy knows what it means to be grown up," Leigh had said, screwing in some private final screw.

"You liked that about him."

"I turn thirty next month," she said.

Then she had met Ray Jackson. Leigh moved back to her folks' house and dated both of them for a month. She told Kat she was breaking up with Tom before she told Tom. "Ray's solid, creative, smart, driven. He's like me. We're both productive people. Creative."

"You said that as if Tommy isn't?"

Leigh flung a look at her full of heartache, angst, and decision. "Tom's adorable, but he doesn't care enough about what really matters. He's not for me. Ray's serious about life and so am I."

"Tom loves you!"

"So does Ray."

"But—" But what could Kat say? "Don't hurt him."

But the talk—or argument, whatever you wanted to call it—didn't go well. Leigh told Kat some of the things she had to say when Tommy wouldn't understand. They were cruel things, Kat thought.

Kat worried, but she thought her brother would move on to another pretty girl as he always had in the past.

But Tom did not.

Acting like a man who had been hit by a truck and left to die on the road, Tom begged Leigh to come back to him and staged progressively more desperate scenes until Leigh demanded that he go permanently away.

And so he did. Leigh and Kat had a fight the next day. Things were said, more cruel things, this time brought on by grief and guilt.

And Kat thought, I have to stop now, stop thinking any more about Tommy, about what I did to Tommy.

She dropped off her notes at the office and got back on the freeway, heading north now, embracing the rush hour like a penance.

Almost thirty minutes after Kat had arrived at the Jackson house in Topanga Canyon, at about five-thirty, a Porsche Boxster drove up, blue, waxed, carapace gleaming like a huge tropical beetle's in the sun, windows shadowy. Rather than pull into the garage, the car pulled up beside Kat's. A man got out.

Tall, taut. Probably six feet two. Dark, groomed, no recession marring a noble brow.

These fine details etched themselves on her mind. A veteran dater, she noticed his clothes, faded jeans topped with a designer shirt, quite formal, silk.

And wow. Very good-looking behind the shades. He and Leigh would make a pretty pair. Kat was disappointed to see that he was alone.

Ray Jackson did not appear happy. He stood by her car like a highway patrolman getting ready to ask for her license. She rolled her window down.

"What's going on?" he said.

"Hi. I'm—uh—an old friend of Leigh's."

"You are?" He considered her, but not for long. The heat made his silk shirt wilt. "Oh, yeah, the one that's been calling. And calling."

"But you never answer."

"We have caller ID. I answer calls from people I know. It's hot. You should come in." He turned abruptly, heading for the front door.

She rolled up her window, adjusted a silver shade over the dashboard to fend off the fading sun, and followed him.

They introduced themselves, and she walked behind him through the security routine into the marble entryway.

She looked around. "Will she be home soon?"

"That would be nice," Jackson said. He took off the sunglasses, folded them carefully, placed them on the polished table. "You should have mentioned you'd be stopping by."

"I tried to. I would have, if you had ever answered your phone." He waited for her next move, and she really didn't have one.

"I knew Leigh for years," she said. She didn't say, You stole her from my brother. Did Ray Jackson know that? Maybe not.

"Apparently not so much recently."

"No."

"Why have you been calling? Why are you here at my house all of a sudden?"

She felt herself blushing and did not have an easy answer. "My sister saw an article about a project you're working on and we got to wondering about Leigh. I just want to see her. Am I completely out of luck tonight?"

"Yes."

"Too bad."

"I'm sorry." He was relaxing a little.

"Can I leave her a note?"

"If you want."

"I just wanted to get it over with. Jacki talks me into these things—"

"Get what over with?"

Startled, she realized she had spoken out loud. "Seeing Leigh. We have old business between us. I decided to deal with it in an adult fashion, by confronting my demons."

"You calling my wife a demon?"

"What? Oh." Of course he was teasing, although he didn't look especially amused.

"What is it?" Jackson tilted window blinds on the main wall that overlooked the Pacific Ocean so that the raging sunset didn't make it impossible to see. "Your business with Leigh?"

"Unfinished business?"

"You don't sound convinced."

"It's complicated." But she always tired of discretion fast. Blurting was her style. Another Buddhist precept said: Guard your mouth. No idle talk.

"We were best friends."

"She mentioned you," he said. A halo of orange-gold sunset silhouetted him between the blind's slats.

"She did?"

"Said sometimes you're too close to someone to stay friends. What do you think she meant by that?"

"She knew I thought I was fat and that I stuck a finger down my throat if I ate too much for a while when I was fifteen," Kat said, rattled. "I knew she fed the dog her oatmeal in the morning even though it gave him the runs, which made her parents insane. Her mom was really house proud." She set her bag down on the marble demilune table, trying to imagine Leigh living like this, so pristinely. The Leigh she knew flung things and thrived on creative disorder.

"I don't think you're fat," he said.

"Uh, thanks," she said. He didn't flirt exactly, but all this guy had to do was flash that straight line of perfect orthodontia and any girl might feel the wind unbuttoning her blouse. She slumped, letting her chest cave in just slightly, not wanting to give him—or herself—any ideas.

"So you're Kat. Leigh told me you'd dropped out of her life," he said. "She told me she missed you. Called you her dark secret. What do you think she meant, saying that?"

"No idea," Kat lied.

"How long since you last spoke with her?"

"Six years."

"That's a long time. Nothing more recent?"

"No." She couldn't tell if he looked relieved or disappointed.

"That's how long we've been together," he went on. He

moved toward a wall, then pushed a button. A mahogany panel lifted, revealing a mirrored bar.

"Nice," Kat said. "Modern. I heard about you, before Leigh and I lost touch."

"Really? What?"

She didn't want to talk about Tom. She never liked talking about Tom. She liked holding him close to her heart. "Leigh was just getting to know you, in love." It came out sounding accusatory, but he didn't seem to notice.

He nodded. "I fell hard for her, too," he said. "Listen, I'm thirsty. Long commute. Can I get you anything?"

"Got anything diet?"

She followed him to the stainless-steel kitchen, to the fridge with its massive doors. He held up some cans and she chose one.

While he filled a tall glass with ice and poured her drink, Kat let her eyes case the great room beyond. No sign of Leigh. The decor did not suggest a woman lived here. She took the glass he offered her.

"When did you meet Leigh?" Ray asked.

"She lived across from me in Whittier when we were growing up. We stuck together all through high school, and for years after college. Leigh was a kick, one of those people who say unpredictable things, plus she didn't give a damn about current fads. She liked comics, and so did I. She liked fantasy rags, ditto. She liked me because—because"—she paused—"my family appeared normal, maybe. I had a sister and brother, and she had neither. Maybe she was a little lonely, stuck with doting parents."

"You lived in Whittier? Where?"

"Near uptown, not far from Penn Park. Franklin Street? We spent all our time hanging around at the park, learning to braid lanyards out of plastic strands and tease the boys. Leigh called that hill where all the young lovers went 'Smoochers' Hill.' "

He nodded. "I lived in East Whittier, once when I was young and then later, from the time I was twelve until I graduated from high school. My mother still lives there. You know I met Leigh at the shopping center in East Whittier? Whitwood?"

"Eating ice cream, no doubt." Without being fully aware of it, Kat had sat down on the white sectional that faced an expensive hill view darkening as night came on. Ray Jackson sat down opposite her, nursing his own iced soda.

"I lived in a two-story frame house, nothing fancy," Kat said. "Leigh lived in a huge Spanish mansion across the street. Her father was a policeman."

"He still is."

Talking about the Hubbels led them into talking about good old Whittier, California. Ray had gone to the same big high school as Kat, Leigh, and Tom, but he was three years older than Leigh. Well, Jacki would approve, Kat thought, looking around. Ray Jackson had also gotten the hell out of Whittier. He could probably see all the way across the hills and into her cramped place in Hermosa Beach through those wide windows.

He seemed nice enough, although the look in his eyes was not exactly friendly. He was polite, too curious to throw her out, although she sensed that she should keep this visit short.

Leigh was not here and wouldn't be coming home tonight, that was clear. As for the rest of it, it was none of Kat's business. She was beginning to suspect that Leigh had pulled another Leigh, dumped this nice guy and went off with another one. No mystery there.

"So, I ask again, what got you here today? I mean, it's been years, so you say."

Kat trotted out her excuse, explained about Leigh's unpaid receptionist. "Unless Leigh wants to close up shop, you better pay that young lady."

He appeared relieved. "Sure, of course. Leigh's taking a little time off. She must have lost track."

"The girl said that's not like her." But Kat remembered, in fact, how Leigh abandoned things. How she abandoned people.

The room was getting darker, but he didn't turn on any lights. He asked her about her work, where she lived, where she'd gone to college. Kat found herself admitting she lived alone and met men on the Internet. She knew she told too many people about these things in her life; she knew she did it so that she would appear bold and self-possessed.

Men often reacted to these bald-faced admissions like wasps, swarming in close. Ray Jackson moved slightly closer, then drew back.

So, he had become aware of the charged atmosphere and had the sense to avoid it.

She knew from bitter experience that animal attraction between two strangers did not mean a man didn't love his wife and wouldn't continue to love her. Closing her eyes for one brief moment, she wished again she had better control over her body and her thoughts.

She stood up, took her pen out of her bag, dashed a note off to Leigh, basically just begging her to call, then she shook Ray Jackson's hand, made excuses, mumbled some more nonsense, and fled.

7

Βut her home in Hermosa would have to wait. The cell phone made its "A1A Beachfront Avenue!" shout-out. "Jacki needs you to come over for dinner," Raoul told her. So she kept going, starting to feel pretty beat up now, her back melding with the Echo's seat as the miles in the car piled up. The moon hung like a gibbous pumpkin over the freeway. At least the traffic had cleared.

Raoul answered the door. His glasses were crooked and her mother's pear apron, well-splattered, was tied around his waist over a pair of canvas shorts. A fan whirred on the floor. "The a/c's out. Jacki's in the bedroom. See if you can do something for her. She won't talk to me." He padded behind the kitchen counter to stir tomato sauce.

"What's for dinner?"

"Spaghetti cheers her up."

"Me, too." She kicked off her shoes, and, going bare-foot to the bedroom door, pushed it open.

"Get lost," said the voice within.

Drapes darkened the room. Two fans blew toward the bed. Kat's eyes adjusted and landed on her sister, who lay curled on one side on the mussed-up king-sized bed, face splotched with tears. "What's the matter?"

"I am a whale preparing to give birth to a whale. The only thing missing is the part where you float in water, weightless, and all's well."

"Can't get comfortable?"

"My liver has merged with my stomach. My kidneys are squished between two sharp bones in my back. My heart is constricted to walnut-size. Food squirts up in acid form in my throat. On this, the hottest night of the year, our air-conditioning has quit."

"We should call your doctor."

"I did."

"What did she say?"

"What she always says. It's normal."

Kat took two pillows from the head of the bed. She tucked one under Jacki's back and another under her stomach. "Better?"

"Kat, remember that time Ma asked you to stop at the store and buy some meat and instead you spent the money on a bouquet of daisies?"

"I thought we needed them more."

"Well, this is like that. I need to give birth, and you bring me pillows. Still, it's a kindness and better than Raoul could manage."

"He knew to call me, didn't he? He does his best, Jacki," Kat said.

Which set off another spate of tears. "Of course he does. He's great. Fantastic. I don't deserve him!"

Kat got up and went to the bathroom for a washrag.

She soaked it in cold water, folded it over, and returned to place it on her sister's forehead. "You rest. We'll call you when the food's ready."

"He's messing up my kitchen in there."

"Don't worry."

Jacki groaned and closed her eyes.

Kat went into the kitchen to help Raoul, which primarily consisted of wiping up after him.

"Will she go back to work when the baby's born?" Kat asked.

"She says no," Raoul answered.

"Do they know she plans to quit?"

"She says she's got three months paid maternity leave and just wants to keep her options open."

"In other words, no."

Handing her four forks, he said, "Who knows? After a few months at home, she might beg them to take her back."

Kat pulled out place mats from the drawer and started to put them around, crowding the three into a corner of the large dining room table. "Set for four," Raoul said. "Jacki insists she's going to get up, and we have another guest."

Kat found another mat. "Who's coming?"

"It's a surprise."

"You both know I hate surprises."

"Somebody Jacki dredged up. I mean, invited."

"Leigh?"

"No, no. I'm not supposed to say."

"Tell me or I'm out of here."

Raoul untied the apron, leaving it in a heap on the floor. Setting candles on the table, he said, "It's a guy I work with who she wants you to meet."

"My God, she's crying all day, wailing all night, and she plans to roll out of bed just to set me up? Call him and cancel. She's in no shape—"

"She wanted to, Kat."

"Don't tell me she enlisted you in this latest campaign to get me settled down."

"Seriously." He poured himself a glass of wine and offered her one. She waved it off and sat down at the table. "Have you thought about therapy?"

Kat gave him The Look. "Well, Raoul, this is an ugly turn. I've endured your lectures on psychology as a pseudo-science. Yet you feel the need to direct me toward what you called, if I may quote you, Professor, 'a potion of bull crap and nonsense'? Plus, reports of my mad sex life are greatly exaggerated. I should know. I'm the exaggerator."

"I've known you, what, eight years? Since you were twenty-seven."

"So?"

"So." His words measured, his voice gentle, he said, "Jacki's worried. I want her happy, too."

Kat took a deep breath. "Tell Jacki to stop interfering."

"Tell her yourself," Jacki said, smiling and peach-cheeked again, emerging from the bedroom in a blue princess-style shirred shirt that splayed out alarmingly. She sat down hard next to her husband, took his hand in hers, and kissed it.

"Now you've got this sweet and otherwise supremely

rational man suggesting witchcraft, you scary *bruja*," Kat said. "You know I like you, Raoul, but I'm not sure I like my sister getting you involved in my life."

Raoul looked at her, then at his wife.

"It's not like he'll tell anyone, Kat. It's not like he has friends"—Jacki ruffled his hair fondly—"except me, of course." She checked the clock on the wall. "Before Zak gets here—did you get hold of Leigh?"

Immensely relieved at the change of subject, Raoul excused himself, saying he needed to change and wash up before their guest arrived.

They moved to the couch, where Jacki struggled to find a comfortable spot, failed, and sank back into the cushions with a resigned sigh.

"I'll help you when you need to get up," Kat said.

"Fuck. You know?"

"Raoul just made a delicious homemade sauce. Did you even know he could cook?"

"He reads recipes and follows directions exactly. A robot could do what he does in the kitchen."

"Ah. Like mixing chemicals in a lab."

"Right," Jacki said. "He's creative in his own field, of course. Oh hell, he's a god. Why not admit it?" Jacki loved her husband too much. Was there a word like "uxorious" which referred to the male part of the couple? "So did you talk to Leigh?"

Kat began with a detailed description of Ray Jackson's house and finished with the muddled conversation.

"You got too personal too fast," Jacki said.

"Shut up."

"He's good-looking, you say?"

"Give it a rest."

"You think Leigh walked out on him?"

"What else could it be?"

Jacki stuck out her tongue. "So what next?"

"Nothing much. Leigh's employee will get paid. I got the impression Ray wants me to think Leigh went on a little vacation without her husband. Women do that, you know. He didn't go into details. She's at a resort in Cabo San Lucas or walking on Moonstone Beach in Cambria or in Paris in a lovely pension on the Boul' Mich, drinking Sancerre, strolling the banks of the Seine, wearing designer heels and not tripping, either. She always liked to travel and she likes Sancerre and high heels and it's none of my business. She'll call if she wants to when she gets my note. Or not. Maybe she pulled another Tom. Dumped Ray Jackson and he's saving face with a little story. Who can blame him for that? I wouldn't put it past her."

"You're kidding. You'd leave things like this?"

"Like what?"

"I don't like it. Women may walk out on their husbands, but they don't walk out on businesses they have built over a period of years. The husband is evasive." Her mouth firmed and she rendered her opinion. "Unh-unh. Something's wrong."

"You think something's happened to her? You're the one who needs therapy!"

"Think now."

"You're an exasperating person, Jacki."

"You owe it to yourself. And you owe it to Leigh, your

best friend ever. Don't tell Raoul about this superstitious streak of mine—"

"As if he doesn't know it."

"But it all happened for a reason, me finding that clipping. Me worrying about you being too lonely. My dream. You're supposed to find her, if only to make sure she's taken a runner from a bad scene at home. You may be the only one checking up."

Jacki sat up straighter, put her hand behind to support her back, and made a face. "Well?" she said.

Kat decided, with a shiver, Jacki was right.

Because she felt nervous about the tone in her son's voice when he called wanting to come over, Esmé decided to make a pineapple upside-down cake, one of Ray's childhood favorites. She had time to make something relatively complicated.

Leigh didn't like her pineapple cake. Leigh. She didn't like thinking about what Ray was going through, and all because of that woman. Well, she had tried to warn him about the heart, and how marriage meant troubles and sorrows. Heartache. She ought to know.

Mixing butter with brown sugar, she considered this thought. She coated a nine-inch-round cake pan with grease and flour. A mother with a child to raise cooked thousands of boring meals, thousands of macaroni casseroles, burritos, and hamburgers. Esmé had never enjoyed that kind of cooking, which was such a chore when you worked all day checking out other people's boring groceries.

Ray's father, Henry, had preferred fast food to her cooking. How had she ever thought to marry such a man?

Such a man. She creamed together butter and sugar until the mixture fluffed up, then added the eggs one at a time, beating them harder than she needed, seeing Henry before her, thinking about life's turns.

Trying to obliterate the image of him that suddenly hovered before her, she beat in vanilla, and alternated adding the flour and milk, trying not to ruin the dough by thumping away too hard, watching for the smooth, shiny look that meant she had beaten the batter properly. Finished, she took a long knife out of the butcher block holder and set a pineapple on a cutting board, proceeding first to peel it, then cut it into neat half-inch-thick slices.

Halfway through the process, she realized the knife needed sharpening. She slipped it across a ten-inch diamond steel sharpener until when she touched the blade to her finger, the skin didn't give, but broke.

No blood, fortunately.

Whack. So much better.

The pineapple slices made a pretty layer of circles, and she filled in the holes with chunks arranged in a pattern, then poured the batter gently over it, popped the pan into the old oven, set the timer, and shut the door.

She made a pot of coffee, intending to tidy up before Ray arrived, but settled into the one really comfortable chair in the living room and got lost in an article about the space shuttle.

The doorbell rang.

She rose, folding the newspaper, and put it into the

holder by the fireplace. Ray liked the house neat, and she liked pleasing him. Glancing around as she walked toward the entryway, she assured herself that only the kitchen looked bad at the moment, and she'd soon fix that.

How grateful she was that they were still close. The bond between a single mother and an only son outlasted almost everything. Tidying her hair with her hands, she answered the door. "Honey," she said, hugging him. She still loved the way he smelled.

"Mom."

But he took no notice of the house, rushing through to the kitchen and plopping down at the kitchen counter on a stool. She had pans to clear, bowls to clean. Since the sink was in the middle of the island, she could work and visit with Ray. She began washing out the cake pans. "You sounded upset on the phone. Is this—something about Leigh?"

He shook his head. "We have to talk, Mom."

"Sure, honey." She still had twenty minutes on the timer, so she shrugged a little and went back to her sink. She reached under the sink for bleach. Nothing else cleaned the old almond-colored porcelain sink as well as bleach. She didn't want him at the sink, checking on that damn persistent leak, getting on her case about it yet again, but he stayed away, tapping his fingers on the counter, apparently thinking hard.

"I went to Norwalk, Mom."

"A new commission?"

"To Bombardier Avenue. The old house."

"Oh, for heaven's sake. Why would you do that?"

"Because I believe you've lied to me, Mom." He stood and put his hands in his pockets, walked to the window, and faced her again. "All that moving. I think you were running all those years, and I ran with you. I'm an adult now, and I can see things don't make sense. I don't believe you anymore."

She swiped at the crumbs on the table. "I knew right away you were in a bad mood about something. But do we have to—"

"Why? Why did we move so much?"

Sighing, Esmé said, "You were so young and made friends easily. I guess it was kind of callous, dragging you around so much, but what I don't understand is why—" She paused, thinking, why can't you leave it alone! "What do you want from me, honey? Details? We moved from Norwalk because I didn't like the traffic there. We moved from Redondo Beach because the chill bothered me. We moved from Downey because I found a place with cheaper rent."

"The house on Bombardier? I went inside."

Shocked, she sat down. "You did? How?"

"I kept the key."

"You still have that old key collection?"

"I just remembered. You used to call me keeper of the keys." He looked surprised by the memory.

She nodded. "Like the Roman god. Janus."

"Who?"

"He had two faces, one looking toward the past, the other toward the future. You were such a serious boy. Ray, please don't tell me you found the key and used it to break into the house."

"That's exactly what I did."

"My God! Have you gone crazy? You really have been so strange lately—"

"I was invited in by the residents, actually." He held up a hand. "Forget about that. That's not what I want to talk about. I want to talk about a tape I found there."

She flashed back to the tract house in Norwalk, the porch, his worst tantrum ever, the circus tent she put up in the living room at Christmas, her first safe place. "A tape," she repeated to buy herself a moment.

"Yeah, remember that loose board? Under the rug in your bedroom? You hid things."

"You knew about that?"

"I paid attention."

Esmé said nothing for a few moments. Ray had phases. Every few years he would start pestering her about the moves, bringing this up, bringing that up, and now he was back into it, and it was apparently worse than ever. Now he had broken into somebody's house and retrieved a tape she had forgotten all about.

Her life for so many years had had a serenity and peace lacking in her early years as a mother. She felt like someone peacefully gazing at a lovely view, when a lunatic appeared out of nowhere to push her over a waterfall.

"You and a guy talk," Ray said.

The oven beeped. Her cake had finished. Esmé reached into a drawer for hot pads. Carefully opening the oven door, she pulled a round pan out. Perfect. She set the pan on a wire rack. The crusty yellow surface, evenly toasty, smelled of the brown sugar and savory fruit that lurked on the bottom. Carefully, she turned the cake upside down onto a platter.

"Invert it right away," Ray said.

"I taught my boy right."

"I was five when we lived there. That made you twenty-six."

"I don't want to talk about it."

"The man threatens you."

"You listen to some old recording and you make assumptions, and they're just plain wrong. Haven't I warned you often enough to use your imagination to serve you, not to make your life harder? Well, I don't know anything about any tape. I don't remember back that far."

"Oh, no?" Ray's face wore the pinched look of a furious teenager, and Esmé thought, after all I've done, I've failed my son. He's stalled and it's my fault.

"Enough." She pulled the pan off a little roughly, taking some pineapple with it, Ray watching without engagement, eyes glazed. "Smell that," she said.

He looked at the table, his hands. She became afraid for him. Not knowing what else to do, she examined the cake critically, then went to the pantry to find a jar of cherries and roasted pecans, which she used to stud the cake. "Now it looks as good as it smells," she said into the tension.

"You tell him you'll call the cops. He calls you a liar."

She dropped the wire rack into the sink. The noise startled them both. Inserting clean beaters into her mixer, she whipped cream in a cold bowl, scooped some onto a piece of cake, and handed him the plate, which he took, both of them acting mechanically. The ordinary moves calmed her enough to say "Some things parents don't discuss with their children."

"He scares you," he said. "Did he hurt you, Mom?"

She slopped another glob of whipped cream onto his plate. "Needs a little more." Why did he do it, come here like a child having a tantrum spoiling the day, the meal, the visit, trying to spoil his whole life that she, Esmé, had worked so hard to keep safe and happy?

The anger simmering in his voice attained full boil. "Was someone stalking you? Who was it?"

"I will not discuss this any further with you. Now, do both of us a favor. Don't go looking for some magical answer to your troubles by digging up the past, trying to make our very ordinary lives into some big adventure! Don't ruin your life, getting into trouble with those damn keys, either! You have a future—count your blessings and focus on making it good." She shoved the plate in front of him again. "This is best when it's fresh. Now you eat this cake I made for you. You eat a bite of this delicious cake."

He shook his head, all the anger appearing to drain out of him. He sat down again, took up his fork, and chewed and swallowed with all the pleasure of someone swallowing bile.

She wiped her hands on her apron, disappointed, wishing she could do something, anything, to make things right for him. She said, "I'll pack some up for you, okay? Freeze it and eat some later. Some people say it's even better then. Do you know I posted this recipe on the Internet?

I get comments from people who have tried it, mostly complimentary. It's the fresh pineapple. I was right, I have to say."

Ray jumped up, knocking over the stool. His uneaten cake fell to the floor. She heard the door slam and the cat springing off the couch, wondering what was going on.

Driving home from her sister's place through a blessedly cool and empty darkness, Kat thought about Raoul and Jacki's pick, Zak Greenfield. Only a year older than her, he had a confidence that she rarely came across and found quite attractive. He seemed to have a firm grasp on life, a plan. Guys like him with actual professions and that air of having figured things out always had friends like Jacki, offering unsolicited, sisterly advice on future prospects.

Zak seemed to like women. He had teased Jacki, did the man-to-man work-talk thing with Raoul, made them all perk up. And he had paid a lot of attention to Kat, touching her arm, asking a lot of questions.

He was interested. Unusually, Kat's legs had first drawn his attention, which flattered her so much she wanted to lie down on the floor and expose their entire length to his inspection and evaluation. They had laughed and talked until eleven-thirty while the fans blew air that kept Kat's hair moving, until Jacki's eyelids dipped closed and Raoul put his arm around her.

Time to go, and they were leaving at the same time. Kat had just decided that the evening really ought to continue, when suddenly Jacki stepped in. Her bulbous tummy came between them at the door.

"Zak has an early day tomorrow, don't you, Zak?" Jacki nudged him out.

Zak frowned slightly, but, unable to deny a woman with such an awesome and unassailable physical presence, finally agreed, saying, "Oh. Yeah, I sure do."

How could Kat not feel drawn to such a man, one who instantly honored Jacki's demented sisterly requirements in spite of the fact that Kat stood panting after him not three feet away?

Once home, Kat took her shower and put on a nightie several guys had enjoyed, the white cotton one with Victorian buttons. Her little brass Buddha sat on its stand and her Zafu cushion awaited. Thirty minutes a day, she had been told to meditate. She went toward it but somehow veered off into bed instead. She had two new men to think about, and what to do about Leigh huddled like a lump of dough in her craw.

8

Ray drove the Porsche straight from his mother's to Stokes Avenue in Downey, a distance of about fifteen miles. He took it at a steady sixty-eight, not wanting to attract any official attention. It was almost ten.

The internal pressure that had got him onto the freeway made him feel fresh and energetic. He felt exultant, actually, because he knew that he was doing the one thing that would relieve his misery and need. His mother's cake, far too rich, had left a metallic echo in his mouth. Pineapple always tasted that way to him, like someone had sprinkled aluminum shavings onto fruit. He never had the heart to refuse his mother's food—she made the offerings with so much love. He didn't even like sweets anymore, but he tried at her house.

He hadn't expected Esmé to tell him the truth. Stubborn at times as she was about changes to her precious house, she had a temper as volatile as his own and the same sense of privacy. But now—the tape—

He burped several times, checked his mirrors for patrol cars, and sped up. They had lasted only seven months in Downey before he came home one afternoon from school to find his mother tight-lipped and packing. He packed his two allotted boxes and drove with her to the next identical place a couple of towns over. He went to another school a lot like the old school, and there was a new bully, messed-up math courses that repeated what he already knew, the usual mountains to climb.

Revisiting these scenes felt like playing with an aching tooth, painful but irresistible. Maybe if something made sense, if he could understand—what?

Was his life simply a random series of events strung together but ultimately unrelated? Or did the series add up to something meaningful?

This red-haired girl on his doorstep tonight—what a time she had picked to decide to make up with Leigh. He hoped she would go home and get laid and forget about them.

He turned on the defroster to clear the ocean fog off his windshield.

"So where is she now?" he had asked Leigh once, referring to Kat.

"No idea. Sometimes people you care about get lost," Leigh said. She sat on the rug in front of the fireplace in the great room, drying her hair, wearing her pink satin robe. She had given Ray a present that day, a silver-trimmed comb from the thirties. They had been married three months, and he thought he knew her well by then. She had married him on the rebound and he didn't care

because he knew—knew in his gut as well as his head—
that she loved him anyway.

"That's it?"

"No, that's not it, but—off-limits, Ray."

Kat's timing couldn't have been worse. She had the
look of a crusader. She hadn't liked what Ray Jackson told
her.

Well, what else could he have said?

He took the off-ramp he had noted on the map, got
lost, and had to pull over to figure out his way, stopping
on a street like a million streets in L.A., lined with a row of
dingy look-alike tract homes built in the early sixties, one-
story houses with one tree in front, a wide driveway, and a
double-car garage like almost all the houses he and his
mother had rented long ago. In the daytime, relentless
California sun would keep the shrubs and lawns brown-
tinged and the few living trees struggling for height. At
night, residents hid behind blinds, too tired to socialize
with their neighbors after fighting the traffic home.

He found his place on the map and negotiated his way
out of the maze of replicant streets. Cruising past the gas
stations and the chain-store strip mall that passed for a
downtown, he took a left and slowed. The trees on Stokes
Avenue had grown a lot—there had only been new twiggy
things to protect the bare lawns from the hard sun when
he lived there.

The house, a new color, paler, looked about the same,
and good news, showed no lights in its windows. He

parked several houses away. As soon as he stepped outside the Porsche he started worrying about the dark clothes, realizing he looked just like a criminal scoping the place out.

Do it fast. He rattled around in his pocket, searching for his keys, striding swiftly up the open walkway and onto the small porch. He tried key one. No luck. Key two. Nothing.

Sirens started the neighborhood dogs howling. For one electric second, Ray feared they were coming for him, so he stopped what he was doing, slowed his breathing, and listened. He stood frozen below an aluminum overhang by the front door, grateful for the cover. Fog rippled through the warm night air like steam.

The sirens got louder. Were they coming here? Was it possible? Bass notes of his heart thrumming in his chest, he peered past a scruffy acacia tree toward the street.

He closed his eyes as the sirens receded. His breathing once again functioned. As he stood trying to blend into the overgrown juniper bush beside the railing, a memory hit hard.

They had moved to Downey in September, so he began school toward the beginning of the year for a change, at least one small relief. Still, the strain of his first day at a new school had worn him out. After getting off the bus, he had walked home fast, looking forward to a haven from yet another new place and all new people, making for the first yellow house with faux brown shutters he came upon. He had walked inside the unlocked door, raised his head, and confronted a nightmare.

Here stood their new place, but wacky, the kitchen on the left instead of right, his mother's furniture, always lightweight so that you could move it easily, replaced by leaden-looking antiques.

Shocked, he couldn't move anything except his eyes for a minute. Here stood his home, reversed. His present life, overhauled in a day. Unfamiliar furniture. Strange portraits on the walls: a man with a mustache, babies in dresses. At first he had shifted his books from one hip to the other, as if adjusting their weight could shift things right, but the setting remained deviant, looking-glass unreal.

Had his mother moved without him?

Left him behind?

She could move very fast but even she couldn't make a house with a garage on the left into one with a garage on the right. Logic should have kicked in about then, that he had stepped into an identical house with a reversed house plan, on the same street, a few doors down from his own house. He didn't belong at his new school. He didn't belong here. Where was his home? Lost like him.

His eight-year-old self had stood with the door open for a long time that afternoon, lawn sprinklers fizzing all around the yards behind him. Where was he? They moved so much, he didn't know. He had walked into someone else's house and now, unsettled, he doubted everything. Was this the right street? Had he gotten off the school bus at the wrong stop or taken the wrong bus entirely? How would he find their house? He didn't know.

Although of course eventually, probably only a few minutes later, he did find his house, this house he was watching now, a few doors away.

The sirens faded but persisted, fretting, chronic complainers, echoing off the million tons of asphalt. They congregated somewhere nearby, weaving closer from different directions like a bunch of tired kindergartners assembling for snack time. Ray caught a whiff of smoke between hits of smoggy air. The engines were en route to a fire, nearby, upwind, but not near enough to concern him. Good. Maybe the commotion would keep the police busy, too.

Ray pulled back behind a juniper bush to give himself a minute to organize his keys, putting aside the ones he had already tried, just in time, as it turned out, because across the street, a woman with a blanketed baby snuggled up against her poked her head outside, examining the sky for smoke, sniffing. She stayed for only a few seconds before ducking back inside. She never even looked toward Ray.

If the police came—but don't worry about them. Stay loose. Taking advantage of the neighborhood din, he continued sticking various keys in the lock a few times, then twisted the handle to the door, which slipped open with oily smoothness. He stepped inside the familiar foyer, closing the door behind him quietly, and listened.

Nothing stirred in the living room. He moved toward the dining area, reluctant to turn on a light. Was everyone gone? He didn't know for sure. He stood for a long time listening, hearing only the creaking of an old house. While he listened, he looked in dismay around the room, experiencing some of the disorientation he had felt that first day of school when he went into the wrong house.

This house, their house, was all wrong. His mother had arranged the couch in front of the brick fireplace, giving the long room some balance and a focal point.

Hearing nothing, feeling excited, agitated, he took one end of the unfamiliar leather couch and hauled it, then the other end, until the couch was in position.

Better. But the two chairs needed to come in, and the coffee table, abandoned across the room, also needed a better home.

There. In the darkness, he remembered what it felt like to live in this house. He liked watching television in his bedroom. He loved the big backyard, with its yellow crabgrass, that he cut every other Saturday. He liked the way his mom had been at this house. She had a job in the back room of a florist shop. She liked the people there, and came home from work cheerful most days.

They had lasted seven months here.

In this house, his mother had hidden things behind some molding in the small back bedroom they had used as a den, where the L-shaped hallway turned.

The doorway to the hall was mercifully open, so he stepped into its murk, too nervous to use the small flashlight he had tucked into a pocket.

Feeling his way along the wall, he walked down the hallway, approached the room slowly, silently, and put his hand on the door frame. The door was open. An empty room awaited him. He went inside, needing only a few moments to complete his mission.

He found it behind the molding, another small plastic rectangle, shocks running up his hand when he touched it. Still playable?

Back into the dark hallway—

A light flashed on in the master bedroom to his right. "Who's out there?" a quavering female voice yelled from inside. "I've got a gun!"

"Don't shoot!" he cried. "I'm going!"

A blast whipped through the closed door to his mother's old bedroom, splintering the wood trim beside him.

When the front door wouldn't open, he crashed through the window.

9

At work on Wednesday morning, Ray felt strangely alive. He had been shot at, broken through a window, escaped with a few scratches. He had obtained another prize.

Martin had greeted him this morning with what might be mistaken for warmth by an observer, but what Ray understood to be a kowtow. "Hey, you look like a guy who could use some TLC."

"I'm fine," Ray had said, not touching a nick from some glass on his cheek that felt particularly painful.

"Like a bum somebody beat, who walked away." Ray waited for him to ask if Leigh had come home yet, but Martin knew better. He watched silently as Ray turned into his office.

Odd how, considering the recent brawl between them, the partnership between Ray and Martin continued to operate. Ray supposed you could put it down to the years of practice they had at suppressing their personal problems at work.

Hair flyaway, pulling at a blouse that didn't quite cover her firm belly, Denise popped her head into Ray's office and reminded him to remember to take his laptop home. Her husband was a former linebacker at UCLA and even Martin hadn't dared to attempt a come-on, not that she would ever bow to his facile charm, something Ray had always admired about her. "I attached the Antoniou presentation on an e-mail. Tomorrow's so crucial."

Ray nodded.

"Are we ready?" she nervously asked.

"We will be."

Her intrusion snapped him back. Along with whatever Denise had cooked up, he had drawings, schematics, and calculations to assemble. He organized his desk, feeling as immortal as a teenager, and as reckless. His work never stopped. For the first time in a long, long time—since he had built his own house—he was doing exactly what he wanted to do on a design.

All because he had said to hell with it.

Although it could come to nothing. No way to tell yet, while they were still in the fantasy phase of the Antoniou project. Strange how it took a crisis to make a person not give a damn, and therefore do some of his best work ever.

Work was an antidote to anxiety. You could forget things working. Spreading the large prints out on his cherry table, he thought, No mistakes.

In the afternoon, he hosted a difficult meeting. Four associates, all younger than Ray, in their mid-to-late twenties mostly, three men and a woman, waved their hands above the conference table, wary. News of his fight with Martin had obviously spread, causing universal consternation. Trust Suzanne to regale them with every grisly detail. They had to be wondering if the partners would break up.

Who would they want to win?

A delicate seesawing of talent was necessary to make a success of an architectural firm like theirs: on the one side, Martin the sales guy with the accountants, Hal and Gary, who didn't pay people until they begged, cried real tears, or threatened to sue; and balanced on the other side, Ray and the overblown assortment of tender artistic types.

The money guys disdained the artists as lightweights with a frivolous disregard for financial realities. The architect/artists hated the money guys back, not so much for forcing them to live within the numbers, but for their contemptible interest in such things. They all needed each other, that was the problem.

"The museum job is going well," Ray announced. The amber sunshine was wasted on the people gathered in the white-walled conference room with its framed black-and-white photos of completed projects. Ray had noticed, after spending a few years at grad school in New Haven, that people in L.A. had the same negative moods, suicidal, enraged, frustrated, and were as angry as people in harsher climes, but in his view, they had them less often. He put it down to weather.

Today, however, the glum faces of his staff did not reflect this mellow summer afternoon. They wanted to know they had jobs. Ray assured them they did.

Martin entered the room, twenty minutes late. His bloodshot eyes belied the hearty smile. He had probably been fortifying himself at the trattoria next door. He looked good, though, dark purple dress shirt, black slacks, black tie, black Nikes. Suzanne's face turned that familiar pink. Ray realized that Suzanne had probably been taken in by his son-of-a-bitch partner also, and that catapulted him out of his pseudo-calm.

"Afternoon, all," Martin said. "What am I missing?" He didn't look at Ray.

"Hey," they all said back, suddenly less gloomy. Martin had the effect of a person with a golden glow.

"We're talking about the firm's direction," Ray said. "Sit down."

"What a good idea, Ray. I think I'll sit down."

Supercilious asshole. "Let's keep this short. We all have work to do. Martin?"

Ears pricked up. Coffee cups clanked on the table.

"As you all know, Achilles Antoniou, the main donor to the museum project," Martin said, "also wants to build a dream house in Laguna. He has three acres of land with an ocean view and no idea what to do with it. After a lot of legwork on my part, he agreed to a set of preliminary designs, which I know Ray and Denise are working up. We've got a meeting coming up on Thursday, tomorrow, and I'm feeling very optimistic. I've told him Ray's a ge-nius, and the rest of us are, too. I think he believed me about Ray. He had seen some articles—anyway, if Denise and Ray need help, you guys get on it, okay? This could so-lidify our name in the business, and that's good for all of us. Plus—money. We all like bonuses, don't we?"

They almost jumped up and down like cheerleaders at

the thought, even though Ray noticed Martin hadn't, in fact, offered any bonuses. As a partner, he had no power to offer bonuses on his own. You had to hand it to Martin. He had probably lavished a good five minutes of brain-power on this latest manipulation.

"If Ray lands this project," Martin went on, "we're all safe for the next year. Better than safe. We can expand."

"If Antoniou likes what we do for him," Ray said. Only he and Denise knew what a stretch that might be at this point.

"If you do your job," Martin said, staring him down, "he will." Excusing himself, he left the room.

They were all looking at him. "He seems to have the firm well in hand," Carl, a junior associate and provoca-teur, said with a crooked smile. "So you entirely with us, Ray? Not planning to jump ship? I mean, there've been ru-mors."

"Obviously, it's too early to get into this discussion, Carl."

"When would be good for you, Ray?"

"I'll let you know."

"Because we have a right to know what plans you and Martin have for the company."

All heads nodded somberly.

"We should talk." Martin opened Ray's door without knocking.

"Not now."

"Come on, Ray, lighten up. I took my punch like a

man, didn't I? And I apologized, but if I didn't apologize enough I'll get down on my knees and kiss your loafer. Listen. I've been thinking about Leigh—wait—wait, I just want to say, I know you'd never hurt her. I'm sure she's fine. You still haven't heard from her?"

"No."

"I'm sure she's fine," Martin repeated. He essayed a small smile. Ray was struck by a vision of Martin and Leigh at the cheesy motel, the way the cheap bed would have creaked, the way Martin would have taken her every which way. That last image Martin had left him with—

Turning his chair toward the window, he didn't answer. Whatever Ray said would be very, very final, and a part of him didn't want all this to fall apart, the business he had sweated and put his soul into for six years.

Eventually, the door closed. But Martin had brought up Leigh. Of course. Thinking about Leigh made him feel crazy, like throwing himself out the window. What should he do? The clenching tension that gripped him whenever he thought about her took over once more. Every muscle in his body fought every other muscle in an internal death-struggle. He stayed like that, jaw tight, eyes squeezed shut.

What should he do?

After a while, relief came as his thoughts drifted back to the tapes.

Two tapes now. Thinking about the tapes was a way to manage the unmanageable tension of Leigh's absence. He could mull over them endlessly, the tapes, the models, the keys, the memories—all these things at least were in his control, susceptible to analysis.

He replayed part of the tape in his mind, the second one. It was just a fragment of a conversation, like the first tape. He knew his mother's voice.

"*Stay away! How did you—*"

"*I'm giving you one more chance. I don't know why I should. I loved you once, I suppose that's it.*"

"*I hate you!*"

"*Yes. Hate. It all turns to hate. So you won't do it?*"

"*I'll never do it. Never!*"

Ray's mother, still young then, ran as fast as a spider. Ray admired how spiders run. So small and smart, they instinctively sense danger. A light comes on, freeze. A nearby movement, run for a dark crack in the cupboards. Why hadn't they run to Canada, to Maine? He had figured that out. He and his mother had hidden far away in the anonymous, huge Los Angeles suburbs because Esmé's beloved mother was in long-term nursing care in Montebello.

Some bastard had, meanwhile, stalked his mother. Esmé had always conveyed that impression, now that he thought about it. She kept few photos of his childhood, telling no happy stories, and remained mum on the subject of men, probably to spare Ray's feelings.

A boyfriend, someone she had dated after Ray's father

left? After he died, when Ray was just two years old? It made Ray feel ashamed. He thought warmly of Esmé, who must have lived in great distress for many years. He would get her to share the story, and then they would put it away forever. Put the models away. Put the need to visit the houses away.

He sat down to his drawing board. He was not going to lose his work over Leigh, over the past. The museum design needed tweaking. Then he would design Antoniou a mansion that would go straight into *Architectural Digest* or heck, even *Granta*. He would show all the bastards the true meaning of original.

10

Downstairs at home that night, while studying blueprints, the cassette burning a hole in his workbench, Ray heard thumping on the door. Ray peered at the large LCD screen in the corner of the basement that showed his front door. Two uniformed police officers stood out there, starched, laden with radios and holsters and clipboards and God knew what else. Behind them he saw a police car, red light spinning.

Walking toward the front door, Ray felt hot fear that flared through him like a sparkler, making his legs move slowly, painfully. Maybe everyone dreamed this moment, a moment when the jig was up. Didn't everyone suffer from some guilty secrets and fear being found out? Had they talked with the kids, somehow identifying him as an intruder? Or was this about Leigh?

Ray shook his head, wishing the mixed-up disarray in his mind would clear up enough so that he could see his way down the hallway, through the door, and beyond, into the future. "What is it?" he asked the two men.

"Raymond Jackson?"

"Yes."

"You work at Wilshire Associates?"

"I'm a partner, yes." He asked for their identification, which they provided: Walter Rappaport, police lieutenant, robbery/homicide, a big man with bags flowery as broccoli under his eyes and a leery attitude; and Rick Buzas, police officer II, field training office, unlined and complacent.

"Nice house," said Officer Buzas, younger, smaller, standing slightly behind the lieutenant. His fresh skin shone in the porch light. "Big. Bet you have a great view." On this soft moonless night he was looking around at the landscaping, sniffing at the jasmine along the steps.

"What can I do for you?"

The big guy in front butted in. "Can we come in? We have a few questions."

Ray closed the front door behind him and stepped outside to face them. "No. Sorry." Ray didn't want them in his house. He didn't want them on his porch, either. He recalled a salient fact. The police had no obligation to tell the truth while discovering the truth. What a skewed world. He should be very careful. He didn't want to get them interested in his business any more than they already were. "Now, could you please tell me why you are here?"

"You know a man named James Hubbel? A deputy sheriff for the County of Los Angeles."

"Mr. Hubbel is my father-in-law."

"He's concerned about his daughter. He got in touch with my sergeant. Thought I'd come out and make sure she's okay. Is she here?"

"No."

"No? Where is your wife, Mr. Jackson?"

"I can't tell you that."

"You can't? Why can't you?"

"I don't know where she is. She left me. Never said where she was going. Has Mr. Hubbel filed some kind of complaint against me? Is there a missing persons case?"

Rappaport's big ears seemed to move back like a dog's.

"How long ago?" he asked.

"Five days now."

"So you're all choked up about this, huh?" asked Officer Buzas.

Ray stared at him. Rappaport coughed, eyeing Ray almost apologetically, as if he too was disturbed by Buzas's bluntness.

If they had a warrant, they would have pushed him aside and would be searching his home right now. Ergo, this was an exploratory visit, the first aside from that unofficial one from Leigh's father, and not entirely unexpected.

He said, "I understand Mr. Hubbel's concern, and I wish my wife would call her folks and say she's okay. But isn't it fairly common, spouses separating? One leaving the home? Not telling her husband where she's gone to get her life together or whatever? I mean, she's a grown woman. She can go where she wants, can't she?" He couldn't keep anxiety from creeping into his voice.

"Where would she go?" asked Rappaport.

The ultimate question they had come to ask. Ray

scratched beside his mouth with a sharp fingernail. "No idea."

"When did you last see her?" asked Buzas.

"Late Friday night, as I said. We had some painful things to discuss. She"—he thought back to that night, struggling against emotion—"walked out. She didn't tell me where she would go."

"What time was this?" Only now did Ray realize that Officer Buzas was taking notes.

"About nine. I don't know. Maybe ten."

"What did she take with her?"

He thought. "A flowered carpetbag she uses for overnight trips. She must have packed that. Some jewelry, I noticed later. Underwear, I assume. Some of her toiletries are missing from the bathroom."

"I would have tried to stop her," Officer Buzas said, looking at his partner.

Ray said nothing.

"What was the subject of this fight?" Rappaport asked.

"I didn't say we fought."

"Okay. What painful things did you discuss?"

"Obviously, it was about problems in our marriage."

"You seeing someone else, Mr. Jackson?"

"No, no."

"What about her?"

"We were just—I've been working hard, and she was upset."

"What have you done to try to make contact with her?"

"Nothing. I think she just wants to have a few days to herself, to cool off."

"She hasn't contacted her workplace for three days running," Rappaport said. "Mr. Jackson, do you want us to find your wife? Because you're acting mighty strange, if you do."

"Look, check me out. I've never been arrested, never done anything. I'm not a drug addict or alcoholic. I'm just a man whose wife left him."

"After a violent fight."

"I never said we were violent."

"How long did this fight go on? You have these fights often?"

"It wasn't a fight! It was just—" He stopped, his mouth open, then said, "Look, is this a missing persons case?"

"Like I said, we're doing a welfare check."

"An informal welfare check because her father's a cop. I understand." Informal because this isn't your case yet, Ray thought.

"You could make it a missing persons case. The father, he knows she's an adult; it's been a few days, he's worried, but we can't open a case based on that. But if you come down to the Topanga station and say your wife has disappeared, we'll find her for you."

"I'm not sure I want to do that. She said she was leaving me and she left. She doesn't want to talk to me right now; that's clear."

"You want her back?" Officer Buzas said. Ray didn't like the way he leaned against the door frame, looking like he didn't believe a word Ray was saying.

"I love her, if that's what you want to know," Ray said.

"I hope when she comes back that we will be able to work through our problems. I'm afraid to track her down and drag her back when that's not what she wants right now. I'm not sure what to do."

"You don't want us even to check on her welfare?"

"I didn't say that. Look, I just don't feel I can help right now, but I will definitely ask for your help if she is gone much longer."

"Deputy Hubbel doesn't believe his daughter would leave of her own free will and not contact her mother even once."

"It's only been five days, detectives." Ray felt very tired. He wanted to be cooperative, but what could he tell them? That they had been fighting over Martin? Wouldn't that make them even more suspicious?

Suddenly he felt the full enormity of his situation. It was like getting knocked down into a dark well, nobody else there, just him, the deep cold water, and slick, black walls he could never climb. These men weren't here to conduct a little question-and-answer session. They suspected him of hurting his wife.

"We'd like to come inside and look around the place. You don't have anything to hide, right? And it might help us locate Leigh."

"No," Ray said.

The younger cop seemed about to knock against Ray with a shoulder and go in, but Detective Rappaport put a hand on his arm.

"You have no idea where your wife might have gone?"

he asked. He was driving Ray crazy with these repeated questions but Ray didn't dare send them away. He could hear the radio static and the flat-sounding dispatcher's voice on the loud radio inside their vehicle, and the red light seemed like a little sun that must be attracting the interest of his neighbors on the right.

Without thinking, Ray answered the first thing that came to mind, so innocent-sounding. "She didn't have many close friends. Maybe my mother's?" As soon as he said these words, Ray realized his blunder. He had needlessly involved Esmé. "Earlier in the day, Leigh had mentioned speaking with my mother on the phone, so when she left, and we both had had some time to cool off, I thought maybe she had just gone there. I went to my mother's house just in case she had gone over there." Lies got so deep so fast.

"Your wife wasn't there?"

"She hadn't gone there after all. I stayed—ate something—and when I came home I went to bed. Leigh didn't come home and she hasn't come home since."

When they asked, he gave them Esmé's address, saying he would call them later with her phone number. He didn't have it on him. They could probably find out all this information in five minutes, even though her number was unlisted. Why not appear to cooperate while obstructing? He needed to slow them down a bit. He needed to speak to Esmé first.

No doubt they realized that.

"You don't know your own mother's phone number?"

"Not offhand." He didn't believe himself, either. "Look. Put it on the record. I didn't hurt my wife, period," Ray said. "I was bitterly disappointed in how things were going with our marriage, okay? I admit that. Now, I have to go. Good night." Ray went into his house and shut the door. It took all his strength to do that, and every moment he expected a hand to come out to smack the door open.

Ray observed the detectives on his monitor. They talked to each other. Finally they got into their loud bright police car and drove away. He sank down to the floor and didn't move for a minute. He spent the next several minutes berating himself, profanely and out loud.

Then he called Esmé. "Mom, two police detectives just left here."

"What? Why?"

"Jim Hubbel asked them to check on Leigh."

"Oh, no. The police. This is terrible, Ray. She still hasn't gone in to work?"

"No, and an old friend of hers showed up today looking for her, too."

"Well, Leigh's a grown woman. She's causing you so much trouble. It's terrible. Are you okay?"

"I made some mistakes talking to them. I got rattled, confused, and—I didn't tell them about Martin, and they're going to find out if they keep looking, and they'll think I lied to them deliberately, and—"

"Martin Horner? Your partner? What about Martin?"

Ray said slowly, "He had an affair with Leigh."

Long, astonished pause. "I don't believe it. An affair?"

"People know at the office."

"Oh, honey, I'm so sorry."

He wanted to shrug, but he knew she wouldn't hear that. "Yes. It's ridiculous and sordid. But to compound it, Martin and I had an argument. We were overheard."

"You lost your temper, didn't you, honey?"

"As a matter of fact, I hit him."

Silence while his mother probably rued the day he was born. "That's not good."

"Yeah."

"I wish you didn't have my temper."

"I was provoked; that's fair to say. He said I drove her to him."

He heard his mother breathing on the line. "Don't you dare allow yourself to take a single bit of blame for their despicable behavior!"

He hated telling her these things, intimacies, but she should know. After all this time, he had to admit to himself, he tried to stay as closed off as she was, tight as a microwave oven, keeping the toxic energy inside.

"You never mentioned you had . . . issues with Martin."

"I didn't have issues with Martin until he slept with my wife." He imagined he could hear the clicking of her brain. Unlike him, she thought things through in advance, even when she was upset.

"I think we should consult with an attorney, Ray."

"No need yet. Let's see if they come back with a warrant. Anyway, what's to find? There's nothing here."

"A search warrant! My God, the papers!"

"Mom, take it easy."

"Listen, here's what we're going to say. Anytime they question your absence, you were here with me. What would be good for us to be eating? Hmm. It might depend on the time of day."

"I did mention you."

"In what way?"

"I said that Leigh might have gone to see you sometime after she left the house."

"Oh. You said that? Why, Ray?"

"She told me you spoke in the morning."

"Oh, I did call that morning. I gave her a message for you to call me, that's all. I have been thinking about how long it has been since I saw Leigh. I haven't seen her since July Fourth. You remember?"

"Ah, yeah." They had eaten, then walked to the nearby park to hear one of those Dixieland bands play for free on the bandstand. Remembering that night, Ray was gripped by the memory. Even then, he had a chance to change things with Leigh, make them right. He remembered how much they laughed, how they sang along with the music. Leigh couldn't carry a tune, but she loved singing anyway and she didn't care when people laughed at her, either.

"If they come here, I can only explain to them I haven't seen her since then," Esmé said.

"Mom?"

"Yes, honey?"

"I don't know why, but I told them I went to your

house right after Leigh left on Friday night, looking for her."

"You did?"

"I lied. Maybe I was embarrassed that I didn't chase after her."

"Okay. Fine. What time were you here?"

"About eleven."

"You didn't call first?"

Ray laughed a little. "Obviously not."

"You didn't call first, because you were so upset, and you wanted to be with me even if she wasn't here," his mother said. "You got here—just before eleven?"

"Why not?" Ray said. "Sure."

"You asked if Leigh had stopped by, and I said no."

"That's what I told them."

"That's what happened then."

"I'm sorry, Mom. I shouldn't have mentioned you at all. But I count on you so much. Too much."

"Don't be silly. You're your own man."

"You're too damn supportive."

"Hush, Ray. This is serious."

"I should never have involved you."

"Well, you just did. You were very upset—no, concerned. We talked it over. You weren't feeling well. You lay down for a few minutes. We had some tea. We ate crème brûlée."

"You make a great crème brûlée. This time the caramel was ever so slightly burnt. How'd you whip up all that when you weren't even expecting company?"

"Don't joke, Ray."

"Leigh's absence is my problem, not yours. I hate asking you to lie for me."

"It's not like you did anything to hurt Leigh."

He saw the cassette on the table.

"I have another tape, Mom. I went back to Stokes Avenue. Remember? Third grade. Or was it fourth grade? The molding? In your old bedroom?"

She gave a little shriek. "Do you realize what you're doing? Ray, I—I'm beginning to think you have lost your mind! You're breaking the law! Now you listen to me, Ray. You already have the police interested in you. You've got to stop this!"

"Why won't you tell me what's going on?"

"Nothing's going on, except that you're ruining your life! Please tell me you aren't going to do that again, go use those old keys and invade people's houses. Especially now. Please, honey."

Understanding she would never explain, fighting down another wave of fatigue, he gave her what she wanted. He told her that he wouldn't do it again.

But before he fell into uneasy dreams, he put on his headphones and listened to the remainder of the tape fragment.

"The phone number was easy," said the now-familiar male voice.

"Oh, God. Stop. Please stop!"

"I'll stop when you stop hurting me, punishing me."

"This can't go on."

"You think you can do whatever you want," the voice said. *"I will find you. I'll always find you. I will never give up."*

"Bastard!" Ray's young mother cried.

11

After work on Wednesday, a day that started dull but ended in an exhilarating courtroom scene between warring business partners in commercial real estate who kissed and made up, Kat met Zak Greenfield at the boardwalk in Venice. He handed her a bouquet of lilies, such fine perfume, but so useless, given that she had only two hands. She walked back to her car, slightly miffed at the delay, stuffed them into the back seat, and hoped they had enough water in the little tubes to survive what she hoped would be a tough, sexy night. Then met him as the sun was nodding off into the ocean like a tired baby.

He rented Rollerblades for them both, and she went along with it, though she had a bad ankle and a worse attitude about cruising clumsily up and down the crowded beach walk on unstable tiny wheels. Lashing the laces, she cast glances at him. He looked happy and even knew how to thread the laces without consulting directions.

"Hold my hand," he advised.

As if she had an alternative plan.

She grabbed hold, teetering, twisting, thoroughly annoyed at herself for pretending enthusiasm, and took off.

They glided south.

On the right, on the beach, foreign tourists who didn't know any better threw sand at each other, the ocean roaring in the background. On the left, raucous summer renters tossed down tequila in their deck chairs. The twinkling lights of the outdoor café they were passing came on.

"You're doing great," said Zak.

Yessir, Kat thought, yessir, Mr. Zak Greenfield, sneaking another good look at him. He had not shaved today, which put him into the category of the sexually suggestive, in spite of his clothing, which was a little too Dockers for her taste. Still, she tingled a bit at the thought of rubbing her own cheeks against his prickly beard.

Something about him.

Jacki talked about chemistry between people, how she saw Raoul and wanted him right then and there. But Kat knew all about the wonders of men, their skin, the way they smelled, what they aroused in her. When Jacki tried to explain this chemistry was bigger than Kat's definition, Kat got as lost as she had when she was forced to contemplate reduction-oxidation equations for a brief moment in her past, not-so-successful college career.

However, the tingling always boded well, that she knew.

"Faster," Zak said a few minutes later.

They flew down the boardwalk, hands wetly locked, the surf white in the distance, all traditional imagery in place. When she wavered, he held her steadily. When she became exhausted, not too far into their journey, he insisted they stop and sit on a concrete bench to take in the waning light. They sat down and got playful, commenting on their fellow Rollerbladers, the muscle-beach guys with their rippling abs, the girls in their cropped tops and wet T-shirts. Zak made fun but displayed a forgiving and gentle wit, not mean.

Kat disliked mean people but loved this kind of activity. Los Angeles was so made to be lampooned. "Don't look at him!" she commanded, averting her eyes and turning Zak with a hand to gaze at the ocean, as a shirtless, particularly overdeveloped creature loped by on the boardwalk. "He craves attention. It'll irritate him, wondering why we didn't look!"

Zak obliged, examining the sunset, laughing.

While they watched the final purple, peach, orange melting display of a clear Southern California sunset, she asked him about his life, and Zak told her that the main thing she needed to know about him was that he loved his work. He wouldn't quit until they fired him and if they did that, he'd find another job in his field.

Kat tried to think of a man in her past who had a job he liked. She failed. A little voice said, "He has a steady income and a happy nature. Plus, Jacki approves." Before Kat could make a further independent assessment of this information, she thought of Leigh. Had she married Ray out of some misguided sense that he would give her the stability Tom never could? Perhaps Leigh had not been misguided at all, but correct. After all, Tom showed his weakness, his lack of steadiness, in the end, didn't he? He had self-destructed.

They arrived back at the rental place as darkness fell,

collected their shoes, and walked to the parking lot. He took her hand in his again, and asked, "What are you thinking?"

Startled, she asked, "What?"

He repeated his question.

She thought about telling him the truth, but how could she? It was too soon to load him up with Tom, her grief, her missing friend. That wasn't in the rules of the game at all. Automatically, trained in the art of dating, she lied. "I was wondering if you might like to come home with me."

"Really?"

"Uh-oh. You sound doubtful."

"No. Really, is that what you were thinking?"

She couldn't recall any time in the recent past when a man had asked her that when the quick lie didn't suffice, particularly that one, which was intended to distract. And so, as they walked into the encroaching darkness, and the waves receded, completely uncharacteristically, she told him about Tom, Leigh, Ray, Jacki's fears for her, the whole shebang.

He listened as they walked.

She realized at some point while she had been so intently unburdening her heart, he hadn't said a word for at least three blocks. "I'm sorry. I don't know what's come over me. Talk about wrecking a good time."

"This is good, too," he said, "learning more about you." Then: "Is there anything I can do to help?"

Touched by the concern in his voice, she said, "You already have."

They arrived at the Echo. "Cool car," he said, running a finger through the dust on the hood.

"Yes, cool's the word, in more ways than you might think. The a/c went out on it, and today I tried it and it had healed itself. I bet Boxsters don't know how to do that."

He turned her toward him, placing her hands around his waist. "Did you mean that, about me coming over? It's late for a work night."

"I meant it, but, Zak, I totally forgot I have to be somewhere ridiculously early tomorrow morning."

The fact that it was true didn't take the sting out of his good-bye kisses, which whispered and promised and left her aching for more.

12

Well before she would ordinarily leave for work on Thursday morning, at six-thirty, Kat hit the road, leaving her dreams behind her and wondering about her reluctance to invite Zak over after all. True, it would have made a short night, but he was smart, funny, handsome, and in general exceeded her usual requirements by a mile. But after their conversation, she had found herself unaccountably—vulnerable, even shy, at the thought.

She called her office, and Gowecki, the only one ever in at such an ungodly hour, unfortunately answered. She explained that she needed to reassess a house in Pico Rivera, that she'd lost some paperwork, which was why she was driving there so very, very early.

Then she apologized a few more times for goofing up, then she drove to Whittier instead.

As Ray Jackson had said, the Hubbels still lived on Franklin Street in their white mansion with the red tile roof and the palm trees. Their home looked as wonderful as it had in her childhood. Across the street, her old house looked about the same, a ramshackle two-story with white wood siding.

The friendly old wooden fence that had sat at the top of the driveway of her old home had been replaced by a mean-looking chain-link. A Rhodesian ridgeback's nose poked past the metal as he watched her nervously, although silently. There had been a couple of owners since their mother, and the place today would be worth maybe fifty times what her grandfather had paid. He had owned the place before leaving it to Ma. He had paid twenty grand. Too bad Ma had sold it and burned through the profits far too fast at a nursing home.

Kat climbed the steps to the oversized plank door of Leigh's childhood home and saw the wrought-iron peephole where Leigh's mother always checked first. Now, an educated adult, she recognized that this house had been built in the thirties. They had paid it off long ago, no doubt. She thought that today it would be worth maybe a million five, more if they had ever put a pool into the backyard, but she hadn't looked at comps for the area, so she could be off. And of course, some depended on whether they had upgraded the kitchen and bathrooms.

"Why, Kat!" Rebecca Hubbel appeared surprised and delighted to see her.

"Hi. I was in the neighborhood." She was pulled in, kicking off her sandals at the threshold. The Hubbels had been watching the Nature Channel from behind TV trays full of eggs and steaming mugs. Rebecca Hubbel wore a sleeveless blouse and walking shorts. There were a lot of veins in her legs Kat didn't remember, but otherwise she looked just the same, glasses, untidy hair, sweet face.

Leigh's father, James Hubbel, sat back down in his red leather chair. The TV was a plasma screen hung above the massive fireplace, which Kat had never seen producing a fire. Lit by windows flooding with morning sun that showed the sheen of the polished wood floor and its silk area rugs, the double-height room with its formal staircase had lost none of its beauty. Leigh's father muted the sound but let the sharks on the screen roam free. He had gotten very paunchy in the six years since Tom's funeral, but he still had the long arms and barrel chest she remembered.

Kat was invited to sit down in a Queen Anne recliner covered in soft green chenille upholstery with curved legs and a doily protecting the headrest. She remembered the chair. What was it like, living with the same chair—partner—for so many years you finished each other's sentences and corrected each other without getting mad?

Surprised at her sudden reappearance in their lives after so many years of silence, the Hubbels traded a few cautious pleasantries. Rebecca Hubbel said she was still feeling weak after a bout of diverticulitis. The people who lived in the Tinsleys' old house were Hurricane Katrina survivors who had given up on New Orleans. Kat told them about Jacki's marriage and pregnancy. They offered her coffee. When she refused it, a cold Snapple appeared in her hand.

"I'm looking for Leigh," Kat said.

They deflated like bad inner tubes. "Then you don't

know where she is, either?" said James. "I guess when we saw you, we thought maybe..."

"I went to her home and her husband told me she's taking some time away. But it's been days since anyone saw her—"

"Six days!" Rebecca interjected.

"—and she hasn't been in touch at her office either."

"Or with us." They spoke together.

Leigh's father said, "I put some LAPD buddies on it—they've got a missing persons unit—but to tell you the truth, Topanga's not their jurisdiction; it's the sheriff's. They have more limited resources. With an adult, they have to be convinced something's wrong: she's disabled, in danger, sick, a crime victim, impaired... We can't prove anything. The sheriff says not to panic. Wait a few more days, a week at the outside. If we don't hear from her by then, everybody gets involved."

"You think that her husband—"

"What can we think? You don't go off like that, take an overnight bag, leaving everything without a damn good reason, and she didn't have any reason. If she had a fight with Ray she knew she had her room upstairs, and we could have kept Ray away if she wanted. Why not come home to the room she left years ago, that we've kept for her, or for her children—"

"How often would you talk before she, uh, went away?"

"Every day, almost," said Rebecca. "I just don't understand. Ray seems like such a good young man. We were so happy when they decided to get married. And he encouraged her to do exactly what she always wanted to do.

Helped her set up a business. She's very successful, you know."

"I have heard that."

"We missed you at the wedding. She missed you," Hubbel said.

"Yes, well, I was still getting over Tom's death and I—"

"I wish she had stayed with your brother, now," Hubbel interrupted, focused on his own problems. "Maybe she would be here with us."

Rebecca Hubbel had teared up. Her husband handed her a clean handkerchief, and she dabbed at her eyes. "Did you know Leigh saw a counselor for almost a year after the—incident?"

Maybe if Kat had seen a counselor, she wouldn't be sitting in this house on Franklin Street again, getting singed by burning memories. "No," she said. "Did it help?"

"Some. But she could have used a friend."

"Don't make Kat feel bad, Jim," Rebecca said.

"It's all right," Kat muttered. She remembered playing dolls in this room with Leigh, how they had turned that painted cabinet in the corner into a miniature house with curtains, windows painted on with markers, even adding a patio alongside on the coffee table. Leigh's father, young then, had helped enthusiastically. Her mother bought toy furniture for the project.

What would they think, if they had known the stories she and Leigh dreamed up? In their fantasies, men played a peripheral role. Male dolls were so ugly. Their doll world featured Junoesque women who bore and raised children alone, with men as fleeting presences, available only when required.

She wondered at her memories, how they influenced the present. Did she want a man literally to come and go?

Had Leigh?

They swung side by side in the swings in the old swing set in Kat's backyard. Fifth grade. "I wish I had your parents," Kat said, kicking hard to get up higher.

"Are you crazy?" Leigh asked. Her legs dangled lazily, and she pushed off each time on only one foot. "I think you must be."

"They do a lot for you! Barbies are expensive. You have five of them."

"No," Leigh had said. "They buy me stuff but they pay way too much attention. My dad follows me around warning me about bogeymen on every corner. He goes bananas if I'm ten minutes late home."

"He's a cop, right? That's his job."

"You guys have so much fun."

"Oh, yeah, my great family. We're broke. They take us to Vegas to blow their money and then we don't get any new clothes for school. They yell at each other."

"Hey, at least it's not all quiet at night with two people breathing down your neck about whether you did your homework and on you about whether you brushed your teeth and warning you that too much television rots your brain. You and Tommy and Jacki watch all the television you want."

Kat pumped hard so that she was flying and out of breath. Leigh had a big house and tons of money and parents who were always home. She felt jealous. Things came too easily to Leigh, so easily that she didn't care if she dropped something and broke it, or just lost it along the way.

Leigh's parents were looking at her as if she might have some solution for them, and she saw how troubled they were, which made her *really* worried. "Will you call me if you hear from her?" Kat asked, getting up, handing Leigh's mother her business card at the door.

"The worst is not knowing. If she's all right—how could she let us suffer like this? Doesn't she realize," Rebecca said, placing the card carefully in her pocket, "how very much we love her?"

Leigh's father walked Kat out to her car. "You do remember to lock all your car doors when you're driving around, don't you?"

She drove a block, pulled over, and called Ray. He wasn't in at the office yet, and didn't answer at home. She called her office and, to her relief, got Gowecki's voicemail. She left an abject message, saying she'd be in sometime in the afternoon, and drove to Ray's house in Topanga.

Wilshire Associates had the all-important meeting with Achilles Antoniou this afternoon, but Ray could barely drag himself out of bed at eight-thirty. To make up for his old-man eyes and the cut on his face and the bandage wrapped around his right hand where the cut was really hurting today, he dressed carefully. He considered a tie, but he had never seen Antoniou wearing one, so he settled on a comfortable cross between casual and formal, a blue Armani shirt over blue jeans, more like their client.

As he dressed and drank his coffee, the police visit replayed in his mind. He went down to his workshop to pick up a few things, but found himself staring at the models. The two houses with tapes, Norwalk and Downey—Esmé and he had fled those homes in the dead of night, running like grunion in the darkness. Sometimes, he now figured, Esmé left things behind because they ran too fast.

He studied the models. He had not taken the time to revise them, and now he saw all their flaws, all the flaws in his own memory. They had left those two houses in the dark, and in those places he had found tapes. Other places—Ojai, San Diego—he didn't seem to care as much about them, which was a good thing since they were a lot farther away. Maybe the reason he didn't have models for them, didn't have this feeling of urgency, was because they had left in daylight, with time to say good-bye to the houses and the neighborhoods.

His eyes stopped moving on the Bright Street model. He couldn't remember the move from Bright Street at all.

Bright Street. Uptown Whittier. Age eleven. He should remember. Why didn't he remember? Bright Street with its fruit cellar, the old trees, and the cracked sidewalk.

Opening the Nesbit book, looking at the list, he felt overtaken again by some destructive looming force.

There it was, the number on Bright Street. His keys still sat in the cabinet where he had hung the ring. He consulted his watch. Ten already. There were two messages from Denise on his voicemail.

Kat arrived just in time to see Ray Jackson's Porsche pulling out of his driveway. She honked a few times to catch his attention, but he either ignored her or didn't notice. Well, she decided, staying as close as she could without rear-ending his fancy car, she would follow him to work if necessary.

The Hubbels' suspicions about him had a contagious quality. She was now sick with it.

Predictably, Jackson took Topanga Canyon Boulevard to Pacific Coast Highway. Then he surprised her, driving right past Wilshire Boulevard and veering onto an on-ramp to the Santa Monica freeway.

What was he up to? He didn't seem to know she was following.

As they continued on, the route became familiar. Ray was taking just the route she had traveled from Whittier, only in reverse. She felt foolishly unbalanced, but continued to follow him.

Maybe he was visiting his mother? On a workday morning?

On the way, driving down Whittier Boulevard with its car dealerships and fast food joints, Ray called Denise and asked her to tell everyone he wouldn't be in for a while longer. She wanted to know how long and, when he couldn't tell her, reminded him about Antoniou at two o'clock and a later meeting with Carl to work out details on the museum contract.

"Right," Ray said, dodging a weaving SUV. "What have you put together?"

Denise said, "I'm concerned. I'm freaked, in fact. We should be going over our presentation for Antoniou. You haven't seen half my work. What are you doing that's so important?"

"I have personal business. I trust you."

Her voice lowered to a whisper. "Ray, the police just left. They talked to Martin and me and Suzanne. Ray?"

"I'm here."

"They asked about Leigh."

"What did you tell them?"

"Nothing. But Suzanne is furious with Martin right now. You probably know why. Anyway, she took the cops into your office—your office, Ray! You ought to fire her! And when she came out she had a smile on her face that was as big as revenge can get. I'm sure she talked about that argument you and Martin had."

So the police knew about Martin and Leigh. Then they knew Ray had lied to them.

Ray wondered how much time he had.

"I won't have to fire her," he said. "Martin will."

"True," Denise said. "Probably today. And then she'll file a complaint of sex discrimination or whistle-blowing or something because of Martin. And the legal merry-go-round will start up."

There was a silence, phones ringing back at the office, a fragment of conversation as someone passed by. "I'm so sorry," he told Denise.

"It's just—Leigh's okay, isn't she?"

"She's taking time off, that's all. Tell everybody I'm sorry for the inconvenience."

"When will you really be in?" Denise said, bluntly fixed on her own concerns.

"As soon as I can."

"Because I can still cancel this meeting."

"No, you can't. I'll be there."

He walked up to the house on Bright Street he thought might have been their cottage, again shocked by time's changes. The block he remembered bicycling up and down now held new apartments where once old houses had led fading lives.

Dogs barked.

Still a few doors down from the house he thought had been his, he approached warily. He recalled the sidewalk, buckled from the eternally shifting California earth, because he remembered leapfrogging the bad spots on his skates. He walked toward the ramshackle cottage, glad to see it, remembering the monster movies, his fears, and the neighbor next door, who yelled when he or any kid happened to stumble into his dichondra.

He hoped the people who lived in the house worked. This, after all, was a working-class street. But a woman came out onto the porch with a tablecloth, shook it vigorously, and reentered the house. He would have to wait. The woman stood in his mother's kitchen. He went back to his car and rolled down the windows, let his head drop back, closed his eyes, and entered his memories.

He recalled this house vividly. A twenties bungalow, it hid a fruit cellar beneath the kitchen, the only one he could remember from all his years of moving. Shelves below had harbored ancient jelly jars, jars of unidentifiable vegetables and fruits. They hadn't lived there long enough for his mother to get around to cleaning them out. Dank dirt surrounded the shelves and webs curled around the old jars.

After one initial exploration of the cellar, Esmé had never again opened the trapdoor, to his knowledge. But she had said, and he had remembered, "These were places where people could hide. Maybe they built it to hide from burglars."

Ray, then only eleven years old, knew the cellar mainly kept food cool in the days before people had refrigerators, and even then marveled at his mother's paranoia. The fruit cellar, so unusual in his world, so hidden and inaccessible, lured him, and he spent hours down there on hot days in the darkness lying on the damp earth, digging, looking at the jars and the rusted tools. He thought of the place as a refuge. A refuge from what?

He had enjoyed those months in uptown Whittier, with its big city library and a fountain in front where kids like him could cool off on hot days. He admired the old-fashioned downtown. On Saturday afternoons, while his mother did the grocery shopping, Ray paid a pathetically small amount of money to attend horror movies at the Whittier Village theaters on Greenleaf Avenue. His dreams were full of flesh-eaters, bats with human faces who flew at him, toxic liquid beings that seeped under doors. At this house, his bedroom had been a closed-in porch with windows on three sides that offered perfect entrances for monsters. He never told his mother how much the movies scared him and how they sabotaged his sleep at night.

His mother had talked about settling down and found a good job at a hardware store. They lived quietly, occasionally visiting his ailing grandmother in Montebello for hurried, always brief visits. Esmé stayed close to her kitchen and collected cookbooks. She experimented on Ray, making muffins with pecans and oranges, pancakes with maple chips, omelets with zucchini. In self-defense, he stopped eating anything except cereal until she relented and got back to serving him plainer fare.

Looking back, it was as though they really were starting a new life. Then one night in August, yes, another August night, she had presumably moved them. He woke up one morning in a new place, with no memory of leaving.

That made this house promising.

The summer sun played over the sidewalk, heating the stone wall he sat upon. The front door to the cottage opened, and the woman stepped out. She held an extendible leash. The big yellow Labrador walked politely to heel as they disappeared up the street.

She might not be gone long, although a dog that size really needed a good long walk. He got out of his car, sauntered up the porch steps, and knocked. No answer. He pulled out his family of keys. Before trying a single one, he played a game with himself. Which one might fit? He picked through them lovingly, but in truth had no idea, so after a few moments, he simply tried them methodically. Not this one, not that one. This one was too old-fashioned, and the next one, too shiny for one from so many years ago.

Twist. Turn.

13

Finally, one worked. He had to push hard against the door. The living room, once home to geometric-patterned curtains, now flowery and strange, held a level of clutter he could hardly believe. Newspapers and magazines piled up in corners, along ledges, even on the couch. He had heard of such people. They hoarded, fearful of what?

He picked his way disdainfully past the moldering stacks, thinking, was it worse to hang on to every single thing, or better to let it all go without regard for its meaning or import?

He checked out the master bedroom and found nothing, then moved into his old room, the one with the three high windows. He hardly recognized it. This room had turned into a repository of neurosis, a place where damp publications mildewed and died. All three walls held moldering papers stacked up to the ceiling. He could barely walk inside.

It hurt, what they had done to his home. He was stifling. Throwing open the back door, he took a deep breath of fresh air to clear his lungs, wondering how much time he had. All the time in the world, really, because the world had come down to this mad search of his.

He moved swiftly back into the kitchen. Scanning the scene, the dirty countertops, the sink full of filthy dishes, he couldn't immediately spot where the trapdoor lay. A sisal area rug covered most of the floor, and he pulled it aside, examining the stained hardwood flooring below.

Ah, yes, grimy lines that showed where the trapdoor existed. No handle stuck up anymore, however. He had to find a steak knife in a drawer and pry at the sides of it. After cleaning and picking at three sides, the door lifted open like an ancient tomb.

He peered inside. Black. Dank. Nothing. Cold air coming at him.

He didn't have a flashlight. Frustrated, he left the trap open and wandered farther through the house, trying to find one. In one cupboard he found a hair cutter, shaver, curling iron, and hair dryer. In one, he discovered appliances: a bread maker, coffee grinder, blender, and sandwich grill. All these things reposed willy-nilly between oven racks, coffee mugs, and canned goods so old their labels looked quaint. In the third drawer down in the master bedroom, right next to an oddly shaped personal vibrator, he found a flashlight. Another ten minutes later he discovered the battery that would make it work.

Phew.

After placing the battery correctly in the flashlight, he poked it into the dark hole of the forgotten fruit cellar.

Webs, the overwhelming truth of the matter. Many spiders, many critters, owned this place. He saw jars he thought he remembered from his childhood, ugh, so old even he didn't want to deal with them. However, he had no choice.

The rotting wooden ladder held his weight all the way to the dank floor. Waving the flashlight around, repulsed, intrigued, he dug through the dusty dank jars, watching for black widow spiders and another revelation.

After all, Esmé had thought of the cellar as a refuge from intruders.

Parked on the street outside, Kat watched Ray leave his car, debating whether to hop out and have a look through a window or two to see what he was up to.

"A1A Beachfront Avenue!" the boyz on her cell phone shouted.

"Hiya. It's me."

"Well, hello, Zak."

"A Chinese movie tomorrow night?" Zak suggested. "Not quite *Crouching Tiger*. More *Man, Woman, Eat Tofu* type of thing."

"Er. Never heard of that one," she said.

"Well, I forget the name, but it's about a guy who doesn't fit in with his girlfriend's family. He's not what they think he is. He can't live up to their expectations."

"He's gay?" She usually passed on gay movies. She went to the movies for the immature purpose of identifying with a main character, wanting to be a beautiful babe who got it all, or got what Kat wanted, anyway.

"No, but there's some kind of kinky sex thing. Does that bother you?"

"I'm okay with kink in moderation." And sure, she liked sex things. She just didn't like subtitled films. She didn't understand Chinese history or French humor or Swedish angst. She liked great production values and a lot of FX.

Rollerblades and subtitles. Zak wasn't easy to pin down, was he? One of these days, she would have to pry into his past, and get equal dirt on him.

"Sounds great," she said, distracted, her eyes on the house.

"I'll pick you up."

She punched off and smiled at herself, an attractive young woman in dark sunglasses, examining herself in the driver's mirror. Just before the call she had been a loser acting peculiarly. Amazing what a phone call could do.

Possibly she could change for Zak. She would watch Korean and Indonesian and Finnish films with him twice a week for the rest of her life and have a normal life, like Jacki's, with him.

Then she remembered with a wince her sister's conversations lately, which had deteriorated into daily reports on her lack of sleep, the daily boredom of staying at home, how much she hated to clean. Maybe Jacki had been right. Kat didn't know what would make her happy. But she was getting a definite inkling about what wouldn't.

She touched her car door handle, preparing to exit, then stopped, as something moved in her rearview mirror.

She sure takes short walks, Kat thought, fear for Ray

rising up in her. He was about to get busted in the worst way, by a frustrated, drooling big animal. She jumped out of the car and approached the woman, even reaching out to pet the scary guy who stood calmly by her side. She, who knew nothing about dogs, learned a lot in the next few minutes. When she couldn't think of another thing to say, the woman said good-bye and approached her house.

Come out, come out wherever you are! Ray! Kat shouted in her mind, but stood indecisively beside her car, wondering what else to do.

The fruit cellar was creepy, even with the square of light above that led back to the kitchen and the day. Ray began to feel claustrophobic, and his movements got larger. He knocked jars off their shelves. Something splattered on the ground and a sickly-sweet fruit smell came up. He ran his hand high along the right wall. Nothing. Kneeling, he flashed the light along the webs and detritus of fifty years of winters and springs.

And there he found it, a filthy zipped vinyl bank envelope, lying against the wall under the lowest shelf, right on the ground. He recognized it instantly, even in this light. His mother had kept her papers in it. He seemed to remember her looking through it for some money to give him one morning when he was late for school, pulling it out of her underwear drawer.

She had put it down here for a reason. He held it, the flashlight trembling so that moving shadows were cast over the walls.

He heard a faint bang up there and his heart fluttered. Pushing the envelope into his pants pocket, he waited in the dark, cursing his stupidity in not shutting the trapdoor when he went down, just to have a little light.

Then he heard growling, then the most horrendous, cavernous barking and scrabbling of feet above his head.

The light through the trapdoor was cut off. "Who's down there?" a woman's voice demanded, muffled through the floor, and spiked by shrieks from her mad dog. He should have said something, "Utility man," anything, but his tongue wouldn't operate.

The trapdoor was pushed over the hole. He barely breathed in the blackness, but the sounds above were incoherent as bedlam.

He could guess what she was doing. He didn't have much time. He climbed up the ladder and tried to push up on it, but she seemed to be sitting on it. It didn't budge.

"Ma'am, please let me out," he said. "Please hold back your dog. I'm with the water company."

"The hell you are," came her muffled voice. "Tell it to 911." The dog, maddened by their interaction, howled afresh.

"Hush, Kobe," the woman said. "You hush."

Amazingly, the dog obeyed.

Well-trained. Not good, Ray thought. "Your neighbor called. A water main broke. You have severe flooding down here." Then he switched to being a gas man, crying out, "Ma'am, listen. We have to evacuate right away. There's going to be an explosion!" He pounded upward on the trapdoor, and he wasn't playacting the terror in his voice. To be found like this—he would be put in jail! Or eaten alive by that monstrous animal.

No answer at first. Then the door opened a crack.

"Ma'am, please let me out. It's dangerous."

"Show me your badge."

"I don't have a badge!"

"Well, you better have something, or you're not—" With a titanic effort he gave the trapdoor a sharp push upward. It fell away and he saw brown legs in rubber flip-flops recede. He burst out into the kitchen and landed in a crouch. The woman stood in the corner by the stove holding a butcher knife. "Don't come near me!" she screeched. "Kobe, get him!" The dog racing after him, Ray turned and ran for the front door.

Once outside, he ran across the lawn toward the street, wishing he had parked closer, aware that he could not outrun the hellhound who wanted him dead.

A green Echo cruised up, window down. "Get in!" The side door flew open.

He jumped in and Kat floored it. The dog hurtled up the street behind them, barking, until he finally couldn't keep up and dropped behind.

"You stink," Kat said, cornering onto the boulevard with one light hand. "No offense."

Ray looked at himself. His pant leg was covered in a slimy goo. Jelly from an eon ago, most likely.

"Oh my God," he said. "Thank you, Kat." He breathed hard for a few minutes, the most elegantly dressed burglar she had ever seen.

"Wait. Stop," he said finally.

She parked in a liquor store parking lot on Whittier Boulevard and folded her arms.

"I have to go back and get my car."

He had stashed it by the library and walked to the house. By then, Kat, intrigued, didn't want him to know she had been following him. She had kept her distance. "I want to know if you hurt anybody at that house."

"No. I swear."

"Did you steal anything?"

"No."

"Why were you there?"

"Why are you spying on me?"

"Listen, you—you know what? I'm taking you right back to Bright Street. I never should have done this." She kicked the little car up to speed and made a hard right out of the lot.

"No, please don't." The look on his face showed real terror. "Just take me to my car. I promise I'll answer all of your questions."

"When?"

"Just not right now. I have a big meeting at work. I'll lose my business if I don't make it." As if preparing for it, he worked a handkerchief over the jelly on his trousers. Kat drove up behind his Porsche and gave him a business card.

"Pick me up at that address at nine-thirty," she said. "I'm working late to make up for this."

"Jacki, pick up the phone. It's me. Jacki?"

No answer. Driving back on the Santa Monica freeway, Kat hung up without leaving a message. She needed Jacki to help interpret the peculiar events of the day so naturally, Jacki, always there when you didn't need her, wasn't there, or wasn't answering.

She called again. "Where are you?" she asked Jacki's voicemail. She didn't like the plaintive tone of her voice but out it came. "Jacki, I need you to call me right away."

Where could she be? Jacki always kept her cell phone one inch from her ear. Kat called Raoul's cell phone, but he didn't answer. Then she called Raoul at UCLA.

Raoul's assistant answered. "Can I help you?" asked a calm voice.

"I need to speak with Raoul urgently. It's his sister-in-law, Kat," she added, just in case he had what Kat's boss called a jiggle list, a list where some people got through and some remained forever banned from access. Family generally made the cut, although not always. Everyone had an uncle Gerald, someone you never, ever wanted to speak with.

"Raoul's out," the voice said automatically. Then, "You're his wife's sister?"

Under the circumstances, the frightening change of the voice on the other end of the phone from calm to solicitous made Kat want to waffle. "Yes," she finally admitted.

"She's at the UCLA Medical Center."

"She's having her baby?"

"I don't know about that. They took her in an ambulance."

Ambulance? Weren't those big white vehicles repositories of urgently sick people who might not make it? Didn't they screech up the street, awakening babies and dogs and making people grind their teeth? "Why?"

"I'm afraid there's been an accident. She got hit by a car."

A tap, tap, tap at his office door interrupted Ray. He had rolled in about three-thirty in the afternoon, entirely missing the Antoniou deadline, missing the meeting.

"Come in."

"Here at last. Praise God," said Denise. "However."

"Hi, Denise." The good news was, she was still willing to talk to him.

She stepped inside the door to his office carefully.

"I want to tell you things can't go on this way."

"What do you mean?"

"I mean we need you here. We need a leader."

"Where's Martin?"

"He came in for the meeting. When you didn't show up, he sent Antoniou away and left. He didn't even talk to Suzanne. I think he's feeling scared, just like we all are. What's going on? You're never here anymore."

Ray shifted in his chair. "I'm sorry."

Denise sat down hard on a bench under the window. The light picked up a brash red in her dark hair. "Ray, I'm thinking of quitting."

"Don't do that."

"We're all frightened. Wondering. About Leigh. I'm worried about you every minute. I don't want to leave you, but . . ."

Ray said, "What's that got to do with Antoniou?" But it was obvious. His personal problems were wrecking the firm. "Look," he said to that unwavering stare. "Don't quit. I need you. This will all blow over soon. I'll get Antoniou to sign on. I promise. Don't worry about it. We put you in a tough position." She relaxed slightly at this. "This temporary situation isn't going to change anything. The firm is top priority for both Martin and me."

"We need this commission," Denise said. "But—"

"What?"

"When Antoniou got here and looked at the plans, I definitely got the impression he's unhappy."

"What doesn't he like?"

"The design?" And this was accompanied by a look almost of pity. He doesn't like my design, Ray thought, the incredible modernist manse that would jut like a ship's prow off the bluff, the glass, the movable walls, the copper cladding, all the great ideas Ray had painstakingly culled and synthesized. Antoniou had nodded and nodded and nodded again as Ray described his vision. The son of a bitch—with a sinking feeling, Ray thought, I don't have the energy to start all over on this thing.

Thinking aloud, he said, "I just have to sell him on it. What time is it?"

"Almost four. Uh, but . . ."

"Yes?" He waited.

She gulped. "Please, Ray. Maybe you should see a doctor. You don't look good. You're all banged up and your eyes look all starey."

Martin arrived a few minutes later from his daily visit to the trattoria's wine bar, bleary-eyed. "Thanks to your no-show, Antoniou is hedging. When you didn't make the meeting, he refused to sign off on the preliminary design fee. He refused to write a check. You insulted him, Ray. Nice going."

"I'm surprised you couldn't handle him without me, Martin. You're the persuader. That's your job. You didn't need me."

"It was you he wanted to talk to. Because he—can't—stand—your—design."

"I'll make it up to him."

"Good. Because he wants you to meet him on his boat this evening. He has a yacht he keeps at Newport Harbor, right off Balboa Island. Near a place called Blackie's."

"Oh, no," Ray said, wondering how he could ever do this.

Martin consulted his watch. "You can just make it by six. He needs to show you he's the boss, make you meet him on his territory. He's difficult, Ray."

"I'll grab the drawings and get going."

Denise said, "I have some old Dramamine pills. Let me get them for you."

"I have a baseball cap in my office," Martin said.

"I have a Windbreaker," Denise offered.

He packed up the portfolio with Denise's drawings. Glancing at the calendar, he saw that it had been six days since that last fight with Leigh, and four days since he had punched Martin.

But all this disarray had been decades in the making, starting with his mother's journeys. He was quite sure of that, but he couldn't say why.

14

Antoniou awaited him at one of the Newport Harbor docks, wearing a captain's hat that covered his bald pate and probably made his kids giggle. In his sixties, he had blinding white teeth under a gray mustache and a handshake that would make a weaker man cry. Ray made sure not to grimace. The bright summer evening was windless, the sea calm.

The client didn't seem angry, about to pull the job. He put his arm around Ray, gesturing and talking about the harbor and the fish catch.

They walked a long way up the dock, passing dozens of boats, small, large, metal, multi- and single-hulled. While Antoniou talked about a race around the world won by a giant catamaran in sixty-two days, Ray steamed.

Martin was the schmoozer. Martin went out with clients to odd ethnic food places, sailed on their crummy boats, danced with the wives or cracked jokes with the husbands. Ray shouldn't have to do this stuff. He was the artist.

Near the end of the dock, they stopped at one of the largest boats Ray had ever seen. White-painted double hulls lifted huge decks and a central saloon. Aisles along each side led to a wide wooden deck, where a green nylon net drape hung over the water.

"That's the place to be when we get going," Antoniou said, pointing forward. "It stays cool. Meanwhile, what can I get you to drink?" He led Ray into the cabin, which held leather plush seating in a luxurious booth arrangement, a stainless-steel long bar on one side, and a chef banging away behind it.

Antoniou saw Ray looking and smiled and rubbed the tips of the fingers of his right hand together. Yeah, I have plenty, the fingers boasted.

They set off, motoring slowly out of the harbor toward the open sea. Apparently, such large catamarans could have motors and did not necessarily teeter on one hull. Antoniou assured him that it had a high stability quotient, that he wanted a boat where he could play with the kids and not worry that one of them might take an unexpected plunge. "Someday I'll go for one that's suitable for racing. Maybe when the grandkids are teenagers, and all this starts to look stodgy."

The crew, at least two additional people, took care of the work. One steered, another scurried around doing whatever needed doing, including serving a platter of shrimp in cocktail sauce, crab cakes, and crunchy bits of toast. He left Antoniou and Ray the heavy task of popping a champagne bottle.

"Now then," he said. "No distraction. We talk. No, don't pull out your drawings. We don't need them. Relax. We are on the sea, on a glorious evening."

"Denise said you had some problems with the drawings."

"Problems. Yes, problems. Ray, you are a brilliant designer. Everybody says so. But—you bring me this house that looks like some science-fiction movie. Angles and concrete. Walls that appear and disappear. Don't you know me better than this yet?"

"When you talked about it—my design—with Martin I thought he said—"

"It's a beautiful design. But not for me. I want white columns, my friend. Through which I glimpse the infinite sea. A portico. A row of olives. A turquoise pool. You put in this long black skinny thing, Ray. It seems to be edged in metal. How can my family swim in that?"

"Mediterranean," Ray said, looking down. Boredom filled him. How many Mediterraneans had he designed in the last five years? They were all Mediterraneans. Every last jack one of them wanted a Mediterranean, and he was sick of designing them.

"You can redo the design? Along those lines?"

"Why not?" Ray said. "White columns, right?"

Antoniou's face broke into a broad smile. "That's a boy," he said. "And one other important thing I didn't mention to Martin. It just came to me, in fact. It makes me feel excited about building this home, Ray."

Ray raised his eyebrows, smiled, looked accommodating.

"A man like me has needs beyond ordinary, you understand? I need a place where I can be myself. I never had one as a child. I'd like you to build me a secret room. A basement. An adult playroom. Stone walls, like a dungeon. A good lock on the door."

"A dungeon?"

"For the ambiance. You know what I mean, Ray. I will tell you how to finish it later. Nothing illegal will happen there, I swear. Just personal play."

"I know just the lock and key," Ray said. "A big, ornate, medieval-looking key."

"Only one key. And Ray—"

"Yes?" Ray, eager, at the ready to serve his master, listened carefully.

"I don't want Martin to know."

"Then I can't put it on the official design, the plans. I can prepare you a private set of plans. I can help you get it built privately, yes."

Antoniou smiled. "It's fun, this idea, eh? I was hoping you were not the squeamish type."

"You need two places to hang people upside down or one?"

"Ha, ha. That's a boy. That's a boy!" Then Antoniou leaned in with a serious expression and said, "Can you put a metal—you know, a hook sort of thing—in the mortar between the stones?"

"Sure," Ray said. Consider it done, Saddam, he said to himself.

"And a safe for valuables?"

"No problem." Now Ray thought of Esmé's hidey-holes.

"I'm going to be grateful, Ray. You'll see." He sat back

and had a drink, wiping his lips with the back of his hand. "You know we meet again tomorrow, with Martin?"

"Okay."

"Be ready for that."

Ray removed himself, with the excuse that he needed to take a whiz in the boat's tiny marbled head. When he came back, Antoniou was stuffing himself on canapés, bouzouki music playing softly in the background. His face in repose was sullen, the lines coming down from his nose to his mouth etched from decades exercising power. How had he ever mistaken this Marquis de Sade for someone who would allow him really to use his talents? Ray looked into the mirror above the sink, holding its sides, feeling trapped.

By now, the boat skimmed along the Palos Verdes Peninsula. The verdant hills displayed hundreds of Mediterraneans Ray automatically hated.

"Sit down by me."

Ray obeyed. Water foamed alongside, making a rushing sound. Even through his sunglasses, reflections blazed like shots of lightning, so much so that he had to close his eyes.

Antoniou placed his hand on Ray's thigh. He squinted up at Ray, who chewed on an olive.

Somehow, Ray had been expecting this. He didn't flinch at the touch. Instead he took Antoniou's hand in his own and held it. "Antoniou, if it was any guy, it'd be you, I swear. I'd be a lucky man. However." He gave the hand a kiss, squeezed it again, and put it neatly back to rest on Antoniou's own leg.

Antoniou, at first startled, began to laugh. "Lotta men like both, you know."

"It never hurts to ask," Ray agreed.

"At least I got a kiss out of you."

Ray laughed. "Some big deal, huh?"

The client shrugged, totally accepting. For a while, they just drank and moved through the water, the clouds scudding by, the white foam spraying their faces, the sun going down. Then they moved down to the netting for a while, lying side by side, arms behind their heads, companionable, like a raptor and a naive proto-chicken. Ray felt thoroughly beaten. He kept his smile and told a few good ones even so.

Back on deck, Antoniou excused himself. He returned looking refreshed and perfectly pleased with his life of mansions and yachts and dungeons.

"I love it out here," he said. "My wife expects me at nine, but let's open another bottle. Now, I want to know more about you, Ray. I'm hoping this evening's the first day of a beautiful"—he paused and waggled his eyebrows—"business relationship. You have any kids? Tell me about your wife."

"No kids." He talked about Leigh, taking care to say nothing real. He talked about her furniture-making, the church where they married, the vacation they had taken a few years ago in Brazil. As he talked, he pictured his wife; her gravity, hollow eyes, the way she would trace his eyebrow with her finger before leaning over to kiss him, the thrilling deep kiss. He remembered her complete abandonment in bed, her soft breasts—

But he told Antoniou nothing of this, nothing of the reality of his wife. This, the client had not earned.

"You continue to love her," Antoniou said, pouring himself a final glass of champagne. "Lucky woman. And she loves you, I am sure."

"Oh, yes," Ray lied, relieved to see that Antoniou had now turned his regard toward the young chef, who, judging by the twinkle in his eye, welcomed the attention. Ray had been a passing yen and there were no hard feelings.

Later, as darkness came, driving home, Ray realized that he had returned to the tricks of his childhood, channeling another person. Not for the first time, he had mined Martin's character, thinking, how would Martin handle this?

He wondered if this talent at impersonation masked an empty soul, as Leigh had once accused. Wasn't he just calling up elements of himself to become other characters, tapping into places in his personality that lay undeveloped inside him? He couldn't display grace under pressure, unless grace lurked somewhere inside there, correct?

He had kissed the client's hand, pimped for the firm, saved the day. All right, it wasn't grace he had displayed. Maybe he had been obsequious. He had nodded encouragingly while Antoniou talked about his columns and olive trees.

Leigh—her gray eyes. Her integrity. He swiped his fingers across his cheeks, erasing what he could.

Kat headed straight for the hospital. UCLA Medical Center held at least six hundred patients. Kat found the parking lot, vast, distant from the building, and tried to find a place as close to the palm-studded entrance as possible. Often, this counterintuitive action worked, and this time it did, when a blue Acura pulled out of a perfectly located spot not five spots from the front entry.

Kat let the Acura out, barely, then swerved her Echo into the spot it had left vacant, cutting off at least one other eager, possibly equally crazed, family member who would now have to spend the next hour cruising aimlessly.

Why hadn't they called her?

She locked the car. Coming through the Westwood Plaza entrance, she made her way into the hospital.

A friendly receptionist told her she might find her sister on level five, so she waited with a motley crew for the double doors of the elevator to open. On her left, a man in a wheelchair, his head twisted to the right in a permanently frozen position, moaned. His wife bent down and caressed his cheek. On her left, a middle-aged woman, maybe fifty, with wiry blonde hair that flew out of her head like Medusa's snakes, rested on crutches.

"What happened?" Kat asked, hoping this was not an awkward question.

"I fell off a sidewalk at a street fair," the woman answered, "while checking out the bonsai booth. The silver lining is, I'm building my upper body strength." She laughed.

The nurses' station, a large central area surrounded by counter space and speckled with computers, did not exhibit a neighborly air; no warm cuddly pictures, no flowers.

"Okay," a male nurse said. "Her name comes up on page one."

"What room?"

The man studied whatever it was he viewed on the computer screen. Games? Instant messages? Kat wondered.

"Hmm," he said ominously.

I hate you, Kat replied internally. She realized the last time she had been in a hospital was when she went to find Tom there, and eventually found him in the morgue. "An ambulance brought her," she said instead, helpfully.

"I'm thinking room five oh eight," he said. "She's in recovery. Just got there from the OR. Hmm."

Stop saying that, Kat thought, or I will hit you.

"Through the double doors and on your right."

She found 508 without too many wrong turns, opened the door, and greeted her sister inside. Raoul, looking like a man holding on to a lifeline, was clasping his wife's hand with both of his.

Jacki had the window side. On the door side, Jacki's roommate was a woman who spoke right up. "Arrgh," the roommate cried in greeting. "Crap! I hate my life!" Thin and pallid as a tubercular character in a novel, she had thrown her white sheets off and lay splayed like an automobile crash dummy, post-collision.

"Hey," Kat said to her sister.

"Hey." Jacki's droopy blue eyes gazed at her. "I know you."

Scared, Kat just took her hand. Her sister, for the past few months whale-sized, now appeared diminished, the sheet over her stomach collapsed like a fallen parachute. Where was the baby? Kat didn't dare ask.

Raoul said, "She's okay, Kat. Really."

"Why didn't you call me?"

"No time. I'm really sorry. It happened really fast, and then they operated—"

All the pent-up concern Kat had been repressing flooded out and she started crying. "Jacki! Boo hoo hoo."

"Quit that. Ma always said you sound like a dying animal when you cry and it's true," Jacki said groggily. "Ow, Raoul, something hurts bad down by my right foot."

"She's doped up, Kat," Raoul said, apologizing for Jacki's crankiness. "Just woke up. I'll get the nurse in here, honey."

"They doped me up, hoping I won't notice every freaking thing went wrong that could go wrong."

Kat said nothing, just squeezed Jacki's hand.

"Ouch," Jacki said weakly.

"Sorry," Kat said. "Tell me what happened."

"I was crossing Sepulveda. Big street, so many cars. This—oh-so-L.A.—this stretch limo came out of nowhere. What I remember is the part where I rolled along the street like a bowling ball. Speaking of which—" She stared down at her stomach. "Oh, my God! Raoul! Our baby!" She clutched her husband.

Raoul bent down and kissed her forehead. He stayed there, cheek pressed to hers, and whispered, "Honey, you're a mother."

"We had—our baby? While I was sleeping?"

He nodded. "You went into labor after the accident, while they were setting your foot. Everything went fine. My brave girl. I love you."

"The baby came?"

"A boy, sweetheart."

Kat's heart filled at the sight of the joy on her sister's face.

"We have another boy in the family," Jacki said. Tears glittered in the corners of her eyes. "I want him! Where is he? Bring him here, my darling. Oh, Raoul, a little boy."

"We can pick a name finally. Anything besides my dad's, okay?" Raoul said.

"Middle name Thomas." Jacki tried to sit up, but she groaned immediately and fell back on the bed.

"Congratulations," Kat said. She smoothed Jacki's hair and kissed her, then hugged Raoul. "I have a nephew," she said wonderingly. A new being with an intimate connection to her had sparked into existence when she wasn't looking.

"But where is he? Why isn't he here?"

"You need to rest. Are you ready to see him?"

"Please. I am."

At Raoul's request, the nurses brought the shriveled and squalling newborn to Jacki, tightly swaddled in a white hospital cotton blanket, a blue band decorating his skinny wrist. Jacki cried at the sight of him. She pulled the tightly wrapped blanket down, which made him cry, too, examining his extremities and genitals.

"They're perfect," she said. "Ten toes. Look, Kat. All good."

"Perfect," Kat agreed.

Wrinkled and of an alarmingly bright pink hue, he was mostly bald, but Kat was as mesmerized by his velvety pate as Jacki. She reached out a tentative hand and rested it on the downy head. His skin felt moist, warm, and pliant under her touch.

Rather efficiently, the baby found Jacki's nipple and clamped on. "It might hurt a little at first," said the nurse. "Of course, you'll toughen up."

"Look, Kat. What a beautiful child. Do you believe it?"

"Be glad he's healthy even though he's small," said the nurse. "One lady tonight had a baby with heart problems. He'll need an operation before he can go home."

Jacki kissed the baby's head gently, as if conferring a blessing. "Send her flowers! Send her money for a college education!"

Raoul held her and his son, all together in one big bundle. When Jacki nodded off at last, Kat and Raoul had a wonderful time holding and passing the bundle back and forth and drinking freely from a bottle of chilled champagne Raoul had scored somewhere. The baby slept calmly in his bassinet by the side of the bed, as if perfectly comfortable already with his new surroundings.

"You did it," Kat said. "You gave me a nephew, Raoul. Thank you."

He stroked the boy's cheek, who instantly rooted, searching for a nipple, hoping for more. He sucked his father's baby finger, temporarily mollified. "What if— imagine me raising him without her. Alone."

"You would never be alone."

"I hope that's true."

"I might not have the colostrum but I have the will. No harm will come to this one, not when I'm around." Hearing the fierceness in her own voice made her almost embarrassed.

"I'll go get us a pizza," Kat said later. They ate, and Raoul slept, and Kat watched Jacki wake up twice to take pills and feed her little one. The nurses didn't bother them much. The door was closed and the small, plain room with its medical equipment and sleepers felt as beautiful as the Taj Mahal.

When Jacki woke up again at almost four in the morning and began feeding her baby, Kat left, but not before Jacki had the last word, as usual.

"I wish you could have this feeling," she said wistfully, "that life goes on, and it's good."

She would admit to silver linings, Kat thought, punching the elevator button, new muscles, new life.

Kat had told Ray to pick her up at her work at nine-thirty that evening, but she wasn't there. Ray missed her. He wanted to talk to her, had been holding on so that he could talk to her.

He looked at his watch again. Too late. She had abandoned him. This pressure in his chest—he had brought the tapes to play for her. They radiated on the seat beside him. He gave up and turned on the ignition, the infernal sound that punctuated all their days and nights.

Ray arrived at Memory Gardens in Brea after the sun sank, the great gardens of the cemetery, their grasses and plaques, immutable no matter what the light. The marker for Henry Jackson reposed in the crematorium. "How we miss him," the simple script read, then showed dates of his birth and death, the death date close to Ray's second birthday.

He didn't believe that death date anymore. His father had died later; he was beginning to feel pretty sure about it.

She hadn't loved his father. He was beginning to understand why, at last.

He wondered why Esmé had bothered with this memorial marker. She had told Ray his father's ashes had been scattered by his great-aunt in New York. Maybe she had put it there for him, with a fake death date. She had told him about it years ago, but he couldn't remember ever coming here with her. Ray had come a few times on his own, during those times when he felt the great pressure about the moves.

She was only trying to protect me, he thought, but I'm a man now. The lying becomes another kind of poison.

He put a bundle of tulips near the marker because there was no place for flowers. He had bought them at a florist just past the off-ramp, bright shiny green leaves with soft curling white flowers at the centers.

"I brought these," he told the marker, "because it's a celebration. You're dead, safely dead, and that's a blessing, it seems." He hadn't cared about his own kid enough to let him grow up in peace. Why had his father terrorized them? Sexual jealousy? He imagined he could guess. He couldn't let go of a wife, felt insulted when she rejected him. He felt enraged.

Just like Ray had felt when Leigh cheated on him.

He pushed the thought down, and studied the marker.

"You ruined my childhood with your craziness. You made my mother live in fear. We were never free. We lived like outlaws, always running, always afraid, something behind us ready to attack, always catching up."

He felt the vast emptiness, surrounded by the dead and his own dead hopes. Every boy without a father probably harbors a secret illusion that his father would have been one of the good guys, if only. He'd load up a camper with canned food for trips to Yosemite to climb to Glacier Peak or Alaska to catch halibut, waking his son at five in the morning. Or maybe he would be the guy who dragged his boy off to museums to study the dusty Indian exhibits, who went on and on about the tar pits, and all the groggy boy heard, all the boy had to hear, was his father's voice, not what he said. All the boy heard was the love.

The time they had together would embed memories so deep, even if the man died, the boy could spend the rest of his lifetime savoring and honoring him.

When Ray had been very young, he had such fantasies. He knew it now because they rushed over him, threatening to drown him. He wondered what his own gravestone might say if Leigh had decided the words.

Ray didn't even know what kind of work his father had done at the bank. Teller? CEO?

He leaned forward, clearing dust out of the engraved words with a finger. His mother, helped by a hundred scholarships large and small, along with student loans that ran into the tens of thousands, had managed to bring him up and educate him alone, with a baying hound at her heels, always on the lookout.

He owed her so much, everything that had turned out right in his life. Especially his work. Thank her and thank God for it. He loved what he did.

Now Ray had his fine education from Whittier College to fall back on, not to mention graduate school at Yale, which had forced his mother into working two jobs for many years. At least now, he could help her. At least now, she worked because she liked it, so she said, because she liked the people and needed the structure.

Somewhere inside, hadn't he always suspected he had a

bad father? His own badness had to come from somewhere, the fear and anger he had tried to hide from Leigh,
from everyone.

"Good-bye, Henry Jackson," he told his father, turning
away. "You bastard."

15

Kat came home from the hospital before dawn, collapsed onto her couch, and fell asleep. Hours later she woke up ravenous, found some rigatoni, boiled it and added canned sauce, then wolfed down several bites standing at the counter like a pathetic, lonely person.

On the plus side, nobody was around to shame her into a normal breakfast.

Her phone rang. She checked the clock. "Kat here," she said. "It's seven-thirty in the morning and you better be calling with good news or else, Raoul."

"Hiya, it's me."

"You're up at the crack, Zak. I'm not sure I approve."

"So are you. Or were you sleeping?"

"Well. No."

"I work out before work. Did we have a date last night? Or was that just magical thinking on my part?"

"We did? We did!" She thought guiltily about also making arrangements with Ray. "But my sister had a baby instead." She told him about her evening.

"Ah, good. Then it's not my choice of movie. Or that I wore an ugly shirt or have hair growing on my neck."

She detected a tentative note she found most gratifying.

"I like you, Zak, although now I'll have to take a closer look at your neck next time we meet."

"How are your ankles?"

"Totally recovered."

"Ah, good. You need those to walk, I'm told. You're beautiful on skates, by the way," he said. "Graceful."

"For someone who trips as much as she glides."

"You're just—beautiful."

Oh, so now, at dawn, he was flirting. She heard a horn. "You're on your way to work?"

"Yeah, and someone cut me off."

"So you're gonna show him?"

"Nah." He paused. "I moved right and let him win."

"His SUV's bigger than your SUV?" she guessed.

"Right."

"I bet Raoul's gonna load you up with extra tasks because he has a new baby and you don't."

He laughed. "No doubt. So, how about tonight?"

"I don't know."

"You don't know? I could come to your place."

"Probably not. Sorry." She'd have to reschedule with Ray first.

"So you lied. You did notice the neck hair, didn't you? You noticed, and now you've judged me. You're thinking, he's a man who needs a better barber, and that's not good enough for me."

"I'm sorry I have to pass on the dinner tonight, Zak. But I swear to God, I am enthusiastic. Soon, okay?"

Her phone getting warm in her hand, she called Jacki at the hospital.

"These places are for sick people, for dying people," Jacki said. "I want to go home."

"They're taking excellent care of you, Jacki," Kat said, scared at the thought of Jacki coming home with a baby, unable to walk for a couple of weeks.

"Raoul says he can only take a week off. He's got some gigantic, important, earthshaking business he must attend to after that."

"My job," Raoul said faintly in the background.

"He wants to hire someone!" Jacki's tone was scornful.

Kat said, "Sounds practical to me."

"I don't want a stranger in my home."

Kat took this in, ate another spoonful of rigatoni, and felt a strong desire to hang up. "What are you saying?"

"I have alternatives. Family. You could move in, for example."

Certainly she could. She, who had no life to speak of, would be absorbed by their vigorously alive family. It was the Buddhist thing to do. Take a leave from work, since Raoul couldn't. Be good, saintly even. The Buddhists had lots of saints, but they had a hell realm, too.

"When hell freezes, Jacki."

"Why not?"

"Put Raoul on."

The phone thunked.

"Yes?"

"I'll help you find someone," Kat said.

"Oh, that's great. I'll be home all next week, so let's try to set up some interviews."

"Jacki's going to be mad at me, so I'm going. Tell her I have a call on another line."

"You don't have another line."

"Use your creativity, Daddy. You're going to be needing it. Bye, now."

She called Ray Jackson.

He didn't answer his phone. He never answered his phone, and at his office she always got some hard-ass named Denise who wouldn't leave him a message.

She dressed hurriedly, and drove to her own office.

That morning, still weary from her almost–all-nighter at the hospital, she soldiered through a court appearance that left everyone in the room chilled by the behavior of the disputing parties, a pair of senior-citizen brothers this time, sparring over their deceased parents' homestead. The handicapped one wanted to continue living there but he wasn't able to afford to buy out his brother. Unfortunately, you couldn't fake comps; you couldn't make a property in Pacific Palisades a property in La Habra, in spite of the similarity between buildings.

Hearing Kat's figures, the currently resident brother emitted an actual sob, which earned him a frown from the judge and only made the situation worse. The hale brother, stoic up to now, jumped up suddenly. His attorney tugged at his arm while he stood, shaking, shouting, "Get over it. Get on with it!"

Kat sighed as she packed up her briefcase during the afternoon break and slunk out the courtroom doors. It wasn't always like this. She loved her job. She enjoyed every new property. When first her father, and later his partner, had hired her, she had stuck to filing. Then, she helped compile lists of the houses, which included photographs. At her desk, sticking pictures onto pages that went into binders, she dreamed she lived in these homes. In one life, she drove the V10 truck in the driveway, had a view of the ocean from a top-floor Manhattan Beach condo, and enjoyed a Viking cooktop. In another life, she occupied a shabby thirties bungalow in downtown L.A. next door to screaming neighbors who beat up on each other.

She opened the back door of the Echo, tossing her case into the back seat. She didn't want to see it again, think about that poor old man whose life had just descended like a kid on an amusement ride, from the airy heights to the brutal lows. He had lived in that house for forty years.

He could move out of the Los Angeles area and buy a house in the Midwest for one-fourth of the money he could make on his half of that unhappy house in Pacific Palisades. Or he could move thirty miles to the Inland Empire, the tentacle of the city that stretched into the superheated San Gabriel Valley, once considered almost uninhabitable with its broiling sun and lack of water, now getting hotter, value-wise, by the day.

Many people commuted from there to L.A. proper every morning. They still came, as they had for sixty years, for the weather, the jobs, the ocean. They stayed because, like addicts, they took sick pleasure in the highs and lows, took pride in the daily stresses. They felt muscular and fit, meeting the challenges of rush hour. Maybe they cut five minutes off their commute by finding a handy side street. Maybe they lived in crowded conditions, but the sun shone and they might make it to the beach one fine summer Saturday.

They all lived as if L.A. was still the paradise it must have been once before they all lived there.

She slammed the door, automatically turned up the fan and hit the a/c button, then hit the freeways, such a lovely name for places where nobody moved, everyone felt trapped, and, rich or poor, you heard traces of the same beautiful, evil siren's song.

At the office, Ray could not avoid Martin who, wearing a starched shirt and fancy tie as if dressed for executive combat, stood sentry behind Suzanne, awaiting Ray's arrival.

"Any mail?" Ray asked Suzanne.

"Overnight." She looked a little flushed.

"Good. Antoniou." He held an envelope up to the light.

"Did he sign or not?" Martin asked.

Ray, who had hoped to savor the moment privately, found himself frowning. He picked up the letter opener on Suzanne's desk, the one shaped like a dagger, and ripped it open.

"Ah," he said, reading the letter inside. "He did."

Astonished, pleased, uncertain how he felt, he tossed the check onto Suzanne's desk.

"Yahoo!" Suzanne said sourly.

Martin followed him back toward his office. "We have to meet," Martin said. "You have time right now?"

"In twenty minutes," Ray said. He had nothing particular planned for those twenty minutes except perhaps to read his mail. He just couldn't give Martin immediate satisfaction. Every time he saw Martin these days, he kept envisioning that stocky, freckled body squirming upon Leigh's, saw her hips rising to meet that compact body.

"Look," Martin said, ignoring him and closing the door. "Let's be civilized. We have a firm to run. People depend on us. Put it aside for this project, what do you say, Ray?"

"Go away."

"Come on. Let's give this occasion its proper due. Here's our biggest residential project in years for our most potentially notable client. Let's ride down to the site together before the meeting with Antoniou, okay?"

"Why?"

"Talk about where to put his goddamn columns," Martin said.

"So you already knew he signed this contract on the basis that I'd redo the design?"

"He mentioned he wasn't happy. I told him to talk to you again. That you were quite reasonable. I know you've been doing some sketching this morning. I'd like to see what you're coming up with while we're sitting on the hill. Helps me visualize and wax poetic for the client."

"Okay. Two o'clock? I'll meet you there. I have a few things to do before then."

After lunch, late for reaching Laguna Beach in good time, Ray hit gridlock and frustration. Still, in his car alone he could listen to music, zone out, stay calm. Sitting next to Martin for the nearly two-hour drive would have driven him nuts.

He had been there before so had no trouble finding the site, a steep, forbidding-looking scrub-covered hillside with an earthshaking view of the ocean on Sleepy Hollow Lane, a half-mile up the hill from the beach. He parked on the street, then hiked down, avoiding the ubiquitous poison oak.

Martin sat in the shade of a eucalyptus tree, legs propped on a granite boulder, putting his feet between himself and Ray.

Ray clambered down the dusty hill, then sat on a small rock opposite, not saying a word. He did not want to give his partner easy satisfaction.

"You hate that I'm Antoniou's man," Martin said.

Ray shook his head. "You're personally invested in this project. It's natural. You're his buddy. Hope he doesn't know how little weight you give that word."

"You want to know more about me and Leigh? Because I have the urge to tell you a few things."

"Let's not get distracted." Ray swept sweat from his forehead with his hand, eyes roaming over the vista, the huge, churning ocean below, the unstable land beneath both of them.

Martin took a deep breath. "You know, I used to admire your relationship. You seemed perfect together."

"Oh?" Well, what else could he say, with this womanizing jackass asserting such an intensely personal connection. Ray loved Leigh, whatever she had done, and he now loathed his former friend Martin down to dust, down to their most insignificant moments eating suspiciously brown cold-cut sandwiches from crummy neighborhood grocery stores together. They used to confide in each other, he remembered, and the thought made his skin hot, like a bad sunburn.

"You've changed a lot," Martin said.

Ray adjusted himself, moving one leg over the other, pulling his sunglasses over his eyes. In the afternoon, the breeze off the ocean could be redefined as wind. No need to shiver. This wind blew hot, like the deadly Santa Anas that had wiped out much of this town in 1993.

"I'm not saying she didn't love you," Martin continued. "But your detachment made her vulnerable, buddy."

"Shut up, Martin, or I'll have to kill you."

"We've been friends for a long time."

"Martin, working with you at all right now is a strain. Now let's get down to the issues about this project and leave Leigh out of it."

"I was interviewed by a police detective yesterday. I didn't say anything that would hurt you. I mean, I don't know anything about Leigh, really, or your personal affairs. Actually, he was looking at me and asking me questions that I didn't like at all. As if I might somehow be responsible for Leigh's disappearance, because we—you know, broke up."

The words hung heavily in the air, while Ray thought to himself, It can't be. He examined his partner, sitting in the pressed tan slacks that his wife picked up from the cleaners for him, the three-hundred-dollar sunglasses that Martin insisted were the cheapest way to look like a mover for the clients, by concealing his eyes.

"Maybe they know something I ought to know," Ray said to Martin.

Who spread his hands and said shakily, "I swear to you, I have not seen her since last Wednesday."

"You could swear from now until the end of the world and nobody would believe you at this point, Martin."

"Yeah, well, you're the one who did it, if anyone did anything."

"Maybe it was your wife."

"My wife?"

"I heard," he lied meanly, "somebody called her about Suzanne. Maybe someone called her about Leigh."

Martin looked stricken. "No. They wouldn't dare."

"But as you say," Ray said, "we have a home to design. Shall we get back on topic?"

Martin's face blackened. He walked out to the bluff and his pants whipped in the wind as he took out a cigar and tried to light it. Ray followed him with the plans and set them on a flat rock with a stone to keep them down. "I need to get back," he said. "Say what you want to say."

"Have you talked to Antoniou about these ideas you sketched out and threw at me this morning?"

"No."

"Did you even consider what he wanted before you spent hours spinning these webs?"

"I heard what you both had to say about what he wants. Denise and I came up with these preliminary ideas. About what he needs."

"There isn't a fucking white column in sight on those sketches," Martin said. "I would describe this, Ray, as Tokyo postindustrial crossed with Italian Futuristic. What makes you dream, or suspect, or imagine in your most outrageous fantasy, you might convince this client to build this crazy shit? Because, Ray, he's an old, conservative Greek dude with strong opinions."

"He signed. He paid. He'll love it. I'm the architect."

Martin's fingers drummed the rock that held Ray's plans. A breeze picked them up. His hand came down to hold them in place momentarily, then released them to the wind. They blew away, toward the edge. Ray went after them.

"He signed because I talked him into it, Ray, and we're giving the man what he wants. Might as well toss that dreamy crap you've drawn here because these look to me like plans for someone else's dream house. Oh, it'll make a lovely spread in some magazine. I know that means something to you. Unfortunately, your design bears no resemblance whatsoever to a home for a family."

Ray plunked down a few rocks to weight his plans, then peered at them, putting his hands in his pockets.

The new sketches were changed very little from the old sketches. In his mind, fully realized, sat a fabulous, innovative three-story building that traveled beyond Herzog & de Meuron and Fong & Chan. Featuring a tower encased in steel mesh, it made boxiness sexy, and was a unique home ideally suited to this client and his family. "I wouldn't expect you to recognize—"

"What? Your genius?" Martin laughed, then shook his head. "We meet, we discuss, then you go do whatever the hell you want." He pulled out a folder full of cuttings from architectural and travel magazines from a briefcase he had propped behind him. "Antoniou specifically mentioned Santorini, correct? Where his parents had a villa. Where he grew up."

"You of all people know clients have ideas that are fetal, unformed. They ask for columns. They request turrets. They despise the modern. They rail against all kinds of things in advance, but your job is to believe in your vision for their very special, unusual, inimitable home, so you must convince them to let you build. Then they comprehend your design and love what you've done."

"We're not talking about stucco walls versus sheetrock or walnut paneling." Martin pointed at one plan. "We're talking radical contemporary architecture that someone has to live with for many, many years. Immutable, unless you've got millions more to burn through in renovations."

Ray tried not to show his impatience. "He's a wealthy man, and not stupid. I promise you, he'll see the virtue in this design ultimately." He held up a hand. "Wait. Let's calm down. Martin, here's why I agreed to meet you here today. I'm asking you a favor. This is a last-ditch effort on my part to salvage our professional relationship, okay?"

"What favor?"

"I want you to put aside your"—he longed to say cowardice but didn't want to alienate him further—"doubts about my ability. I want you to be a real partner in every sense of the word and back me up on this project. We can do something great here, or we can give him what he thinks he wants and settle for mediocre."

"I took one look at that first set, 'A.' You call for a 'Flying Carpet' roof."

"It's a proven design. This one would suggest the one at Lo Scrigno. It softens the—"

"Yeah, I bet that's a huge hit in Italy, but first of all that's an art gallery, not someone's home."

"Private. Family owned."

"Nobody lives there. Secondly, it's the opposite of a simple white structure overlooking the sea. It's an expensive indulgence."

"You know what I hate?" Ray said. "I hate artists who analyze their own work. I hate writers who explicate their own poems. I loathe musicians who attempt to describe their music. Martin, listen. Put our differences aside for one second and understand that there's an ineffable quality to design, and that's what makes it rise above what's out there doing the basic job. And you like what I do. We've done some good things in the past."

Martin stared at him as if observing a meteor landing in a field. "When we started out, we were such good friends. I wanted you to be brilliant. I supported your brilliance."

"We're still in business," Ray pointed out. "We've had good press."

"This man's my friend, too. I want him happy."

"He will be happy. He'll adjust. Give him time. Give him the opportunity to look at these designs, and put your own heart behind them."

"You mean, let him pour another million bucks into a design he hates?"

"Talk him into it, Martin, like you've talked people into things they didn't want to do your whole life!"

"I see now why Leigh ran, if that's what she did," Martin said. "Talking to you is like talking to a rock."

"Damn you, Martin."

Martin sighed and took one more flip through the plans. "Antoniou wants a family gathering space, curving, welcoming spaces. Light in spirit, but warm and friendly. Rooms to remind him of his past, of a white house hanging over the Mediterranean Sea, with soft seating where his immense family can drink retsina and recall warmer days."

Ray pointed at the ocean. A wave, suitably dramatic, rushed up the shoreline and flew through the rock-sculpted air. They both watched and listened, waiting for it to quiet. "What about the plush sofas, wall-hangings, curving half-walls? Are you looking at the whole thing? And please. This isn't the Mediterranean. We're talking the Pacific Ocean at Laguna," Ray said. "What's grand in architecture is how an old story gets told a new way, in a new language. I can promise him a warm home, a show-place, a gathering place for his family."

"You loved Kahn for a while, Wright, then I. M. Pei. That house in Agoura? You channeled Neutra, building all in glass. Those people ended up having to put mini blinds on all the windows. I mean, come on. They had neighbors twenty feet away on each side."

"Martin, my ideas have changed over time. I was a young kid, and overstepped sometimes. I finally know what I'm doing. Why can't you trust me?"

"Why can't we give Antoniou what he wants? A California dream? A home for his family that recalls his roots?"

Ray thought about that. "Los Angeles has a shallow past. Most of the people living here, and that includes Achilles Antoniou, have no ownership over the land, the climate, nothing. They don't know what fits their new neighborhood because there is no neighborhood. Every-one around here arrived five minutes ago. Our job is to give the client a home that's right for this setting. Some-thing with roots they can't possibly feel, a place that goes beyond their dead past."

"Minimalism with fresh horseshit scattered around to gussy it up," Martin said. He grabbed the plans, rolled them up, and stuck a thick rubber band around them. "Don't show these to Antoniou."

"I guess that means you won't be watching my back, Martin."

"Get us plans that meet our client's requirements. And oh, when that happens, run them by me."

Ray thought, he's sitting on such unstable ground there, on that rock that shifts when he moves suddenly. He could easily go over the edge, die, topple over in a tragic accident.

He experienced the event in his mind. Martin, beaky nose buried in the plans, hand reaching toward his briefcase, unnerved by something Ray had said or done, rising, stumbling, tumbling.

He imagined Martin falling way the hell down, dashing his head against the boulders in the ocean cove below.

Ray, shocked, would stand, then run for his car up above where he had left his mobile phone.

Well, okay, he had his mobile phone in his pocket, but nobody else knew that. He would climb up the hill, maybe even intentionally step into the poison oak he knew well to avoid. Distraught, he would say after, explaining the inflamed rash on his legs and arms. Too distraught to worry about such an unimportant outcome. Then he had trouble finding his keys. Who wouldn't under the circumstances, his oldest friend lying still, bloodied, upon the rocks so far below?

Martin spoke, interrupting Ray's latest homicidal fantasy. "In fact," Martin said slowly, "given that Antoniou was my client to start with, and I brought him to you, I insist that I see another set of plans based on our discussion today before either one of us speaks to our client again."

"I always appreciate your input, Martin, you jackass." Ray stood up and dusted off his pants.

Martin snorted. "Sure. Just so we're clear that what I say goes." He stuffed Ray's plans into his briefcase in a last-ditch effort to show who was in charge and started up the hill.

Ray followed. Martin seemed to know the best route, where the sand didn't shift too much, and the rocks stayed lodged in the hillside. He kept looking behind him as if he could read Ray's mind.

16

Back in his office, Ray worked on sketches he had made of Achilles Antoniou's secret playroom. Go medieval in that basement. Underground, seen by a select few, the big, exotic room would not affect the exterior or core design at all, so Ray didn't feel any kind of call for a design aesthetic. The fruit cellar on Bright Street flashed through his mind, the single bulb that dangled in its center. He pondered lighting—spooky uplights?

Bare bulbs, like Picasso's *Guernica*. What was Antoniou going to do down there, put in a purple bed or a rack?

Denise came into Ray's office, youthfully enthusiastic, wanting to talk color and furniture. She had tortured her short hair with rubber bands and she wore a leather vest; in the cold office, she could. She looked out the glass walls toward the reception area. "One thing. I've been thinking. You need a backup plan."

"Too late for that. I'm committed."

"It would be no trouble to quickie-revise some existing drawings that would satisfy him for the moment. Let things calm down between you and Martin."

She let that notion twist for a moment, then said,

"Pretend to go along, then whittle away at Martin and Mr. Antoniou."

"Finally, a tempting suggestion." He opened and closed a few drawers. "Now, where do I keep that big sharp X-Acto of mine? Good for whittling when all else fails."

"Ha, ha," she said. "You work them, together and separately, until the client's ready to take that extra step forward. You've done it before."

He sighed.

"Nowhere is it written that good architects must be uncompromising."

"*Et tu*, Denise?"

"I'm on your side, Ray." She gave him a half smile, then frowned, gazing beyond him out into the hall. "Uh-oh."

"What is it?"

"He's here."

In the conference room, the streaked rosewood surface of the table cold to the touch, Ray sat, plans spread out in front of him. At the head of the long table, Antoniou reposed, no other word for it. His big eyelids had sunk over his brown eyes, like windows with shady awnings pulled down over the bright parts. Martin sat directly across from Ray.

"We've been talking these last few minutes," Martin said, without preamble.

Ray nodded, looking toward Antoniou, whose sunken head sank lower.

Not a good sign.

"Achilles has already told you that your basic design, while no doubt brilliant, is not really what he has in mind."

Ray wondered about the basement, but another peek at Antoniou told him the truth. The client's hooded eyes rose to meet his momentarily, blazing. He was reminding Ray to protect his secrets.

Did that mean he might still go with Ray's ideas? Was there wiggle room? Or had Martin bent his ear?

Martin pulled out a sheaf of photographs of the inspirational Greek island. "As per our earlier conversation," and he went on for quite a while, the gist of the lecture being: here's Santorini; ain't it beautiful, and this is what Antoniou insists upon.

"Simple blocks, stacked. Curved, plastered. Bright white."

Ray felt his pulse beating in his neck. He wondered if they could see it. He struggled to control an impulse to leap up, grab Martin by his neck, and strangle him until his pasty face turned black.

Antoniou, looking at Martin, nodded. Anyone this guy hired could come up with an adequate basement for Antoniou's purposes. Antoniou didn't need Ray. He didn't need this firm. He had the money.

But Ray could let it be known. Around town. Dungeons and Dragons at the Antoniou palace.

He pressed his mechanical pencil against a blank page in front of him. The tip broke off. He realized he had been clicking it while Martin spoke. It lay in a gray line, like a fallen cigarette ash.

This beautiful design was the one good thing he had going in his life now. Without Leigh. Without the belief in himself as a good man.

Going, going—

To gain time, Ray repeated, "Santorini." Should he reproduce another ancient place with soul in a new place where it wouldn't belong, where it would look like a hangnail on a beautiful hillside, swollen, burning white, ugly, obtrusive?

"We need a new set of plans, Ray, ones that reflect Antoniou's original concept. And we need them soon. Joey Zaremski promises he can help."

Oh, yes, another jab from Martin. Martin had worked out how to keep the commission within the firm, initially selling the client on Ray's brilliance, with the sly idea of substituting one of Ray's smart protégés if Ray didn't pan out. Ray had hired Joey when Joey first got out of Cal Poly, a probational graduate with no awards, nothing to his name, not even rich parents who could hire him to build a statement house he could show to prospective employers. Ray had studied his designs, loved them, and taught him everything he knew. He believed Joey had no notion of Martin's underhanded wrangling. He trusted Joey.

"Joey refuses to work without your involvement, Ray," Martin said, as if reading his mind. "He considers you his primary influence, a kind of mentor. So here's the deal.

You do the design, no restrictions except doing what your client wants, working in concert with this young architect I know you respect. Any parts you don't want to do, you have Joey handle."

Now was his chance to launch into an impassioned sales job that would turn all this around. He could make them see. He could appeal to Antoniou's snobbery, give him a diplomatic lesson in how run-of-the-mill his dreams were in Laguna. He could.

But he didn't have the energy, and maybe he didn't have the skill. The moment passed.

Martin stood up. Antoniou also stood.

"It's gonna be fine," he said to Martin, not looking at Ray. "Ray and I understand each other. We're gonna get along great."

Kat got off work at five and headed straight for her sister's.

"Hand me the powder," Jacki commanded, hand out-stretched, leaning against the changing table. The baby wore no diaper.

"Go sit down. I'll do that."

"Third shelf down."

Kat located the blue container and handed it to Jacki. The baby boy lay on a paper diaper. After powdering the reasonably clean bottom, Jacki endeavored to pull up the middle section of the paper diaper and flip over the side pieces, so that the Velcro would grab. The baby fought, sobbing, face twisted up like a pretzel, tiny fists tight.

Jacki breathed deeply, then tackled the child again. This time, the baby did not roll over beyond the white padding. "Gotcha!" Jacki crowed, folding down the side of the diaper that would keep her out of trouble, at least for the immediate future. She picked up her newborn boy. "L'il animal," Jacki mooed. Perspiration had turned her once-shiny streaked bangs a dingy, greasy color. "L'il fella," she went on, kissing first his toes, then his stomach, and finally his moist cheek.

She let Kat carry him into his bedroom and tucked him into his turquoise-linened crib.

After listening at the open door for a few minutes, Jacki closed the door. They sighed, then laughed, snickering at each other's dishevelment. Kat straightened her shirt, now with a blob of vomit on the shoulder. Jacki smoothed her hair. She wore a robe and fluffy slippers and a walking cast on her foot, and was exactly two hours out of the hospital.

"Want a cup of tea or something? Beer?" Jacki asked in a whisper, as she tottered toward the kitchen.

"Hard choice."

"Beer it is." She opened the refrigerator, pulled out a bottle, and popped the top, handing it to Kat. "Too bad they accuse mothers who drink beer when they nurse of abuse these days. I could use one."

"Best beer I've had in my entire life."

"He'll be up again in two hours and I'll nurse him. I need to grab a nap in a minute."

Kat set her beer down on a grease-speckled table she could not recall ever being speckled before. "I have a lot I need to talk to you about."

"Did you hear something?" Jacki said, placing her finished bottle on the kitchen counter. "I could swear I heard something."

"Leigh—"

"Beau's crying," Jacki said.

"Is that his name?"

"Beau Thomas Chavez." Jacki opened the door to the baby's room. "Dignified and historic; that's our boy."

Kat followed her sister into the twilit room. Two glass night-lights shaped like daisies poked through the dark-orange gloom.

Jacki pushed open the window curtains, letting in the last light of the day. "I should have nursed him longer before putting him down. His stomach is minuscule. Babies need to eat all the time." She sat in a wooden rocking chair and pushed off from the floor like a person trying to have fun. She closed her eyes and pressed her back against the chair, supporting her child on a pillow. "Incredible, isn't it. Owowow—"

Her eyes closed and she snored, head at an odd angle, her baby safely propped on pillows as he nursed. When he let go of the nipple with a tiny pop, she awoke instantly. She handed Beau off to Kat. "Wet again."

Kat changed him. They put him down. He dozed for a few minutes, then awakened, his cries amazing considering the size of his voice box.

"Forgot to burp him," Jacki said, patting his back while he rested against her shoulder. He burped and threw up, then went peacefully down to sleep.

For twenty minutes.

Etcetera.

"I have to go," Kat said.

"No," Jacki wailed. "Raoul's due home in an hour. I'm a sweaty pig and there's no food."

Grimly, Kat ran out to the store, bought a roasted turkey breast, rolls, packaged salad, and carrot cake. She had trouble parking, which involved giving one person the finger and screaming at another one before she landed a spot. She lugged the bags up the elevator. She unloaded the sacks in the kitchen, laid out the food on the counter.

She checked on Jacki and the baby. They were asleep in a rocker and a bassinet, respectively.

She sliced the turkey, found an almost clean platter, which she wiped with an almost clean dishrag, and assembled the salad into a pretty bowl. She found the dregs of some Caesar dressing in the fridge, which she splashed into a cute bowl with a spoon. She located two new place mats still in plastic. After wiping the table, she set them down, found candles and holders in the cupboard, and placed them in the center along with a box of matches. Then she stepped back again to observe her handiwork.

The crusty kitchen counters, rising above the dining table, detracted from the overall mood. As the sun weakened, crawling across the hardwood floors in a golden streak, Kat found bleach under the kitchen sink and blitzed through the kitchen, flinging dishes into the washer.

Raoul arrived exactly on time, full of kisses for Jacki, all smiles, and Kat was free.

Outside, pulling his Honda into the spot next to her, Jacki's downstairs neighbor, who had invited Kat to come with him to watch the sunset several times, loitered. He had a thin mustache, a sliver of hair in the middle of his chin, and shaped sideburns. All this decorative shaving gave Kat the creeps, although she realized in a previous life, only a couple of months ago, she had thought him a bit of a hunk. He approached her car.

"How about a late drink, honey?"

She hated that her window was cracked low enough to let this guy's voice get heard. "Uh. Sorry, Josh. Busy."

"Hot date? Where are you going?"

"Stuff to do at home."

"What stuff?" Big smile.

She had never figured out how to extricate herself gracefully when someone paid her too much attention. If she openly rejected him, saying, mind your own business, she'd upset him and the blow to his male ego would turn him hostile and he would say something hurtful. If she said, I need to wash my hair, same deal. She contemplated her options, feeling perplexed. Had Ray Jackson felt this way when he spotted Kat outside that house on Bright Street? Hunted?

"You bring over different guys all the time."

She had brought a few of the good ones to Jacki's. Not-so-hidden meaning: why not me, too?

"You're a player, just like me. Admit it."

"Josh, would you please back off so I can pull out?"

A certain light penetrated his flat eyes. Hostility, coming on like a 747.

Would she, two months ago, have gotten out of her car at this point, put her hand on his butt, and said, follow me home, let's go?

"Aw, come over for a coupla minutes. What's your problem? You're here. I made a cool drink you'll like. Gin and lemon. Fresh mint on top."

How did he know her favorite drink? Probably observed her once in a local hangout. Note to self: excellent reason to cruise far from her own home and Jacki's, too.

The Echo's interior was heating up. Perspiration pooled below her thighs on the scratchy fabric of the seat.

Get me out of here.

Could she reverse the car without knocking him down?

Without warning, as if suddenly transforming from an insensitive clod into a sensitive one, he backed away, shrugging. "Okay, another time," he said.

Relieved, Kat said, "Josh?"

He turned back to face her. "Yeah?"

"You have a lot to offer the right woman."

He shuffled his feet. "Yeah," he said. "I do."

"I'm looking, but I'm confused."

"Me, too."

"I'm not for you, Josh."

"Guess not."

"It's tough. Don't give up."

He sighed. "You, too."

Being a player was getting so old.

17

After the meeting with Antoniou, Ray phoned his mother.

"I've been hoping you would call. Are you still angry?" she asked.

"I found another tape. That makes three."

A long silence. If his mother had ever prayed, he could imagine her praying right this minute. "Ray, please, this is getting—you have to stop."

"I found it at Bright Street. In the fruit cellar. He says he's coming and then you hang up."

"My God," she said.

"Did he hurt you? Beat you?"

"Who?"

"You know damn well who!"

She hung up on him again.

He slammed the phone down so hard it fell off the desk.

Suzanne, sitting at her desk outside his door, said, "Are you okay?"

"I better go home, Suzanne."

"Sure, Ray." She blinked big brown eyes and said, "I'm

sorry about everything, Ray. I'm embarrassed about me and Martin."

"It's okay."

"I just couldn't control my feelings. I didn't realize I might be hurting you, too, when I told the police about Martin and . . . I hope you and Leigh will be all right."

On impulse, he leaned down and kissed the top of her head. "You do a great job here," he said.

Ray sliced radishes in his silent stainless-steel kitchen. He put the finished salad in a glass bowl, wrapping the leftover bits of vegetable in plastic wrap and stuffing them into his refrigerator drawer. Pouring two diet sodas over ice, he carried a tray into the living room and sat it on the sculpturally beautiful dining table.

Sipping his drink, he sat down on the sofa to wait for Kat. Leigh had hated this sofa. She wanted something plush, she always said, something velvety and plump. Leigh had been right. A home was more than its walls of glass and hard furniture. He hadn't given Leigh a comfortable home.

So many things he would do differently . . . his life was avalanching down . . .

The doorbell rang, and he answered.

Kat came inside, all business. She didn't take off her shoes.

"This place—any chance I could get a tour?"

He led her around, explaining the mechanics of construction, telling her about tricky decisions he had made at the time, as if she was a potential client.

He wound his way down to the workshop. She clutched the wall, balancing.

"Ray," she said, "you're going crazy, right? Or you're already halfway in the bag."

He didn't exactly nod, but he didn't disagree.

All the time she followed him downstairs, she felt anxious. His eerie serenity bothered her. She had pepper spray in her bag and her hand tight on the strap and she wondered if it was a good idea to be alone with him.

Somewhere along the way, she seemed to have accepted the idea that Leigh might be dead. But then she would think, Why? Leigh's just left home. She looked around the basement, but there was no sign of Leigh.

Ray gestured toward an architectural model that took up part of a shop table. "I make three-dimensional facsimiles of some of the houses I lived in as a kid."

"Wow." Kat cocked her head, looking the meticulous models over. On wide shelves beyond, several other little tract houses sat, detailed with trim, porches, even house numbers clear as anything in a high-definition video.

"It started months before Leigh left. It started when—when she—"

"Yes?"

"Nothing."

Kat ran a finger over the roofline of one. "You've got drainage gutters here. Downspouts. Individual bricks on the fireplace." She put her hand inside a small kitchen. The faucet over the sink turned. She withdrew her hand. "At least there's not running water. Yet."

However, they were wired for lighting. He snapped a switch to show her. The houses lit up like a Christmas village. Even the furnishings included upholstered pieces suitable to the era.

"I can't believe this," she said, thinking, He is one sick pup.

"I've spent these past months remembering the houses I lived in growing up, thinking about how I felt in them, who I was." He cleared his throat. "One night, after an argument with Leigh about our future, I thought, If I could only understand. See these kitchens? I never remember anyone there but my mother. I even tried to build in her hiding places. I tried to reproduce whatever I stuck on the wall of my room with pushpins every year."

"I don't understand," she said, examining them. "If what you say is true, you haven't lived in these houses for years."

"In the beginning, I thought I could somehow control the past by reproducing it. I could—move the mental dolls around, you know? Make them behave. Explain themselves."

"Man, you're a real Henry Darger. Only he did it with paintings of children."

"It didn't work, though."

"No."

"You still work on them."

"I wonder if I get it right, whether I can get what went wrong right, too."

"That's pretty oblique, Ray. Promise me you won't take up screenwriting."

"You asked what I'm doing. I told you. Now you tell me why you're here again. Why we had to meet."

The room was so bright, the walls so white—what was that behind him in the dimness past the half-open closet door?

Ray moved a thin wall on the model in front of him slightly. "This was a bad idea, coming down here," he said. He turned his head a little. His eyes flicked to the right, toward the closet, and Kat saw something flash in them. "Let's go back upstairs."

A shaft of cold air traveled down her neck. Kat got up and, moving fast, threw open the door to the closet expecting to see—Leigh?

Rough coir rope, thick, dangled from the high interior ceiling from a huge industrial metal hook. A noose hung on the end. Thick knots made it secure. The rope swayed as air currents entered.

Horrified, she moved back. Ray stepped past her, shut the closet door, and stood with his back against it. "Nothing to do with you or Leigh, okay? Don't look at me like that. Wait."

He pulled something out of his pocket. "Look," he said, walking toward her, holding his hand out. "See, I just bought the thing—"

"Stay away from me!" She pulled out the spray and pointed it at him.

He flung a piece of paper to the floor. "It's a receipt

from the hardware store. I bought this stuff a couple of days ago."

Warily, she picked up the paper and examined it.

"Just—just go," he said. "I'm sorry I scared you."

"Wait. Wait. Let me think." Kat kept the pepper spray can ready. "You killed her?" she said. "And you can't take the guilt?"

Ray put a hand on his forehead and rubbed. "My wife's gone," he said. "Kat, honest to God, she left me. I didn't hurt her, not that way. I think I'm going to be arrested. My work—well, some days I think I know what I'm doing. Other days I doubt every decision I make. My father—he was a crazy asshole who never loved me and spent years trying to hurt my mother. What's left, huh? What's there to live for?"

Tom had asked that question, too, and it outraged her, hearing it again.

Kat grabbed scissors off the table and marched straight toward Ray, stopping in front of him when he didn't move out of her way.

A strange smile played on his lips. "Gonna help me out, Kat?"

With a grunt of disgust, she pushed him aside and entered the closet, then hacked away at the noose until it split open. She turned back to face him. "You are not going to do this. No way. Not while I'm around. You say Leigh's alive out there, well, then we'll have to find her. Get her to explain why she's left behind a train wreck of a man who, I'm beginning to believe, loves the hell out of her!"

"She doesn't want to be found."

"How do you know that?"

"Things I said to her—things she saw in me."

"You sound like me now, Ray, all tangled up." She shook her head. "Maybe she's waiting for you to fight for her! Maybe she wants you to drag her back, show her how much you care."

"I don't think so."

"I could wring your neck myself! You know my brother, Tom, killed himself? You know what agony that spread around in the people he left behind? The guilt, the nightmares, the self-loathing, the accusations, the grief? Our mother couldn't take it. You could say it killed her, too."

He walked past her and closed the closet door gently. "I'm sorry about this, Kat. Sorry to drag you into what's essentially a private problem."

"You self-pitying—jerk! You kill yourself, and this woman you loved enough to marry spends the rest of her life crying through the days *and* the nights."

"That's why I didn't." He nodded his head toward the closet. "I couldn't do that to Leigh or to my mother."

"C'mon, Ray, let's do something about this goddamn mess! You say she's out there somewhere, so, okay. Let's find Leigh. Talk to her. Give her a chance to explain, redeem herself. No more running around after phantoms when there's a real woman out there who is waiting to be found!"

He seemed stunned by her shouting.

She sat down. "If we find her and she rejects you totally, I'll buy you another noose, okay? I'll even hang it up there and kick the stool away for you, if you want. I'll sing you a good-bye hymn or recite a Buddhist chant, your choice."

"It was expensive rope." An unhappy curve played along the side of his mouth. "But listen, no need. I stood on that stool for a long time staring at that thing before I realized that I'm not quite ready."

"Suicide casts a blight on a lot of other lives. Don't even think about it!"

"Okay, okay!"

"Okay what?"

"Let's find her. How do we start?"

Kat got up and opened the closet door again. "Help me get this thing down." She climbed on the stool but couldn't reach the hook in the ceiling, and climbed back down. Ray took her place and unhooked the cut rope.

"This goes in my car trunk with the broken subwoofer. I'll get rid of both of them while I'm at it. Tomorrow's Saturday. I'll be back in the morning. Let's give this place a real search."

"Okay."

"You're ready to find her?"

"I have to, don't I?"

"You have to."

"Okay," he said again.

18

Ray answered the door on the first ring. The eucalyptus waved its seared brown frilly silhouettes in the canyon below. "You shaved," Kat noted, entering the perfect, air-filtered climate of the house. "Thank goodness."

"Well, if I'm forced to live, I need to be able to stand myself."

"I need to be able to stand you, too."

"I assume you have a plan," Ray said. "You would."

"We go through Leigh's journals and papers. We invade her computer files."

"Her computer's at her office. Later."

"Her mail. Her cell phone bill."

"On the counter."

"Has she used the credit cards?"

"I called last night after you left. No. Let's go upstairs first and rip the place apart."

They sat across from each other on the expansive, nubby carpet in the master bedroom. The contents of Leigh's dresser and closet, clothes and scarves and bags and underwear, lay in stacks around them. "What did Leigh wear that last night when you fought?"

"I don't remember," Ray said. "I made up things when I talked to the cops." He thought. "Shorts. Her purple shirt? A favorite, with a V-neck."

"Is it here?"

Ray rummaged around and Kat began to help him.

He said, "It isn't here."

"She was wearing it?"

"Yes. I think so. Her Rykas—the shoes she wore to run in—I don't see them, either. She went upstairs before she left, I remember now. Maybe she took the time to change. I was too upset to notice how long she was up here."

You're not making this up as we go, are you? Kat wanted to ask. She managed to keep her mouth shut. Ray was on a roll. "What else did she take with her?"

"My guess," he said, "as I told the police, although I was stretching the truth, I'd say she probably took her overnight bag with some shirts, a fresh pair of jeans, and underwear. Nothing I would notice was missing."

As he had told the cops. "Did she keep cash at hand?" Kat asked, frustrated.

"She carried cash with her, kept an eye out for unique things for her furniture designs from vendors at flea markets, the kind of places where it's handy. Oh, the Tibetan chest. I didn't think about that." He jumped up and went to the wall side of the bed, where a small wooden chest just the height of the bed held an industrial-looking metal lamp and a couple of paperbacks. Kat heard him laughing to himself.

"What's funny?" He had opened the little chest and was doing something with the shelf. "Come here," he said. "She saw an antique Tibetan chest at a warehouse about a year ago. In the old days the Tibetans made these things with secret shelves. They used really simple mechanisms to unlock the shelves that must not have fooled very many Tibetan thieves. But in this country, we use safes. You know? We don't use tricks, we try to just make big strong impregnable obvious things. But I can't quite remember the secret."

"Is this the antique?" Kat stood by his side. He peered in, pulling at the side walls, poking around. Kat saw immediately that the chest was clearly one of Leigh's, red, hand-painted with a pair of cockatiels that looked like the pair Leigh's mother had kept when Leigh was in eighth grade.

"No, she saw wood shavings inside the old chest that she said meant there was still insect activity. But she couldn't get it out of her mind. It delighted her, the idea of this secret shelf. So she built one for herself. She showed me how it works but I can't—it's not a mechanism, it's something stupid—"

"Let me try," Kat said. "My hands are smaller."

She prodded and pulled. Nothing. She fell back onto the carpet. "No secrets here."

Ray shook his head and stuck his arm back in. He smiled. "I just remembered." He showed Kat the piece of wood that caused the door to close without continuing all the way inside. "Watch this." He lifted it. It rose about an inch. Ray reached below to the painted panels and pulled.

They popped open. He pulled out a jewelry case, a notebook, and a passport case with some papers inside. Kat thrust out her lower lip, raising her eyebrows.

"She's a furniture maker. A throwback to simpler, more devious times." He grinned.

They smiled at each other, and it seemed to Kat that she was doing the right thing, coming straight here to the lion's den.

"I'll take the notebook—" Kat said.

"No," said Ray. "Let me look things over first."

While Ray examined the Tibetan cache, Kat checked in with her sister. "How you doin', Jacki?" she asked, waiting for the usual invasive questions. Instead, Jacki treated her to a storybook full of baby, how he made the ahhh sound, how much he cried, how puckered up his face got when he felt disturbed or constipated. She listened, saying "Uh-huh," looking out the window. Her ears were glazing over, would soon harden like rocks.

"Are you listening to me? I have the feeling you're not listening at all!"

"I am. I swear."

"So how many poops did I just tell you Beau does on a given day?"

"You're the one who's good at tests. Remember how I had to take the state exams twice even though I know more than anyone else in the office?"

"Three to five," Jacki said.

"Oops, gotta go, take care. Kiss the baby for me." Kat pushed "end."

Ray had looked through the small contents of the chest. "Leigh exposed herself to you when she showed you the Tibetan chest she made, Ray. She didn't want to hide from you."

"She knew I wouldn't look in there no matter what."

"She showed you its secret," Kat said. Why was he so dense? "She tried to let you inside her life."

He shook his head sadly.

Impatiently, Kat asked, "Okay. What is this?"

"She wrote poetry," Ray said. "She had a little Chinese notebook—"

"A diary?"

He blushed. "Love notes. Little poems."

"Hmm."

"These are drawings. Furniture designs, visionary, nothing she ever built that I know about. Here are some mementoes—news clippings about your brother, some notes he wrote her. Her gold earrings from her mother aren't here. Her passport's gone, and our marriage certificate. And her will. She took all that. I know she kept her checkbook and cards in her purse. She took all that."

Sitting down on the bed, Kat picked up the silk-covered notebook. She flipped through. Ray hung nervously beside her.

Leigh loved her husband, oh, she sure did, that much

Kat gleaned, even though she whipped quickly past certain pages that made Ray bite his nails.

Some other, sadder poems featured Tom. Kat felt her self-possession beginning to melt away. Leigh hadn't recovered from Tom's death any more than Kat had.

Picking through what was left, Kat found a gold chain with a small star pendant, a rhinestone pin from some other century, and gold earrings, small hoops that Kat remembered Leigh wearing.

A new longing to see her old friend welled up in Kat's heart.

"There's nothing to help us here," Ray said, sitting down on the other side of the bed. "Unless it's useful to know that, like you said, Leigh wasn't trying to keep secrets and wanted to tell me things. She wanted me to know how she felt."

It was useful to Kat, who now had a glimmer of understanding about the depths of Leigh's love for Ray.

"I quit wanting to know because I was afraid to hear."

"Nothing here will help us," Kat said, giving in to her frustration. "Let's go down and check all the mail."

"Feel free. I'll come with you. But I opened it all as it came in."

"Today's?"

"I went out and got it just before you came."

In the living room, Ray leaned in the metal chair, arms looped on the back of it, wearing his usual tense, troubled expression. She sat across from him patiently, hand cupping her chin.

"I feel like telling you a few things now," he said finally.

"About time."

"My mother has always been my best friend. We're very close. Lately, we argue. She's cutting herself off from me."

When he finished telling her about that, Kat nodded, saying "That's rough."

"Yeah. Rough. Now let me tell you a few things about my partner. My former friend." He began to speak, and once he started, it shot out like rain through a downspout. He talked and talked until he had told her about the affair, the office politics, Antoniou's dungeon. "I didn't really understand before how good it feels to just give in and hate someone," he said. "It's an exciting feeling. It's also addictive and corrosive. I now understand people who say they wake up in the morning hating themselves."

"What are you going to do about your firm?"

"I can't stand working with Martin anymore. I see him so differently. I had a girlfriend years before I met Leigh who I thought was great. Over time, I couldn't ignore the real her: she shoplifted, lied to avoid confrontations, and backstabbed. It's that way with Martin, like a love affair gone sour. He looks like his own evil twin to me now."

"Have you considered that Martin might have something to do with Leigh's disappearance? Maybe she tried to leave him and he got angry." This story about the partner and Leigh—was it true? Kat wasn't surprised Leigh had had a relationship with somebody else—it happens—though she felt a disappointment she would deal with later. What mattered was that Martin was married, and an amoral opportunist, according to Ray, and Leigh was gone.

"I put it to him and he denied it. If I go that way I have to think about Martin's wife. I think she knew about the affair. And Suzanne, my secretary at work. She was in love with Martin."

"We need to explore all possibilities."

He sighed heavily. "I have a feeling the police are already doing that." Out of the blue, he went on, "I've thought about killing Martin. Maybe I almost did."

Shocked, Kat kept her cool, and said, "I almost got a college degree. I almost won the lottery. I almost got eaten by a shark when I drank too much and went for a midnight swim at Huntington Beach. I almost smacked my sister right in the kisser for saying something really rude to me."

"Martin used to know me better than anyone. Know how he pegged me? As a paralyzed veteran. Yeah, not of wars, but of a disturbed childhood. He used to say I played a good game, had a good face for it, but, in fact, lacked a strong sense of self. Well, he was right. I feel like seaweed, bobbing along, no idea where I'll end up.

"Up to a month ago I could hide it pretty well. People envied me. Imagine that? They thought I had a good life. Now all I have is a nightmare and a hard-nosed appraiser who doesn't trust me."

"I have a feeling you're going to rise to the occasion," Kat said. "Okay, Ray, I'm going to tell you why I expected there was something there. As a hard-nosed appraiser, I spend all my time snooping around other people's houses. Complete strangers. When I walk into a house, people expect me. I have an appointment."

"What does that matter?"

"It matters that they know I'm coming. What they leave for me to see has meaning. And they leave out things that would straighten your short and curlies. That's the secret. They expose themselves by what they choose to leave for me to see."

"Like what?"

"Underwear. Women's clothes in the man's closet. Guns, knives, clubs. Checkbooks, bank statements showing their balances. We see a lot of sex toys," she said. Some resembled male members, some resembled alien members. "Leather straps, clothing with strategic bits missing, if you get my drift." She shoved her own experiments in such directions out of her mind. She was good at that. Somehow her own peccadilloes were acceptable and other people's were frightening. "I know more about people in Los Angeles than I ever wanted to know."

Ray spoke quietly. "You think whatever is left, she meant to leave."

"Yes, I do."

Silent for a moment, in his ironed slacks and silk shirt, he crossed his legs, then crossed them again.

"Can I ask you something?"

"Sure."

"When you come into my house, what do you see?"

"It's a beautiful house," she admitted.

"I think—my ideas on what makes a home are changing.

I'm designing another house right now, and I want to get it right. I want it strong, but soft. Light but warm. I don't care about this place anymore. It's not right."

He unfolded an open envelope, reached inside, pulled out a bank statement, and pointed to one of the items. "Look at this. While you were talking to your sister, I read the mail."

He held the statement out to her. She read it.

"There's an ATM withdrawal from the Idyllwild branch of US Bank. She wasn't dead when she used the card to take out five hundred dollars on her way out of town," he said. "Check the date. I just realized that's the morning after she left."

Someone had used the cash card in Idyllwild, a forested mountain community not too far from Palm Springs. Kat sat very still, trying to control her excitement. "Then she's alive."

Kat wanted to call Detective Rappaport immediately. Ray did not. Ray kept saying it proved Leigh was safe.

"What if somebody took her and forced her to withdraw money? Don't the banks keep videos of automatic cash machines?"

Ray, fingering the statement, obviously loathed this idea. "Nobody abducted Leigh. She ran away on her own. She took the money out herself and moved on. Please, let's not complicate things. Let's not involve the police unless we have to. It's only been a week. We have no proof of anything good or bad."

"This is the eighth day, Ray. No, something is still very wrong."

"Look, whoever took the money that day would have to know her personal identification number, her PIN. That's not something Leigh would give out freely."

Kat thought about her friend. Leigh hated trivia and even more hated math. At Cal High, she had almost flunked trigonometry, in fact had relied on Kat to cheat on her homework. "She might have written the number down in her wallet."

His compressed lips confirmed her hypothesis.

Kat jumped up. "Let's go," she said.

"Where?"

"Idyllwild. Bring a picture."

"Idyllwild—wait—"

"Come on, Ray. Grab whatever you need to grab. Her parents had a cabin there years ago." Up in the mountains that fringed the Los Angeles Basin, Idyllwild was a few hours away. "Uh, the street was called Tahquitz Lane. They called the place Camp Tahquitz, that's why I remember. That was so long ago. I wonder if they still own it?"

"I never went there, but she mentioned it a few months ago. She said that her parents had some run-down old shack that they never went to anymore and were trying to sell."

Kat ran out to her car to get her laptop, tapped into his AirPort, and pulled up Realtor.com to have a look at multiple listings for Idyllwild. The town was too small to have a separate set of listings, but she called up the area listings and very quickly found a cottage for sale on Tahquitz Lane.

"Two bedroom," she said. "Sixty-five years old. They're only asking two-twenty for it. How refreshing. Cheap these days."

"She described it as a dump."

"The description matches. I'm going to call the realtor up there."

"We could just call her parents. But then they would—"

"It would be out of our control after that," Kat said. They looked at each other.

"Go on. Call the realtor," Ray said. "You will with or without my permission."

The lady handling the cottage wasn't in but her broker was, and Kat, using her appraiser credentials, managed to get the owner names.

Hubbel. No bites had come into the office after more than a year. The cottage had sat there unsold for months, in desperate need of updating, but the owners refused to fix it up.

Kat hung up. "She's either dead, abducted, or on the run," she said. Ray put a hand over his eyebrows, as if seeing something in the distance he didn't want to see. "But she went through Idyllwild," Kat continued inexorably. "I bet she left you that charge on your bank statement in case you were looking for her, just like those people leave signs of who they are in the homes I appraise. She's smart—she didn't want you to know right away where she was going, but she didn't want to be completely cut off from you, either."

Ray said, "I'll be right back." He left the living room. Kat took out the notebook and read some more of Leigh's love poems. In five minutes he returned, loaded down. "A couple sweaters," he said. "Two sleeping bags. It might get cold up there at night, even in summer, and I sure don't expect sheets. Bring another bottle of that French stuff from the fridge."

"Yessir," Kat said, scrambling up from the floor. "Don't forget toothbrushes."

19

I'm outta here," Eleanor Beasley said, walking past Esmé's station. "See you tomorrow."

"Wait a second, Eleanor."

Eleanor waited while Esmé finished checking through a big shopping cart, whizzing through the bar-coded items and bagging them with efficiency born of long experience.

"Thanks for shopping at Granada Market," she told the customer, who nodded. Esmé swiftly fastened the chain to her station. While she finished her closing-up chores, Eleanor talked to the bagger at the next register about his new Prius. Eleanor wasn't a hurrier; this could be a problem in a grocery store, but the customers liked how she noticed when they were tired and asked how they were doing.

Granada Market had started out as a small specialty health food store in the seventies. Over the years, as people became educated about the virtues of healthy food, the store had tripled in size. Granada gave Safeway and even Trader Joe's a run for their money. The store had twelve full-time clerks, but since it was open until midnight, they all worked long shifts during extra-busy times or vacation times. Esmé most appreciated the ten percent employee discount on food items.

"Where are you going tonight?" she said as they pushed open the double doors and entered the cool, dim rear of the store.

"Jackstraps," Eleanor said, "same as every Friday night." She pulled her scrunchie off and her blonde hair stayed put until she ran her fingers in and out a few times. She had the thin, hard-living face of a smoker and drinker and had been divorced for decades from her rodeo-rider husband. She pulled lipstick out of her bag and ran it over her lips without checking a mirror, then traced her work with a finger.

They punched out. "I thought—maybe I could join you?" Esmé said.

Eleanor's eyebrows went up and she smiled. "You changing your ways, Esmé? It's pretty rowdy there."

"I feel rowdy," Esmé said. She felt like exploding, was how she felt, after the latest call from Ray. Something had torn between them like the tear on a piece of fabric that continues straight across, all the way across the cloth until the piece is neatly halved. If she went home now she would call him, apologize, say things she shouldn't, anything to try to mend this tear.

And besides, she couldn't stand the thought of going home right now. She couldn't contain all she felt right now. She had to get out, right now, but not alone. She didn't want to be alone.

Their boss, Ward Cameron, a small man who liked to cut a big swath, sneaked silently up behind them. "Not so fast," he bellowed, startling them. He chuckled at their reaction as they turned to face him. "Rotation tomorrow, Saturday morning. You two, eight a.m. Don't be late."

They both maintained smiles for as long as he was looking, then Eleanor rolled her eyes.

"We oughtta unionize."

"He beat back a union vote twice."

"Then I oughtta quit. I hear they might open a new Safeway across the street from the Whitwood Center."

"Ellie, you love it here. You're so sociable. I admire how friendly you are with the customers. You love getting people laughing."

Eleanor smiled, appreciating the compliment. "I love the money." They walked into the employee lunchroom, where each employee was allowed a small locker for personal items. Eleanor pulled off her work shirt, a modest blouse, replacing it with a green tank top and hanging a string of beads around her neck. "Voilà," she said, and laughed.

Esmé wondered at her changing in this room, but no men arrived to applaud her.

"Ward likes me," Eleanor was saying. "Have you noticed? Whenever he gets a little bored, he drops something just so he can watch me bend over. What would he do without me?" She already knew the answer. "Hire another one. I guess that's why I've gone through two husbands already. I think I'm special but they think different. You ever married, Esmé? I always wondered."

Although she had worked at the store for many years, Esmé had always kept her distance. She never went out with the other clerks, and kept to herself at lunch. She preferred to walk somewhere, to the dollar store to browse for little household things, or to a nearby park where she could escape the store, which had no windows, no natural light, and a lot of talk about very personal things.

"I'm a widow," she said.

"Oh. Sorry."

"Long time ago," Esmé said, changing out of the thick-cushioned shoes she wore to protect her feet from the day of standing. Everything important in her life had happened so long ago, but Ray was now on a rampage through the past. She remembered the phone call again and this uncontainable anger returned—against Ray, for his pig-headedness, and against Leigh, who had dealt him a massive and destabilizing blow and set him on this course.

"Let's go, Eleanor!"

"We're gone." Eleanor snapped her purse shut and gave Esmé a glossy smile.

They joined a crew of three other female coworkers, all finishing shifts at six o'clock that day. Even for those on an early shift, Friday had that glow. Even Esmé felt it, a hopeful electricity as if this weekend would bring all they desired. Chatting and laughing, they walked toward the café-bar, which was only a block from the grocery store.

Esmé worked hard to enjoy the walk. The hot yellow of

the day had drifted away, a burning sun low in the sky now at its sweetest and most benign. The heat of the sidewalk radiated up through the thin sole of her sandals.

She tried to hear what Eleanor's friends were saying, but one thing about evening, every car for thirty miles around had hit the boulevard. Drivers squinted against the long low rays. She saw angry faces behind the windshields. She crossed her arms.

"You cold, honey?" Eleanor asked. "Here." She removed her thin crocheted sweater. "Take this. I'm hot enough for both of us." She expanded her chest and everybody laughed. The other women were younger than Eleanor and Esmé and in pretty good shape. You couldn't hold a job at Granada's unless you could stand for eight to ten hours.

Esmé looked down at her blouse and black pants and thought, I look older than I am. She felt a little ashamed, as if she was letting down the other women, detracting from their beauty. She wished she had put on some makeup, or a skirt—her legs were still good—oh, what was she doing? She'd given up cocktail lounges years and years before. She felt like turning around and going home, but it had been such a long time since she had let herself live a little—there would be a long bar, shiny bottles, low light. She could relax, have a refreshment—

A long long time.

Jackstraps had flashed its green sign for a lot longer than Esmé had worked at the market. A long wooden counter with shiny black marble inlays made a wide half-circle through the center of the room. Two immense flat screens blasted quick-cut images of Nascar racing. The place had begun to fill up. The women sat down along the far end of the bar, Eleanor choosing to stand.

All the men at the counter had swiveled to watch them enter. Several continued to check the group out. The air practically glittered around the women as the sexual energy in the room rose. Esmé felt increasingly uncomfortable.

"Shoot. Too far from the bartender," Amy said, opening her purse and taking out a mirror. She fluffed her hair and returned it to the bag. "I'm in a hurry. Craig's picking me up later."

Multicolored halogen pendants lit them festively, and the bartender came over right away, bantering with all of them equally, although Esmé saw immediately that he focused the gleam in his eye on Eleanor.

"Jack, this is Esmé," she said.

"Welcome, darlin'." Jack, as well-seasoned as his bar, put an arm around Eleanor's waist.

The other women all had special drinks.

"Esmé?" Eleanor asked.

"Coke," she said.

"Coke?" Eleanor leaned over and patted her on the knee. "Don't tell me you came with us tonight thinking you'd get away with that. I never saw a woman who needed something stronger. You leave it to me. I'll pick something'll knock your socks off."

"I don't drink."

"Why not? Not healthy?" asked the youngest one.

"I have to drive home. It's just a bad idea."

A few of the women looked offended. "One drink is not illegal," said one. "Nobody has to come out of here any drunker than they want."

"You live over on Close Street, right? That's not too far from me on Ceres," Amy said. "Craig'll give you a lift home and I can pick you up for the early shift in the morning if you're worried about driving."

No driving. That meant she could drink whatever she liked. Anything. Why not? She had come out tonight because she wanted a drink, so there. Esmé said, "Okay. Wine?"

Spirits restored, they laughed at her. "This is no place to drink wine." A debate ensued over which lethal mixture Jack might serve. "Oh, I know," said Amy, the slowest clerk with the fastest smile. She kept the customers and the boss happy on sheer charm. "Give her the stoplight tease."

"What's that?" one of them asked.

"Show her, Jack."

"That's strong stuff for a lady don't like to drink much," Jack said.

"Too true," Eleanor said. "Maybe a beer's about the right speed."

"Who said I don't like to drink?" Esmé said, rallying to the mood. "Now I've got a ride home. Okay, barkeep, I'll have a stoplight tease. Please."

Jack left them. They watched him flip bottles around sparkling glasses, dashing a little of this and that, pouring some of the other, but quickly turned to each other to catch up on gossip.

The moms complained about their kids' crowded schedules, ex-husbands late with child support, nasty landlords. The unmarried discussed various dates, almost all bad but some humorous. Eleanor, the senior checker at Granada's and the most-married so far, ruled the conversation, kidding around, taking the worst situations and wrestling some fun out of them.

One of the grizzled guys with hat hair on the other side of the bar came over and Eleanor drifted away with him. Esmé sat on her stool, smiling at the right times. Her mind wandered as she looked into the mirror behind the bar and watched the headlights of the cars on the boulevard, the red, white, green colors blurring like watercolors as the evening darkened. The noise level rose as more people came in, and she was vaguely aware of a sleeve brushing against her, someone leaning briefly into her back, bursts of laughter.

Esmé blew out a long breath. Where was her damn drink? Let it come. The bottles glittered. There she was in the mirror, dark-haired, neat, almost sixty years old. Not like thirty-six years before. She wondered what her friends would say if they knew this would be her first drink in all that time.

She sped up the road toward Avonbury Street, her foot pressed all the way down, singing as loud as she could, radio blasting, windows open. You couldn't think back and remember an event like that, you recalled it in flashes, and that's how she recalled it. A curb rising up to meet her, the sudden realization that she was on the wrong side of the road and that her tires were up on the curb of a central divider.

"Shit!"

She swung the wheel hard, slammed on her brakes, and backed up the empty road. Thank God, nobody there to witness this ridiculous thing. Back on the right side of the road again, she drove slowly, methodically, and when the car drifted across the center line she corrected carefully. She didn't have far to go, only a couple of blocks to get home and make dinner. He'd be home in an hour.

How did she get so drunk? Oh, yeah. Mad at him. Stopped at the bar, saying to herself, to hell with being a responsible person! To hell with my screwed-up life!

In those days, she drank manhattans. To this day, she could not tell you what went into them. She had liked the name. Also, the drink had an attractive color, and came in a triangle-shaped glass she thought sophisticated.

Four. Five. She drank so much so fast she passed out for a second or two on the bar. When she awoke she ordered another one and was politely invited to leave. Someone wanted to call her a cab. She told him she would walk home, no problem.

She climbed into her car, the cheapest used automobile on the lot that day she and Henry went to buy one together.

They had fought, but Henry prevailed, as he always did. Logical, solid, respectable, smart, he could outtalk her, outsmart her, and leave her laughing while he did it. So things had been in the beginning. Later, they had skipped over the part where he made her laugh. He looked at her differently, and the way he looked at her made her dislike herself, and that made her act badly.

She hated this dinged-up car almost as much as she hated being married to a man named Henry, whom she called Hank because it sounded more manly. Everyone, right down to the flakiest housewife on the block, drove cars like this because of their fuel efficiency and budget pricing.

In those days, she didn't care about money or budgets. She expected life to have some flair, drama. She never expected to get stuck in a mundane house in a suburb. What happened to that girl who planned to move to San Francisco as soon as she got out of school?

Giving in on a more glamorous car was giving up on her idea of herself. She smacked the wheel. But Henry, handsome Henry, talked her into everything, a fast wedding in Las Vegas when she had always pictured herself in a white satin gown, maybe getting married at a chic hotel overlooking the beach. Having a child. She had never thought of having a child, but along came Ray. And God, she loved little Ray.

Hurry home. She had taken longer at the bar than she'd expected. Now, weaving, she panicked a little. Where was their street? Squinting into the late afternoon sun, she tried to read the street signs, but she was seeing double.

A car honked behind her and she realized she was crawling along. At the next big intersection, eureka! She realized that she had gone too far by a few blocks. She pulled into the far left lane, careful to leave some space between herself and the divider, congratulating herself on finding her way back. Easy to miss the turn, an honest mistake anyone could make on a hot evening like this, when you're upset, when the sun rakes through the windshield and directly into your eyes when you're trying to drive straight, do an easy thing, get on home.

She waited for the green arrow. Arrows took so long. Turned up the radio again and sang a little, then sang a little louder. Why not have a good time? She was fine, fine, on her way home after a long day. Happy for her husband for once. He used to say he loved her smile. Even now, he didn't want her to complain. He wanted happy. So, tonight she'd give him happy!

One hand on the radio tuner dial, one on the wheel, she pulled into the intersection. The U-turn cut too wide and again she found herself heading for a curb. She put her foot down.

On the accelerator.

The last thing Esmé remembered hearing was not the crash, not the windshield shattering: she heard a baby's wail.

Jack placed three small shot glasses in front of her with three colored liquids, one green, one yellow, one red. "Here's your tease. A stoplight."

"Tell Esmé what's in it," Amy said. Esmé, caught up in the frenzy of noise around her, the high spirits, the cars outside, had already knocked back the first one, green, absolutely vile.

Jack explained. "Step one," he said. "The green drink. You mix an ounce of melon liqueur or Apple Pucker schnapps and an ounce of vodka into a shaker. Heave it to and fro. Then you strain the mixture into a rocks glass.

"For the yellow shot, the halt, caution, do not enter the intersection stuff, you mix an ounce of vodka into a shaker, best available stuff that's yellow-tinged, or add a little food coloring, shake well with a little ice, and strain that into a shot glass or rocks glass.

"Step three, you add an ounce of Hot Damn or Cherry Pucker to one of Bacardi 151 rum. Put those two ounces in a shaker, bounce 'em around, then strain them into a shot glass or rocks glass. That's stop, baby," Jack said, leaning close to Esmé, almost whispering. "For some reason, people who drink this stuff never do stop. Careful."

By then she had thrown the murky bile to the back of her throat, swallowing a few times to get it all down.

"Hey, honey, sip that stuff," Eleanor's friend Carmen said, putting a restraining hand to her wrist, "or Ward'll be calling in a replacement for you in the morning."

Esmé shook her off. The red went down sweeter than melted butter.

"I'll have another," she said. "No. That was awful."

"Now that is the truth," Jack said. "I'll fix you something nice to get the taste out." He gave her a manhattan. Esmé felt herself loosening, as though rubber bands had been holding her brain in place and were popping off one by one. Now she was laughing, too. She felt young and adventurous.

"Another."

"Sure, honey." Jack mixed it for her. There were peanuts on the bar, but she ignored them even though she hadn't had dinner. Eleanor had disappeared and her friends were all involved in their own conversations, but Esmé no longer felt alone. She was part of all this shifting light, this lubricated bonhomie. Everybody happy, like life should be.

"More."

Amy and her big hunky friend Craig stuffed her rather awkwardly into the back seat of their car, Craig holding one arm, Amy the other. Craig drove her home. She had trouble opening her front door, so Craig worked the key.

"You sure you're okay?" Amy asked, watching from outside of Craig's car.

Esmé waved her hands sideways. "Better than okay," she said. She shut the door in Craig's concerned face. "I'm good," she told the door.

She tried leaning against it to keep herself propped up but she was pretty dizzy and it felt better to slip down and feel the cool hardwood. She passed out in the entryway.

20

Sitting beside him so close she could smell Ray's Pi aftershave and touch his shoulder each time he shifted, Kat studied the map. Just outside San Bernardino, they were heading east and most of the way out of the L.A. Basin. The Porsche's outside temperature gauge showed a hundred four Fahrenheit on this Saturday afternoon in August. Not a single car they passed had the windows rolled down. The air carried a distinctly orange tinge. Little could be seen along the freeway—sound walls covered with ice plant, roofs. Not exactly scenic, but it got you there.

She said, "I went to Idyllwild on a field trip when I was in fourth grade. All I remember is bugs, dust, and manzanita. There's no lake very close by. But one of the women in my office likes the place, and she told me it's an artists' town. A tourist town, prosperous these days."

"It's the closest mountain to L.A.," Ray said. "Of course they would plant a town there, to escape to in the summer. It'll be packed this time of year. And there's some real forest, too, in the Mount San Jacinto park."

"Did Leigh tell you about the ghost?"

"What ghost?"

"She claimed her parents' cabin was haunted."

"Then maybe she didn't go there."

"If there's no sign of her, we'll ask at the motels."

"She could have just been passing through."

"Going where?"

"I have one other idea," Ray said. "She bought supplies for her work from a man who lives on a reservation some-where around there, a Native American." The Porsche whizzed into the middle lane and passed a slower car in the fast lane.

They did eighty on the uphill winding road, but Ray had his eyes fixed on the road and his hands squarely in the ten and two o'clock positions on the leather-covered steering wheel, so Kat just said, "What reservation?"

"I can't remember."

"Think!"

"I told you, I can't remember."

"This map doesn't mark any Indian reservations."

"It's a highway map. What do you expect? Tell me about the Hubbel ghost."

"He hovered in the air. He wore old-fashioned clothes." She told him what she could remember, which wasn't much. She did recall Tom relating a story or two. She guessed he had gone up there with Leigh, but this wasn't information she thought Ray would appreciate, so kept those memories to herself.

She thought about the ghost up there with Tom, how he had laughed at the stories but came home looking remarkably chastened at the encounter. She thought about Tom, a ghost himself now.

The trip took nearly three hours, but the Porsche managed the twisty roads magnificently. Arid semi-desert turned to fir and pines, greener as they attained the higher elevations.

Kat closed her eyes and let her head be cuddled by the headrest. She worked to recapture more about the time when Leigh first told her of the ghost. It must have been soon after she fell for Tom. It was this very cabin that she had taken Tom to when they ran away together, benighted lovers, hiding out at her parents' spooky getaway.

Leigh had claimed she and Tom had made love for the first time at the Idyllwild cabin in a room that turned out to be haunted. "I saw something, Kat, something creepy but I wanted him so bad I never said a word. I wonder if Tom saw it, too?"

"What did you see?" Kat, on the floor in Leigh's girlhood bedroom, remembering her brother's story, sat close to the faint breeze coming through the upstairs window on Franklin Street. It felt just like sitting directly inside the pink oven in the downstairs kitchen. Kat wore a tank top and cutoffs, but even in these minimal clothes her moist legs stuck to the hardwood floors.

At twenty-six, Leigh still lived at home. Her bedroom held the furniture she had grown up with that her grandparents had brought from Mississippi, heavy dark mahogany, probably modest in its time but rather admired these days, especially with the gaudy fabrics Leigh had draped over them. The walls, baby blue, were covered floor to ceiling with posters of—what else—furniture through the ages, William Morris designs in particular.

"A guy in old-fashioned overalls appeared," Leigh said, completely seriously. "He didn't make a sound, except to moan. He hovered at the foot of the bed while we went at it."

"Overalls. Omigod, how horrifying!" Kat had reacted, and both young women found this hilarious.

"I love Tom, you know."

"I can't imagine why." But she could. Everyone liked him. All the women fell for him.

"Well, you're his older sister. Where I see a charming and fun-loving man, you remember his snotty baby nose."

"Definitely."

"Kat, I hope you believe I would never hurt him."

Leigh's mother came up and rapped on the door. Leigh called out, "*Entrez* at your own risk."

"Your father wants to talk to you," Rebecca Hubbel said.

Leigh slid off the bed, pushing her feet into a pair of flip-flops.

"He's upset," her mother said.

"Why?"

"He'll tell you."

"See you in an hour if I'm lucky," Leigh said, handing Kat a magazine devoted to woodworking. Rebecca Hubbel gently closed the bedroom door behind herself and Leigh.

Kat looked at the pictures, sometimes reading the captions. Twenty minutes later, Leigh reappeared.

"What did your dad want?"

Leigh pulled out a suitcase, threw open her bureau drawers, and started filling it. "Oh, the usual horseshit about Tom and me. They're worried. They heard about us going up to Idyllwild together. Things are progressing too fast and seriously, according to my dad. I told him I'm moving out."

"Really? Where?"

"Can I stay with you and figure that out for a bit?"

At that time, Kat lived in a studio apartment in Manhattan Beach. "Of course," she said, her heart sinking. Where would she put Leigh?

"It's been good, living here. No rent. Happy parents. I've saved some money. They wanted me to stay home until I'm married, I guess, but geez."

"Your folks were upset." Kat hated to think of that.

So did Leigh, who stopped packing for a moment to wipe her eyes. "They both practically cried."

"Our ma expected us to leave after high school. When it took longer, I think she held it against us."

"I don't want them in my sex life anymore."

"What will you do?"

"Whatever the hell I want."

She actually bypassed Kat's studio and went straight to Tom's Balboa place.

Fifty-three hundred feet high in the San Jacinto Mountains, Idyllwild boasted hundreds of miles of hiking trails, horseback riding venues, shops, and an eclectic selection of restaurants, plus fishing and distant access to two flanking lakes, Lake Fulmor and Lake Hemet. So said the brochure they picked up at the Visitor Center, anyway. They cruised along a tree-dominated main street filled with chalet-style shops displaying paintings and gift items. Tourists wandered about.

By the time Kat and Ray arrived at the Hubbels' rustic cabin, they had between them drunk four waters, eaten three PowerBars, and squabbled twice rather bitterly, eventually descending into silence.

Ray pulled the Porsche into the gravel driveway and slammed on the brakes. Kat lurched forward as they came to a halt. "Holy shit, Ray."

He stared at the cabin. They both did. Wooden shutters closed the front windows. The place looked deserted.

"Maybe she's in the village and she'll be back," Kat said. "She sure doesn't seem to be here. Wait a minute. We may have just eradicated some tire tracks. Back up." Ray backed into the street and left the motor idling as Kat jumped out to check. The gravel was compacted and she couldn't see any tracks from either Leigh's van or the Porsche.

What they could see, once they pulled into the driveway again, encompassed less than a quarter of the large, heavily treed lot. The cabin had once been painted barnred, but the paint had weathered and peeled. A shuttered, ramshackle porch kept sunlight from entering the place in front. Behind the cabin, the hill sloped precipitously down, and the pylon Kat could see didn't look thick enough to keep the cabin from sliding down the hill in the first rain.

And yet it had endured for sixty-five years. A For Sale sign had been placed by the driveway by the real estate agent, with a plastic container for holding sales brochures tacked to it, but any glowing descriptions that might once have filled it were long gone. Kat remembered Leigh telling her about feeding jays on the back porch. She wondered briefly about the Hubbels, their lives, whether they had enjoyed coming here with their little girl years before.

The pines, brown and rustling in a late-afternoon wind, appeared close to death. They must have something strong in them, Kat decided as she mounted the wooden steps, because they were living on almost no water. Ray slammed the car door and followed.

"Shoot," Kat said. "I assumed the realtor would have a lockbox on the door. I have a master that will open just about any lockbox." She showed it to him and he turned it over in his hands.

"Nice," he said enviously.

"Now what?"

"No problem," Ray said. He turned and his eyes sought out the porch's hiding places. Then he went down the stairs to a round granite stone to the right of the porch. He bent over and pushed it aside. And there sat a dirty house key.

"How'd you know?" she said.

"I like keys. This is where they would keep it."

"But you went straight to it."

"I have never been here before. Okay?"

"Okay."

Kat knew, had known the minute they pulled up, that no living being resided inside that boarded-up cabin, but that didn't stop her from looking around hopefully as she entered.

The cabin felt chilly. Ray, doing the guy thing, immediately went to locate a thermostat or heat source. Kat pulled her sleeping bag inside and shut the door behind herself.

The entryway, meager, held a small closet which hid coats. She peered inside, noting coats for every season, light, dark, thin, thick. Musty smelling.

The first room past the entry, presumably the living room, had a red leather couch, comfortably worn, two floral chenille chairs, and a coffee table with an undone puzzle on it. She reflected, casting a cold professional eye on it, that this look would not appeal to the desirable market, an affluent suburbanite. It looked to be exactly what it was, a moldy old cabin nobody had ever improved. No wonder the Hubbels had no nibbles. Instantly, turned on like a faucet, she imagined the possibilities. Paint the paneling a light taupe or soft apricot. Replace the moldy carpet. Replace the lighting fixtures, dated and dusty. Replace the appliances. Spend twenty grand and make fifty.

Ray stood in the doorway. "I got the heat going."

"That's a plus," she said. "Shall we have a look around?" They went together, turning on lights and opening shutters, glancing into the tiny kitchen, the upstairs bedroom with its pink chenille-covered queen bed. The downstairs area was shut off from the rest of the house by a closed door that led off the living room. The staircase down, narrow and rickety, bothered Kat. Maybe it was the harsh, naked lightbulb that lit the stairwell, or the lack of windows. She followed Ray down and they found themselves in a large room with a fireplace at the far end, a den, perhaps, with a couple of couches and a window with a nice view of the nearby hillsides.

"This isn't so bad," Kat said. They went into a narrow hallway. Way in the back was a small bedroom with a double bed complete with pillows but no overhead light, just a dim lamp which Ray snapped on. "The second bedroom," Kat said. One window faced out from the hillside, covered with a cotton curtain. A closet took up one corner. Kat looked inside. No bodies.

"She's not here," Ray said. He sat down on the bed, which creaked alarmingly, and put his head in his hands.

"We haven't looked everywhere yet."

"You mean, the cupboards, in case I stuffed her under the sink or something?"

"Let's make sure you didn't," Kat said. "You've surprised me before."

It didn't take long. They found old clothing in the bureau drawers and a storage closet filled with things the family had left behind. They wandered around the property in the gathering darkness. A sliver of moon shone down as Kat held a flashlight under the house. Then they went inside and found an opening to the low attic in one of the closets, and took a look up there. A lot of insect droppings, signs of asbestos. Probable termite infestation, a sale-killer. But no sign of a body.

Leigh was not there, and they found no sign that she had been.

The two were defeated, even anxious. They came all this way, and now had nothing. Ray brought the second bottle of French wine from the car. Kat located small glasses in the kitchen, and wiped them well. They drank the wine warm in front of the rock fireplace, where Ray had built a small fire. He placed two more logs on the fire and shifted the logs, sending sparks flying. "Y'know, we are trespassing or burglarizing or something."

"I'll just say I'm doing a detailed appraisal. You remembered to open the flue?"

He smiled. "Obviously. You sound just like Leigh, who never trusts me. Yes, I opened the flue before setting these logs on fire. I'm not suicidal anymore, in spite of what you might think."

"And I have plans," she said, knowing she sounded haughty but unable to help herself. "Every single one of them involves me living past the age of forty."

"Kat," he said, eyes lit with the reflection of fire.

"Yes?"

"I'm grateful to you, whatever happens."

She didn't believe him but felt bad to be such a doubter.

She slept in the basement bedroom paneled in a plastic wood veneer. In the middle of the night, she woke up. She pummeled her pillows, rearranging them, closed her eyes.

Still no sleep.

She checked out the clock. Three a.m.

Too early to rise, too late to read.

She punched her pillows again, putting one where a man would be, if a man were around.

Closed her eyes. The air felt close and heavy and she wished she had opened the window.

Thought about Ray and Leigh.

Opened her eyes.

Saw a shadow on the wall that didn't belong there.

Felt an aching hollow inside her as the shadow moved and grew larger. The curtain was closed. It was dark. How could there be a darker shadow? The illusion hovered off the ground.

Now she saw that it wasn't on the wall but stood out from the wall, a black mass shaped and sized like a floating door. But it was alive, she could feel it, aware of her, watching her.

She froze; stopped breathing. Held her eyes in exactly the same place. Did not dare to widen them.

"It's me." In the doorway, silhouetted by the hall light, a figure stood.

And for a terrifying, emotional moment, she thought she saw Tom, and he was furious with her, madder than she remembered seeing him ever before. He moved closer. She found her voice. Her scream must have echoed for miles up and down the old Tahquitz valley.

Where was Zak when she needed him?

21

A light came on in the hall and Ray materialized, stepping into her room, appearing quite sturdy. "What? What's happened?" he asked, looking around confusedly as she flipped on the little lamp.

"I saw it! I saw—"

"What did you see?"

She rubbed her eyes. "I screamed, didn't I? Sorry."

"A bad dream?"

"It must have been."

"Okay, so you don't need me here?"

"I guess not. No."

But he lingered in the doorway. "Listen, Kat. There's something you need to know. I got cold and went looking for a blanket in the upstairs bedroom closet. I found something."

"You did?"

"Leigh's purple shirt. The one she was wearing when she left."

Kat shivered and pulled the cover up to her shoulders, unable to care for the moment about some old shirt he found.

"Kat, are you really okay?"

"No, I'm not. I saw the damn ghost. At first I thought—then I realized it was a black door, floating by the doorway. I saw it and it saw me. I'm not staying down here! God, what if you hadn't showed up? What would it have done to me? Stop laughing!"

"You saw—a door?"

She threw off the covers and jumped out of bed. Ray's eyes widened and she realized she was wearing bikini underwear and nothing else. Ray wore boxers, cotton, and his skin had a warm glow from the light behind him. "Lovely girl, aren't you?" he murmured.

The air between them quivered like their breaths.

She looked at him standing in that awful doorway, the hairy chest and legs, the loose boxer shorts, the goose bumps forming on his muscular arms.

A mutual, accumulated longing soaked the room.

Ray didn't move, just stood there gathering up that frightening masculine power that usually slayed her on the spot.

Under such heavy pressure, in the quiet she heard a tiny voice saying "No, no."

Maybe he heard the same voice. He turned away.

"Don't leave, Ray, please? Wait for me," she said, pulling on her jeans and T-shirt. "Okay, let's go." At the top of the stairs she closed the door firmly and tilted a chair back against the knob.

"If we had done anything," Ray said, as they walked toward the living room, where the embers of their earlier fire continued to flare, "we would have ruined everything." He pulled a flannel shirt off the coatrack by the front door and put it on. The tails swung down nearly to his knees. Must have belonged to James Hubbel, a large man.

She nodded. She felt better, back by the fire, in better light, her jeans on and zipped. "Yep," she said. Ray poked the fire, bringing up some heat. They sat on the floor, feet as close to the burning wood as they could stand. Finally warmed up again, Kat said, "I thought you weren't positive what she wore the day she disappeared."

"I am now. Take a look." He led and she followed him into the upstairs bedroom. A purple V-necked shirt lay across the pillow.

"That's Leigh's, and I don't mean from years ago. It was thrown in the back. The rest of the clothing was folded."

Kat picked the shirt up. It was inside out and wrinkled. She spread it, looking closer. "My God. What's this?" She held the shirt up to the light, and even he could see it, holes. Rusty-looking spots. "What the hell?"

Ray examined the shirt. "Oh, no," he said. "I didn't really look at it. God, no."

"She was injured."

Voice constricted, like someone who had been punched in the stomach, he finally said, "Yeah."

"What happened to her?"

Ray broke through a long silence, saying "But she left the shirt here. Doesn't that mean she's okay?"

Kat, the shirt dangling from her right hand, didn't know. "Maybe. Should we call the police?"

Ray looked flummoxed. "I just don't know. Maybe she was working with her power tools? It wouldn't be the first time she hurt herself."

"Oh no, Ray. These are like—jabs. Too many to be an accident."

After a long discussion, they decided to bag the T-shirt and take it to the sheriff the minute they got back.

"She left it here. She's okay," Ray said.

"If that's so, they'll figure that out," said Kat.

And so at last they had something, and it was hard to look at each other, because they were both thinking the same thing. Ray fetched his sleeping bag and resettled himself on the living room couch, not far from the dread door to the downstairs. Kat took the upstairs bedroom bed and left her door open and the light on. Even so, she only dozed. Ghosts, dead bodies, old houses, and bloody shirts flitted through her dreams.

She was running out of the manhattan mix from the liquor store. Esmé sloshed some more into her coffee cup and took a drink. Really, she preferred a more delicate glass. What was she up to, drinking from such crude pottery? Even Ray would not approve.

She poured it full. It had been a long day, starting with calling in sick at the store. She settled herself on her couch.

No need to cook tonight; she wasn't hungry.

During the couple of years they were together, when the world seemed so wide open and possibilities stretched out infinitely, the fact that Henry's parents didn't like Esmé seemed like nothing, a flick of a feather duster. Who cared what they thought? Her grandparents did not approve, but nobody expected to gain their approval. Good God. These people had been born in the early nineteen hundreds, so very, very long ago.

If they had looked at Henry objectively, not as a crazy, lovestruck young man who didn't know what he was doing, they might have recognized him for the catch he was. Henry had graduated with honors from high school, attended Cal for two years. He almost finished his degree before they got married, and planned to take graduate courses so that someday, he might teach at Cal State. Before everything went so bad.

Who could have predicted such a tall man with such winning blue eyes could turn against her so utterly?

Pouring herself another glass, walking out into her garden, she remembered that she had been so young. Henry wanted her, yes. He loved her fluffy hair, her innocence, her sweet youth.

Oh, give Ray a girl like herself back then! She had been irresistible!

Then she'd had Ray. She ballooned from a hundred and ten pounds to a hundred and sixty-five. After graduation, Hank worked at Cal State Long Beach as a TA, a teaching assistant. He came home at the end of the day disgruntled, unsatisfied with his lot, and dis-approving.

"Other women keep their figures," he would say. "Other women go back to work right away after their baby is born."

He wanted her to support him so that he could finish his graduate degree and couldn't understand when she didn't rate that goal as a priority.

She didn't care about prettier women or his education. She would not go back to work until this amazing boy spent most of his days in school. She did not give a damn about her figure.

"Real men want their wives to stay home and take care of their precious sons," she said.

Esmé wondered where Ray was. She had called him twice today. He didn't answer. She tried his cell phone, leaving a message.

The last dregs of the bottle dribbled into her glass and she drank them. Although her thinking was fuzzy, she was sure her driving reflexes were fine. Certainly her emotions were full and flourishing. She called a cab, gathered up her keys, locked the front door, and picked up her own vehicle in Granada's lot.

She stuck her key into the ignition, which did not start.

But she did not believe in divine intervention. She did not believe in fate. After about four tries, the car started up. She recognized a certain unsound quality to her driving, but she seemed able enough to stay within the boundaries of her lane. Be very careful. She opened her eyes very wide and put both hands on the wheel and kept reminding herself that she was driving toward Topanga Canyon.

She made her way out of Whittier through the maze of numbered freeways. This exercise frequently reminded her of those mazes people marked with stones that started in the center and led to some outside goal. People claimed to find the walk edifying, even spiritual. She had tried walking the labyrinths, with mixed emotions. They frustrated and angered her. If a choice had to be made, which, depending on the maze, choices did have to be made, she invariably picked the wrong route.

Kind of like picking Henry, who turned out to be so wrong for her.

Now she followed a well-worn path, and when traffic stalled, she listened to talk shows.

"I hate my father!" one tearful caller said.

"Let's figure out why," said the patient radio host.

The host probably had no credentials, no counseling experience whatsoever. He probably had three ex-wives and seven children, vaguely related, all wondering what love meant witnessing his mean existence and emotional detachment.

Esmé arrived at Ray's house around seven Saturday night. Maybe he was out.

During daylight savings time, even the canyon stayed relatively light. She saw no signs of life except for the landscape lights bursting on when she stepped out of the car. She wove up the driveway, her Rockports crunching on the gravel, aware that she was not at her best.

Tonight, she wanted to tell her son the whole story, the whole sad tale of herself and her hero, Henry Jackson. How it all fell apart. How she regretted so much.

She dreaded the encounter slightly more than she welcomed it. Her power over Ray had weakened through the years. Leigh came along, a normal course of events. Leigh loved Ray; even Esmé could see it, how much Leigh loved her son. But as a mother who had invested absolutely everything in her child, she could barely stomach the change. She went to work at the grocery store every day, yes, but with what purpose? No little boy came home to her anymore needing a hug, fresh crayons, help with his science project.

Sometimes she indulged in a vision of grandchildren. Whenever she broached the topic with Ray, she got put off. "We'll think about that when the time comes."

In other words, Leigh didn't want them, not ever, and Esmé could just up and die of a broken heart, for all Leigh cared.

Drinking brought up negativity. She remembered that. She must crush these unpleasant thoughts. Finally reaching the entrance to Ray's house, she rang the bell. Nobody came.

She knocked. No one answered.

"Ray?" she called softly. Then, "Ray!" regardless of the neighbors. After waiting a polite amount of time, she gave up and took the hidden key from behind a bramble bush. She pushed the old-fashioned key first into the door lock, then into the dead bolt. Both slipped open like well-oiled musical instruments. She opened the door to his immaculate, magnificent, sterile home.

A perfectly tempered air swept over her, forcing her eyes closed. "Ah," she said, accepting this benevolent feeling that came from money and good planning.

Replacing the key, she went into the house. Lights greeted her, turning on as if bidden. Ray adored modern technology, and at this moment, so did she. She felt so welcomed.

She poured herself a vodka from his wet bar, and looked around. She admired and hated the artwork on his walls. She peeked into his closet, but when she spilled her drink, decided she probably ought to lie down for a bit.

His sofa, worth thousands no doubt, was hard but at least had some loose pillows. She put her head on one end and stretched out on the unforgiving sofa.

She would tell all.

In a way, she couldn't wait. All these years, she had kept her life bottled up inside so tight, corked, screwed down. Ray should know, she decided, plumping the pillow with one hand, feeling a little dizzy. He ought to know who his father was, and who his mother is.

Probably he deserved to know, although such niceties of morality seemed a little like the leaves outside, blowing in hot summer winds, untouchable unless they fell to the ground and you stomped on them. She would have a nap, and then he'd be home.

22

For breakfast, Ray found some food they could eat, canned pears, dry cereal with powdered milk. The pantry, located on a porch beside the kitchen, showed signs of vermin infestation. Kat, continuing to feel quite hungry after the ordeals of a haunted Idyllwild night, did not care. When Ray didn't finish his cornflakes, she finished them.

The T-shirt sat in its bag on the couch. Ray kept away from it. Kat couldn't stop looking at it.

"Plan of action," Kat said. "Besides take the shirt back to the sheriff?"

"We didn't finish searching this place. Maybe there's more."

"We hunt some more?" Kat said.

"Don't want to miss anything, now that we're here."

"But it's a crime scene. We shouldn't mess it up."

"Is it? I don't believe it. Besides, we already slept here."

They hunted. Kat made Ray search the small downstairs bedroom. She refused to go downstairs at all, in fact.

They tossed the place attic to foundation, finding nothing else that suggested Leigh had been there recently.

Kat found a picture album that documented many years of visits. Mr. Hubbel, not exactly a fine figure of a man these days, appeared godlike, handsome as a movie star. He water-skied, hiked, rode a bike, swam wearing a mighty tight Speedo. In occasional extras presumably taken by friends, his wife appeared alongside him, small and adorable. Leigh, young and accompanied by friends male and female over the years, grinned a camera-false smile. Kat, although frequently invited, had never managed to visit before.

At the back of a leather-bound volume on the bottom shelf of many albums, she found three pictures of Tom with Leigh.

In one, they sat together on a boat, heads inclined toward each other, hers so very blonde, his darker, his thick eyebrows furrowed, worried looking. Leigh looked up at him, and although the picture was black and white, her gray eyes appeared translucent. They sat in the stern of a speedboat, a white trail behind them, globules of water decorating both their faces. Tom gazed back at her, lovestruck. She appeared happy, without connection.

In another, they smiled into the camera, Tom, several inches taller than Leigh, standing against a desert backdrop of treeless, cracked ground. He had looped an arm over her shoulder. They looked relaxed, like two people who belonged together.

In the third and last picture, Tom was peripheral, not part of the framed group. He sat on a bench in the background, watching Leigh whoop it up at an evening party, champagne glass in one hand, a plate of hors d'oeuvres in the other. Behind her, an orange desert sky blazed. Tom, lurking in shadows, appeared to glower.

Leigh glowed like the moon, handsome young men hovering nearby.

Kat pulled out the photos and pushed them into her pocket. She shut the album.

"Find anything?" Ray called from outside.

"Nothing."

"I have something." He held his hands cupped as he showed her some broken nutshells.

"These haven't been around long. I found them strewn all around under the back balcony where the blue jays hang."

"Peanuts. She likes peanuts."

"She sat out there eating peanuts."

Neither of them said the obvious: maybe whoever had hurt her had sat out there, watching the jays.

"Put 'em in another bag, and we'll bring them, too," Kat advised. "For DNA testing."

"You've made up your mind she's dead," Ray said. "Haven't you?"

Kat held up her hands.

"I want to spend a few more hours in the area before we go back," Ray said. "Please. I can't go back quite yet. It's too awful. That shirt. I need some kind of hope."

"It's an important discovery, Ray. I think we have to go back."

"Just check a gas station or two. I think I remember vaguely where the reservation is."

Kat shook her head, but in the end, she felt as though

whatever harm had come to Leigh had come and gone, and a few more hours wouldn't cause any more harm.

They packed quickly. "We need a better map of this area," Ray said. He seemed calm, rested, on patrol this morning. They closed up and drove into the village, to a local market which carried maps. Ray studied the one they bought, saying "Maybe," as if to himself.

They drove north and then east along the long hill, catching glimpses of taller mountains in the distance, stopping at every convenience store, every grocery store, every gas station, moving farther and farther from Los Angeles. They showed photos of Leigh.

Nobody knew anything. Morning turned to mid-afternoon under the blue mountain sky.

Without discussion, at the foot of the next mountain, Ray turned his Porsche onto the road that led toward Palm Springs.

Kat, dozing in the comfortable coolness of the Boxster, felt the car turn left and crunch onto a road that was not highway. Ray said, "I saw a road sign. There's a reservation down here. Let's check it out, see if I recognize anything. It's the only one marked on this map. It's called Baños Calientes."

"You think it's the one Leigh visited?"

"I can't remember. I don't know if she even told me the name of it. It could be." On both sides of them, scrub and sand stretched away. The chaparral plants were so evenly placed, so organized in their desperate struggle to find just enough water for their roots, that the landscape looked like a park. Of course, this park was assiduously tended mostly by snakes and scorpions.

"What exactly did she buy there?"

"Wood. For furniture she wanted to make."

"What else do you remember about it?"

"Just that an old guy sold it to her. She told me she liked him. I wasn't paying much attention. It could be this place, or there may be a dozen small reservations around here."

"Well, hip hip hooray." It popped out.

"What?" He sounded offended.

"I've felt like I dragged you along with me on this hunt for Leigh, Ray. Now here you are actually trying to help us move forward. Maybe you didn't kill her after all." Now that one foot was lodged in her jaw, she had to cram the other one in, too. Even as she spoke, she realized she would regret it.

Ray's chin moved to the forefront. "She's not dead. Stop assuming that she is. You never gave me the chance to take charge, Kat. You're a prodder. A poker. I hate women who prod and poke. Especially ones who look like stick insects with red hair."

"Yeah?"

"Yeah."

"Well, real men don't wear boxers. Especially plaid ones."

"How would you know? You've never had a real man."

"I was just trying to say—"

"The same shit you've been handing me all along to keep me moving."

"Which worked, finally."

"I worked up to it on my own, little lady."

Kat folded her arms and stared straight ahead, though the bouncing from the potholes detracted from this dignified posture. They were sending up a rooster tail of dry sand behind them, even though Ray was doing under thirty miles an hour now.

After a minute, he said slowly, "Although the hot poker up my ass did make me jump a little faster."

"You really were frozen. Immobilized. Except for running around L.A. peeking in houses like a hamster running in a wheel."

"Had to do it," Ray said.

"What did you get out of it?"

"I figured out where some keys fit."

"That's not all of it."

"It's good enough for now."

Kat felt they had just barely avoided an impasse that would have sent them careening back home. Ray seemed relieved, too—he whistled a little under his breath. She resolved, as she had a thousand times before, to keep a close watch on the openings to the body, guard the mouth—guard the—whoa, guard all the orifices, that meant—she had a silent epiphany involving her love life, an epiphany which she managed to keep from sharing with Ray.

"I think his name was Pablo," Ray now said. "Of course, I could be making that up to throw you further off the scent."

Replying carefully and reasonably, she said, "Okay, Baños Calientes, here we come. We still have a few hours before we should turn around and go to the police. How far are we from Topanga?"

"Two and a half, maybe up to three hours, depending on traffic. I'll get us back."

Behind them, the San Jacinto Mountains loomed, their rugged shapes piercing the sky like vampire teeth. An outcropping of sedimentary rock appeared, and over a rolling hill a settlement of nondescript ranch houses and trailers in an oasis of willows.

Four-thirty in the afternoon. A small hawk perched on a telephone pole, feathers barely moving; women wearing Sunday-go-to-church dresses chatted in the parking lot of the trading post, which was basically a mom-and-pop grocery store; a leathery senior in a white hat and lived-in jeans filled up his Ranger at the gas pump out front. Ray pulled the car into a parking spot.

He locked the car remotely with a click. Kat followed him into the store.

Racks of bait mixed incongruously with fresh spices. Apparently the people down here not only liked to catch fresh food, they liked to cook with spices, rare beer batters, unusual root-based roux. Unlike the grocery stores near her house in Hermosa, the aisles were not speckled with plastic grasses or lit with halogen spotlights to create the illusion of cozy gourmet. This store reminded her of the one down the hill from Franklin Street in Whittier when she was a kid, what they used to call "the little store." Fusty candies in moldering baskets decorated the shelf below the counter cash register. The rest of the store held basics like toilet paper, tampons, and peanut butter stacked up to the black painted ceiling without any fan-fare.

A gum-chewing teen manned the register. Ray did not pretend he wanted to buy anything.

"Pablo around?"

The jaw worked. Gum popped once, then twice.

"Haven't seen him today."

"I need to see him."

A stare as indifferent as the stars blinked back.

"I know him," Ray said.

"Who are you?"

"My name is Ray Jackson. My wife's name is Leigh. Leigh Jackson."

The gum popped again. The boy at the counter took a dirty rag out and wiped his counter down. When it continued to be grubby, he spit on the rag and wiped it again. "Don't know you."

"You sell my wife manzanita."

A dim light penetrated the distant universe of his eyes. "Sounds familiar."

"She builds furniture, and sometimes she uses the manzanita as bases for glass tables."

"It grows wild out here."

"Yes."

"He doesn't steal it, you know."

"Nobody said he did." When the boy began to straighten the newspapers, Ray said, "It's not like he was selling her drugs."

"He wouldn't."

"He around?"

"No. You want to buy something?"

No problem, Kat had a handful of goodies she wanted at the ready. She plopped them in front of the boy. Ray looked at the candy bars and said, "That's not your lunch."

"No, I missed lunch. This is high tea."

The clerk smiled, revealing gold-tipped incisors, and rang their purchases up.

"Where can we find Pablo?"

Ching. Ching. Ching. "He's my grandfather. You want to buy some manzanita?"

"Maybe."

"We call it *madrón*. He rambles around the desert collecting what he calls found things. He used to follow the Grateful Dead around, you know? Fell in love with a woman who played harpsichord with them a few times, named Margaret. When she dumped him, he married Grandma Rayella."

"Sounds like a live wire," Kat said, while he bagged up the food she couldn't wait to eat. The cornflakes at the Idyllwild cabin had not assuaged her need for nutrients.

The boy began to hand her the change from her twenty; she waved him off.

He narrowed his eyes and tucked the money into the right front pocket of his jeans. "Grandpa comes in around five almost every night. Since Grandma died, he doesn't cook." He waved toward a steaming bar along one side of the shop. "He'll eat any soup we dream up."

"Is that what I'm smelling? Smells good." Kat was now regretting the Mounds, the Snickers, and the paper-wrapped Necco Wafers she had just opened.

"White bean soup. I make it with fresh parsley, garlic, and a delicate imported parmigiano." He smirked, and Kat imagined how many cans he opened in the morning, getting that fresh soup going.

"I'll take a quart," Ray said, pulling out his wallet.

They left to await the appearance of Pablo. They had only a few minutes to kill. Cars passed by but nobody stopped. Lights winked on behind them.

They didn't want to return to the car, so they walked up the block toward a distant blinking sign that said "Desert Tots." On both sides of the street, empty lots extended for miles beyond the road. Tumbleweeds blew by. An early moon floated in the blue. A shaded wooden bench sat in front of the store, which on weekdays sold secondhand items for children. It was very quiet.

Ray opened his soup container and pulled a plastic spoon out of his pocket.

"You going to eat all that?"

"You could have told me to get two spoons," he said, offering her the first bite.

"I couldn't. I was embarrassed." She slurped down a bite, then two, then three. "Oh, man."

He took the spoon from her and sampled the soup.

"That kid can cook!"

They polished off the soup and walked up and down, past the library trailer, the bank branch, and the post office in the heat. That was one block and then they were in a neighborhood where a few kids played in a yard.

When they got back to the little store, they had a new contact, a middle-aged babe with bold silver streaks in her hair, who wore a low-cut T-shirt that displayed her amplitudes. Ray asked for Pablo again.

Seconds later, a man in a straw cowboy hat with a dark, seamed face appeared from behind a door at the back of the store. He had a cloth napkin decorated with roosters tucked into his neck like a bib. "Cheche outdid himself," he said to the woman at the register. He paid no attention to Kat and Ray.

She answered, "He thinks he can talk you into paying for cooking school next year. He's praying. He's hoping."

The older man, scrawny, small, no more than five feet five inches tall, nodded. "He's been cooking since he had to stand on a stool."

She pointed toward Ray. "These people want to talk to you."

Pablo removed his bib, folded it, and placed it on the counter next to the woman. "Find a place for that, will you, *querida*?"

She stuffed the dirty napkin under the counter, turned away from them, and began watching a miniature television, with a serious expression.

"Hi," Kat said, letting Pablo look them over. He leaned against the ice-cream cooler, the picture of a well-fed man. He must be past seventy, with large scarred hands and cords standing out in his neck.

"We're looking for someone." Ray pulled a picture of Leigh out of his coat pocket and handed it to Pablo.

Pablo held the picture of Leigh in his hands. "Long time since I saw this lady." He had a deep, distant voice, like he was channeling it from somewhere else.

"Old man," the woman at the counter said, "your memory needs tweaking."

"Months," he said stubbornly, and gave her a look. "Don't pay any attention to her," he said. "She just likes to talk."

"Leigh is my wife," Ray said. "She's missing. If you saw her, we really need to know. We are afraid something has happened to her."

"I remember a long time ago when I saw her, she mentioned you," the man said. Kat couldn't see his eyes under the hat. "I was asking why she came out here alone. She said she had a wonderful husband. A wonderful husband, but he didn't have time for deserts and mountains."

"She meant me, all right," Ray said. He didn't blink.

"She makes wonderful furniture. She made a table for me last year."

"She did?"

"She's a real artist."

Ray looked away. Kat wondered what he was thinking. She said, "When you saw her, was she on her way somewhere?"

"I wouldn't know."

"She didn't say anything about her plans?" Kat broke in.

"Who are you?" the man said, his gaze moving back and forth between her and Ray.

"I understand why you wouldn't be sure about trusting us. But this is urgent. She has disappeared. We have to find her."

"Who are you?"

"Her best friend."

"She didn't mention you."

"Nevertheless, here I am," Kat said.

"If you know anything, anything at all—" Ray said.

"Sometimes people want to disappear for a while."

"Is that what she told you? She came through here last weekend, didn't she?" Kat said, the words rushing out.

The man squeezed his lips so tightly together they disappeared, and Kat was reminded again about guarding the mouth. She turned to the woman at the counter and said, "Please."

"It's up to him," the woman said, jerking her head toward Pablo.

"You want the police here?"

"My cousin's the deputy on duty here. I'm not afraid of him, or you two. You better go now."

23

"They're lying," Kat said, as they got back in the car and pulled back into the road.

"I agree."

"He saw her. Or he knew something about her. He knew something!"

"Could be."

"You think he'd act like that if he knew nothing?"

"I think," Ray said, steering the Porsche west as they turned back onto the highway, "we have to go back to L.A."

"Did he see her or not? It's a simple enough question."

"He said she wanted to disappear," Ray said. His jaw clenched. "As if he knows she's alive."

"Not exactly. Maybe we should keep going until we find her."

"Where should we go?" Ray said. "Palm Springs? Vegas? Salt Lake City? Albuquerque? St. Louis? Cleveland? Owego, New York? We have to go back now, Kat."

"I'm angry at that old man," Kat said. "He could have helped us."

"Don't think about him. Get mad at Leigh," Ray said. "I

know I wasn't a great husband to her. But here I am, ready to change, and she's not here to see it. And she wasn't a great wife to me. I knew she was still sad about your brother. But years passed and she stayed just as sad. I wonder if she ever loved me. Maybe I was just the guy between Tom and Martin."

"She loves you," Kat said. "I read the poems."

For a long time into the night, heading up toward the stars that shone so brightly, they drove in silence. The desert, yellow, gold, ochre, mustard, whipped by.

Ray drove too fast for another couple of minutes, then asked, "What was he like?"

"Who?"

"Tom."

"You never asked her?"

"Why would I? I'd only start comparing myself to him. But it doesn't matter now, I suppose."

She found herself telling him about Tom. She told him about how he was the glue that kept their family together, how he kept them laughing, how he didn't have an enemy in the world. Surprisingly, she didn't get choked up like usual. To be able to talk about Tom without descending into utter grief was a new thing for her.

Ray listened intently, while dodging the semis and the road hogs trying to make it to their destinations before dark.

"She still loves him," he said finally.

"She had broken up with him before he died. She left him for you, Ray! Why are you so stupid! Of course she loved—loves you!"

"You don't understand. She—" He fell silent.

"Look, what she did with your partner—I don't excuse that," Kat said. "I can't explain it, and I doubt she can explain it. Let's find her. That's all I know."

"I don't know where else to look," Ray said.

"She took out some cash. We'll find her."

"Someone used her card. Not necessarily her. Like you said before."

"Was Leigh's PIN hard to guess?"

"No idea." They talked about that. Leigh had apparently never told Ray her PIN or for that matter any of her computer IDs, facts Kat found telling. Now she was glancing at him again.

The shirt in the back was like a funeral shroud and they were just a couple of hearse-drivers. Her mind was like a Ping-Pong match. It was too late. No, it wasn't. Yes, it was.

No, it wasn't! "The police have to get right on this!" Kat cried.

"As soon as we get back, I'll go straight to Rappaport. No more phone calls. I just hope they don't clap me in jail when I do."

Kat rifled through her purse for a brush. She knew how bad she looked from the tiny mirror under the sunshade in the car that revealed all in the unforgiving glare of the map light. She pulled a brush through her hair and discreetly tossed loose spikes out of the car window when she thought Ray wasn't looking. Let the birds make nests.

She vowed to take more vitamins, meditate properly, love the people in her life, because you never knew how long they might be there. She considered calling Jacki. Checking her watch, she saw that it was late and decided to wait. Jacki and Raoul, and with luck, the babe, would be snoring away.

They had dropped into the L.A. Basin into light traffic. Thank God for Sunday, the one day you could still drive here. Full dark had come on. Sandwiched between sound walls on this strip of blacktop, they could be anywhere.

Kat, looking out the window at nothing, realized that she was very low, so low she could feel tears coming on. Every once in a while she needed to have a long talk with Tommy, and it felt like tonight would be another one of those nights. Where was Leigh? She just wanted to be in bed now, safe, even if she couldn't sleep, even if she'd spend the night thinking about the losses and the pain . . .

But then she bit her lip and smiled to herself. Her sister had a new baby. Good things did happen. There was a chance for all of them still.

"Did you notice what she did as we were leaving the store?" she asked Ray.

"Who?" Ray passed in the left lane, doing ninety, headlights in front flashing by, headlights behind eating his dust. Kat held on tight.

"The woman at the register. The one with the big hooters."

"She looked good."

"She looked at the old man."

"So?"

"I don't know. I might be imagining this. But I thought she gave him a signal, sort of a wink. As if she's not worried about Leigh, not taking this seriously. Would they really have shined us on like they did if they didn't know Leigh is okay?"

"Yeah, sure, she's fine," Ray said. And Kat managed not to look at him this time, but she was wondering again, wondering what was really in his mind, whether he knew exactly where Leigh was. She remembered a California murder case in which an adulterous husband, Scott Peterson, killed his pregnant wife and threw her body into the Berkeley harbor. In the absence of much direct evidence, the jury had been mightily influenced by his conduct during the subsequent search, his calls to his girlfriend, his purchase of new toys.

Was Ray just making a case for himself, using her?

Kat, exhausted, barely spoke to him when they finally pulled into the driveway in Topanga. "Rappaport," she said, fished out her car keys, climbed into her tin can of a car, and drove off, buckling her seat belt for another stretch before she'd be home in Hermosa.

Ray pulled the Porsche into the garage, watched the door lower, and went through the inside garage door into his house, beat through and through.

Something felt strange. The door led into his laundry room. He couldn't see anything out of place there, but he had an instantaneous impression that something was not right. A smell? A peculiar air, not his.

Setting his jacket gently down on the floor instead of on its usual hook, he made his way slowly toward the darkened living room. "Who's there?" His voice reverberated hollowly along the hard surfaces.

Nobody answered but the clock his mother had given him for his mantel. It chose this moment to let out its muffled chime.

Midnight. How perfect. He remembered Kat's scare at Idyllwild and told himself to get a grip.

Rather than march directly into the living room, he sidestepped into the kitchen, where he had a view of the front room but some protection if he needed it, and flipped on the overheads: he chose a low counter to hide behind. He took his big chef's knife out of its special place in a drawer, taking care to keep the drawer quiet. Stopping to see anything he could view from the kitchen, he moved silently into the living room and fumbled for the light on his Palmetti lamp.

Vomit desecrated his custom bamboo floor. The mess had been hastily wiped, with ugly gobbets left behind. Ugh. A throw had been moved from his bed to one arm of the sofa, and dragged sloppily on the floor.

Ray moved in closer. Who? Who would invade his home then sleep there? Certainly no typical burglar. Not the police?

Leigh?

Martin?

Now he walked rapidly through the house turning on lights, holding the knife tightly—but he wouldn't need it, there was nobody there, not even an open window, no other signs of major disturbance.

Back in the living room he examined the pillow on the

couch, silk, that had been taken from a nearby chair. A hair, mid-length, gray-rooted, lay at the center.

He drew a final conclusion easily when he spotted her favorite sweater draped over a chair. His mother had come, crashed in his living room, and left again. She had thrown up. She was sick.

After Ray cleaned up the mess, placing the rags he used directly into the washing machine with copious amounts of detergent and bleach, he drank coffee he probably didn't need in spite of his lack of sleep.

His mother had slept here, tossed her cookies.

She never drank. Could she be ill? But he wasn't quite ready to call her.

A quick perusal of the kitchen told him that she had invaded the cupboard above his refrigerator and the mirrored bar. A bottle of vodka Leigh had bought months ago that had gathered dust was less than one-fourth full. Last time he had noticed, the bottle had been three-quarters full. Even if Leigh made several of her favorites, cranberry and vodka, she hadn't drunk that much that fast in all the time he had known her.

Had he driven Esmé to this?

They had always had such a reliable relationship, loving in the way a mother and son had to love, superficially distant with an understood undercurrent. Now, the real nature of their relationship nagged at him like sinister whispers. What went on in her heart? What went on in his?

He tried to put himself in his mother's position. He

had risen up like a cobra hiding behind tall grasses, awaiting the right moment, attacking, determined to tear to bits her hard-won privacy. He had been very hard on her recently, denigrating the effect of all those years of love. Regret stabbed at him.

Afraid, he picked up the phone and called the house on Close Street in Whittier. She didn't answer. He would have to drive over there, but he was too damn tired.

He left the shirt and the peanut shells in the trunk of the car and lay down just for a second on the living room couch.

And then it was Monday morning.

Esmé still didn't answer.

He called the office. "Denise, my mother's ill."

"You have Mr. Antoniou at one!"

"Yeah, okay. Can you take the group of drawings on my desk and get them copied this morning? I made a few last-minute changes. Sorry."

"Oh, man. That'll cost extra for a rush job. You're coming, though?"

"I'll be there."

"Because Martin's here and he's had a bad night and he's rampaging around waiting for you." She lowered her voice. "But screw him. I'll take care of him."

"Thanks, Denise. You're a real—"

"Friend. You have quite a few here, Ray."

He took twenty minutes to shave and get dressed, then called Detective Rappaport.

"Been trying to call you," Rappaport said. "What's wrong with your cell phone?"

"Why?"

"We checked on your bank account and found an ATM withdrawal, Mr. Jackson. From nine days ago."

"Yes. I got the statement. That's one of the things I wanted to tell you."

"We have the videotape from the ATM machine for that date."

"Is it Leigh?"

"We can't tell. You may be able to help."

"What do you mean, you can't tell?"

"Don't shout, Mr. Jackson. It's hard to identify the person. The tape is not the best quality."

"I guess this is a case now."

"An investigation has been opened."

"I found some things at the cabin at Idyllwild. They're in the trunk of my car."

"What?"

"I'll bring them in."

"I'm sending a car over to get you. What have you got?"

"Don't send a car. I'll get there as soon as I can."

Back inside the Porsche with its candy wrappers on the passenger side floor and the scent of Kat's floral cologne, he decided that if this kept up he would need a bigger car, since this one had somehow become familiar as a second home. Unfortunately, the amount of time he had spent cleaning up his living room forced him into competition with every commuter on the planet earth, or so it seemed.

The Boxster crawled through a long morning's heat.

An hour and a half later, when his mother still did not answer her doorbell in hot, smoggy Whittier, he used his key to get into the house.

He looked around in astonishment. She obviously hadn't lifted a finger to clean in days. Wine bottles, several, sat or lay on the kitchen counter and floor. Lipstick-edged glasses decorated most of the tables she usually kept dust-free and gleaming.

A wretched scenario played itself out, unfurling like a movie in his mind. Tipped over the edge by Ray's investigations into their past life, she had waited into the night, driven to his house over the limit, then drawn out her misery with alcohol when he did not appear.

He checked out the bathroom and glanced into the darkened bedroom. She had dropped a glass there and had not bothered to pick up the pieces. She wasn't home.

This late on Monday morning, Esmé must be at her cash register at Granada's, although how in the world she dragged herself in considering the state she must be in was beyond him. He set to work restoring order to her kitchen and living room, moving glasses into the sink and finding a paper bag in which to put the wineglass shards.

He found bread and made himself toast, then cleaned up the crumbs, emptied out old milk, and wiped down the refrigerator, which also appeared neglected. Checking the time, he tried to estimate when she might finish her shift. He knew they constantly jockeyed around on shifts;

she complained about it sometimes. He had arrived at about ten a.m. She worked six to eleven a.m. on Mondays.

Fishing out his cell phone, he called the market. Glenn, a coworker, said, yes, Esmé was scheduled for that shift. He hadn't seen her, but that didn't mean anything because he'd just arrived. Did Ray want him to find her and put her on the phone?

He hung up, needing to decide what he wanted to say.

Laying his hands on the old Formica surfaces, he considered Esmé's stubborn refusal to let him upgrade the place. It looked the same as it had when they had moved there when he was twelve. She had painted the back wall of her main room mauve, and mauve it remained. The gold wall-to-wall carpet had experienced different looks, as she did not seem opposed to using new area rugs here and there, but even the Danish modern furniture she liked because it was light and easy to move stayed roughly in the same place it had been in when Ray had learned to play chess on that very same glass-topped, rounded, wooden-edged coffee table so many years ago.

He sat for a few minutes, numb. His mind turned, like a mole digging toward air, toward the old houses, the tapes, the voice on the tapes. The model of the house on Bright Street, unfinished in his basement.

The thought struck him: I will never get it right, never get any of it right. The dark stain on the shirt in his trunk seemed to spread out through a crack in the trunk, spread along the driveway and into Esmé's house, into his heart. At this rate, he'd never get through the day, and he had chosen to keep going, for a while at least. He needed something to occupy him while he waited for Esmé.

Finally he remembered the old albums. Where might she keep them? A tall bookcase held stacks of magazines and paper digests with short stories, her favorite reading. He began an exploration of the house, something he almost never did. Esmé liked her privacy. She demanded it, in fact, and he couldn't remember the last time he had been in her bedroom, but he remembered a case with glass doors. Maybe she kept the albums in there? That seemed possible. In previous houses, she had kept them in her bedroom.

In the dimness, he could perceive almost nothing. The curtains in her room were closed. He flipped on the light to see everything much the same as it had been in his childhood except for fresh bedding in tones of rose, black, and beige to match the walls and new curtains. She had left the bed unmade. Incredible!

Uncomfortable at the sight, he tossed the comforter over the messy sheets. He found the bookcase, browsed the titles, these slightly more substantial, probably helpful in getting his mother to sleep on nights when she couldn't sleep. Still no albums. He slid into the mood he went into at the old houses he had been entering. That perfume atomizer of ancient Chanel No. 5; she never used it and had kept it on her dresser for as long as he could remember.

Her closet door stood open, and up on a top shelf, six large decoupaged boxes sat in a row. They could hold shoes or—anything. He pulled them down, placing them on her bed. He opened the first one. Scarves and belts, neatly rolled. The second held tax records neatly labeled and bundled in rubber bands. With the third he hit pay dirt. Old photographs, an accumulation of memories, private ones. He had never seen these before.

"What the hell is going on here?" His mother stood in the door to her bedroom, hands on her hips.

Ray, saying nothing, plucked the pictures from Esmé's bed, replacing them in the box neatly. He didn't know what order the pictures originally took, so he made up an organization on the spot based on whether the pictures were black and white or faded color or brilliant color. That should constitute a kind of rough chronology.

His mother watched, saying nothing.

He placed the box neatly between two other boxes on the shelf in her bedroom, then closed the closet doors.

"All done?" she asked.

He straightened the bed, then straightened himself. "Yeah."

"Follow me."

He followed her into the living room where she opened a case that held many bottles of wine and poured herself a plastic tumbler. She didn't offer him any. He didn't sit down, though she arranged herself in her favorite chair. He had never before noticed this look she had now, a glower, like hot ash.

"You're okay?" he said, folding his arms.

"Dandy."

"You came to my house, and you were sick."

She stared him down. "I'm fine now."

"I can't figure it out," he said. "Just to start with: you're drinking?"

"I drink."

"Huh. You never have, in my experience."

He watched in amazement and disapproval as she drank the wine down like water. It seemed to make her angrier.

"You're here to collect the Holy Grail, aren't you, son?"

"The Holy Grail?" he asked.

"Christ drank from it at the Last Supper. I'm guessing the imagery had to do with a holy vessel that held important information, or at the very least, holy water." To his surprise, she went on to quote Tennyson. " 'Three angels bear the holy Grail: With folded feet, in stoles of white on sleeping wings they sail.' " She poured herself more wine and glared at him.

"Mom, nobody cares about that old stuff. I want to know why you came to my house drunk, spent the night on my couch, and are here at your house now, nose red, eyes bloodshot, wrecked, not yourself. Mom?"

"I don't know where Leigh is. Do you believe that?"

He didn't disbelieve her. Why should she know? He couldn't imagine how she might. "What about the rest of what's going on? The recordings? Our very screwy past? I really thought—well, Mom, you came to my house. I presume you have things to tell me."

"I have only one thing to tell you."

"Shoot."

"I want my keys back, Ray. Give them to me. I want you

out of my home right now. I don't want you coming here without my permission ever again."

He took the keys to her house and handed them to her. She set them somberly on a side table in a small Italian plate she had bought at a flea market, blue and orange, flowery.

"I think you ought to see a doctor," Ray said. "Let me take you."

"I'm fine. Go home."

"You're not yourself."

He didn't like the way she laughed. "Oh, but I am," she said. "Go on, now. The moment has passed."

24

Outside, climbing into his car, Ray felt his mother's eyes on him from behind her curtains. Even though she had demanded it, he imagined she must have hated his relinquishing the keys. This left her alone. Accelerating, backing out, heading in to work, Ray thought, you couldn't feel good about that, being entirely alone. She was definitely ill—he should march in there and have it out and make her go with him—but there was Antoniou.

He decided to check on her by phone right after the meeting. He would pretend nothing had happened. She'd like that. She'd be feeling sorry by then.

"Did you call?" Kat's voice on the cell phone. He was approaching the big cloverleaf that led toward the beach communities. "I want to know how it went with Rappaport."

Kat must have heard his groan over the phone. "What's happened?"

"I haven't seen Rappaport yet. A couple more hours. I talked to him on the phone—"

"This can't wait! It's been more than twenty-four hours since we turned up that shirt! I'm going to call the police myself."

"I'm on my way. No need." That calmed her.

"Did something else happen?"

"I drove to Whittier to check on my mother. She poured herself two glasses of wine at eleven in the morning, and she kicked me out. Not to mention what she did last night at my house."

"Tell me," Kat said.

He told her.

"We're all disintegrating."

"Ah yes, Inspector Clouseau. That's it, undoubtedly."

Kat seemed to ponder on the other end of the line, unfazed by his sarcasm. "Does she like Leigh?"

"I think so. What has that got to do with anything?"

"You don't know for sure?"

"I thought she did."

"Did she love her, though? Maybe she's suffering, too, because she's worried."

"I can't understand this thing with the liquor. It's not like her."

"Leave her alone today," Kat advised.

"But what if she falls? She's all alone."

"Jesus, Ray. Maybe you're suffocating her with your dependency."

"She's the one who depends on me."

"Really?"

"I have to go."

"Wait. Listen, I got an idea. I want to go and talk to Mr.

Hubbel again. Leigh's father. But not with Mrs. Hubbel around. It's all I know to do, Ray. I'm going to Whittier right after work."

"What's he going to tell you?"

"I don't know. But he's her father. Maybe he'll remember something. Wanna come with me?"

"I can't think about it right now."

"Okay. Do what you have to do."

Achilles Antoniou arrived promptly at one p.m., bursting through the conference room door without introduction. He looked hungover but his tan had deepened and the jeans and deck shoes were so new and so covered with fancy logos, he was still an ad for the good life after fifty.

"Where's Martin?" was his question.

Martin had left the office at noon after another argument, so Ray just said, "Martin's late. Let's get started."

Antoniou reared back as if attacked. "I need to see Martin."

Ray tried hard not to react to the contempt in his voice. "Come on over and sit down, my friend. Have some coffee. You came to me originally because you thought I had something. You thought I understood what you wanted."

Antoniou shuffled from foot to foot. He allowed himself to be led to the couch and took the excellent coffee.

"Let's chat a little," Ray said. "Drink some coffee. I'm sure Martin will be here any minute. I've been looking forward to showing you the playroom. The plans are right here on the table and we can look at them in a minute. I added some great new touches last night. I'm working hard for your approval, Achilles. That's some boat you have, by the way. It's got those clean modern lines, you know?"

"It's a nice boat."

"I admit I was surprised when you came back with Martin and asked for a specific design, nothing like what we discussed. I didn't want to embarrass you in front of Martin, Achilles, but the whole Greek Mediterranean thing—save it for Greece, you know? The style is so out of it here in L.A. Spielberg's doing modern. Weinstein's doing modern. You know what Niarchos's son is doing with his new place in Bel Air, Achilles?"

"Modern?"

"That's it. You're smart to know that. I'm here to save you from a serious mistake. Big money down the tubes. I've got a set of plans here that are gonna knock the socks off the Spielbergs and Niarchoses. Make them raze their own places and start over. They're gonna be shit-jealous, Achilles.

"You have the opportunity on that site to make something beautiful for you and your family, something that's going to be famous for its beauty. Why not open yourself up to the potential of the site? You'll need a bigger gathering space. Welcome the ocean spray and a lot of movers and shakers onto your new, expansive, gorgeous deck. Hey, come on over here." He gestured toward the rosewood conference table. "I know you're gonna be pleased once you really look at these plans. I don't know anybody more open-minded than you are. Even Spielberg, he's gonna be a step behind you now."

Checking his watch one more time, Antoniou stepped in closer, intrigued. He studied the plans.

"I know you were impressed by what you've read about me, Achilles, but I'm going to tell you something. I had a revelation recently about what a home is, and we have a chance here to make it happen in a way that's going to explode people's ideas, not just about architecture, but about life."

"That's a big promise, Ray," Antoniou said.

"Something entirely new. Your dream house, a template for the next movement in architecture. The whole world's gonna want to see it. Movie stars, the works."

That got him. He leaned down, studying the plans beside Ray.

"But where are the walls?" he said urgently. "Where is the line between the kitchen and the entertainment area?"

"Fluidity, you see? Walls that move wherever you need them to move, not just the inside ones, but many of the outside ones. They raise, they lower. They cuddle up to make a big space cozy for a few people. They expand space infinitely. Slate decks off each floor. Imagine waves crashing below, that salty air. This place will flow out of the landscape and the landscape will flow into it. This home will change and grow along with you and your family in the most unimaginably creative ways."

Ray went into a place he loved, an imaginary place. Antoniou followed along.

Ray had Antoniou's signature on the new drawings by one-fifty-five, and ushered the client out the door.

At two sharp, Martin was back from lunch.

"You got Suzanne to lie." Martin was furious. "You said the meeting was at two, you bastard. You spent the time selling him on your insane notions."

"No, Martin. I spent the time explaining insanely beautiful possibilities to him. Believe me, he left happy."

"Garbage. You finessed him."

"Like you finessed him? In my opinion, I straightened him out."

"He's our biggest client!" Martin, by now bursting blood vessels in his face, shouted. "I didn't finesse him, I tried to do what he wanted. Why, oh, why can't you give him what he wants?"

"He wants special. He wants unique. I'll give him that and I will make this firm famous beyond anything you ever dreamed."

"You're an egomaniac, Ray! You want to ruin us?"

"All you care about is the money. Art doesn't enter into it. You think so small, Martin. So puny. You cheat on your wife and family. You've forgotten what it means to be honest and true. You've forgotten what it means to be a man, or a creative professional."

"It's about Leigh!" Martin shouted.

"Don't even speak her name! You want to take this outside?"

"And have you pound on me again?"

"Then let's discuss this."

Martin tried to fight him with words, but Ray, sure of himself for the first time in a long time, refused to engage. Martin hated him and his ideas; he hated Martin and his ideas.

The clarity of this notion burst on them both at the same time.

"I guess we've come to a parting of the ways, Martin," Ray said, after more futile discussion.

"What? Is that what you're leading up to? You're leaving? You're nothing without me. You need me to sell your so-called visionary bullcrap to an unsuspecting public!"

"Actually, I explained to Antoniou that this might be in the works, but he was so excited about my ideas by then, well, he didn't care, Martin. He really wants me to design this house, and I regret that you didn't have enough faith in me to back me when I most needed backing."

Maybe Martin would have a regret or two himself, Ray thought after Martin had banged the door shut on his way out, and Ray began packing boxes, pinging and panging here and there about the things he had to leave behind. He took three trips out of his office, all the while stalking past Martin, who stood, frowning, hands in his pockets. Suzanne had already spread the news; staffers came and went, some just checking it out, some wishing him well. But Martin stayed the whole time.

"You make quite the statement, Ray" was all he said.

Ray lugged boxes out, understanding that Martin felt nervous about the contents of the boxes, but also understanding he could not figure out how to interrupt this process without risking another pop on that cleft chin of his.

The final box stuffed into the trunk of his car, the bagged shirt and peanut shells now sitting on the passenger seat beside him like an accusation, he twisted the key. The car roared to life.

Pounding at the window.

What the hell?

He let the window down.

"Oh, honey. Don't think you're leaving without me." Denise was smiling like the brave little creative professional she was. "Give me a second to go steal some pertinent drawings and files. I'm going where you're going."

"I have no plan."

"It's okay. I'll help you with that." Denise came back in five minutes, finished filling up the trunk of the Boxster, leaned in the window again, pulled out a business card, eyed it like someone paying attention, then said, "New name."

"What?"

"Bell Jackson."

"Oh, Denise, no. I can't offer anything like the benefits Martin's got lined up, at least not yet."

She didn't care, she informed him. She would go where he went because, and he felt the first joy in a long time hearing this. Ray had a vision, he was the talent in the firm.

"My ideal is to be a full partner in two years. Martin would never let that happen. He's so greedy, Ray. He wants to retire at fifty. Did you know that?"

"What's that got to do with your promotion?"

"He has his own agenda, and I don't fit it. Makes me sad for myself. He's got two protégés, neither one of whom is me. I want to go where you're going. What do you say, Jackson-Bell Associates? Now, doesn't that sound fine!"

He couldn't help laughing.

She smiled, and two dimples popped out in her cheeks. "You might not like hearing this, but all these years with Martin have rubbed off on you. You've become quite the salesman these days. You sold me as well as Antoniou."

He sent her home to draw up a business plan for Jackson-Bell Associates.

And he finally went to see Rappaport.

Kat had a house in Hacienda Heights to assess. She could make Whittier her last stop fairly easily.

After surveying the Hacienda Heights house, standard three bedroom but lacking that all-important second bath, she drove to Whittier, to Franklin Street. Whoever had bought their old house after their mother sold it had kept the paint on the house gray and white, just like it had been when she had lived in the place decades before. Strange. It had reverted to its true nature.

Across the street at the Hubbels' Spanish-style mansion, the curtains were closed. No cars. No telling if they were around on this windless, eye-stinging hazy day. The green, anomalous yard made her think about the high desert past Idyllwild. Southern California was just a continuation of the Mexican Mojave, and the sooner they started living like the desert-dwellers they were, the later the basin would run out of water.

Kat sat in the Echo, parked on the curb of the wooden-frame house she had grown up in, across the street from the house Leigh had grown up in, sipping a Fresca, playing with her cell phone.

No one came in or out of her own old house for a while, then a boy aged maybe twelve blasted out the front door. He propped his skateboard against the thirties glass brick flanking the entryway, fiddling with a helmet. She prayed, since apparently his parents were unavailable to pray, that he did not plan to go down the steep hill. Surely, at ninety miles an hour toward the bottom, he would die when he hit the busy intersection below.

He finally got the strap attached, then headed up a side street toward the college. She let out a long relieved breath. Then she called Ray again, who did not answer.

Lights came on in her old house. Panicked parents? She wished she could reassure them. "Your son went up the hill, not down." Instead, she called Ray one more time. This time, he answered.

"I'm in Whittier," she said. "The house looks empty. Did you see Rappaport?"

"He's got the shirt. I'm not sure what they think but I should get a lawyer," he said. "I think they're going to arrest me and it won't be long. He thinks the shirt is important."

Thinks she's dead and I did it was what Kat heard.

"He listened to everything I had to say about Idyllwild

and the reservation. He taped it and said he'd be back in touch about it. He's got your phone number and he wants to see you, too. And—"

"But what?"

"He showed me the bank video of the ATM withdrawal. He was very interested in seeing if I could identify Leigh. I saw a person hiding under a watch cap and sunglasses. I saw someone who was nobody or who was anybody."

"Damn it! Was it Leigh or not? Could it have been her? Can't you recognize your own wife? The way she moves? Her nose? You really couldn't recognize her?"

"Could have been Leigh! Could be you!" he said. "It was just a feeling."

"What?"

"That it was her."

"You had a feeling it was her?"

"Just a movement—something. Like—I don't know."

Was he lying? "So what are the cops going to do?" she asked.

"He says Leigh's been gone ten days and it's a matter of concern and he is assigned to it. He's going to see Leigh's parents and go to Leigh's office. It's really starting now, Kat. And he asked me again if I knew where she is. What's your plan right now?"

"I'm just sitting here. A fool on a hill. I don't know where the Hubbels went."

"Let's see, it's almost six. He walks his dog at Penn Park after he gets off duty. He's done it for years. It's a beagle. I'll bet that's where he is," Ray said again. "He stays out there feeding the ducks and cooling off from his job until sunset. I'm coming out. Wait for me."

"But you said—"

"I called my mother right before I called you and she picked up and then she hung up on me. So I know she's physically okay. Let's do this together. I need to have it out with him anyway."

25

On a summer's eve, the lingering heat of the day drifting romantically around like incense, the sun glowing, no other word for it, people in Penn Park had a right to feel superior to most other folk. They had their kids, their steaks and barbecue sauce, their dogs, and their greensward. Greensward—Ray loved that word. Up the grassy hill, couples kissed in that golden light and ducks quacked along the slow-moving creek that ran through the center of the park.

They stepped through air thick with the sweetness of blooming flowers over boulders and dips in the path.

Leigh had grown up close to Penn Park. She had told him about the summer programs and the heat, and how much she longed for those lengthy days to come again when she had no needy clients coming after her, no deadlines to work her up.

"We spun on the merry-go-round," she said. "Oh, you have no idea how hot it used to get, how dizzy we got. We fell on the ground. It tasted sweet, the dirt."

His memories of heat mostly involved bungalows without air-conditioning, the air so tight it choked you.

He remembered Penn Park only vaguely, like Disneyland, a one-time event, magical, hazy. Why hadn't Esmé brought him more often when they lived on Bright Street? He really didn't know. Maybe she was too busy working, trying to keep them fed.

"They had craft programs. I learned how to weave a plastic bracelet. Kat and I brought our dolls here and made a whole world for them. And if we forgot them, the lantana made a pretty hoop-skirted doll."

Searching for James Hubbel, Ray and Kat strode into the swing area. Ray found himself amazed at how high these swings seemed to be. He sat down on one. Kat shoved him hard, and he flew.

"You see him there?" Kat muttered, because James Hubbel stood in the nearby meadow while his dog crouched only a few dozen yards away from them.

"Yeah." Ray slowed to a stop.

"He didn't even bag it!" Kat said, outraged.

"I imagine the minute he arrived in the park with a dog he was breaking rules."

"Well, people shouldn't—"

"Listen, Kat. I want you to stay right here."

"What? It was my idea."

"Haven't you ever noticed how much harder it is to speak from the heart when there're more than two people talking?"

Still holding on to the swing's chain, she gulped. "Well, okay. True."

"So I'm going to talk to him."

"I have a more friendly connection. He remembers me, Ray. I knew him when I was a kid."

While they argued in whispers, a couple of kids screamed by them, fighting over a bouncing ball. "Gimme."

"No, you gimme!"

Before the fight ended up deadly, a graybeard picked one up by the neck of her shirt, like a tomcat lifts a kitten. "It's her turn," he said firmly, then carried the kicking child back to the red gingham-covered picnic table. "Your mom has a hot dog for you, if you can shut your mouth long enough to open it."

The child shut up and stuffed her face with a hot dog loaded with mustard. The child who had won the ball returned and sat across from her. The two little girls made ugly faces at each other. They tossed fries and competed as to how much ketchup.

"He thinks I killed his daughter," Ray said quietly. "He needs to talk with me." He got off the swing and walked toward Hubbel.

Kat let him go. She sat down on the swing and watched.

"Here, Marley. C'mere, boy!" Hubbel had let the dog off the leash. Marley chased a little boy. The boy's father arrived, purple-faced, to chastise Hubbel, who apologized, although not profusely. Once the beagle finally decided to come back, he was spoken to in a mild but firm tone. "You're a bad boy and you know it," Hubbel told it, snapping the dog's collar to his nylon tether. "You know we love you but you're a bad boy." Like all bad parents, he gave the dog a good petting, and even a kiss on his head.

"Hello, Jim," Ray said.

Hubbel, clearly startled, jumped up and examined him. "What the hell are you doing here?"

"I used to come here years ago."

"Nostalgia strikes me funny coming from a man your age."

"I came here once with Leigh."

"Have you heard from her?"

"No."

"No," he repeated. He shook his head, and Ray saw him as a father who was sick with worry about his daughter.

Ray said, "I know you are angry and suspicious of me right now."

"Damn straight I am. I just had a talk with Detective Rappaport about you."

"I want to show you—explain—that I'm looking for Leigh. I'm worried, too."

Marley, snuffling in a hedge, pulled his owner a few feet. Hubbel followed, as if he didn't know what else to do under the circumstances, and Ray fell into step beside him.

"Tell me more about this shirt you found up there," Hubbel said. Ray went over it carefully. When he was finished, Hubbel said, "I don't know if you're trying to help or if you're destroying evidence. The trunk of your car! Don't you watch cop shows?"

"All I know is, I'm looking now, Jim."

"You're really looking for her?"

"I should have gone looking a lot earlier," Ray said. Hubbel took this in. They entered a narrow path, deserted, between rosebushes.

Ray heard a sound like a sob. Hubbel had stopped and turned his back to him. He found himself patting the beefy shoulder of his father-in-law.

"I'm sorry," he said. "I can't swear it's her on the videotape. I can't promise you she was all right at that time."

"It's her mother. She seems to have given up on everything. When she heard about the shirt, she broke down. She is sure Leigh is dead. I don't know what to think about this video, whether it's a hopeful sign. I've been a cop a long time, and when girls go missing like this, the news is usually bad. Ray. Swear to me—swear you didn't—"

"I swear, Jim."

Hubbel looked hard at him. "Okay," he said. "I want to help. Anything." He continued to keep his opinions in reserve, though.

"I came to talk to you about the cabin."

"Ask me anything." They kept walking, the little dog keeping to the side, sniffing at the flower beds.

"Has she ever gone there on her own, to get away for a while, as a refuge?"

"No. I don't think so. I don't think she liked it much. Maybe there is a ghost scaring people away. I don't think anyone will ever buy it. This rumpled-up T-shirt you found. You're right, it's odd."

"If it's hers—if she went to the cabin, where could she be heading?"

Hubbel rubbed his mouth. "If Leigh was in charge—"

He stopped and the dog looked back at him. "I would think Palm Springs. She used to rave about a trip she took there a few years ago. She ever tell you about that?"

"No."

"Oh, I guess she wouldn't because she went there with her old boyfriend."

"Tom Tinsley?"

Eyebrows raised, Hubbel said, "You know about him?"

"You know I do."

Leigh's father shrugged. "Yeah, well, she and Tommy stayed at the Blue Sky Motel and took a hike in Borrego Springs. She wanted us to go see the waterfalls at the end—you know how Leigh gets sometimes. We don't go out to the desert, though. My wife can't take the heat."

The park lamps came on suddenly.

"Here comes night," Hubbel said conversationally. "Let's sit down. I'm walked out." They sat on a low brick wall against a viney hillside. They had walked deep into the forested part of the park and were alone.

Hubbel, stroking the dog, who had his head back and eyes half-closed in pleasure, sighed, and Ray suddenly realized how much emotion James was suppressing. He kept turning his head away, swiping at his nose. He was like a big old dog himself, wary, with that barrel chest. "You and Leigh ever talk about having a baby?"

"Yes."

"You don't volunteer much, Ray."

"I didn't want a baby."

"Oh. That cause problems?"

"And the thing is, I'd love to have a child. But I didn't

think I'd make a good father. Didn't trust myself. Leigh had no doubts."

"Doubt's like a pesticide in a marriage. Kills the love. You should trust her."

Ray felt an intense longing to talk to Leigh. There was so much to say.

"You're some schmucky kid, then you have a baby, you know? Oh, I guess you don't. But let me fill you in on the parenting thing. It's like getting hit by a semitruck on the interstate, a horrible surprise. You don't know how to cope with this emergency. You're thrust into a new world of disability. You can't go out at night to dance, to dream, to drink. You can't even sleep, for Chrissake."

Hubbel said, "I never got my degree from Cal. She ever tell you that?"

"No."

"Yes." Leigh's father petted the dog below him who circled twice, then plopped down directly on his feet. "Studied criminal justice with the help of the G.I. Bill."

"She never said, Jim."

"I married her mom in my sophomore year because we were going to have a little girl. I got a steady job. I'm a good deputy. I'd rather be on the street than sitting behind a damn desk anyway. I don't regret my life, but I wanted Leigh to be safe, to have a skill. I wanted her husband, when she married, to have a good degree."

"Uh-huh."

Hubbel smiled. "You don't get why I'm saddling you with this ancient history."

"Not really. No."

"Then she had to go and fall in love with Tom Tinsley." Hubbel pushed the dog off his feet. In the glimmering twilight, in the distant bursts of light from the park's lampposts, children screamed and played. Ray wondered if Kat was eavesdropping.

"It went on for years. He used to eat dinner with us. My wife liked him. He seemed like a nice enough kid. But we had issues. Tommy was—nice didn't make him a good match. He had no direction. No drive. He wanted to be an actor. He would have made a good truck driver, if he had lived. You know he drowned himself?"

"Not the details." Ray could no longer read his expression, but he heard Hubbel breathe deeply.

"You know, I smoked for thirty years. I miss it every day, even though I know it was making my lungs black and tarry. It was right about then, when I was trying to quit, that I had a little talk with Tom. I couldn't stand how much I missed smoking. I thought about it every minute, night and day, until my wife sent me packing to the park. That's when I got the habit of coming here every day," he said. He laughed humorlessly. "I'm not excusing myself, I was mean as hell for a while. That's just how it was."

"He met you here, at the park?"

Hubbel nodded. "It was earlier. A really hot afternoon in the summer. Smog like today. Anyway, he and Leigh had had a dustup. A bad one. He looked miserable. He'd been crying, I don't know."

"Puffy eyes?"

"Yeah. She had met you. He was afraid he was going to lose her."

Ray looked around the park at the pools of light the lamps created, at the extended families still eating barbecue, laughing, some shouting slightly drunkenly. Life at its best, in a way. The best part of Los Angeles, a homey warmth here in this suburban park named for William Penn, the peacemaker. "What did you tell him?"

"It seemed like my chance to get rid of him once and for all. First, I talked to her. Then I told him—" Hubbel smoothed the leg of his corduroy shorts. "Don't come around my daughter anymore. Told him he was finished."

"And?"

"She had another man lined up. A better man. She had told him, too, but Tom was crushed. I saw that and I ignored it. You know, I never told my wife any of this. To this day, she doesn't know what I said to that guy. I don't know which of you Leigh would have ended up with. She still loved him, I think. I pushed her very hard."

Ray tried to see Hubbel's eyes, but could not make them out. The dog made satisfied dreaming sounds, the equivalent of a cat purring.

"Yeah, I told him to fuck off. I told him all about you, Ray. How much she loved you. How you were gonna be a big man. A rich professional. The man could see I was moving him out and Leigh had done the same. All for you, Ray. We believed in you."

"He died that night," Ray guessed.

"He folded. Gave up." Hubbel patted his pocket as if seeking phantom cigarettes.

"Leigh must have felt like she killed him," Ray said. "You should have told her about this a long time ago. You could have taken some of the burden off her, done something for her I couldn't."

"We all better take some responsibility now," Hubbel said. "I'll keep pushing law enforcement, but I won't push 'em down your throat anymore. I can't say I'm sure you hurt her. I just don't know. They need to widen the search. You work with them, Ray. You promise me. I'll let you know if I think of anything else."

Ray shook his hand. It turned into a bear hug. It felt like they were clinging to each other, because they couldn't cling to Leigh.

26

Kat hovered above the stream, looking down at the black water. So she hadn't followed them.

Ray flicked a flashlight onto her face.

"Turn that off."

"What's that in your hand?"

"A chicken drumstick from the Colonel I picked up en route."

"Got any more?"

"In the Echo." They walked back toward the parking lot, down the pathway past the shrill, tired children on the monkey bars, past the flushed faces of the men at the barbecues, and climbed into Kat's car, which smelled like a restaurant, rolling down the windows to the cool of evening. Ray felt ravenous. He seized a piece of chicken and began to eat.

Kat gave him thirty seconds. Then, "What did he tell you?"

"Two important things," Ray said, wiping his mouth with a napkin. "I want to know exactly what happened between you and your brother the last day of his life. Can you stand to go through it with me?"

She frowned. "Why?"

"It has to do with Leigh. Our marriage. Our problems. Why she left."

"It was more than six years ago. What could it have to do with your marriage?"

Ray said half to himself, "It must get worse over time. You don't forget. It grows inside you."

"What?"

"Guilt. It's a poison, like doubt."

"You're tellin' me," Kat said, her voice shaky.

He put a gentle hand on her arm. "I wouldn't ask if I didn't think it was important."

She started off slowly. "They had an argument. Tom called me, and I finally agreed to meet him for lunch, even though things were really busy at work and I didn't really have the time to waste. We went to a Tastee-Freez on Pacific Coast Highway." She paused.

"The day he died?"

"Right. He told me Leigh had broken up with him. Well, you know, I saw it coming. Leigh told me she was getting discontented. She had someone new. That would be you, Ray. People our age, in our late twenties, broke up every day. Women complained in the coffee rooms about their ne'er-do-well boyfriends. They had so many issues. And I, well, at that point I had no boyfriend at all. I was working so hard, trying to find my own way. It just didn't seem to matter so much. Tom had a hundred girlfriends before Leigh."

"But nobody after her." For a moment or two, they both stared into the dark trees.

"He wanted to talk. He had to go over each detail over and over and it didn't seem to matter what I said, it didn't help him. I had been invited to go to a party at a coworker's who lived in a big fancy house in Hollywood. I rarely got invited to do anything social, particularly anything that involved wearing something new and cute, so I was resentful."

"But he insisted you stay."

"He said I was the only person he could tell it all to, because I knew Leigh so well. Really, a lot of it was, What did she say about me? How does she really feel? Do you think I could get her back? Those kind of questions. Over and over. He said I owed him because of the time he covered for me when I rolled through the ground-floor window drunk and when the folks asked about it, he told them I had the flu. I owed him for the many times he saved my ass. And that was true."

"But."

"He said, Forget the damn party. Come with me to the beach. I didn't want to go. I wanted to go to a party, and I was just—just—thinking of myself and my own concerns, okay? I didn't want to get involved in this shit between him and Leigh.

"He said it had to be the beach. And I'm afraid of the beach at night. Strange people come out and they're messed up and they want to get friendly. And I'd be stuck with my younger brother crying over Leigh and no way to get away if it got to be too much. And I was upset because I felt like Tom was hurting my friendship with Leigh.

I was very torn between the two of them. Too much complication!"

One of those summertime squalls had come up, and rain spattered the windshield. Any local understood this traumatic event might last maximum fifteen minutes. Kat didn't even turn on her wipers. Ray wolfed down French fries while Kat went on soberly, "He said to me, 'Oh, promise you'll never tell anyone what I'm about to say!' He asked me, 'What would you do if I decided to kill my-self?' "

Ray said nothing.

"You know what I said?"

She made fists with her hands, covered her mouth, and rocked back and forth. The words choked out of her. "I said, 'Try to forget you as quick as I can.' "

Ray said, "You were young."

"I was c-cruel and selfish. I'll never forget the look he gave me. His eyes. Oh, God."

"How did he die, Kat?"

"He dropped me back at work and he drove back to his apartment in Newport. He drank some and wrote notes." She recited, " 'Don't blame yourself, Kitty-kat, for me cav-ing in to sentimentality and tomfoolery.' You see, he was joking around, even when he was letting go of his pre-cious, precious life. He complimented me on my jacket that day, too, before things got so heavy."

"Oh, Kat. Don't cry."

"He left the notes under a vase of irises he had in his kitchen. He must have been pretty drunk. His handwriting was worse than ever. Then there was Leigh's note. He quoted Yvor Winters, the poet. You know him?"

"No."

"The note started off quoting or paraphrasing him: 'Death. Nothing is simpler. One is dead.' Then he talked about loving Leigh, and how right everyone was, what a loser he was not to be able to hold on to the person he loved more than his own life. He said she tilted him cosmically, and he would never be the same, and he could not go on without her."

"Did Leigh see the note?"

"Of course. I'm sure it's branded on her soul."

"She said that he died. I knew it was suicide but she refused to discuss it."

"He must have waited until it was good and dark, and then gone back out to the beach. And he swam out, and out until he was too tired to swim back in. I often imagine it at night, so dark, cold water, phosphorescence maybe out past the breakers..."

Ray gave her a handkerchief. She cried into it then blew her nose.

"Tom's body washed ashore on the rocks at the tip of the peninsula. At the party, I panicked, and when I couldn't reach him by phone I went to his house. When I couldn't find him there, and saw those notes, I called the police. Beach Rescue started looking for him. Our darling Tommy. My darling brother."

Ray's right hand patted her knee. "A lot of things sent him out there," Ray said. "Not just you."

"Oh, it was me, all right. I put him over the edge. I

could have talked him out of it if I'd stayed with him, not been so cruel. Ray? Y'see, I have never told anyone about being at the beach earlier with Tommy. I couldn't stand to tell anyone. You're the very first person to hear this in six years. I don't even know why I'm doing it, but—anyway, I turned a lot of my misery on Leigh, tried to blame her instead. She was so hangdog, but I couldn't explain. I just couldn't. I let her think it was all her fault. That's why I couldn't talk to her all this time. Because I'm a liar and a phony."

They sat in silence. After a minute Ray said, "There's somebody else who talked to Tommy that afternoon. And he has been just like you, just like Leigh. Hugging his sins to himself, thinking he's a monster."

"What?"

Ray explained what Jim Hubbel had told him, adding, "He gave your brother facts. Facts register with guys. He made it seem as if it really was hopeless, and he was cutting about it."

"Are you trying to tell me that"—she leaned back against the car's headrest—"he thinks he's totally responsible?"

"Didn't you? Didn't Leigh? Now, you have to take this in. Your brother made the decision, not you. He talked to a lot of people. God knows what Leigh said to him. Maybe other friends. He put it all together. You didn't cause his death. Hell, I could take some of the blame myself. I was in love with Leigh, and I wanted the breakup, too."

"I sure helped."

"Maybe it's time to forgive yourself."

"I didn't take good care of him, you know? I guess I didn't know how. Oh, I hate never being able to clear things up with Leigh!"

"Maybe you'll get your chance."

"Huh?"

"Talk to Leigh about it. The other thing Jim said was that Leigh stayed at least once at the Blue Sky Motel in Palm Springs. I told him about Idyllwild and he told me about the place."

"Palm Springs! You think—you think—"

"Shall we go back to the police?"

"I say we go to Palm Springs. I think Leigh's dad is going to reflect on your conversation and follow up with the police."

Ray nodded. "I agree. But I can't go tonight. I have to check on my mother."

"But—"

"I have to. We'll both get a few hours of sleep and pack a bag this time. It's only a few more hours, Kat."

"I won't sleep at all," she said. "But, yeah, I'll leave a message at the office tonight. And I need to stop by and make sure my sister is okay. I'll gas up the Echo on my way back to Hermosa. Let's take the Echo."

"Why?"

"Because your expensive little toy only has two seats. If we're lucky, we'll need three. I'll pick you up before the traffic starts. Five a.m."

"Thatta girl," Ray said. "If you're driving, I'll come in from Topanga to your place. Five a.m. is fine." They looked at each other.

"It's all about taking better care of each other," Kat said. "Your mother, my sister. If we find Leigh, let's take better care of her, too."

"We could call," Ray said. Kat clapped her forehead and grabbed her cell phone. She had the Palm Springs number in another minute and had to punch out the number three times, her hand was shaking so much. When the clerk answered, she said, "Uh, may I please speak to Miss Hubbel?"

"Who?"

"Hubbel. Leigh Hubbel."

"Nobody here by that name."

"Tall, blonde girl. Please. This is important." But she had made a misstep saying that. The clerk's tone became suspicious. "I'm sorry, we don't give out information that way."

"But—please—"

"No one by that name is registered here." The line went dead. Miserably, Kat told Ray what he had said. "What if he tells her some strange woman was looking for her? Maybe she'll leave! I'll call back and ask him to leave her a message—"

"Leave who a message?" Ray said. "Anybody tallish and blondish around the place? Let's just get there and find out one way or another ourselves."

Kat meditated for half an hour on the bedroom rug. She felt unhurried afterward, prepared to accept whatever they found. She packed lightly, not a problem since she had very little clean.

In the kitchen, the phone message light blinked. She finally noticed it on the way to the fridge to try to find some old salad she had just remembered.

Zak!

"Hiya. Friday. We said Friday. Where are you, Kat? I waited. If you're like this before we even get to know each other—don't call me, baby. I won't be home." She picked up the phone and dialed his number. Voicemail.

Bad timing was how it felt, as if she had somehow skated right past Zak on the boardwalk of life. "I just can't find the time right now for us, Zak. I'm sorry."

27

R ay arrived in the predawn, well stubbled. He prowled her premises while she hit the bathroom, opening drawers, taking in the view from her deck, analyzing her architecturally. "You have to get some lamps," he said. "These overheads are disgusting. And the popcorn ceiling has to go."

"Quit that," she said as she came out.

Ray, at the moment immersed in studying the contents of her bookshelves, said, "You don't like me figuring you out."

"These things aren't me."

"You're the one who told me about how much you can learn from looking at people's homes. I spy with my little eye your dark side. No porn DVDs for this lady; no, you've got a much more embarrassing secret. You're a reader." He plucked a book from the shelf. "Hemingway?"

She smiled, caught in her own game. "Okay, Ray. I'll tell you about that guy and why I have this book of short stories. He stole everything that made him special from Gertrude Stein. You think that deceptively simple little style of his was original?"

"I could get into that with you another time." He put it back, then took out another. "Woolf?"

"Boring but so beautiful."

He placed the book back exactly where it had been, then turned to her. "I thought—men and bars."

"Them, too, sure, sometimes. After all, men're not all as patronizing as you."

"Is that what I am? Patronizing?"

Kat smiled. "Earnest and clueless, that's how you mostly are. But you seem to be trying, I'll give you that."

Kat wheeled her small suitcase to the front door while Ray stood at the window, admiring her tiny view of the Pacific. "You sit here at night and see the sun set. Here," he said, going through the sliding door and finding the spot on the balcony where he could best view the ocean. "You watch the day end."

"Yep, that's what I do," she said. "Now enough with the getting-to-know-Kat number. I'm ready."

He carried her bag down the stairs. Kat took a quick sip of coffee from her thermos and stifled a laugh, looking at her living room one last time before she went into the hall and locked up, seeing it from a stranger's point of view. The place wasn't trendy or enthusiastic or glam. It was stuffed with things, messy, and comfortable.

She fluffed her hair. There was a there there, that was the main thing.

They were almost to the San Bernardino Valley by the time the sun came up over the mountains. Kat stole a glance at Ray in his sunglasses, while she braked and maneuvered through a snake pit of semis, and wondered again what he expected to find. Paranoid scenario: he already knew they would not find Leigh, but his show of cooperation would keep Kat from suspecting him of hurting her.

It all could be a show. But she had been forgetting to keep her guard up, had even started to like him and hope for him as well as for herself. Tighten up, she told herself sternly.

At eight-thirty they found the motel on the edge of the ritzy desert oasis of Palm Springs. Yes, Kat thought, a person on the run might say I made it, and pull into the first motel with a Vacancy sign.

For here it was, the Blue Sky. The motel sprawled along a busy road, one story, adobe-colored, with Spanish arches and a tile roof, a fountain in front. The water was a nice touch, gurgling, faking an oasis.

Farther east there would be championship golf courses, pools, hotels, restaurants, shopping. Kat remembered the town as a compact, wealthy, sedate Vegas. Tuesday morning, and the only people going to work seemed to be Hispanic. The retirees would still be putting in the laps in their backyard pools.

They drove around the parking lot, looking for Leigh's minivan. Nothing. Driving past the corner market farther up the road, and up and down a couple of side streets, all they turned up was a guy washing his driveway with a hose—felonious waste of water. "We'll just have to get the room number somehow," Ray said as they parked under the portico. The external air temperature was eighty-seven degrees, according to the thermometer Velcroed onto the Echo's dashboard. The earth-withering heat slapped her down as she climbed out. "Ow." She flung her hand away from the car.

"Let me go in," Ray said.

She stood in the shade by the car, imagining a star drifting too close to the earth in a disaster movie and searing the landscape, blinding her through her shades and shriveling her skin. Ray negotiated with the clerk inside behind the barrier of glass, smiling, gesturing like a Napolitano. For somebody who hadn't communicated very well with his wife, Ray seemed to have a way of persuading people to go his way, so she waited and hoped.

When he came out, she said, "Well, is Leigh staying here or not?"

"He says no. He remembers your phone call. We're lucky to get rooms at all, he's so suspicious. Luckily the place isn't jammed full, it's a Tuesday in August, not exactly the best weather for a visit. He says it'll be ninety-nine by noon."

She examined his face and read nothing. "That's it? Aren't you disappointed?"

"We just got here. Keep your shirt on." He picked up his bag. "Got us communicating rooms at the corner, away from the traffic," he said, self-satisfied in the way guys were when they killed a deer with a rifle or made money on a stock. He handed her a card key. "Meet me at the coffee shop in ten minutes."

She walked along the concrete path in front of the third-floor rooms, second-floor rooms, first-floor rooms, cursing the efficient blinds. Now and then she caught a glimpse of motel life, a man sitting on the bed watching TV, loud noises of squabbling kids, a woman on the phone brushing her hair, heedless of the open window.

She wasn't Leigh, though, and Leigh wasn't in the standard-issue coffee shop. They showed the waitress her photo and got another look and a shrug.

They ate. Kat had a headache behind her eyes. She thought, another wasted trip, and this thought was very frightening, because the road seemed to end here at the motel. It seemed to Kat that if they didn't find Leigh here she would have to admit she was dead.

"If she's not using the coffee shop, I guess it's not much use to check out the pool," Ray said. "We can do that, though, and keep a watch on the rooms, and we can keep looking for her van."

"You think the clerk was lying?"

"I think the clerk was doing his job. Protecting people's privacy."

"After this we'll have to go home," Kat said.

The waitress gave him the check and he got out his credit card. As he was signing the bill, the door opened and the motel clerk came into the coffee shop. Waving a hand familiarly at the waitress, he zeroed in on their table and slid into the booth next to Kat. He was younger than she had imagined through the window, Latino, with large clear brown eyes, not hostile but not friendly, either.

"Why do you want this lady?" he said.

"Why do you care?" Ray said. "If she hasn't been here?"

"Curiosity. I keep track of cops traveling through. Do I need to watch out for her?"

"It's nothing like that," Ray said. "I'm her husband, just like I said."

"Who's she?" he said, motioning with his thumb toward his seatmate.

"I'm her sister," Kat said.

"Like I told you," Ray said.

"Still lying," the clerk said.

"How do you know I'm lying?"

"Because the lady I'm thinkin' of, she ain't got a sister."

Ray's mouth dropped open. "She's here?" Kat experienced a peculiar feeling in her chest. Hope, rising eternally. But she felt very fragile, as though she couldn't bear for this hope to be crushed, too. She and Ray looked at each other. The clerk was watching them.

"I didn't say that. There's a similar lady. I gave her a call. She said she had a husband, but no sister."

"Okay," Kat said. "Look, we shouldn't have tried to tell you a lie. I'm not her sister. It's true, she doesn't have a sister."

"Let me see your driver's license," he told Ray. Then, "And yours, too." Kat produced hers, and he looked them both over carefully. "Wait here," he said, and left.

Five minutes passed. The hum in the coffee shop

seemed to get louder. Kat was trembling; it was freezing in there and too brightly lit, and her headache was getting worse. She and Ray seemed to have lost the ability to speak. This is it, she kept saying to herself. One way or the other.

Just when she thought she couldn't bear one more second of this purgatory, she saw the clerk come in again. He plopped down and said, "This lady—she says she's willing to talk to you." He held up a hand. "Wait. That's all she said. She doesn't talk much. That's it. I don't know anything else."

"What's her name?" Ray said.

"Gale Graham."

"How long has she been here?"

"A while. Do you want the room number or not?"

"Is she—did you recognize her photo?"

"I can't say." He handed them a map of the complex, which turned out to be much larger than they had imagined from seeing its front, including two adjoining buildings. Building A hosted the overnighters. Another building, for monthly renters, held struggling young families receiving Section 8 funds from the government. Building C held what he called "executive suites" and were for paying clients who stayed a week or two.

"Here." He tapped a fingernail on room 116 of Building C. "Her room. First floor, by the pool. I'll be checking on her in an hour. And I made copies of your IDs. You know what I'm sayin'?"

Ray led the way. She followed him, step for rapid step, along the harsh white concrete walkways to Building C.

They arrived at 116. Two dried-out potted palms flanked the doorway. The sun was fierce on the concrete. When Ray didn't knock but stood, hanging back off the walkway like someone who did not belong, Kat knocked firmly.

No answer.

She tried the doorbell.

Again, nothing.

Then, like a chapter starting up in a children's story, the door opened.

28

L eigh stood there, in a tank top, shorts, and running shoes, long hair in a ponytail.

Ray and Kat faced her uncertainly, but not for long. "You came for me!" she cried, leaping forward into Ray's arms. She buried her face in his shoulder. He held her tight, his eyes squeezed shut as if he was in pain.

Kat stepped back, dizzy, watching as they pressed against each other so hard they almost toppled over there in the entryway. Realizations tumbled through her mind. Leigh was alive. She had run away after all.

Ray hadn't murdered her. Ray was just Ray. The police, the suspicion—it amounted to nothing.

Leigh ran away, leaving them to search for her. She had caused so much pain—

But she was alive. Ray and Leigh held each other, then pulled apart enough to look at each other. Then there were a lot of kisses, more hugs. After a long, long time, the couple broke apart, and Kat took a good look at her lost friend. Taller than Kat remembered, older, pretty in a grave way in spite of dark circles around her eyes.

"Kat," Leigh said, her voice muffled, and her arm drew

Kat close. "You here? Incredible. Come in." They stepped out of the heat and into the arctic breeze of a Palm Springs motel room.

The room, slightly larger than most hotel rooms, had textured wallpaper, soothing green and white in an abstract fern pattern. Double-glass doors, at the moment standing ajar and letting in a river of superheated air, led out to a courtyard. Beyond low palms and succulents that fringed a flagstone walkway, the turquoise, freeform pool beckoned, the water reflections dancing on the ceiling of Leigh's room like something alive. The king-sized bed was unmade. A jumble of groceries was stacked on the desk, and the TV was on, muted. Leigh had been here awhile.

They stood in the room and stared at each other. Where should they start? With her frightening absence? With all the distrust, and the many changes?

"We thought something had happened to you," Kat said at last, her voice hoarse.

In a quiet voice, Leigh said, "I had decided to come home. I want you to know that. I'm ready to face—everything."

Ray and Leigh sat down on the edge of the bed together. He put his arm around his wife and held on tight. Kat took a chair by the door.

Ray said, "I'm so very, very sorry, Leigh. I didn't treat you right."

His wife shook her head. "No. No, darling. It wasn't you. I should have come straight home. I was confused and—hurt."

"I never should have—"

"I need you so much—" They fell together like drowning sailors, murmuring and sighing. Kat tried to restrain herself.

"Kat?" Leigh was examining her.

"Hey." Kat's voice felt less forceful than usual.

Leigh's eyes whipped between Ray and Kat and cruised back again, settling finally on her husband.

"Is this like—I take up with your best friend so you search for mine and hook up?" The corners of her mouth trembled, but turned up slightly. Kat realized she was joking, obviously as unsteady with the situation as they were.

Kat said, "Gee, Leigh, there was that ugly possibility that Ray might have killed you and buried you under a new swimming pool in Laguna or somewhere."

"What?"

"The police—your father called the police."

"Oh, no. I knew I should have called them. But—Dad's a police officer—it would have set things in motion—I couldn't—" Leigh stood and went over to Kat, put her hand on Kat's shoulder, and looked into her eyes wonderingly.

"When I—saw you both standing there in the doorway, I had the awful thought this was some kind of payback for Martin. I'm sorry. I'm—so surprised."

"I'm glad to see you," Kat said, and broke into a smile. "It's been a long time."

"I'm glad, too. It's so good to see you, Kat. I can't believe it."

"We joined forces to look for you."

Leigh's eyes welled. "I didn't expect that. I thought you both hated me."

"I never hated you, Leigh," Kat said. "Are you all right?"

"Not exactly. I mean, I'm not sick, if that's what you mean. But there have been times when I thought I might never come back. I just couldn't see my way out. I needed time."

"I don't give a shit about what happened with Martin anymore," Ray said. "And I swear, you don't have to run from me. I will never hurt you. I'm sorry if I scared you that night."

"Oh, my darling. Of course you would never hurt me! I didn't leave because of Martin. I didn't leave because you were so mad." She closed her eyes for a moment. Then, when Ray tried to speak again, she laid her finger across his lips.

A fan spun overhead and a chill ran down Kat's back.

"I'll explain. Just let me catch my breath. Hold me, please. Tight."

"Tell me one thing," Ray said. "Tell me you'll come home."

The look she gave him puzzled Kat. Leigh put a hand on her husband's shoulder and it was a look like a goddess comforting a penitent, a look full of love and—what? Pity? "You came a long way to find me. I hope—I pray you won't regret it," Leigh said.

"Never," Ray said. "Come home with us."

"I need to explain but I'm afraid."

During the pause that followed, Kat stood up and said, "I'm sorry. Where are my manners? I'll leave you two for a little bit, okay? You can catch up. I'll take a dip or some-thing."

"Don't go," Leigh said firmly. "We've all kept too many secrets. No more of that. Let's just go. I'll tell you every-thing soon. So much to say, but first, we need to pack up and get on the road. I want to go home."

She went over to hug Kat for a long time. "You haven't changed a bit. You're as extreme as ever," she said with a flash of her old impudence, giving Kat's cheek a quick ca-ress. Then, "This will just take a minute," she said, opening drawers and tossing clothing toward her suitcase.

They checked out of the motel, Ray slipping the clerk a hundred-dollar bill and being rewarded with the name of the clerk's brother, who would be willing to drive Leigh's van back to L.A. He collected Ray's money, collected the card keys, and turned back to a small television at the back of the office, which was at that moment offering up a compelling advertisement about pizza.

When they opened the door to leave, the clerk spoke at last, still watching the TV.

"You all find what you were looking for here?"

They nodded.

"Leaving me with just the tumbleweeds, the old folks, and the highway patrol for company." He chuckled raggedly. "Well, *hasta luego.*"

"I bet he's a transplant," Kat said, as they walked through the parking lot toward the Echo. "I think he got stuck here because his elderly parents owned this run-down motel. He spruced it up, advertised in some good magazines, and gets all his news from travelers."

"You still do that," Leigh said. "Make up things about people. Oh, it's so good to see you, kiddo."

"Sit with Ray in back," Kat said. "I'll chauffeur." She should be dying of curiosity, she supposed, but she wasn't. She didn't care why Leigh had left. She only cared that Leigh was returning, with new chances all around.

Or perhaps some part of her just wanted the moment to stay bright and unalloyed, pure, happy. Ray and Leigh were holding each other, and she could feel in a visceral way both Ray's overwhelming joy and Leigh's deep relief at being found.

Leigh's face when she said "I pray you won't regret it"—let that wait, let the universe hold still for a few moments and just rejoice.

After stopping for gas and a snack at a convenience gas station, they climbed back into the mountains at top speed. For as long as they had open highway, Kat drove fast, dashing from one lane to another, eyes glued to the side mirrors, watching for trouble.

Leigh's mood changed. She pulled away a little, looking out the window silently, though she kept Ray's hands in hers. Every once in a while they would lean their heads together, murmur to each other, their love for each other obvious.

Kat passed her bottled water back to Leigh. They were at the top of the grade, looking down on the L.A. Basin.

All they could see was brown air swathing everything. External temperature, ninety-four.

Leigh stirred. "Um, take the 605," she said, "when you can, okay?"

Kat, caught up in the flow of getting home, was thrown off. "That's not on our route. Why should I take the 605? I mean, Whittier?"

"I promise it makes sense," Leigh said. "Could we stop and get coffee or something? This isn't going to be easy."

Kat pulled off and they found a chain restaurant. When the coffee came, Leigh talked. And talked. And talked.

A pounding at the door. At first, Esmé covered her ears with the extra pillow. That didn't work. Her head began to pound along with someone's fist, pow, pow, pow. She wished she had not drunk so very much whiskey that night, or at least had eaten dinner. Sodden and fragile, she realized that, now awake, she wouldn't be able to sleep again. Fury built. That noise! She had to make it stop!

What time was it? Three in the afternoon, not good, not good.

Sliding out of bed, which caused a nasty shifting of perspective, she peeked out the side window toward the porch and saw a tableau of three shadowy figures in blinding sun. Her heart froze as she recognized Ray. Two women flanked him. One was tall. Leigh.

So you're back, she thought. Back to ruin my life. The fury grew, as if it had an existence of its own, had lived independently inside her for many years. They had come like furtive critters who dig up carcasses in the night forest, that bring the soil aboil.

She peeked again from the raised curtain-corner. The two women stood silently along the pathway to the house, having retreated from the porch. Ray had disappeared. Well, she had taken his key away, hadn't she? What could she expect? Her boy wanted in. He would not be denied.

She would fight. He had no right to violate her space. He was a traitor to the family, no longer welcome.

But he was her darling son. She had lived her life for him.

No more.

Which?

Swaying between emotions, her mind achieved a moment of clarity, and she understood he would attack the weak point of the house, the single basement window, the chink in her battlements.

She ran into the living room and located her sharp knife. She could not allow Ray to bumble around in that basement. She would have to go stop him.

Was there some way to explain away anything Leigh must have told him by now? Could she save him, sacrificing only the peripheral people who did not matter? Padding through the dark hallway toward the closed door that led to the basement stairs, she thought, I'll just deny everything she says, whatever she told him.

But Ray would believe Leigh, not her. It's a matter of love, she thought. He has cleaved to his wife and left me.

She breathed in the bitterness of his abandonment and it mixed with the anger.

Glass broke. She heard the basement window creak open, the window she expected to open. She had every right to protect herself and—and—her hand shook, holding the knife ready. He was breaking in, all right. I thought it was a burglar, Judge, she thought, her mind swirling. It isn't always about you, son, some of it is about me, my basic survival, and now when you turn your back after I have given you everything, everything—

Down below, like a big rat scurrying around in the dark, Ray was trying to find his way up.

29

"Y our mother attacked me," Leigh had said in that highway diner to Ray, earlier in the evening, after finishing a cup of strong, steaming hot coffee, "the night I left you. With a chisel."

Ray stood up. "Have you lost your mind? My mother—I don't believe this." The man in the next booth let his paper fall to the table and turned around.

"Please. Ray. Sit down," Kat whispered. She pulled him back into the booth beside her.

"It's outrageous. A damn lie! What are you trying to do to us, Leigh?"

Leigh looked him in the eye. "I wish I could spare you this, but I can't hide what happened any longer. You have to know. I'm sorry but I am telling the truth. She stabbed me in the stomach with a chisel."

She continued as if an inner propeller had started up and could not be stopped. "I ran upstairs and out of the house, holding my hand inside my shirt to stop the bleeding, to hold myself in one piece. Ray—I heard her coming behind me. I was so terrified. She's strong when she wants to be, you know. I barely got inside the van, with the door shut, when I heard her whack the rear grille and I started up and drove like crazy. I didn't know where.

"Once I got to the freeway I looked down and saw my shirt was wet and my hand on the steering wheel was wet. I was bleeding, feeling a lot of pain, so I stopped and asked directions at a gas station." She ran a hand through her hair. "What amazed me was how calm I felt then just being in my own car, as if I was out of danger. Funny, isn't it? The guy directed me to an urgent care clinic. I had a towel over my stomach, so he couldn't see anything, I guess, or maybe he would have offered to drive me or called an ambulance.

"Anyway, they asked what happened, and I said I did it to myself, that I made furniture and had stumbled against a tool in my shop. I don't know if they believed me, but what could they do about it? They sewed me up, gave me a shot, prescriptions, all that. The gash skimmed along the front of my stomach and if I had been facing another direction I would have taken a hit in my liver and probably would have died."

Ray's face was screwed up like a child's. "You can't be saying my mother would do a thing like that."

"She did, Ray. She would have killed me. I've thought and thought about it."

"But why? Why?"

"Isn't it obvious? Then I tried to think. I wanted to call you. I wanted your arms around me and the safety of our house, but we had fought—I thought you never wanted to see me again. And I felt like—like it would kill you to hear this. Look at you now!"

Kat said, "Take it easy, Ray. Just listen for now, okay?"

"I hate having to talk to you like this. I know how much you love her. I have rehearsed many ways of telling you over the past days, but I can't make it easier." She began to sob.

"It's okay," Kat told her. She reached across the table to hold Leigh's cold, trembling hand for a moment. "Just tell us what happened."

"Well, after the clinic, I—was still feeling very shocked and pretty battered. I needed to think and the cabin at Idyllwild seemed like a logical place to rest and take some painkillers. I drove up there and collapsed. The next day, even though I was still in some pain, I got worried you might think of the cabin and follow me there, so I moved on. Maybe I wasn't thinking straight, but I thought you didn't love me anymore. I thought I had lost your trust forever. And still, I didn't want to hurt you any more than I already had."

Ray said, "Leigh, you have it all wrong. Martin was right about one thing. I drove you away from me. Ever since you started talking about having a child—I got so scared. I drove you to him. You needed to be loved and I took my love away. And then I wanted to blame you for everything! I could see myself—hurting you back. Hurting you more." Ray closed his eyes and shook his head. "I wanted you to go. I'm afraid you felt that."

She nodded. "That's why you called your mother and

told her about Martin and me. I can only imagine what you said. And she—she got so angry at the hurt I caused you, she wanted me to die."

"No! No! I didn't call her! I wouldn't do that! She didn't know until Sunday!"

"Are you sure?" Leigh said. "It's all right, I don't blame you."

"I didn't! She didn't know until after that night! You're all messed up! None of this is true!"

"Wait," Kat said. "Keep your voice down, Ray. Sssh. Ray, think about the shirt we found."

Ray put his face in his hands.

"Leigh, go back, just explain again. You left the Topanga house. Why would you drive to Whittier?"

"I was going to my parents' house," Leigh said. "But just as I got to town I saw Esmé's inhaler lying there on the car seat, you know, the one she needs for her asthma. I saw that and thought, oh, damn. She's running out."

"She used one while I was there on Sunday. Must have been the same one," Ray said.

Kat asked, "But why did you have the inhaler, Leigh?"

"Esmé called the house on Friday morning, but Ray had gone in to work early, so I got the call. Her local pharmacy had run out and wouldn't get any until Monday. She asked me to ask Ray to pick it up in L.A. and bring it on Sunday, during our regular dinner. I offered to bring it over instead.

"I just thought I'd drop it off. It was only a few more miles, and then I'd go stay with my folks. I got to Close

Street, but I couldn't raise her. She didn't answer the door, so I went in the kitchen because I know she leaves that door unlocked sometimes when she takes out the trash. I called out—getting more worried. Then I saw the basement door open."

"She keeps it locked."

"Right. I thought maybe she had an asthma attack down there, or slipped down those steep steps. So I went in and ran down the stairs. It was so weird." She paused, narrowing her eyes, remembering.

"What, Leigh?" Kat said.

"Well, I came down fast. She whirled around, and there was an instant there when I'd swear she was deciding this was exactly the right thing to do, then she stabbed me with the chisel. I dropped the inhaler, which was still in my hand in a bag, and I stumbled back up the steps. She followed me, but I guess the situation got her worked up. I could hear her wheezing, trying to catch me."

Ray had kept his hurt, shocked eyes on Leigh. "A chisel?" he interrupted. "Why would she be in the basement with a chisel?"

"I don't know," Leigh answered. "Trying to get something open? Do you know what she keeps down there? I mean, it looked empty to me."

"Working on the pipes?" Ray said. "You know, the sink was leaking upstairs. Probably the water had drizzled down there. I warned her about that. It could weaken the walls or even flood the place."

"Old people have a lot of problems that might change

their personalities," Kat said, straining for a reasonable explanation.

"She really did this to you? Really?"

Leigh broke down again. "It's true."

"She isn't old. She isn't senile or crazy," Ray said. "My mother knows how to control herself. Oh, she sure does. But hang on. That was true up to a few days ago. But she has been drinking over the past few days, a lot I think, like binge drinking, and it started very suddenly. Was she drunk?"

"She was stone cold sober," Leigh said.

"Do you think she—is she taking drugs? Methamphetamine? Cocaine? PCP?" Kat said.

"My first thought was, yeah, she's on something. She ran toward me like a ghastly character in a movie. I could almost hear the music."

"She hates drugs," Ray said. "She hates having to use the inhaler sometimes for her asthma. She won't even take an aspirin."

Kat bit her lip and looked at him. He was back with them, but the expression on his face was so sad she could hardly stand it.

"Ray," she said, "your mother must have known about your fight with Leigh. It's the only explanation for her attack on Leigh, and it's wild enough."

"I didn't call her, Leigh," Ray said. "I swear to you, I didn't."

Kat said, "Could she have been—eavesdropping at your house?"

"But I drove straight to Whittier like a bat out of hell and there she was," Leigh said. "She couldn't have beat me." She looked at the table. "Then why? She must be mentally ill. But—"

"I ate dinner with her that Sunday, after you had been gone two days. She was just like always. She seemed sorry you had left."

Leigh said, "I suppose I should have gone to my dad. But imagine. He would have had your mother arrested. I was so confused. I—I didn't want to hurt you any more."

Ray took it in.

She pulled up her shirt and lifted her body a little. "Look."

Three angry red welts with stitch marks, about four inches long, scored through her pale skin just above the navel.

"Jesus," Ray said. He touched his wife's skin and Kat could see any remaining doubt had melted away.

"You poor thing," Kat told Leigh, staring at it. Then a second wave of feeling overtook her, sadness for Ray.

In finding his wife, had he lost his mother?

Leigh pulled down her shirt, dropping back into her seat. For a few moments nobody spoke.

"We need to talk to her. Let's go to Whittier," Ray said.

"Let's not and say we did," Kat said. "You're kidding, right?"

"We should just call the police," Leigh said imperatively. "I'm not afraid of her, with the two of you with me, and I want to know why she did this to me. But we need to stay safe."

"She attacked Leigh," Kat said. "She's violent."

"She would never hurt me," Ray said, so decisively his tone would brook no further disagreement. "Leigh, I want you to go home with Kat. I'll drop you both in Hermosa and then go talk to her. I'll pick you up afterwards."

"It's more than sixty miles to Hermosa," Leigh calculated, "and then at least forty-five minutes getting back to Whittier. You'll be so tired. In no shape to talk to her."

After a few more minutes of wrangling, they decided to call Rappaport. They got his voicemail and left a message.

"Whittier's on the way," Ray said. "I'm going."

"Then we'll wait in the car for you if that's the way you want it. I swear we will let you work it out yourself," Kat promised, thinking, Holy shit, if anyone ever needed backup! They could not let him go there alone.

"Let's go," Leigh said.

They went outside to the car and got inside, Ray in the driver's seat, Leigh beside him, and Kat in the back. Then Kat and Leigh waited and waited. He didn't start the car. "I need to say something, Leigh. You know, I used to hear about people having breakdowns and it had no meaning for me. Then, this year, it happened. You started talking about children, remember?"

Leigh nodded.

"Well, I got afraid. I never had a father. No role model. And I knew my parents had divorced. Although my mother never talked about him, I understood he was off-limits for a reason, probably something pretty ugly. I suspected that made me a bad bet."

"Ray, we can talk about this later."

"No. Because here's the bad news. It turns out—at least, from what I've found out in this kind of compulsive genealogical research I've been doing"—he laughed slightly—"I was right. My father was a vicious thug. He stalked my mother for years. He's the reason we ran like scared bunnies for all those years."

"How do you know that, Ray?" Leigh asked.

He told her and Kat about the keys, about the houses, and, finally, about the tapes.

"Why did your mother make recordings like that?" Kat asked, "and then leave them hidden in these houses?"

"I have a theory. She was afraid of this guy catching up with her. If she thought he might hurt or even kill her—or me—she might have wanted those tapes to get the police after him, like some kind of evidence."

"But they were hidden."

"If she had been killed, and her home was searched, they could have found them easily."

Leigh frowned with concern. "So you found out about your father. Nobody has easy parents, Ray. Some are worse than others, but that doesn't mean—"

"I've been thinking so much about how you can cripple yourself," he went on doggedly, "obsessing on whys and feeling permanently bruised by things that have happened in life that you can't change. Since you left, I've understood love so much better. It's like"—he struggled for words—"a house with walls that change color, shape, position every day, a place that's so full of life it never stops changing. I want to tell you—I'm not afraid of that anymore." For a long moment, they stared at each other, then melted into an embrace, a surrender to each other that made Kat's breath catch.

When they finally pulled apart and straightened up, Ray started the car and rolled up the road.

30

Esmé, loitering at the cellar door, hung back. She heard her son, the love of her life, down there. She wished he of all people understood.

Opening the door to the cellar, the light off, she began to creep down, her hand finding its way down the rail.

Ray squirmed into the pitch-black. Kat had shoved a small flashlight into his hand. Its aura cast dim shadows on the walls.

At the door, at the top of the stairs, he heard something.

Mom, he thought.

Rather than worry about her, he shone his light around. He noted the cobwebs, the living spiders, the dank wetness of a space that needed, according to his architect-sensibility, a dry atmosphere.

"Mom?" he said, stepping into the space.

Her voice came from very close by, inches away from him, like a scent on the wind. He felt her touch his cheek.

"Right here."

"Mom?" He heard her step in even closer. He heard his own throbbing heart and thought he heard hers, too.

"So you broke in."

"You locked me out. Took my key. You weren't going to open the front door. I need to talk to you, Mom."

She said, "I hoped Leigh would never come back. I thought, if she doesn't come back, we're okay. We can go on as always."

"I love her, Mom. I want her home."

"I know you love Leigh. But I'm mad at her."

"Her friend, Kat, got me going. She had her own reasons for looking for Leigh, nothing to do with you or me, but I'm glad she helped me find her."

"Same outcome. Leigh's out there on my doorstep. So's her friend, Kat. They are up there waiting. Meantime, what should I do? That's a big question."

"You hurt Leigh, Mom, stabbed her with a chisel, for God's sake. You almost—"

"I did my best." Esmé's laugh was dry, crackling. She had stepped back into the darkness. "I was hoping she died. But no such luck. I never had any."

"You've been drinking. I can smell it."

"I'm not that drunk. Not so drunk I don't see you break into my house just like she did."

"We have to figure out how to help you, Mom." The dark made it hard to do anything. "Why won't the light go on?"

"On your own you would never have gone after her.

You would have let her go, because I taught you that, Ray, how to let go of things and people. How to move on, adapt to new circumstances. It took a lot of guts, living the way we did."

"She's my wife. It's different. I never wanted to let her go."

"Every single time we moved I reminded you that I was your rock. The two of us made a good family. We never needed anybody else."

Ray's flashlight landed on something. "The bricks are loose."

He fingered it, and the crude mortar peeled up like an onion. "I told you, it's crap. Not a professional job."

"Don't mess with the wall, Ray," his mother said. "This is my house. My life."

"This is a real problem here, the bricks. This has to be repaired right away," he said. He knew it was an incongruous thing to say, but he couldn't help it. He felt so comfortable in the role of a man who knew how to solve construction problems.

His mother laughed again. He shined the flashlight on her face and heard her laughter, saw her terrible smile. He saw a glint in her hand. "What's that you've got?"

"Oh well," she said. "The time has come, I suppose."

"What am I missing?"

"You have all the keys you need," Esmé said.

"Where's the friggin' light?" Ray shouted. "What is this?" He had been fiddling with the wall. A brick came loose, then another. "Some kind of opening." He reached inside.

"You do not have the right to come here and invade my past."

Ray moved the light down. He saw a big knife glinting. One of her sharp ones.

That night, Ray, twelve years old, had slept in the small room at the back of the house. Esmé had decorated it in blues and greens with an athletic theme because at that age he followed a number of national teams. He would watch games on Saturdays and Sundays, just like Henry had done years ago, genetically programmed to enjoy watching men bat balls, run around, and get knocked down.

Esmé had stayed up a little late watching her favorite sitcoms, savoring her time alone.

Curled up on the sofa, hot tea in hand, she had watched television, following the shenanigans of a group of unbelievable characters, reveling in the rewarding ending. She turned the tube off then, stretched, and carried her drink into the kitchen. She didn't like facing litter in the morning. She liked it all put away.

Right when she was opening the dishwasher, she heard it, a car door closing, not slamming, but closing carefully.

Alerted, she crept toward the front door and peered through the window beside it.

Him.

She felt the familiar terrified rush of blood through her veins. Her hand flew to her heart and landed there, feeling the thudding below the skin. They had lived here in this house on Close Street for almost an entire year without being bothered by him. She liked Whittier, she thought, pressing against the wall. She didn't want to move again. She didn't want to leave this town. She was sick to death of his interference in their lives! Sick of it!

She felt rather than saw him approaching the house from the street.

Knocking.

He always knocked. Some vestige of civility remained, in spite of how much he must hate her by now.

She didn't answer. Instead, she opened the drawer in the kitchen where she kept her knives.

A finger of feeling reached up and tried to grab her but she pushed it away. No. She had made her decision months ago. She would not succumb to sentimentality anymore.

No more running.

Ray deserved a normal life. He seemed happy this year and she wanted him to stay in this house, on this street where he was happy. He had friends at Ceres. She envisioned him at Hillview, then Cal High in a few years with the friends he had made.

She peeked through the window. Nobody at the door. Henry would be seeking a way in.

She kept all the windows of the house locked all the time, and had schooled Ray into doing the same long ago. He could not enter easily. Broken glass, she would hear.

She listened, hearing nothing.

But she would only hear it if something broke, something like the basement window.

The place got dank in winter, wet, moist. Maybe years ago, a window made some kind of sense in a basement. Maybe the owners had long-term plans to turn it into a poolroom or playhouse. Whatever they had planned had caused her problems. She stored jellies down there, and a few pickles she made when they stayed somewhere long enough for her to make them. Last time she had gone down there, she noticed the thickness of the air, and had cranked open the small window. The basement room reminded her, not pleasantly, of Bright Street.

She had not closed the window. Bad mistake.

Walking silently toward the basement stairway, which was at the far side of her kitchen, she tried to remember exactly how big he was. Could he squeeze himself through the window?

Mice, she had heard, needed only one-half inch to squeeze into the pantry and eat everything in sight.

Rats, maybe an inch.

An angry man? How much space? How fit was he these days? Henry worked out. She remembered that, how he stayed fit.

Without turning on the light, she stepped down the thirteen stairs into the basement. Down here, she did laundry.

She let her eyes adjust.

Saw one foot, then the other foot push through.

Yes, he was fit enough to squeeze himself through.

She waited like an assassin, gearing herself up, so eager, dying to have it all over. For so many years Henry had ruled her life. She couldn't take another minute. She could not.

His entire body shimmied through the window. He landed on a long, rustic table that someone had built beside the washer-dryer and turned to face her.

"Oh, Esmé," he said.

"Yes." She realized the light from the hallway was leaking down the stairs behind her. She must look like a silhouette to him.

A certain, small piece of her heart yearned for him, but the feeling concreted into confidence that she had made the correct decision when he said, "Where is he?"

"Sleeping upstairs."

"I'm taking him. Get out of my way, Esmé."

That's when she stabbed him with the sharp, sharp kitchen knife. Then she stabbed him again.

"What's this?" Ray had pulled something out of the hole behind the brick. The flashlight revealed tatters, dirt. "Cloth." He had answered his own question.

"His shirt, I guess."

Ray jumped back, knocking into the washing machine, and yelled, "What's in there?"

"You mean who's in there."

"It's—it's a body!" he yelled.

"Henry Jackson. Your father, Ray."

"Why? Why?"

His mother sighed deeply. "Oh, I wish you could just let go but you're like me, stubborn and loyal. If only I hadn't needed to stay near my mother for all those years when she was so sick we could have moved to Australia or somewhere. None of this would have happened."

"You killed him! Oh, God, you did!"

"No, Ray, I stopped him. He broke in, just like you."

"Wait. Wait." They stood in the semidarkness, both breathing hard.

"He tried to hurt you, Mom? He attacked you?" Ray said at last, his voice breaking.

"He didn't get the chance."

"It was self-defense," Ray mumbled. "He stalked you. We'll deal with this." He felt the tattered cloth again.

"It won't look that way to a judge, son."

"But he broke in—"

"Ray. Ray, precious child, your father didn't come here for me. He came for you."

"He came to hurt me? Why?" A hundred possibilities flashed through his mind. "Did he think I wasn't his?"

"Henry," she spat out his name, "had full legal and physical custody of you."

"But—"

"Yes, it is incredible, isn't it? Ripping a child away from his mother."

"But why would they do that?"

"He faked being perfect, and I wasn't so good at that in those days. Look, I was a young woman when I had you, only twenty-two. I wanted some fun out of life! I deserved some fun!" She cast a desperate glance at him. "And one day, one miserable day, I did something really stupid. I drove drunk."

He thought about that. "That was enough to cost you custody, getting caught driving under the influence? I mean, why not make sure you got some treatment and quit?"

"You were in the car with me. We cracked up. You spent two months in the hospital. My visits to see you had to be supervised after that. He took you away from me. He divorced me. He couldn't forgive me for what I had done."

Bright lights at night. A high bed. Nurses.

"You had a head trauma. Bleeding and pressure in your brain. You have a scar under your hair. No one could believe I would stop drinking, not Henry, not the case-workers, not the judge. But I did."

"Until now."

"Who wouldn't? Have you thought about my life at all? Thought about anything but your obsessions and your needs and Leigh? Ray, I need you to help me now. I'll leave this house. I'll go away like Leigh did, and I won't come back. Will that satisfy you and Leigh?"

Silence lodged heavily between them.

"So you kept the tapes in case there was another custody fight," Ray concluded. "You wanted to prove he was some kind of angry, crazy monster to the court. You needed something against him. Is that why they were so short?" He answered his own question. "You only kept the bad parts, and there weren't many, were there? He got frustrated and angry sometimes."

"Any judge would hear it in his voice. He was a dangerous man."

"Dangerous because he wanted his son," Ray said. "He had a court order to take me. He wasn't a monster."

"I did it out of—"

"And so you killed him. You were the monster." He breathed heavily, and he stepped back farther from her. Each step felt like a year of the pain she had experienced, running with him, running, trying to take care of him and her mother, no life for herself, all for him—

"We had peace after that, didn't we, son?"

"We lived on top of his body!" Ray said, backing away from her toward the stairs. "You did that to me."

"Where are you going? Are you leaving?"

"You almost murdered my wife!"

"She broke in, son. She came down here when I was trying to fix the wall."

"With a chisel?"

"That damn leak! I couldn't fix it, and just like you said, the water was undermining the brick wall in the basement. I mean, you always said it was a hack job. It was a hack job because I did it! I put up that wall myself, and it was crummy and starting to get dangerous, so I was going to loosen the mortar and repair everything. And then she broke in at night and surprised me. I had to protect myself! I had to protect us! Wait—where are you going? What are you doing, son?"

He shut the door and locked it. "I'm keeping you down

here until the police come. The window is full of broken glass. Don't try to get out that way. I'll stand out there waiting."

"Let me run. Please. Ray?"

He checked the lock. It was secure.

EPILOGUE

Seven months later, Ray drove up to Corona, California, the dry heartland of the state, practically at its center. He filled out a form in the entryway, showed his ID, went through the metal detector, braved the scrutiny of several guards, and finally got into the visiting area.

He put on headphones, as did Esmé, sitting across from him and through an acrylic barrier.

"They treating you all right?" She had aged, of course. Her jaw was set and he noticed how square and stubborn it still was.

"I've applied for kitchen duty," Esmé said. "The food is too high-carb. I've decided to become a vegetarian. I don't trust the meat."

She didn't ask about how Ray was doing, he thought with a twinge. Esmé was thinking about herself. Maybe she always thought of herself. It felt like a wind had swept through the big depressing room, blowing away his illusions. "I left some money for you for the canteen."

"Did you bring my magazines?"

"You bet."

"My roommate needs a kidney transplant. She's back

in the hospital. I sleep so much better now that she's gone but I think they're bringing in a new inmate next week."

"That have you nervous?"

"They're not as bad as you might think. Mostly abused women, druggies."

She had never used that word before. Ray sat up straighter.

"It's so unfair. I had that one lapse. That one time when you were in the car, and I drove drunk. So should I spend the rest of my life paying for that?"

And what about killing his father and attacking his wife? Esmé continued to have blind spots big as tunnels that would fit a big rig. "Mom, maybe you should listen to what they say. It's not all stupid."

"It's so galling. Me, here. Do you blame me for things I had to do?"

"Yes," Ray said.

"All I can say is, you're not a parent yet. Someday you might understand better."

Ray, now three months along on the road to becoming a parent, said nothing about Leigh's pregnancy. "Do you blame me for the things I had to do to stop you?"

Esmé paused, wet her lips. "You were the center of my existence for most of my life, honey. Lately I don't worry about you anymore, about how well you're eating, if your work is going well. I suppose it's one way to cut the apron strings." She smiled. "But of course I blame you. You're ungrateful. That's how it is."

"Try to understand what you did, Mom. After I found

those tapes, I decided my father was some kind of stalker," Ray said. "I thought he tracked you down and we moved because you needed to hide from him."

"You should never have gone back to those places. Wasn't it sad?"

"Yes."

"You must understand why I had to hide you. I needed you close. You were just a baby, Ray."

"Henry had custody, Mom."

"So? Did I raise you badly? Did I ever take a drink while you were growing up?"

"You stole me from him. You stole him from me."

She considered this. Then she sighed. "Here we go again. After all I did for you, you blame me."

"You robbed me of the truth." Henry Jackson would have been sixty-two this year, not old. His remains had now been officially interred at Memory Gardens in Brea.

"Would you rather he had robbed you of your mother? I doubt that." Esmé changed the subject and talked about all the wonderful things she planned to do when she finished serving her time, eight to ten years. She would renovate her house at last, she said, not asking but assuming Ray would keep it for her. She didn't know yet that the house had already been sold to pay her legal fees. Where she would go when she got out was something Ray didn't want to think about. She told him she would quit her job at the market and do volunteer work in the schools.

Quit her job! She had been terminated long before her guilty plea to second-degree murder.

Esmé rambled on. She loved kids. She needed kids in

her life. But Leigh and Ray had decided their baby wouldn't be visiting Esmé at the prison. Ray didn't want to hurt his mother, so he might never tell her until the day she walked through the locked gates to whatever was left of her existence.

He let her meander on, worrying about her. Mainly, as always, he felt amazed that this woman had loved him so fiercely that she had killed his father.

He listened, took her in, and felt so sad.

Beau smiled, waving his arms. He kicked his round legs all day long. After Raoul finished changing his diaper, he quieted, lying peacefully down against the bold blue bolsters edging his crib. Kat came in to finish cleaning up the changing table. Raoul leaned over the crib, playing with Beau's little fingers.

He and Kat had found Jacki some help, and Jacki was back to working part-time.

Kat was seeing a lot of Zak.

After several weeks of silence between them, Zak had finally called. "Hiya."

"Hiya." Kat had been attempting a chicken curry, chopping onions in her kitchen, holding the phone to her ear against her scrunched-up shoulder. She had a special new knife they sold on television, a big book of recipes, and a hobby, being a homebody who liked her own company better than almost anyone else's.

Although tonight Leigh and Ray were coming over. They saw a lot of each other these days. Ray was going to tell her that they were pregnant, and she was going to look surprised, as if Leigh hadn't told her that a month ago during one of their long lunches.

Zak said, "So—"

Kat picked up the board full of chopped onions and dumped them into the wok. "So—"

"I've tried to work out why things haven't worked between us, and I want to clear the air."

"Okay."

"I hadn't had a date in two years when I met you. I have a brother who's a little like Jacki, concerned about me becoming a creepy bachelor. Sometimes that makes me nervous and it made me really nervous because—I like you, and you don't seem very responsive. So I'm going to lay it on thick and tell you everything, and that way I'll know I'm being rejected for myself, and not for the image. You know what? I hate Rollerblading. You just sounded like such a fun-loving person, it seemed like the right thing to do. I'm a reader, mostly nonfiction, but I can get into a thriller. I'll go to any movie ever made, and eat a large popcorn clogged with butter. I like to take walks in my neighborhood. And I basically like my life the way it is. It's—contented. Wonderfully boring."

"Oh, Zak!" How bizarre. He had a dating game, too. "We did start out awkward, didn't we?"

"You surprised me, though, talking about yourself. And I felt you deserved the same from me. A little bit of the truth. I see other people bogged down in mortgages and babies and—that's not for me right now, Kat. So now you know."

She smelled the curry, then reached to pull the cloves down from the shelf. Nobody else liked cloves the way she liked cloves. "You like cloves in curry? I mean lots? Don't lie to me now, Zak."

"Love them. I swear."

"Want to go out with me Friday night? We won't get tattoos. We won't skate. And we won't shop for rings. Anything else suits me, too."

"You have a deal."

Kat smiled, thinking back to their conversation. Then Jacki came into the nursery, real pearls on her neck, looking older in the most lovely way, made somehow more sophisticated by her recent motherhood.

"We'll be back by midnight. You sure you can do this?"

"I look forward to it." That was true. Jacki gave her a hug and she and Raoul departed, leaving Kat with Beau.

He willingly came out of his crib and Kat sat in the rocking chair, resting him on her legs. "I hope you're feeling amusing," she told him. "Gum display. I guess that means you're happy? You like the mother and father you picked? Oh, good. I totally agree. And what about me? Am I the world's most fabulous aunt?"

Beau followed her lips with his all-out blue stare. She gazed down at him and something happened which had not happened before. They really looked at each other. Beau didn't blink. He had the Tinsley glare down already. He looked and looked and Kat felt that she was being sucked into his new-old soul.

She leaned down close and whispered, "You'll forget it all soon and this'll be the only world for you. But before you do I have to ask you a question. Okay?"

His eyebrows raised. He waited with milk-scented, bated breath.

"Have you met your uncle Tom at any point?"

No change in his expression, but he continued fascinated. No kicks, no waves. He listened intently.

"No?" Kat said, disappointed.

"Aaah," Beau said, suddenly opening his mouth hugely.

At that moment Kat understood. She just hadn't phrased the question properly. Beau's scanty hair, soft brown, smelled good as she lowered her head and rubbed her cheek against his. His ears were going to be big, and the nose had the Tinsley crook.

"I get it," she said. "I think I've suspected it for some time. You look at people with the same... perspicacity. Right through me, just like him. He knew I meant no harm. He knew how much I loved and admired him."

Beau brayed at her. A couple of brand-new baby teeth poked through his bottom gums like kernels of fresh corn.

"I'm going to take such good care of you this time, little buddy."

Ray went home to Leigh.

When they had moved from Topanga, he had closed up his hobby room, stuffing the house models into the trash bin or sending them to a donation center. How relieved he had felt, letting go. The models had served their purpose, revealing their secrets, and the truth about both his father and his mother. His collection of keys, wrestled away from him by Leigh during foreplay to a particularly fine night of sex, disappeared, never to be seen again.

"Suzanne called," Leigh said as he walked into their new shingled house in Santa Monica. He threw his car keys onto the painted bench from Leigh Jackson Designs, and then watched her setting down a plate on the trestle table in the kitchen. The bulge in her stomach didn't slow her down one bit. She was at her shop daily—if not sawing and sanding, she was drawing. "I'm fertile in every sense of the word," she had laughed when he had remarked upon her incredible energy.

He came up behind her and wrapped his arms around her, smelling her neck. "Oh, I am so very hungry tonight, Leigh."

"Good. We've got plenty. It's great to be out of the boonies and close to so much fantastic take-out food again."

"Who said anything about food?"

She slapped away the hand that had begun a slow exploration of her hip. "This is important. Antoniou is trying to reach you. He wants you to design another house for him."

Ray took a piece of crust off the pie and put it in his

mouth. Chewing, he said, "Tough man to satisfy. Wasn't the one I already designed enough for him?"

"He loves the Laguna place," she said.

With the construction moving along at a rapid clip, it already looked fantastic and had gotten press Antoniou appreciated as much as Ray.

"But this time, he wants you to design one in Santorini!"

Ray sat down, laughing too much to keep standing. "You're kidding."

"I've seen pictures of the island. What a beautiful spot. Denise's so excited. She's ready to make a site visit. I told her I'm coming along."

He put a hand on her stomach, and felt for movement there. "What about needing a new home for ourselves? Our next project together?"

"What, you can't draw when you're away from California?" She grinned at him, and put her hand over his to move it to a lumpy place that roiled like a wave. "We can't dream anywhere else?"

"Okay," he said. "Greece first."

"He said to give you a message. Antoniou."

"Yeah?" Ray pulled her down on his lap. "Sit," he said. "Whisper it to me."

He smelled her perfume as she leaned in, felt her warm breath at his ear.

"He wonders: can he have columns this time?"

ACKNOWLEDGMENTS

So many people are involved in the making of a novel. We have been lucky over the past years in having the backing of a fine publisher and are very grateful for the hard work undertaken by the imaginative and efficient staff at the Bantam Dell Publishing Group. As this novel presents a different direction for us, the process has been even more trying than usual, but we've heard nary a discouraging word.

We would especially like to thank our outstanding literary agent, Nancy Yost of Lowenstein-Yost Associates, Inc., for her steady guidance, enthusiasm, and creative participation. Nancy is that rare combination, a powerhouse professional associate and wonderful friend. Danielle Perez, senior editor for the Bantam Dell Publishing Group, contributed her usual unflinching critical eye, maintaining her patient support through an embarrassing number of drafts. Many thanks, Danielle, for your fair and gentle guidance.

For insight into the business of house appraisals, we relied on Mary's knowledgeable and experienced Plantation Café buddy, Jim, of James J. Nicholas & Associates, real estate appraiser and consultant, Redwood City, California. A warm pat on the arm to you from Nina Reilly, Jim. That's all you'll ever get from her, whatever you may dream.

We also want to thank Cambridge Seven Associates, Inc., Cambridge, Massachusetts, which unwittingly contributed inspiration for our architectural firm. Nobody in Ray's firm remotely resembles the good people working there, past or present, and none of the opinions about the business or building aesthetics expressed in our novel is theirs—these are all the authors'. However, anyone considering a major project ought to run straight to these talented people to get a taste of real, world-class architecture.

We have thought a lot about our own childhoods in writing this book, and how important our double cousins, Stephanie and Marc O'Shaughnessy, have been to our lives. We grew up together and remain very close. We stole heavily from their childhoods, too, along with cribbing from those of our sister, Meg, and Patrick, our late brother. We used our cousins' house on Franklin Street as Kat's childhood home. We will always treasure those hot summer days together in Penn Park, where Marc and Pat got up to no good, and we girls played so nicely.

And a final appreciation goes out to the good friends who put up with our insecurities, busy schedules, and late-night calls: Joan Westlund, Joanna Tamer, Helga Gerdes, and Ardyth Brock.

ABOUT THE AUTHOR

PERRI O'SHAUGHNESSY is the pen name for sisters Mary and Pamela O'Shaughnessy, who both live in California. They are the authors of eleven bestselling Nina Reilly novels as well as a collection of short crime fiction, *Sinister Shorts.*